MAKE ROOM

The clerk cleared his throat. "I'm sorry, sir, but we do not host coloreds or Injuns. The squaw can stay in the stable. That would be two bits."

Sett's fingers on the purse strings twitched. He clenched his jaw and stared down at the balding man for a long moment. "This is my wife," he said carefully. "We've just traveled a long ways overland and she is not well, and we have a small child. I will pay for the room now."

The clerk turned to Ria again, this time his eyes lingering on the faded red wool of the trade blanket swaddling the child. He then stood, leaned over the counter to look down at her high-topped moccasins and leather leggings. He slowly reseated himself on his stool and turned to face Sett.

"Sir, I have stated our policy." He adjusted the spectacles yet again, and firmly closed the ledger book.

Sett's knife pierced the ledger with a thunk, driving deep through the book and into the imported teak of the desktop.

The old man, to his credit, slowly withdrew his hand from within an inch of the quivering blade, though he fought the urge to count his digits. He peered up at Sett Foster's face. It was not a comforting sight.

Titles by D. H. Eraldi

SETTLER'S CHASE
SETTLER'S LAW

SETTLER'S CHASE

D. H. Eraldi

BERKLEY BOOKS, NEW YORK

THE BERKLEY PUBLISHING GROUP
Published by the Penguin Group
Penguin Group (USA) Inc.
375 Hudson Street, New York, New York 10014, USA
Penguin Group (Canada), 90 Eglinton Avenue East, Suite 700, Toronto, Ontario M4P 2Y3, Canada
(a division of Pearson Penguin Canada Inc.)
Penguin Books Ltd., 80 Strand, London WC2R 0RL, England
Penguin Group Ireland, 25 St. Stephen's Green, Dublin 2, Ireland (a division of Penguin Books Ltd.)
Penguin Group (Australia), 250 Camberwell Road, Camberwell, Victoria 3124, Australia
(a division of Pearson Australia Group Pty. Ltd.)
Penguin Books India Pvt. Ltd., 11 Community Centre, Panchsheel Park, New Delhi—110 017, India
Penguin Group (NZ), 67 Apollo Drive, Rosedale, North Shore 0632, New Zealand
(a division of Pearson New Zealand Ltd.)
Penguin Books (South Africa) (Pty.) Ltd., 24 Sturdee Avenue, Rosebank, Johannesburg 2196,
South Africa

Penguin Books Ltd., Registered Offices: 80 Strand, London WC2R 0RL, England

SETTLER'S CHASE

A Berkley Book / published by arrangement with the author

PRINTING HISTORY
Berkley edition / July 2010

Cover illustration by Ben Angresano.
Cover design by Diana Kolsky.

ISBN: 978-0-425-23541-6

BERKLEY®
Berkley Books are published by The Berkley Publishing Group,
a division of Penguin Group (USA) Inc.,
375 Hudson Street, New York, New York 10014.
BERKLEY® is a registered trademark of Penguin Group (USA) Inc.
The "B" design is a trademark of Penguin Group (USA) Inc.

PRINTED IN THE UNITED STATES OF AMERICA

10 9 8 7 6 5 4 3 2 1

For my mother, Helene Ladd Eraldi,
and
In memory of Great Grandmother
Sarah Flewharty Ladd
Who shared her stories

ACKNOWLEDGMENTS

I am deeply grateful to the Jackson family, and especially to Ronald and Pam Jackson of Jackson Ranches in White Sulphur Springs, Montana, for their generosity and hospitality, and for allowing me to range over their land in all weathers.

Heartfelt thanks to Peg Kingman, Emjay Wilson, Jennifer Uhlarik and the members of the former Monday Night Writers Group—without your careful reading, thoughtful comments, spirited discussions, and continual encouragement this story would not be.

Appreciation is also due Joel Shechter for information about river ferries in Montana, and Laura Redish of Native Languages of America for assistance with the Blackfeet names and translations.

There is not enough space here to list all of John Jackson's contributions; they are measured in miles and years. Thank you, with love.

D. H. Eraldi
Potter Valley, California

PROLOGUE

Late September, 1886

Wreckage scattered along the slope, broken wheels and flapping canvas leaning haphazardly against boulders and tree stumps in the steep avalanche slide. The woman peered down the canyon wall. She leaned as far over her spotted pony's shoulder as she dared, and then sat back to glance down the narrow wagon trail.

The back trail was clear, no sign yet of the soldiers, but she knew they were coming, were in fact not far behind. She listened carefully for the sounds of hooves, jingling spurs, or rattling scabbards. The only sound was the wind in the trees and the distant rush of the river far below. Her knee bumped the empty cradleboard still swinging from the tall horn of her saddle. Her husband had chided her for carrying it along, but she could not yet put it away. Now he stopped beside her, leaning over his own horse's shoulder to examine the spoils below.

The white man's stagecoach had tumbled off the narrow trail, one of the large wheels catching on the soft edge of the roadway. The ruptured belly of the coach lay like a bloated carcass on the rocky ledge of the canyon wall. Below that, the team of horses, still attached to the single tree and front wheels, were piled legs-akimbo at the bottom of the ravine.

It was tempting—there were useful goods down there—but there was little time. The man jerked his head and began to turn to follow the others. She started to rein the spotted pony to follow, but a sound stopped her. A thin, reedy cry.

"A bird," the man said.

"No," the woman answered. She got down and handed the jaw-line rein to him. "Don't let Spots bite you." He nodded, never glancing at the spotted pony, who was already laying back her large ears and baring her teeth.

Then the woman hefted her body over the edge of the roadway and carefully made her way down to where the wreckage of the Overland Stage rested on the rocky promontory at the headwaters of the Tenderfoot.

ONE

Late October, 1886

Sett Foster could not imagine a sweeter sight, and he barely restrained an appreciatory whistle. Below him, scattered like gemstones across the high mountain pasture, a small herd of mustangs grazed, their bodies sleek and fat from the summer feed. The foals raced through the golden fall grass, the mares no longer trailing them worriedly as they had earlier in the spring when the babies were very young. At the outskirts of the herd, a group of older colts lingered, being chased away by the tall red stallion if they ventured too close to either mares or young ones. Sett was pleased to see that even the stallion was in fine fettle, a few new scars but still fat and holding his own. Sett allowed himself a low chuckle. The saddle horse had adjusted to life in the wild easily, and now there was this fine group of stock for Sett to profit from. After he captured, gentled, and trained them, they would bring good money from the cavalry officers.

Sett ducked back down in the rocks and fished the monocular from his pocket, carefully extending the brass tube and wiping the dust from the lens. Through the magnifying scope, he examined the three geldings at the perimeter of the herd. They were the first results of his plan, born three years before and briefly corralled as two-year-olds, but otherwise as wild as they came. All were first-rate animals, strong-boned like their mustang mothers and athletic like their race-bred sire. The officers would be fighting to bid on them.

Sett collapsed the monocular and returned it to his pocket. Everything was in place: the box canyon trap that he had built over the course of several years, the ropes and long poles he'd stashed above the narrow entrance to the canyon, the habit in this dry time of the year for the lead mare to bring the herd in to drink every evening at the little spring in the back of the canyon. It had all worked out. The horses would go in to water, Sett would slip down and lash the poles in place to make a solid gate, and the horses would be contained. He would rope the three geldings and turn the rest loose again. In a couple of weeks, he would be returning home to his wife Ria at their cabin with a string of nice horses to sell. All he had to do was wait until the horses went to their evening water.

A pair of blue jays were squawking in the tree over his head, and the still afternoon air was undisturbed by breeze, a rare warm day so late in the season. Sett brushed an exploring ant off his neck, scratched his beard, and pulled his hat down over his face to doze until the herd came in. He let his mind wander. He would make a good profit–perhaps he would buy some iron pipe and put in a spring box at the cabin. Perhaps he could get something for Ria. She seldom asked for anything for herself.

The shadow of the pines was stretching long across the hillside when a snort roused Sett from his rest. The sound was repeated, an alarm from the head mare in the trees below. Sett pulled himself up to peer over the shielding rocks. His first thought was that his big saddle mare had gotten loose, then that somehow the wild ones had smelled him in his hiding place; either one would foil his carefully planned capture. The horses were still moving toward the watering hole, but the lead mare kept pausing to look out over the gray slope and let out that loud expulsion of air that warned of something discomforting. Sett followed her gaze and slowly reached for his monocular.

To the north, at the edge of the trees, was another horse moving after the herd. It was hard to see in the shadows of the late day, but something about the new horse was strange, and certainly the wild ones below agreed. Once he had focused the small telescope, Sett made out a spotted horse and the reason for the spookiness of the herd. The horse was wearing a saddle of some sort, with a flapping blanket hanging off of the right side. The horse moved cautiously along, its head tilted oddly to one side. As far as the wild horses were concerned, the new horse was a frightening thing, but to the lone horse the herd looked like a comforting presence. The saddled horse made its way slowly toward the mustangs.

Sett could see his plans falling to pieces like leaves blowing from the autumn trees. If the strange horse spooked the bunch, they would abandon their evening water for some place more open, but for the life of him Sett could not think of anything he could do about it. Showing himself in any form would be every bit as disastrous. All Sett could do was sit and watch, as the oddly moving animal approached the others.

As it came closer, Sett could see that the horse was sidling away from a rein that dragged in the dirt. Closer now, the horse stopped and looked anxiously at the group of mustangs, nickering softly as if calling in hopes of finding a friend. The chestnut stallion swaggered away from the herd to examine this interloper.

The rest of the herd was not so sure. The saddled horse was like having a monster in their midst, and the mares nipped the inquisitive foals nearer to them. The stallion was now up to the new horse, muzzle to muzzle, exchanging the breath of their species. Satisfied that this was indeed another prospect for his harem, the chestnut elevated himself into a high-stepping trot and circled the spotted horse, biting at her flank and sending her toward the reluctant herd. Sett held his breath. The scary animal had the rest of the mustangs milling in the trees. Sett would not be at all surprised if the lead mare bolted away onto the open prairie. The stallion, after all, had been a saddle horse, was used to seeing equipment of all sorts on other horses, and so was nowhere as concerned by the spotted mare's appearance as the wild-born were. All Sett could do was hope that the mares accepted her and would decide to continue into the trap for a drink.

The head mare, an old scarred black with a handsome foal at her side, came forward and bared her teeth. The spotted pony drew back, timid and submissive to the older mare's display. Not a threat, the old black decided, and she turned away from the cause of all the commotion and headed up the narrow trail between the trees toward the spring.

Sett had not realized that he was holding his breath. The sight of the black mare turning up the canyon made him force himself to let his air out slowly, then to take a deep quieting breath. The rest of the herd turned to follow the leader, and the stallion urged his slow-moving new prize to follow behind. As the new mare came closer, Sett could see that the bridle was a crude jaw-line, the one long rein trailing ten feet along the ground, the odd-looking saddle made from carved forks of wood with a hide for a seat. Part of this hide had slid to the right, the flapping edges that had so frightened the wild horses. An Indian pony, a little scrubby spotted horse with a stand-up mane, ewe neck, and knobby knees. Not worth much, in Sett's opinion. He'd capture it with the geldings and sell it for whatever it might bring as a packhorse, as he certainly didn't need any progeny

from such a poor specimen. The stallion herded the sorry-looking mare right under Sett's hiding place, and he took the risk of actually poking his head above the brush to get a good look.

Sett sucked in his breath again and held it. There, bobbing along the shoulder of the sad Indian pony, was a cradleboard, a tiny wizened face peeking out of the tight lacings. A Blackfeet cradleboard, like the one Ria had started to build and decorate when she was pregnant with the first baby. As if crabbing sideways to protect the baby, rather than to avoid the dragging rein, the little Indian pony still carried her passenger.

TWO

Ria had tried to ignore the dull ache in her back. From the moment the pale fall dawn had awakened her, through rekindling the small cookstove and setting the pot of water on to heat, she determinedly ignored the weight that hung along the back of her slim hips. With Sett away, she bypassed making coffee, choosing some mild tea instead, but still her stomach jumped and twisted in spite of her outwardly steady appearance.

Coy knew something was wrong. The dog padded around the cabin on Ria's heels, peering up at her as she dressed in her odd assortment of Blackfeet leggings and man's wool shirt over a cotton undershirt. It was a practical layering of functional attire, without a thought to appearance. She pulled her dark hair back into a loose braid, then gathered the few dishes from her evening meal. With Sett off checking his mustang traps, Ria had not bothered to cook full meals, grazing instead on handfuls of plums or some pine nuts. Now she told herself that the nagging discomfort in her belly was nothing more than the fruit, and she grabbed up the bucket and headed out the door of the cabin.

The sky was bright, clouds teasing the horizon over the Cottonwoods, the light spilling out across a landscape she had grown to love, a view as distant as the imagination. She paused a moment, the empty bucket dangling by her side, to watch the landscape and to wonder exactly where in those great folds of mountains Sett Foster might be.

He had pointed out the range, the rolling golden slopes to the east, where his horses roamed; not actually *his* horses, but she thought of them as such. A wild herd with the lead stallion turned in by Sett himself, to improve on the durable mustang mares. Sett had described his trap—the unscalable walls of a box canyon, with the gushing spring to draw in the wild ones this late in the season. He'd been excited. There were some nice young horses ready to be captured, broke, and sold. Finally his plan would begin to pay off.

He'd invited her along on this trip, but Ria made up an excuse about finishing the pemmican for winter, and if Sett recognized a lack of enthusiasm for a trip, he paid no mind to it. Ria swung the bucket aimlessly, lost in thought as she gazed into the early morning.

If he did not notice, that was good. She had not wanted him to think about it.

Now a stitch in her side brought her back to herself, the self that was trying so hard to pretend that there was nothing wrong, nothing different. Ria placed her palm across her stomach and started again toward the fanning branches of the mountain stream, insistent that if she ignored this cramping it would go away.

At the edge of the stream, she placed one small foot securely on the stepping stone that Sett had rolled near the bank. With one leg braced on the rock and the other on the worn grass tufts of the bank, she could swing the bucket into the deeper water of the creek and scoop up a bucketful without any gravel. In the spring, the rushing water could nearly pull her from her stance, or the stone would be icy and slick, but here in the late fall the water wandered along

at a softer pace, still deep and clear but nowhere near the snowmelt rush of earlier in the year. Ria let the bucket sink into the pool, filling without disturbing the bottom. But when she straightened to pull it from the water, the ache she had been ignoring zipped up her side, and she doubled over, dropping the bucket back into the pool with a splash.

No, she insisted to herself. This wasn't happening. This couldn't be happening. Not again.

Trying to catch her breath between muscles spasms, she dragged the bucket through the water and retreated to the stiff marsh grass on the bank of the stream. Coy came over to lick at her face, but she could not pause to greet the dog. She kneeled down on the earth and clutched her belly, folding in half over her knees in an effort to stop the spasms, but each brief rest was filled with the terrible ache, an ebb and flow that was now familiar and impossible to ignore. Tears trickled down the woman's freckled cheeks, tears not caused by pain, but by the recognition of it. She was going to lose this baby, yet another baby.

She was grateful that Sett was not here to see this, for she had not told him about this child. She could not, not after so many disappointments. The first time she had told him, he had stared at her uncomprehendingly as if the idea that he might be a father had never entered his mind. But then a boyish grin had lit his face, and he had scooped her up into a bear hug that left her struggling for breath and stretching to get her toes on the ground. The second time he had been happy too, but by the third pregnancy, his joy was mixed with concern and he had given her a warm hug and started insisting on bringing in the heavy water bucket in the morning. After that she did not tell him, could not stand to bring sorrow upon him too. With this child, this one who had stayed the longest, she had only dreamed of finally telling him, consoling herself with his imagined delight.

And so when he had suggested the horse-hunting trip, she'd known she'd been successful in keeping her secret,

for he would not have left her had he known. How he had not was beyond her. She had been walking around with a silly half smile on her face for weeks, catching herself holding her hand to her abdomen and humming, gathering the best and softest hides into her sewing basket.

But it was not to be, and maybe would never be; the thought that she would be doomed to spending the rest of her life losing babies brought on fresh sobs. How could she repeat this? How could she live if this were the fate handed her? Ria rocked back and forth on her knees in the stiff grass, arms folded over a body that rejected that which she wanted most, and wondered why this one thing—the only thing that she had ever wanted for herself—was denied.

She could smell her blood even before she felt the stickiness on her legs. It brought her back to her world, that world in which she was alone and in the wilds. She could sit here and cry, and the coyotes or wolves would smell her and come in to finish her off. She could put up no resistance, simply huddle in the grass until her existence was complete. Perhaps that would be better than living forever in this hell.

Then Coy sneaked a quick tongue across her cheek, the concern of Ria's oldest friend breaking into her bleak sorrow. If coyotes came, Coy would be killed defending her. Ria pushed herself up and crawled to the shallow water to retrieve the abandoned bucket. She would have to heat some water and wash up. The absorbent flannels were in the cabin.

Hot tears streaked down her clammy skin as she hauled the half-filled bucket onto the bank. With each movement, the fluids that had been her child ebbed from her body. Not a child, not anymore. Ria thanked the powers that she had decided to wait until Sett's return to tell him the news.

Now there would be no news.

THREE

Sett jerked back down into the brush, the shock making his heart pound. Sitting absolutely still on the gravelly soil of his shady spot, he tried to sort out the questions that flashed through his mind like fireflies. Where had the baby come from? How long had it been alone with the horse? Was the child even still alive? And much more pressing, how was Sett going to catch the horse and safely retrieve the baby?

When he closed the makeshift gate behind the horses in the box canyon, they would become frightened and mill about. Sett could easily imagine a set of flinty hooves kicking toward the new horse with her precious burden. Or in the melee a horse might shoulder the mare into a tree or against the rocks. Even without that kind of violence, the mare could decide to roll in the sandy streambed. Certainly her back must be itchy from wearing the saddle. Sett had no illusions of simply walking up and catching the horse; Indian ponies were little better than wild, and in the stressful situation with the new herd there was no way that the little mare would allow a strange man to approach. Once the wild ones realized their escape route was blocked, they

would be panicked and milling and it would be dangerous for him to be in the box canyon on foot at all.

The horses had disappeared single-file between the rocks of the narrow canyon, and if Sett were going to slip down and lash the gate poles across the opening, now was the time to do it. But he hesitated. If he did nothing, the herd would drink and then return to their normal routine of grazing on the plain below. If they did not see him, he could easily spring his trap at a later date. But could he catch the Indian pony out on the open plain, or would she run with the rest of the herd?

The earlier enjoyable daydream about spending his profits from the sale of the geldings drained away and Sett scowled. There was only one thing to do: catch that scruffy pony and get that baby and to hell with catching the geldings.

Sett scrambled down the far side of the bluff. Hidden again in a cluster of sagebrush, he inched forward and sighted down into the little flat meadow below the watering hole. The lead mare was done drinking, the younger mares and the geldings now snorting and pawing at the shallow water that pooled in the sandy bottom. The new spotted mare was hanging back, nervous about approaching the rest of the horses, and Sett sent a quick thank-you to whatever god controlled horses. The stallion was busy moving between her and the established herd and so the pony stood alone. She was thirsty though. Sett could see her nostrils flaring to take in the scent of the cool water, and he had the sudden idea that maybe she would wait until the rest of the horses had finished drinking to go to the spring. Perhaps the rest of the horses would head out of the canyon and Sett could pinch off just the pony.

It almost worked that way. The black mare finished drinking and then wallowed in the wet sand, followed in suit by her colt and then the other mares. Sticky and coated with clinging sand, the lead mare sauntered back down

the canyon, passing through the narrow trail where Sett had planned to lash the poles. One by one, the others followed. Finally the little pony went to the water and drank. The stallion joined her then dropped to his knees to roll. The pony pawed and Sett held his breath again. *Please,* he thought, *please don't lay down on that child. Please don't lay down now.*

The chestnut stallion leaped back to his feet, shook, and then started quickly after his disappearing herd. The pony, not willing to be long out of sight of her newfound companions, turned to follow. Sett leaped up from his hiding place and jumped onto the shale slide that made up the south wall of the canyon. He skidded and slid in a scattering of rocks, grabbing brush and bunchgrass to slow his descent. Startled, the stallion halted, tossed his head up, and stared at the sudden appearance of the man between him and his departing mares. With a snort of alarm, the chestnut charged toward the cottonwoods where the narrow trail wound between the trees and the enclosing rocks. But Sett was there before him, blocking the escape with a wild leap and frantic wave of his battered hat. The horse spooked back and sought another route up the broken cliffs, with the pony gamely trying to keep up. Sett sprinted down the trail, his chest hurting from the labor of running in the high mountain air. He could hear the mustangs ahead of him crashing through the trees, panicked by Sett's wild plunge off the ridge. He briefly wondered how long it would be before they would venture back into his spoiled trap, but then he was at the hidden poles and he did not have time to worry about them. Grabbing the first long sapling from his hidden stack, he dropped it into the forks of a tree. With a quick lash of the rope, the first rail was fixed in place. As quickly, he dragged the second pole into place. Only after he had securely lashed all five poles to the trees, making a solid rail fence that completely blocked the captured horses from escape, did he pause to gasp and collect his thoughts.

and that, before wrapping the rope around a sturdy tree limb. *You're a good boy*, Sett thought as he stroked the stallion's shoulder. *I hope those colts you sired are as reasonable*. Then he turned his attention to the scrubby pony who danced just beyond his grasp.

The little mare was not as trusting of the tall man as her newfound companion. She maneuvered to keep the chestnut between the man and herself and, when pressed, offered to duck under the stallion's neck. Alarmed, Sett backed off. The last thing he needed now was for the little mare to panic and try to squeeze between the stallion and the trees. The image of the cradleboard being dragged between unforgiving trunks sent Sett back to his sitting position on the ground. He wished he'd thought to bring the nosebag of grain from his saddlebags, but it was too late for that. He'd have to convince the pony to come to him without any bribes.

Sitting still on the ground by the stallion's head, he watched the pony. She seemed torn between sticking close to her new friend and being too close to the strange man. Her left ear was split, an old injury that had healed into an ugly forking of her spatulate ear. Her hooves were strong, but naturally worn, and there were no brands on her brown and white spotted coat. She was not a finely made horse, or a young one; her large jaw and thick neck joined into upright shoulders and a short back, and her tail was a solid mass of burrs. But her eyes were bright and large, and Sett thought that she was perhaps a fine little mount in spite of her looks.

Now the pony settled down and stood on the off-side of the stallion, where she did not have to look at the man sitting in the short grass. The long rein draped across a small sagebrush behind her. Sett didn't want to grab the rein; the pony might panic against the sudden pressure, but there was only so much time before nightfall. He had to take a chance.

It still took time. The sun was below the horizon when Sett finally stood at the end of the braided rope. Standing directly behind the chestnut stallion, Sett kept one hand on the horse's rump and slowly eased his way down to pick up the rein.

When the rope was in his hand, he rose back up to a standing position as quietly as he had crouched. The mare snorted suspiciously, but did not rush away. A surge of elation swept through Sett, but he didn't let it show. That child was still at the other end of a nine-foot rope and not in his grasp.

The pony didn't panic at the realization that she was caught. She flared her nostrils and pinned her floppy ears as he worked his way up the rein. Close enough to touch her, but she was not going to give in to that extent, not yet. She did not offer to sniff Sett's extended hand or allow him to rub her neck. She laid back her ears and threatened to bite. The cradleboard hung only a couple feet away, the thick cord looped over the crossed forks of the Indian saddle. The child's face looked like a reddened and wrinkled doll surrounded by the silvery rabbit fur. The desire to grab the cord and yank the child to safety pounded in Sett's chest, but any fast movement would send the pony away and possibly out of his control. Sett forced himself to take another deep breath.

A chill filled the air when the pony flinchingly allowed Sett to lay his hand on her neck. Rubbing soothingly, he inched toward her shoulder, murmuring a few phrases in Blackfeet though he did not know what he was saying. His hand scratching at the base of the scruffy mane, Sett hooked his thumb under the cord and lifted it up and away from the saddle horn. Swinging free, the cradleboard bounced against the pinto's shoulder, and she leaped away. Sett grasped the strap desperately and yanked the child and the carrier free of the frightened horse, and the sudden motion startled the tiny mouth into an O. A thin, weak wail

quavered briefly before the child's strength gave out, but it was a joyous sound to Sett Foster's ears. The child was still alive.

Now all the suppressed urges to hurry came over him and he carried the cradleboard in both hands. Nearly running, he scrambled between the bars of his pole gate and back up the slope to where he had left his saddlebags and canteen. Propping the board against a rock, he leaned close to see the child's face. The baby's eyes were squeezed shut, the lids swollen from sun and dust, but when Sett chucked the tiny face under the chin, the baby scowled, its tiny mouth puckering as if that was all the cry that it could muster. Sett sank to the ground in relief. The past hours of tension, now relieved by the sight of the living baby, made him suddenly weak and almost sick. But he could not rest now. The baby was too weak to cry, and who knew how long it had been without nourishment.

Sett poured water from the canteen onto his bandana, twisting it to a point and then tickling the baby's lips with the moist end. The child squirmed, working its mouth as the wet cloth dribbled water down its chin. Sett felt awfully clumsy, as if his hands were way too large for this job, but he smiled broadly when the child opened its mouth and some of the water droplets ran in. Satisfied that the baby had taken in some of the vital moisture, Sett gently tried to wipe some of the dust and grime from the dirty face. With careful, deliberate motions, he dabbed the damp cloth on the tiny chin, then wiped above the squinted eyes. The child again squirmed in its protective covering, and worked its mouth into a silent cry.

"There now, little one. It's all right," Sett crooned as he would to a nervous horse. He rewet the rag, but this time when the cool cloth touched the child's skin, its eyes forced their way open, and Sett was looking down into sky blue eyes that belonged to no Blackfeet child.

FOUR

Ria never slept well when Sett was away, but tonight she was more restless than usual. Coy curled up on the end of the pallet, but even with her faithful friend warming her feet, Ria was chilled. The cramping in her belly had lessened, and she had forced herself to drink a warm broth before lying down, but sleep eluded her and she gave in to the visions that had taunted her all day.

Children laughing, running, stirring up dust. Babies, tiny and helpless, dimpled and chubby-legged. Wild boys clinging to bouncing ponies, shiny-haired little girls sitting on Sett's knee. The images whirled around over her head, captured by the sapling rafters of the old cabin roof. Tears slid from Ria's eyes, wetting the sackcloth pillow she had sewn for their bed. There was a similar pillow filling the cradle box that she had pushed out of sight under the pallet. She did not want to think about it—how the mice would move into the sturdy box and use the pillow stuffing to line their nests. *That is fine*, Ria told herself harshly. *At least mouse babies will sleep in the down. Certainly no babies of mine ever will!*

Her mind punishing her with the specters of children she would never have, never hold, she stared up at the lantern-lit roof and wished there were a smoke hole instead of the metal chimney. Perhaps with a hole in the roof, her evil dreams could escape and not torture her so. But Sett had explained how his chimney would keep out drafts, making the cabin cozy for all of them in the long winters. He said unwanted dreams could escape through the cracks in the doors that opened to what had once been stables at the back of the cabin. But then he had caulked those with mud and grass, and so now Ria sat alone in the dark cabin with her haunts, and her sadness gave way to anger.

Why was she so cursed? What had she done to deserve this? Since she'd been a child a mere seven winters' old, when she'd held her newborn brother on her lap while First Wife helped her exhausted mother, she had wanted to one day hold a child of her own. The scent of that baby had made her child's breasts ache, and now she hurt again in that tender area that would never nourish a child. Long ago, Ria had learned to cry without making a sound. Now she wished she could let out all that was inside.

She looked again at the solid roof over her head. It was not that she did not appreciate it; Sett had worked hard to make the cabin secure and snug, but now that opening for the dreams to escape seemed necessary and she wished she had a traditional lodge, not one of white man's design.

She jerked upright from the pallet. The dog, startled, jumped to the packed earth floor, and Ria followed her out of bed. By the woodstove was a small hatchet, the one she used to split kindling. Grasping it, she climbed up onto the pallet. With the added inches, she could just reach the corner of the ceiling where it met the heavy logs of the back wall. Attacking the corner with the hatchet, she vented her rage and grief. The chips flew into the bed, onto the stove top. With each sharp whack, the bits of her dream neared escape. With a final, elbow-jarring blow, a tiny hole opened

up and fresh cold air rushed into the room. Ria dropped the hatchet on the floor and sank down onto the pallet. Now her sobs came loudly, chasing the lost hope out the hole in the roof and into the wild night.

She was barren.

She would never give birth to Sett's child.

Ria's eyes flew open. The cabin was dark, no morning light seeping in the one window, and for a moment she was disoriented. She had been dreaming of a clay jar, empty and cracked. Unusable. Perhaps her own nightmares had awakened her from the exhausted sleep. Then she heard her dog whine again from by the door.

She had a brief flicker of fear. Her hand raised involuntarily, her finger stroking across the slightly tilted eyebrow that would always remind her that not everyone was good and kind, like Sett. But if whatever had awakened Coy was dangerous, she would not have been wagging her tail, and Ria could hear the gentle whish of it in the stillness. Then she heard the snort, a greeting from her own horse in the pasture behind the cabin, and the soft hoof-falls of another horse approaching the yard. Sett must be returning, but why would he arrive in the middle of the night?

Ria's heart pounded again as she thought of Sett being hurt, of his horse returning without him. Her feet hit the packed-earth floor and she rushed to the door, nearly tripping over the dog that still waited there. She grabbed the drop latch and was about to fling the door open, but something stopped her. Her moment of hesitation was broken by Sett's soft voice from the yard.

"Ria? Are you awake?"

She yanked the door open, could see the dark shape of Sett's big mare against the starlit sky, could see Sett stepping down out of the saddle in his graceful way. He car-

ried something, grasped between his hands like a precious relic.

"Light the lamp," he said, and she turned back indoors to find a splinter on the lip of the wood box and catch it alight from the glowing coals in the stove. Carefully she removed the glass chimney of their only lantern and touched the burning splinter to the wick. A golden glow bounced around the room when she replaced the chimney.

Sett had come in the door, still holding his burden in front of him with both hands as if afraid he might drop it. Ria's eyes adjusted to the new light, and she thought for a moment that he held a shield. Then he took another step and thrust the leather-and-board bundle toward her.

"It's a baby," he croaked in a voice she barely recognized. "I don't know if it will live."

Ria's dark eyes met his, questions bright in them, then she took the cradleboard and he dropped his hands to his sides as if in great relief.

The cradleboard was light, the child tightly bound in the lacing of doeskin and rabbit fur. Strips of red flannel fluttered from the visor, the only decoration. The child screwed its eyes tight against the light, and gave a small chirp from cracked lips as Ria lay it on the pallet.

"Where did you get him?" Ria asked as she began unlacing the thongs that bound the child into its shelter.

Sett rubbed his hands over his face as if to wipe away the weariness and tension of his nighttime journey. "There was a new horse following the herd. Wearing an Indian saddle and bridle, and . . . that."

Ria was taking small notice of Sett but pulled back the cradleboard's skin flaps to release the naked infant. With the sudden freedom from the bindings and the rush of the chill air in the cabin, the infant let out an enraged squall and waved his tiny fists. Ria smiled.

"He's a boy, a son," she whispered, lifting the child up

to her shoulder, seemingly impervious to his shrill cries. Sett stepped away.

The child hesitated in his screams for a moment, a hiccupping pause that only brought a wider smile to the woman's face. She held the naked boy out at arm's length, examining his strong kicking legs and fine pale hair, admiring his resiliency after the time bound captive on a mustang pony.

"He is a courageous one already," Ria said, now placing the baby back on their bed. "There is warm water behind the stove. Pour it into the basin for me." Ria selected a soft cloth from her sewing basket and dipped it into the water that Sett brought. Carefully, she wiped the child clean.

Sett was hovering behind her, peering over her shoulder as she wrapped the child in a flannel cloth. The baby's cries were still piercing. He wrinkled his face up and let forth with noise to shake the rafter poles.

"I tried to give him some water. I have no idea how long he was alone on that horse. But I didn't know what to do, other than to bring him here." A hint of despair crept into Sett's voice.

Ria looked away from the baby. For all of Sett's strength and size, he looked like a small boy himself at the moment. It was not often that Ria saw Sett so discomfited, so concerned. Normally she would go to him, but now there were more pressing matters. "He will be fine, he is a strong boy. You did the right thing," she said.

"Do you want some broth for him?"

"Not now." Ria sat on the pallet and pulled the blanket up around her shoulder to shield the child from drafts. The baby's angry cries and flailing hands made her breasts ache. She thought of the hole in the corner of the cabin, the one she had hacked so desperately to let her wailings escape into the night, to let her despair and desires flee into a cold world. It had returned to her, her pleading. Returned to her in the form of an answer to her prayers: this small miracle,

a small, needy miracle, one that had swung in his cradleboard until Sett could find him and bring him to her. Ria rocked the baby in her arms, quieted him against her breast. Great tears of joy rolled down her cheeks and dropped onto the child's sunburned face.

Sett was very tired and hungry and very relieved that the baby was cuddled in Ria's arms now, not his. She had even been able to comfort him, for the frantic crying had ceased and the cabin took on a soft silence. Sett glanced at the stove. He'd love some hot food, but one look at the woman, now settled on the pallet with a blanket wrapped around her, and Sett knew he would have to get dinner himself. He stoked up the fire and filled a pot with water from the bucket by the door.

The woman's dark head lightly nodded, so absorbed was she in the child. Sett could hear her crooning, the Blackfeet words indistinct. Sett put a second kettle on the stove. He said as if to himself, "The herd spooked away. Don't think I'll get 'em caught again this year. I brought the pony back here, though. I better go out now and put the mare and pony away. Big mare came home fast and sure in the dark." Sett looked again at Ria, huddled and humming in the blanket. She seemed to have only a bare awareness of his presence, nodding whenever he ended a statement, without regard to what it was. It gave Sett a cold shudder of aloneness.

"Ria?"

The dark head nodded again.

"How are we going to feed him?"

Now she turned her face up to meet his gaze, and he was surprised by the wetness in her eyes. "Do not worry, he is eating."

Sett crossed the room, knelt down beside her, and lifted the edge of the blanket. Ria had loosened the buttons of the man's shirt that she favored, and the child, nestled in the crook of her arm, was nursing contentedly. The sight was not what Sett had expected, and for a mo-

ment he had the odd sensation that he was looking at a different woman.

"How . . . ?" he whispered.

Ria smiled, more at the child than at him. "Go take care of your horse," she said.

Sett Foster rose slowly, checked the firebox, added another stick of wood, and without another word, went out to unsaddle his mare.

Morning arrived crisp and clear, the fall weather carrying the snap of the approaching winter. Sett brought a bucket of fresh water up from the creek, to find Ria already rustling around the cabin, stoking the fire and warming the frying pan. She hummed to herself, a cheery-sounding repetition of notes that he did not recognize, though she had known the lullaby all her life. He glanced over at the pillow-lined box, but the infant was not there. Only when Ria turned and smiled at him did he realize that she had bound the baby under her shirt in a sling of fabric.

"Are you hungry? I can fry bacon," she said.

Sett nodded. "Starving." He smiled back. It had been so long since he had noticed Ria smiling. Now she went back to her humming while she sliced thick chunks off the side of bacon and dropped them to sizzle in the pan. As the bacon fried, she stirred the kettle of beans that resided on the back of the stove. Sett sat down on the bench at the small table, watching the young woman as she cooked breakfast with a barely noticeable, precious bundle slung under her shirt. Sett again had the strange sensation that he was looking at someone he didn't really know.

Ria placed the tin plate with bacon, beans, and a rewarmed biscuit in front of her man, then took some for herself and ate with relish. Sett almost forgot his meal, watching how happily Ria scooped the meat onto the bread. He realized she had been barely picking at her food recently, eating only a little and never anything greasy or spicy. He wondered about it while chewing. He didn't know much about women,

either hadn't been around or hadn't paid attention, though he did recall his friend Poke mentioning that his wife felt ill when she was expecting their daughters. Still, it made no sense now. Neither did Ria's full breasts, which seemed to satisfy the child when he whimpered. Sett took a bite of the biscuit and pondered the curiosity of Ria.

"Will you be all right here by yourself? I need to go doctor the pony. She has a big gall from wearing that Indian saddle so long," Sett said as he finished off the beans.

Ria nodded. "I'm not by myself." She smiled and glanced down at the lump beneath her shirt. "Yes, we will be fine."

"Do you need anything here before I go?" Sett usually didn't worry about Ria. She was as well equipped to care for the house and animals as he in most situations. He wasn't sure why it bothered him to leave her now.

"Do not worry, Sett. Go take care of your horses." She stacked the plates on the end of the rough table, preparing to wash them later in the stream while the child slept.

Sett rose and picked up his hat from the peg by the door. He said, "We can decide what to do with the baby when I get back."

Ria tensed, said, "His name is Tapikamiiwa, Cricket. I am keeping him." The smile had vanished from Ria's face, her dark eyes now somber. It was a look that Sett knew well.

"Ria, he must already have a name. Someone must be looking for him." The woman did not blink, just stared at him as if she were hearing the ranting of a lunatic. Sett tried again. "He is a white child, Ria. Look at his blue eyes. Look at that pale hair. Somewhere he has a family that wants to know he's alive."

"And if he were black-haired it would be different? No one would care? He is a Blackfeet child. He was in a Blackfeet cradleboard. His mother must be dead. No Blackfeet mother would leave her child unattended on a pony. Now

I am his mother." It was a long speech for Ria, her anger overcoming her usual shyness.

Sett realized he was clutching his hat and crushing the already battered brim. He crammed it on his head to save it from his hands. Arguing would do no good. He had never won an argument with her. Sett sighed. Now she did not seem unfamiliar, even if she did have a bulge under her shirt. Now she was exactly as he had first known her, a she-badger defending her own.

"No one else is going to believe he is your child," he explained, trying to maintain a calm voice. "What's going to happen when people find out we have him, and didn't try to find his parents? We are going to end up with the law here, Ria. And you know I don't want to have any more to do with the wrong side of the law."

"No one has to find out he is here. They will forget. They will believe he is ours."

"We can't just avoid going to the Millers' for the rest of our lives. You know that. They will know this baby isn't ours." Aggravation was seeping into his voice against his will.

"They are your friends. They will not tell."

"Damn it, Ria, I am not going to ask them for that. Poke and Samantha have taken enough risks on my—our—behalf." Sett squelched the desire to give her a good shake. "We have to make an effort to find the baby's real parents. I'll go talk to the sheriff in Verdy."

Ria hiked up her shirt and adjusted the baby in the sling. With her arms folded under the child, she looked back at Sett. "Then we will go where no one knows us. No one will know Tapikamiiwa is not mine."

"We? We will go somewhere? This is my home, this is where I live." Sett pointed at the ground.

"Me. I will go with Tapikamiiwa. You stay here in your empty home." It was unusually sarcastic, not Ria's style, but the threat of her taking off over the mountains was

not new. He had heard that before. Had heard it and not believed her, until she'd proved just how determined she could be.

"You are not going anywhere without me." Sett lowered his voice to a whisper, caught himself with his hand on the hilt of his sheathed knife. He turned and stomped out the low doorway. Halfway across the grassy yard, he spun around again and came back to lean in the door. Ria still stood in the middle of the small cabin, the babe cradled in her arms, her eyes glittering with anger. "Pack your kit. We are going to Verdy." Sett stalked away toward the corral before she could answer.

Ria watched his receding form through the narrow doorway of the old line cabin. She clenched her fist and hissed one of her few American curses. "Bastard." The infant startled awake with a cry, and Ria's fury turned to guilt as she comforted the child.

FIVE

Mary Alice McFee gripped the scarf that battened her black hat onto her thick gray hair. The gusting wind threatened to blow her right through the door as she pushed it open, and she burst into the office of the *Rocky Mountain Post* with a swirl of snow and black cloak. The clerk behind the counter snapped his head up from his paperwork at her entrance.

"Mrs. McFee! Why ever are you out on such a day?" The man pulled his spectacles off and hurried to shove the door closed behind his visitor. Mary Alice adjusted the scarf, loosening it now in the relative warmth and comfort of the room.

"I came to see Mr. Morgan," she said as she advanced toward the closed door at the rear of the office. "He's in, I presume?"

The clerk bustled around to block her but was too late.

"Ma'am, he is not to be disturbed!" The clerk pleaded as Mary Alice grasped the brass doorknob and swung the door, revealing Mr. Morgan, editor of the *Post*, sitting with his feet propped up on the desk and a brown bottle within easy reach. The man hardly looked surprised.

"Hard at work again, Alfred?" Mary Alice stood in front of the desk, casting a knowing eye on the man and trying not to smile.

"Why, Mrs. McFee! Here to collect more nonexistent rent? Is it the first of the month already?" Alfred Morgan did not bother to take his boots down from the cluttered desk. He was making muddy smudges on the rumpled papers under his heels. He flicked his fingers at the clerk, who was hovering in the doorway with apologies on his lips. "Go away, Curtis. Take a break and get a drink or something." The clerk looked surprised but retreated from the doorway quickly, grabbed his coat from the rack, and battled his way out of the office into the storm.

"Please, do sit down, Mary Alice. Would you like a drink?" Alfred picked up the bottle.

The woman allowed a small smile to tickle her generous mouth. "I'd certainly take you up on that, Alfred, were it not nine in the morning." She settled herself in the available chair, carefully removing some pages of what looked like mine statistics first.

"It's that late, is it? I've been up all night. With this storm, one can hardly tell the sunrise." Morgan tipped another sip of liquor into his mug and appraised his visitor from behind his smudged spectacles. Mary Alice McFee! Still a handsome woman after more bouts of bad luck than he could count. Old Ben had been the lucky one, to catch her eye when she was young. It had made Ben a successful man, having such a mate. Not successful enough to live past sixty, though, so now the McFee empire was run by the deft hand of Mary Alice through her eldest son, William. A rich widow, she was, but not an available one. That, she made most clear. Alfred Morgan tasted his brandy.

"What brings you out on such a lovely fall day?" he asked.

Mary Alice reached into her handbag and brought out a folded sheet of paper. "I wish to place an advertisement in your paper. In fact, I would like it wired to every paper in the Western territories." She leaned forward to hand the page across the desk. Morgan examined it, pursed his lips, and grunted, "Huh."

"You realize that every scalawag in the territory will be trying to sell you a baby?" he said.

"I believe I will be able to discern the truth when I see it, Mr. Morgan. Besides, what other choice do I have? I have exhausted all the other resources. There has been no response from the army or from any sheriff. No one seems to have time to search anymore. And I just can't rest until my grandson is found."

Morgan fortified himself with another sip of brandy. "Are you sure you wouldn't like a small drink? Because what I have to say next you are not going to want to hear."

"I know exactly what you are going to say, Alfred. And it will make no difference."

"It might." Now Alfred Morgan pulled his feet down from the desk and sat up, straightening his vest to compose himself. "Mary Alice, I've known you since you were a little thing, and you were never one to give up or give in. Ben was my good friend, and a very lucky man. So I am going to say this in the name of the many long years of our friendship. My dear, this child is dead. When that stage rolled over and your daughter was killed, that child died too."

Mary Alice stared at the man for a long moment. She cleared her throat and nodded at his harsh words.

"Print the advertisement, Alfred," she said, her voice steely with self-control. "I will deal with what comes of it."

Alfred Morgan shook his head sadly. Poor Mary Alice, she'd lost so much in the last few years. Perhaps she was simply unable to believe that her tiny grandson was gone too, gone before she had even seen him.

Morgan tapped his fingers thoughtfully on the paper that Mary Alice had handed him. A reward of the size she was offering would have every ne'er-do-well in the country offering up an infant. There could be kidnappings, or children sold away from poor mothers. Besides, he had seen the reports of the accident, a tragic situation to be sure. The stagecoach had overturned on a narrow road in remote mountains, rolled over and over down the canyon slope and come to rest on a riverbank. When the coach had not arrived for its scheduled stop, nearly a day later, a search party was sent out. It had been five days before someone located the wreck. Mary Alice's daughter Amanda, her husband, and the driver were dead. But no sign of Amanda's young child was found.

Morgan looked across at his friend's widow. He could certainly understand her desire for the child to have somehow survived, but the evidence was overwhelmingly otherwise. The baby could have been washed down the rushing river, could have been thrown from the stagecoach anywhere along its disastrous descent, could have been dragged away by the scavenging wild animals. As much as he wished to believe with her that the child was safe somewhere, just waiting to be returned to his family, he could not. And by running this advertisement, offering the huge reward, he knew that Mary Alice McFee would swamp herself with descriptions of orphans, each one first raising then dashing her hopes.

Mary Alice stared back at the newspaperman, her bright blue eyes clear and tearless. "Print the notice. Alfred, you know I can afford the reward. But I can not afford to not try!"

Alfred Morgan sighed. He picked up the paper again, read the simple words, and put the sheet on a stack at the side of his desk. "All right, Mary Alice, I'll publish your notice. But I want you to promise me that you will allow William to screen the responses, or that you will hire a solicitor to do that. There is no reason for you to consider every pitch from some rascal with a three-year-old Indian child to sell."

Mary Alice inclined her head, her black hat dipping a bit as she did. "Yes, Alfred, I understand your concerns. When will the advertisement come out?"

"I will get it in the next issue, but it will take time for the posts to carry it west."

"Fine. Thank you, Alfred. Now, how much do I owe?" She opened her handbag and drew out a coin purse. Morgan waved her away with one chubby hand.

"No, Mary Alice, I can't charge you for misery."

"But you could for possibility and hope. I know this newspaper isn't making you a living. Now, how much?" Mary Alice chose a coin and laid it on the desk, then, rising from her chair, she pulled her scarf tight over her neat hair. "I'd like it run weekly. That should cover the first time. Thank you again, Alfred."

He waited until her black-coated figure had pulled the office door closed before pouring himself another, stiffer drink and downing it in one swallow.

SIX

Ria rode in a sullen silence, following Sett's horse and leading the Indian pony, packed with their supplies. Even Coy sensed the tension between them and carefully kept out of the way as they rode down the mountainside. After a few hours, Sett tried to talk to her, commenting on the water level in the creek, or that he should get a message to Lieutenant Kelly about not having horses to sell this year, but she refused to answer him in spite of his friendly tone of voice. If he was going to treat her like a prisoner bent on escape, he didn't deserve her attention. She pulled her blanket up and hid the baby from him. Sett tried to ignore her cold shoulder.

"We'll make camp here at the aspen grove," Sett finally said. "I'll go fish us up some supper while you get the fire started."

"You are not afraid I will run away?" Ria said bitterly.

"You won't."

Ria stared at the tall man. She wouldn't run away, not yet when he could just track her down faster than she could move. The years of living with Sett Foster had taught her much about the man's skill in the wilderness. It complemented her own. That she was now at odds with him caused tears to threaten in her eyes, and she turned away so that he would not see them. Ria swung down from her horse and carefully placed the baby's cradleboard against a log while she gathered up dry sagebrush for a fire.

The aspen were nearly bare, a scattering of golden leaves still clinging to the more sheltered branches under the canyon wall. The ground underneath was littered with fallen leaves. They covered the old fire ring and cushioned each step. They had camped here before, in the warm days of summer. It was a pleasant memory that made Ria's throat tighten. She had never thought that Sett would turn so stubborn and knot-headed. Ria dragged the saddlebags off of her red horse and then started to lift the heavy panniers from the pony's saddle. Sett was beside her in an instant.

"Let me do that," he said, pulling the heavy box from her hands. Ria bit her lip and turned back to the camp preparations, pretending not to notice that Sett was standing silently by, watching her with sad eyes as she walked away.

Sett unsaddled and turned the horses loose in their hobbles. The bay mare and Fox Ears never strayed far, but he did not trust the spotted pony and so left her tied securely to the tree. He retrieved his fishing tackle, the leather case similar to an arrow quiver. To make it, Ria had used fire-toughened hide rolled into a tube, lacing the edges together with strong lashes that dangled in graduated fringe, the cap hinged on one side and held closed with a toggle. Inside were stowed the two shafts, which fitted together in a rawhide sheath to form a long slender pole with tiny wire loops for the line. A carrying strap which he could sling over his shoulder also had small pouches for hooks, extra line, and the weights he had molded from soft lead. He started to call to Ria again, to tell her that he would be just downstream if she needed him, but she resolutely turned her back on him and busied herself with the fire. With a sinking feeling, Sett headed down the creek bank.

Sett generally enjoyed fishing because of the time it gave him to think. Now he had plenty to mull over. He hiked a ways to find a pool this late in the season, finally choosing a dark pothole formed under the exposed roots of a cottonwood tree. He fitted the two halves of the pole together, turned over some rocks until he found something to bait the hook with, and cast the line into the water.

The loss of the income from the three colts was a small part of his troubles. In the past few years having income hadn't really mattered. He and Ria lived off the land. The appearance of being a duly employed citizen mattered more than whether he actually made money, but he had found a ready market for the horses he captured and trained. That was how he had met Lieutenant Kelly. The soldier had been passing through with a detail and noticed one of the nicer horses in the sale corral. He'd purchased the horse and on his next trip through had queried the gelding's origins. After the lieutenant met Sett, it was a standing agreement between them that any quality horses Sett trained would go directly to Kelly. He was expecting these three, so it was only fair to let the man know that the horses would be delayed. That was not a problem, since he would be in Verdy anyway.

The first bite from the trout almost startled him, so far away was he in his thoughts. He gathered the line up in his right hand, wrapping the filament around his palm in quick twists. The trout flopped up on the bank and Sett dispatched it quickly with his knife handle.

It had been a long time since he and Ria had quarreled about anything, so long that the memory of how staunch she could be had faded. Those years ago, when Sett had finally returned to his family's Cottonwood homestead to find his family murdered and violent strangers living in his childhood home, he had tried to protect Ria, to send her to safety with his friends at the trading post. He had asked her to promise to stay away while he dealt with the killers, but instead she had stolen a horse and returned to help him in a battle that likely would have killed him had she not. It had been the beginning of a strong partnership between them. Now it appeared that her allegiance might well be diverted from saving his sorry hide, and the thought that she held such anger for him hurt.

It was a short matter of time before Sett had enough fish for their dinner. Still he dawdled along the banks as he returned to the camp. The fall grass was brown and soft, each footfall muted by leaf mold and debris. There was a singular snap to the air, not yet cold but mindful of the coming winter. It was a dying time of year, and Sett could not push away the feeling of gloom as he made his way back to the camp and Ria and the child.

It was not that he didn't care. The thought of taking the baby away, of causing Ria such pain, was terrible, but Sett knew that if someone was searching for the towheaded child, and found them, even years from now, the end result would be the same. Perhaps too it was the still-painful loss of his own family that nagged him with the image of a sad-eyed mother searching forever for her lost child. Could he balance that picture with the hatred in Ria's eyes when he did what he had to do?

He could smell the smoke of the camp before he could see it. Coy came out to meet him, though she looked back at Ria as if aware that being friends with Sett might be risky at this time. Ria was kneeling by the fire, checking something in the coals. The coffeepot was at the side of the grate, and the baby was propped up nearby in his cradleboard. It was a peaceful scene, one which Sett had imagined many times, one with which he was happy. One which he was compelled to destroy.

Ria heard him approaching but refused to look at him. She chewed a bit of jerky as she worked over the fire. When her hands were free, she leaned over and placed a dab of the softened meat from her mouth on her finger and offered it to Cricket. The baby stuck his pink tongue out at the taste, but she hoped he had swallowed some of the nourishing juices. She smiled at him and he opened his mouth again, a baby bird that she could not refuse. It was almost enough to make her turn to Sett, standing behind her, and smile at him too. But she would not. Wiping the child's face with her fingertips, she rose and composed her face into the flat mask that she had learned so well in her youth. She turned and reached for the cleaned trout.

"You are feeding him regular food?" Sett asked, maintaining his grip on the stick which held the trout, just to make her stay near.

She shook her head curtly. "No, just the juice."

"That's good. I mean, I guess that's good," Sett said.

Ria tugged on the stick. She did not want to talk to Sett about Tapikamiiwa. She could not start talking about it. She wanted Sett to stay on his side of the fire and leave her to brood. But he didn't. He grasped his end of the stick as if it were a lifeline and stared into her eyes. She finally gave up tugging on the stick, finally gave up avoiding his eyes.

"Ria, I will do everything I can to keep this baby," he said softly. "I promise you that."

The tears that had been welling all afternoon now spilled over, slipping down Ria's brown cheeks though she hated the idea of crying in front of him. He would promise. He would promise to try. And she knew that a promise meant much to Sett.

She let go of the string of fish. It dropped to the ground. He slid his arms around her and pulled her close, muttering into her hair, "I don't know if everything will be enough."

Her tears came harder now, staining the front of the shirt she had sewed for him, draining her of her anger and leaving only a fear of what was to come.

SEVEN

Verdy, Montana Territory

Deputy Sheriff Sketch Jones took a surreptitious sip from the brown bottle before slipping it back in the pocket of his overcoat. He caught his wife Eliza looking at him and cleared his throat

"This cold weather makes my joints ache," he complained.

"And in the summer, the heat gives you the hives," she replied sarcastically before turning back to the sock she was darning. She knew full well that the bottle made occasional trips to the deputy's lips; though, as he always pointed out, never when he was on duty. It was one of his failings, and not his largest one, but who was she to point that out? She had her own troubles and her own bottle of solutions for them.

The couple sat in a tiny rented room on the second floor of the Bonaparte Hotel in Verdy. The winter wind whistled between the cracks in the wall boards, and the raucous noise from a Saturday evening in the barroom below drifted up so loudly they might as well be sitting at the card tables with the miners. In all, it was a disgusting situation.

Eliza stabbed her darning needle with vengeance into the thick sock.

"I suppose you are working the night shift yet again?" she complained. "And still without a raise. When did the sheriff say you would get that raise? Last month? Or the month before? The citizens of this so-called city should roast in Hell for expecting their peace officers—ha! peace officers!—to work such ungodly hours for the pennies they pay!"

"I think that Hell is a popular place around here—it's the chance of being warm." Jones fingered the tempting bottle in his pocket once more but did not have the courage to bring it out again in front of his wife.

She continued, "And that skunk Coleman should be the first through the fiery gates. Him taking the easy shifts and making you do all the hard work. All the dangerous jobs! Look at this! Unable to afford a decent cabin! How long am I supposed to live like a nomad in this flea-ridden hotel?"

Sketch Jones was silent. He pulled out his watch. Still over an hour before he came on duty. Over an hour before he could escape. He grumbled. "Come on, Eliza, Coleman is getting old. He's making noise about retiring, not running for reelection next year. If I stay on, I'll be a shoo-in . . ."

"Unless Coleman changes his mind. Why not? He has you to do all the dirty work while he struts around tipping his hat to the socialites and kissing babies!" Eliza leaned low to peer at her darning. "And you, Mr. Jones, you just take it all. No effort. No ambition. Father was right."

Sketch Jones gritted his teeth. Yeah, her father was right. He was right there shaking Sketch's hand when Sketch had asked for his spinster daughter's hand in marriage. Hell, he was probably so damned excited to have someone offering to take the complaining biddy off his hands . . .

Sketch needed to change this subject. He picked up the

folded copy of the newspaper that he'd swiped off the hotel desk that morning. There was a large advertisement there, the lettering at the top both dark and elaborate. Sketch squinted at it. Finally he asked, "Eliza, what's this say?"

Eliza put her darning in her lap and adjusted her spectacles. She gave a small *humph* as she reached for the newspaper.

"Reward. Lost child. One thousand dollars in exchange for the safe return of the infant son of David and Amanda McFee Bruce, who lost their lives in an accident September 1886 between Verdy and Butte."

"One thousand dollars. That's what I thought it said," Jones said.

"I'm surprised you could read that much," Eliza handed the paper back to him. She returned to her needlework, concentrating on knotting off the yarn without leaving a lump at the toe of the sock. She had reason to be careful. It was her sock.

Sketch ignored her sarcasm. "That's a lot of money," he said. "The sheriff mentioned that accident. Rich folks; their stage went off the road."

"Yes, indeed. The child is probably dead."

Sketch Jones carefully folded the paper so that the notice lay open on the rough table. "Or being raised by savages," he said.

Eliza gave a snort of disgust. "Better dead." She snipped the thread from the mended sock and returned the tiny scissors to her sewing kit. "Though, since the Injuns are all confined to the reservation, I suppose there's not much chance that they have the child."

"There was some renegades about, left the reservation to go hunting, but the cavalry rounded them all back up, I heard." Jones slipped his hand into his pocket, fingered the tempting bottle again. "The family thinks the child is alive, I guess. A thousand dollars would come in mighty handy 'bout now."

Eliza cast a gaze as cold as the bare floor at him. "As if you would be the one to find it! Why don't you better spend your time finding another job? Or go stake a claim in Alder Gulch? Anything to get us out of this misery-bound hole that bills itself as the finest hotel in Montana!" She rose and pulled her shawl up around her scrawny shoulders, stomped the three steps across the tiny room, and returned her sewing kit to her valise.

"Eliza, my turn'll come up if I stick with this job. I'll be the next sheriff of this city, and it'll change our fortunes here." Jones took advantage of his wife's turned back to bring the bottle swiftly again to his lips. Then he grabbed up the newspaper, the big letters standing out as if addressed just to him. "See, it's an opportunity, knowing this. One never knows when opportunity will knock."

Eliza gave a final harrumph. "Well, don't let the pounding on the door wake me. I'm going to bed. Perhaps it will be warmer with the fleas!"

Jones leaned back in the chair and brought the newspaper closer to the glow of the lamp. He stared at the notice, took another swig from his bottle, and let a smile tease his lips.

EIGHT

Sett's misgivings grew as they approached the outskirts of the town of Verdy. As they passed through the first scattering of houses, then joined the well-used road from the north, the weight of his decision sagged around his shoulders as if he were wearing a miserably wet buffalo robe. But it was not a choice he could easily shrug off. The idea that he should have cared for the lost baby himself for the long day's ride to Verdy was easily rejected. If he'd shown up in town alone with the child, some kind citizen would have relieved him of that burden, and any remote chance that he and Ria could adopt the boy, should his real family not be found, would have been dashed.

So Sett's only choice had been to bring Ria and the baby, keeping her in sight and hoping for the best. Which was, at the very least, not going to be pleasant.

Ria huddled into her coat and let Fox Ears lag behind the bay mare as if she could stave off entering the town by simply slowing down. She did not smile or return greetings when they encountered other travelers, and her dog snarled at everyone who passed. Her woolen blanket hung down over the cradleboard, both to shield Cricket from the raw wind and to hide him from view. The spotted pony was on the lead behind her, carrying the Blackfeet saddle and the saddlebags with their supplies. Sett paused his mare and turned to check on Ria. Her eyes darted from him, to the houses in the distance, to the cloud of dust that heralded yet another wagon approaching on the road.

"How are you doing?" Sett asked, reining his mare around close to her. She nodded, but then shrugged the shawl up over her head even further, shielding her face from the next group of strangers.

Sett understood. He was not fond of cities and their chaotic bustle, but in her whole life Ria had never dealt with more than a handful of people at once. When visiting at the trading post, she would often withdraw into a side room if a stage-load of strangers arrived. When she did stay at the table, she was silent to the point of attracting glances. Here they had encountered more people in the past hour than Ria had seen in the past year, and it was soon to get worse. Verdy had grown into a thriving town after the railroad came through. These few wagons on the road were just a dribble compared to the flood of humanity that would wash around them before sunset. Sett clenched his teeth and watched fear spark across Ria's eyes.

"You don't have to go. You can wait back in camp," he suggested.

"But you will take Tapikamiiwa in to the sheriff." It was not a question, though spoken in a tiny voice. "He should not be alone."

"He won't be alone. He'll be with me." Sett didn't want to argue with her here in the middle of the road. It could only make matters worse.

Ria shrugged her shawl again and laid her hand on the top of the cradleboard where the child slept. "I will stay with him." Her voice now was cold, as if she were agreeing to march to a waiting scaffold.

"Okay. But stick close. You don't have to talk to anyone.

Just stay near me." He turned the mare back toward town, warning bells clanging in his head.

Ria had not ever imagined anything like it. The southern edge of town spilled down a slope, as if in its rush to grow around the mines it had boiled over the edge of the low bluff and taken haphazard course in the talus shale. Houses of every description perched along the road, with some version of outbuildings—chicken coops, low barns, privies—decorating each of the yards. Fowl and children darted across the road in front of them, and the pinto pony snorted and tugged on her lead. Dogs dashed out to defend their territories, and Coy warned them off with an impressive show of teeth, all the while trotting just under Fox Ears's nose. A two-storey house commanded a corner of the street, its porch ornate with turned spindles holding up the railings and curlicues painted a bright red. Ria could not help but gawk as they rode past. She wanted to ask Sett if a very rich person lived there, but it seemed her tongue was frozen in her mouth.

At the crest of the hill, the street turned again, and now the full glory of Verdy hit her with an assault that began in her nose and then proceeded to her ears. Fresh horse dung, soap in the making, the occasional whiff of some good thing cooking, then an angry clatter, cracking whips, and strange metallic music which tinkled out the open door of a popular building. The street now filled with conveyances: wagons and horsemen and odd drayage vehicles pulled by teams of oxen which plodded resolutely, forcing everyone else to wend their way to the side. Ria finally pulled her stunned gaze from all the activity and realized that Sett was a ways ahead, separated from her by some boys driving a flock of geese with a stick, and a dark-skinned woman carrying a large basket. Panic rose into Ria's chest, a type of fear that was both unfamiliar and overwhelming. What if she lost sight of Sett here in this melee? How would she find him again? She kicked Fox Ears hard with her heels, and the horse raised his head at the unexpected jab. Pushing her way through the geese, the boys yelling and waving their sticks as they scattered, Ria caught up to Sett and concentrated on keeping Fox Ears's nose on the bay mare's tail, so close in fact that they bumped right into her when Sett suddenly stopped.

"Kiernan? That you?" Sett exclaimed as he swung down from the saddle.

"Foster? I wasn't expecting you this soon!" The man called Kiernan marched out into the street and stuck his hand out for Sett to grasp. He was almost as tall as Sett, but with a long and lanky build that reminded Ria of a pliant sapling. He wore blue wool army trousers with a stripe up the leg and a fancy jacket with gold buttons, which made him look to Ria like he was very important. The man grinned widely at Sett, and she could not imagine who he could be. But then, maybe with all else that was whirling around in her brain, perhaps she had forgotten something that Sett had once told her. She sat on her horse in the middle of the street and felt even more awkward than she had before.

The man pumped Sett's hand, and Sett responded with a warm clap on his shoulder, and their words blended into the general hubbub until Ria heard her name.

"Kiernan, this is my wife. Ria, Lieutenant Kiernan Kelly. He's the one who bought us out of colts last year."

The lieutenant did an admirable job of trying not to stare. His quick glance took in Ria's large man's coat and beaded moccasins and what he guessed to be a cradleboard hanging under the blanket. She was, to all appearances, an Indian, but Lieutenant Kelly both was quick-witted and considered Sett Foster a friend, as well as a valuable business acquaintance. He stepped forward and touched his hat brim.

"Pleased to make your acquaintance, Mrs. Foster. Your husband is becoming a most in-demand horse breaker." He looked at her expectantly for a long while, then cast a quick glance at Sett.

Sett's grin hardened when he caught Ria's eye. She knew she was supposed to acknowledge this man, maybe was supposed to say something to him, but she could not. She winced back into her shawl.

"Ria's not been feeling well, and it's been a long ride. I think we better put our horses up and get a room," Sett said.

"Well, hope you are feeling better soon, ma'am," the soldier said before turning to Sett. Their voices drifted back into the mishmash of town noises and Ria stroked the fringe of the cradleboard. The sleeping child was all that kept her from digging her heels into the sides of her horse and exiting this crazy place at a gallop.

Maybe Sett had been telling the truth to the soldier. She was not feeling very well at all, and the ride had tired her out beyond any exhaustion she could remember. But if she left, who would care for Cricket? And when his family was not found, who would claim him? She sat on her horse in the middle of the swarm of humanity and waited for Sett to lead them to the next challenge.

NINE

William McFee waved a handful of papers as he came in the front door. From her seat at her tidy desk, Mary Alice could see his chagrin and guess its cause.

"Mother, every scoundrel west of the Mississippi must be in Montana Territory." He came to a stop in front of her, brandishing the letters as if fanning flames. "Just look at these! 'We have your child. We found her by the side of the trail north of Billings. She says her name is Mandy.' Or this one, 'My dear wife has raised for years the boy abandoned in Virginia City. He is bright and does well in school.' That one goes so far as to ask for repayment of the costs of raising the child, along with the reward!"

Mary Alice regarded his bluster with a calm shake of her gray head. "If they are not the ones, Willie, toss them away." She motioned to the parlor stove. Her son suddenly stood stock still, the angry redness in his cheeks draining away in shame.

"I'm sorry, Mother. Every time I go to the post, I pray that there will be a legitimate lead to Amanda's baby.

And these, these shysters! I cannot believe there are that many orphaned children in the world, or that there are that many people willing to claim a child parentless, just for money."

"There are most likely many more parentless children than we can imagine, and many more people who would sell their souls for a small sum. It is not your fault," Mary Alice said to console him. William rubbed his fingers across his brow and sighed deeply. Mary Alice reached over to pat his other hand, which still clutched the letters. Her only son, William had proven himself to be the reliable, responsible sort, just like his father. Perhaps too responsible, in that he devoted himself to running the McFee businesses and assisting her to the point that he ignored social duty—a handsome young man should be courting some likely girl, not doting on his mother. His sister's death had hit him hard. Mary Alice wondered if she were not doing her son a great disservice to be so determinedly clinging to these last shreds of hope.

"Willie, have you spoken with Miss Preston recently? I saw her mother today in the mercantile and she asked after you." There, a safe change of subject for her son's good.

William said, "Yes, actually, we crossed paths this morning at the bank and I walked her home. She said to give you her regards."

"Lovely girl, don't you think?" Mary Alice casually took the letters from her son's hand, placing them in a neat pile on the desk.

"Yes," he said with a trace of a smile. His mother's machinations were not entirely lost on him. "Well, I shall clean up and change for supper." He leaned down to give his mother a peck on the cheek before heading upstairs. Mary Alice watched him go, from the back looking so like his father. She listened as his footsteps resounded up the stairs.

Then she turned back to the pile of letters on her desk, a stack of unanswerable lies that taunted her in imagined voices—"we have your child," "we found a baby safe and sound," "an infant was brought to the church . . ."

Mary Alice picked up the top letter and began to open it, then dropped it back onto the pile. Folding her arms across the desk, she rested her forehead on her wrists and let tears stain the paperwork beneath.

TEN

The crowded streets of Verdy were bad, but Ria was completely overwhelmed by the lobby of the hotel. A relatively new, sturdy log building, its towering facade dominated the main street. Tall double doors of carved wood swung into a dim parlor lit by wall lamps in ornate metalwork sconces. A thick carpet stretched in front of a large fireplace and was flanked by a red-upholstered chair and matching settee. An older man sat behind a desk at the back of the room, and he peered at Sett and Ria with interest. Dirty and travel-worn, the couple looked terribly out of place in the elegant surroundings. Ria had taken Cricket out of the cradleboard and now carried him wrapped against the cold in a trade blanket. She moved closer to Sett, wishing she could stay hidden behind his tall frame. Sett glanced around the lobby, then headed toward the desk, his spurs jangling his presence as loudly as a bull elk in rut. Ria hurried to keep up with him.

The clerk opened a register book and adjusted his spectacles at Sett's approach. He gave the briefest of inspections to the tall blond man in the dusty buckskin jacket and disreputable hat. He'd seen it all, here on the frontier, and would not reject a possible customer until he'd seen the color of his money or . . .

The man adjusted his glasses again, this time perusing Ria with squinting blue eyes. Ria tucked her shawl under her chin, tipping her face away from the scrutiny, but it was too late.

"We'd like a room for tonight, and baths." Sett leaned his arms on the high counter and the clerk jerked his gaze from Ria.

"Private rooms are one dollar, a hot bath for fifty cents, but . . ."

"That's fine," Sett broke in. From his pocket he pulled the beaded leather purse that Ria had made him and opened it up to reveal the glint of gold coin. "I'll pay now."

The clerk straightened himself up and cleared his throat. "I'm sorry, sir, but we do not host coloreds or Injuns. The squaw can stay in the stable. That would be two bits."

Sett's fingers on the purse strings twitched. He clenched his jaw and stared down at the balding man for a long moment. "This is my wife," he said carefully. "We've just traveled a long ways overland and she is not well, and we have a small child. I will pay for the room now."

The clerk turned to Ria again, this time his eyes lingering on the faded red wool of the trade blanket swaddling the child. He then stood and leaned over the counter to look down at her high-topped moccasins and leather leggings. He slowly reseated himself on his stool and turned to face Sett.

"Sir, I have stated our policy." He adjusted the spectacles yet again and firmly closed the ledger book.

Sett's knife pierced the ledger with a thunk, driving deep through the book and into the imported teak of the desktop.

The old man, to his credit, slowly withdrew his hand from within an inch of the quivering blade, though he fought the urge to count his digits. He peered up at Sett Foster's face. It was not a comforting sight. "As I was saying," Sett's voice was low and modulated in a way that Ria had heard seldom and not since years before, "we've traveled a long road. We are only looking for a room and a bath. I pay cash and up front."

The clerk stepped back from his stool, as far out of reach of Sett Foster's knife as he could before his back was against the flocked wallpaper. Without raising his hand, he knocked three times on the wall. He tilted his bristly chin up.

Sett had not missed the rap on the wall. Help would be showing up for the desk clerk soon. *Damn, I shouldn't have pulled my knife*, Sett thought. It had been a long time since he'd had that knee-jerk reaction. It was one thing to be treated with suspicion—he'd learned to expect it—but to have it extended to Ria . . . now, that seemed to twist him the wrong way.

He reached over to remove the knife from the desk just as the door at the back of the lobby burst open. Three men, one wearing an apron and carrying a sawed-off shotgun, were backed up by the crowd that had been drinking in the bar next door. The clerk's expression changed from frightened to smug. Sett let his hand drop without retrieving his knife. He turned to face the men with his hands at his sides.

"We don't want trouble. We were just looking for a place to rest." He shrugged, purposefully letting his coat fall open to reveal the empty sheath on his belt and more importantly to give him quick access to the short blade in the hidden sheath at his back.

"Well, you won't find one here, or anywhere else on this side of town. We do not take to Injuns." The man brandished the shotgun to emphasize his words. One of the men standing behind him nodded, a sneer twisting his lips.

"Yeah, we don't need no more Injun-lovers neither."

Ria huddled behind Sett, shifting Cricket into her left arm as she slipped her own hunting knife from its sheath on her belt. Beneath the layers of clothing, the handle of the blade was comforting, and for the first time since arriving in the town, Ria felt grounded. She would not just cower here and let her family be shot without a fight.

The man with the gun stepped farther into the room. The mob of men behind him pushed forward too.

"Maybe we should just teach this squaw-man a lesson," one of them muttered. There was a general murmur of agreement. Behind him, Sett could feel Ria tense, her small hand grazing his with the handle of her knife. Of course she'd fight, he thought. She always had.

There was a gust of cold air as the ornate carved doors swung open behind them. For a moment Sett thought he was really surrounded, but he didn't take his eyes off the man with the gun.

"Okay, Henry, put your goose-blaster back under the bar. I'll take over here." The voice was calm and filled with authority. The man with the gun swung it down to point at the floor.

"This Injun-lover pulled a knife on old George here!" Henry said in an injured tone.

"I said I'll deal with it from here!"

The crowd behind Henry started to fade back into the bar, and Sett turned to meet his defender. The sheriff was a stocky man, not particularly tall but built solidly, as if from stone. He wore a neat Stetson and had pinned the badge on the outside of a long drifter coat. Behind him stood Lieutenant Kelly.

With the mob retreating, Ria quietly put her knife back in its sheath and cuddled Cricket to her chest. She thought every man in the room must be able to hear her pounding heartbeat.

Kiernan Kelly stepped over to Sett. "I was visiting with John when a fellow came dashing in from the bar. Figured by his description it was you."

Sett gave the soldier a tight-lipped smile. "Thanks for

coming. I seem to have gotten crosswise here, just trying to find a decent place to sleep."

"Well, if it was just you . . . ," Kiernan said quietly, leaving the rest unsaid as he glanced at Ria.

The sheriff came over as the door between the lobby and the bar was pulled reluctantly closed.

"Settler Foster, huh? I heard you were living south of here. I'm John Coleman." The sheriff looked from Sett to where the clerk was standing behind the desk. Sett's skinner still speared into the register book like a war lance in a hide. The clerk was eyeing it as if insulted. Sheriff Coleman reached over and pulled it out, turned the blade over once in inspection and handed it back to Sett.

The clerk sputtered, "But, Sheriff!"

The sheriff said, "I doubt Sett Foster will be causing any more trouble in my town."

"I wasn't trying to cause trouble in the first place," Sett said. "I just wanted a quiet room for my wife and myself."

The desk clerk broke in. "Sheriff Coleman, you know the hotel policy about Injuns!"

"Yes, I know, George."

"But . . ."

Kiernan Kelly turned to include Ria and said, "There's no need to rent a room. Mrs. Kelly and I would be honored to have you and Mrs. Foster as our guests. We've rented a house in town, as Belinda is not fond of camp life. We've plenty of room."

The clerk rolled his eyes and muttered under his breath, "Well, if the hoity toity missus wants to disinfect the linens . . ."

Sheriff Coleman ignored him and nodded to Kelly. "Sounds like that solves the problem without knife-play."

"Thank you, Kiernan. That's kind of you." Sett placed his hand on Ria's elbow and gave her arm a little squeeze. She had been standing there as silent as a frightened doe, and he wished she would nod or smile or something, just to let these men know that she was not just what the clerk thought she was.

Ria knew what Sett must want from her, and she was well aware that she had been the cause of the trouble and that the soldier in his impressive jacket had just bailed them out. She should thank him, but as often happened when she was distressed, the American words simply would not form in her mind. Sett understood her odd mixture of Blackfeet and trader French, but she didn't think Blackfeet was a good choice under the circumstances.

Ria roused up her courage to look up at first the sheriff, then Lieutenant Kelly. "*Merci*," she whispered with a hint of a smile.

The reaction from the men was visible. Both stared at her pretty face, until now obscured by the folds of the shawl. Large dark eyes and a small nose with a spattering of freckles, her lips full and young—the woman was a looker. And French! Kiernan Kelly thought immediately that Belinda was going to be charmed that he was bringing home such an interesting guest, even if she was dressed in mountain clothes. He grinned back at Ria.

The sheriff, more controlled than the impulsive Irishman, touched his hat brim politely.

"Now, Foster, I'm assuming you have reason to be in Verdy?" He brought the subject back to business.

Sett gave Ria's arm another squeeze, to let her know she'd done just the right thing, before stepping aside to talk to the sheriff. Kiernan, still grinning, took over Sett's place at Ria's side.

"Yup. Actually my business is with you. If you'll be in the office in the morning, I have a situation I'd like to discuss with you."

The sheriff nodded again. "That's fine. Probably best to get your wife settled. It's been a long trip?"

"We came from the Cottonwoods," Sett informed him.

"Wild country, that. Hopefully this 'situation' doesn't have to do with disappearing gold or dead cardsharps?"

Sett noted that the sheriff was quite well informed. "Nope, nothing like that."

"Okay then, I'll see you in the morning." The sheriff turned and headed back out to the street.

Kiernan was still smiling down at Ria, though she had not said another word. He was admiring the baby, assuming that even if she didn't understand English, she would know he was saying something nice about the infant. Sett glanced around at the ornate furnishings of the hotel. He went to take Ria's arm, shaking his head at the lieutenant's enchantment.

"This ain't our kind of place anyway," he said. "Let's go."

ELEVEN

The morning dawned gray and gloomy, and the wind rattled down the main street of Verdy as Sett walked up the boardwalk. The saloon next to the hotel was silent, and other than a few oxen teams and freight wagons, the street was empty. The hurriedly built structures of the boomtown seemed to lean into the constant wind. Sett's long coat flapped around his legs, and he tilted his hat so it was not blown off his head.

Kiernan's rented home had seemed palatial. A two-storey sawed-board house with a wide porch, it was perched on a hillside street with a view of the mines across the canyon. Kiernan had explained that Belinda came from a prominent family in Washington and had not acclimated to living in a tent or one-room cabin at the post. But for all her reputation as a society belle, Mrs. Kelly had fussed over her unexpected guests like lost children returned from the wilderness. She'd not shown any distaste at Ria's attire or lack of speaking, for which Sett was extremely grateful, and after serving them a warming bowl of meaty soup, she had settled them into a well-appointed guest room upstairs.

Sett had left Ria this morning still sleeping in the feather bed, feeling that she was in good hands for the time being. He wished he could think of a way to repay the Kellys' kindness.

He had gone by the livery first, checking his horses and the dog. They were all well, though Coy did not allow the stable boy in to muck the bay mare's stall until Sett arrived. Sett then continued on his way to Sheriff Coleman's office at the far end of the street.

The sheriff's office was an unpainted pine building that backed up to the substantial stone jail. Jails made Sett uncomfortable; he'd had enough experience with tiny stone rooms and damp sour odors. He paused outside the door and sucked in a long breath of crisp fall air, as if to carry him through the coming meeting. Then he pushed open the door to Coleman's office.

John Coleman was seated behind his desk, his Stetson and coat hanging on a hat tree behind him. His handmade boots were propped up on a box next to a tiny potbellied stove. The stove glowed red, and still the drafty room was not warm. In the corner, a surly looking deputy was just shrugging into his overcoat before heading out for his morning off. He paused to glare at the big man in the doorway.

"G'morning, Sheriff," Sett said, touching his hat.

"Morning. Everything go well at Kellys'?"

"Fine. Mrs. Kelly is a kind woman."

The sheriff peered up at Sett's bearded face. "I'd offer you to take off your coat, but you probably still need it in here this morning. The fine citizens of Verdy don't want the sheriff to be overly comfortable in his office. But do have a seat." He motioned to several straight-backed chairs against the wall. Sett chose one and dragged it in front of the stove before sitting down.

"Sheriff, you want me to stick around?" the deputy said, adjusting the coat around his shoulders.

"No, Sketch, go on and get some rest," Coleman replied.

"Well, maybe I'll check the stove in the back before I go. Split some kindling for ya."

"No need, Sketch." Now John Coleman sent a quizzical look at his deputy.

"No problem, no problem," Sketch insisted. He shot one last quick look at Sett Foster before letting himself through the door into the stone jail.

The sheriff waited until the deputy had pulled the door closed behind him before shaking his head slightly and issuing a soft *humph*. Soon the faint smacks of a hatchet were heard through the grated window of the door.

The two men stared at the struggling stove. Finally John Coleman said, "You probably aren't real comfortable this close to the jail, or maybe this close to me, but far as I'm concerned you are only a friend and business acquaintance of Kiernan's, and he has a high opinion of you. Though others might disagree."

Sett cast a glance at the door that led to the jail. "Can't say it brings on happy memories, but that was a long time ago."

"Yes, almost eighteen years."

Sett squinted at the man. The sheriff had done a bit of research on the Boy Outlaw. Sett wasn't sure if that boded well or not, but he was not here to rehash mistakes made in childhood.

"I've run into a situation that I hope you know about." Sett squared himself in the chair, and the image of Ria, asleep in the feather bed with the infant snuggled beside her, crossed his mind. *It has to be done*, he told himself. *Maybe it will turn out as she wants.* "That baby my wife has . . . it's not hers. Ours. I found the child hanging in a cradleboard on the saddle of that little paint mare in the livery. The horse was running with my herd."

John Coleman tipped his head, his iron gray hair flopping forward over his forehead. But he said nothing, only raised his cup of coffee to his lips thoughtfully.

Sett paused, screwing up his courage. "That's no Indian child. He's as blond and blue-eyed as they come."

John Coleman carefully set the cup down on the edge of the hissing stove. He pulled first one booted foot then the other off the box and turned to seat himself officially at the desk.

"Your wife seems very attached to the child."

Sett appreciated that the sheriff had not hesitated on the word "wife."

"She is. She can't have children, probably from abuse she suffered as a girl. She wants to keep the child."

"So why are you here?" The sheriff's question hung in the air. Sett thought for a moment of getting up, walking out the door, and packing Ria and Cricket back into the mountains. He thought that Sheriff John Coleman would not have tried to stop him if he had.

Instead, he said, "Cricket is someone's son. They could be looking for him."

Coleman nodded once. "Yes. They could be." He began to shuffle through papers in the several stacks on his desk. Somewhere in the middle of the nearest one, he found what he was looking for. He peered at the paper a moment, then handed it over to Sett.

The word "REWARD" was large across the top of the paper, but as Sett slowly read down the handbill the words seemed to blur and he felt like he'd been kicked in the stomach. He didn't finish, just dropped his hand clutching the notice to his lap and stared straight ahead at the stove.

It was too simple. Somehow, even though he'd insisted that bringing the child in and searching for the real parents was the right thing to do, he'd had the same hope as Ria. Now, he could only picture her face when he returned to Kelly's and told her that the boy's family was actively searching for him.

John Coleman watched the younger man's face as realization and grief passed over the striking features. He didn't envy Foster's having to break the news to the woman. Even if she was Indian, or a breed, Foster obviously cared about her enough to insist on calling her his wife. And with what he'd said about the woman being unable to have children . . . well, John Coleman had been married long enough to know how that would go. He cleared his throat to break the silence.

"This doesn't mean for sure that the baby you found is the one these McFees are looking for. I'll send 'em a telegram. They might have found their child already."

Sett looked down at the crumpled paper. "It says here that the mother was killed in an accident."

"Yes, the Overland stage went off the road up in the mountains. Hell of a wreck, rolled right down into the river. Took a couple days to even find it and by then it'd been looted—the firearms, anything of value—taken. And of course the varmints had been at it. Husband and wife both killed, but no sign of the infant."

"So who placed this ad?"

"My understanding is it's the grandmother there in Denver." John Coleman knew where Foster was heading with this. "There's a chance she'd let you raise the child."

Sett shook his head. "Not after paying a thousand dollars for his return."

Coleman agreed, but said nothing. He had to admire the man for doing the right thing, in spite of the sadness it would cause in his own life, and certainly Sett Foster had already had his share of misfortune.

Sett smoothed the crumpled paper and handed it back to the sheriff. Rising, he adjusted his hat. "Guess I'd better go tell Ria," he said with a sigh.

"I'll send that telegram off right away, but it might take a day or two to get a response, depending on where these McFee folks live." Now Coleman squinted at the big man standing in his office. He had no reason to mistrust Sett Foster other than history, but he felt he couldn't ignore all possibilities. "It would be best for you to stay close by. So I can keep you informed."

Sett clenched his teeth. There was no missing the man's point. "We'll be at Kelly's, Sheriff, here in town. Until we hear from you."

The sheriff nodded, and Sett turned on his heel and was out the door into the busy street, sucking a shockingly cold breath of air before heading determinedly down the street.

Sheriff John Coleman stood and retrieved his Stetson from the peg. He turned his collar up in preparation for the journey out the door, so lost in thought that he didn't notice that the chopping sounds had long since ceased in the back room.

Sketch Jones peered cautiously from the door to the jail. The office was empty, and only the two chairs pulled up to the stove gave indication that one of the most famous outlaws in Verdy's history had been sitting right there, chatting with John Coleman like an old friend. Sketch snorted at that one. The sheriff had some odd opinions at times, championing Mexicans and the godless. And now lawbreakers and their Injun whores. Sketch paused at the sheriff's desk. The crumpled handbill lay on the top of the stack of papers, the bold letters looking very familiar. Sketch picked up the paper and squinted at it, then slammed it back down onto the desk. That squaw had a white baby, and didn't want to give it back. No white child deserved to be raised by a filthy squaw like that.

Sketch let himself out of the sheriff's office and sauntered across the street. He stifled a yawn and wondered if Eliza was up yet. The lumpy bed in the hotel was much more comfortable if he didn't have to share. But it could wait. Sketch Jones had some business to take care of first.

* * *

The morning bustle was in full swing when John Coleman strolled down to the train station and telegraph office. He tipped his hat to the ladies he passed, gave curt nods of greeting to the men. Once there, he chatted for a time with the clerk before writing out his message and waiting while it was tapped off on its errand. Then he headed back out to see and be seen.

He no sooner had turned the corner than the telegraph office had another visitor: Deputy Sketch Jones.

"G'morning, Sam," Jones said, leaning on the counter.

"Morning, Sketch. Going to send a telegram?"

"Not today. Only wondering, did the sheriff just send a telegram to Denver by any chance?"

Sam rubbed his chin. "Now, you know, Sketch, folks' messages are supposed to be confidential."

"Well, John said he would send it today. Just wanted to make sure he hadn't forgotten," Jones said with a casual smile.

"Aw, you know the sheriff don't forget that kind of stuff," Sam said.

"So he sent it, huh?"

"Of course." Now Sam started to shuffle his papers as if realizing that he was talking out of turn.

"Well, then you won't mind letting me know if a reply comes in," Sketch tweaked the front of his wool coat, making sure his badge flashed at the distressed telegraph agent. "You know, Sam, just to let me know that everything is on track, right? Then I won't have to ask the sheriff if he got the reply."

Sam grimaced a bit and stared down at the handful of papers he had gathered up in his hands. "Sure, Sketch. I mean, Deputy. No need to tell the sheriff."

"Thanks, Sam. See you around." Before Sam could get any more uncomfortable, Sketch Jones turned and left.

TWELVE

Belinda Kelly was just finishing a cup of coffee at the polished table in the dining room when Sett came in. She wore a greenhouse dress which complemented the loose piles of golden curls that were pulled casually to the top of her head. She delicately set the cup back on its saucer before nodding to the maid, Martha, to take it away. She smiled at Sett when he entered the foyer, but his gloomy countenance changed her cheerful greeting to a more cautious one.

"Good morning, Mr. Foster. Would you like some coffee?"

Sett shook his head. "No, thank you, ma'am. I just had some coffee with the sheriff."

His hostess rose gracefully from her seat. "Kiernan told me about the reason for your visit to Verdy. I most certainly hope that it all works out for you and Mrs. Foster."

"Thank you for your kind thoughts, Mrs. Kelly, but it isn't looking too bright right now." Sett removed his hat and looked around for somewhere to hang it. Martha appeared out of nowhere and held out her dark hand for the dusty Stetson, probably to whisk it out of sight. Sett was reluctant to hand it over. He liked to keep track of his hat, so he just grasped it in front of him and tried to nod the maid away. This fine house made him feel like a boy, awkward and too big. He asked, "Where is Ria?"

Belinda Kelly waved a manicured hand at the stairway. "She seemed to prefer to stay in your room. Martha brought her up some breakfast and some warm water in case she wanted to wash up."

"Thank you," Sett said again. Belinda Kelly had been a most kind hostess, not so much as raising an eyebrow at his or Ria's disheveled appearance. Nor did she ask probing questions about the baby, whom Ria would hardly uncover long enough to be admired. Now Mrs. Kelly waited politely, surely filled with curiosity. Sett said, "I'd better go talk to Ria. The sheriff had a notice about a baby whose parents were killed in a stagecoach accident. He's sending a telegram to Denver. I'd better go break the news." Belinda Kelly's expression changed to one of appropriate concern and sadness. Still Sett remained at the doorway of the dining room, as if getting up his courage to head up the stairs.

"Mr. Foster, Kiernan and I have a certain amount of influence in the community and will put in a good word for you. Perhaps, even if this is the lost child, they will allow you to adopt him."

"I hate to hope for that, Mrs. Kelly, what with, well, the situation . . ." Sett swung his hat down against his leg, making a small cloud of dust for which he was instantly sorry—the room looked like dust was not allowed.

"Well, it will take time for telegrams to travel back and forth. Perhaps we will come up with a solution," Belinda said, her eyes growing distant as if she were thinking hard about something.

"Thank you," Sett said yet again, then could have kicked himself. He must sound like a complete imbecile, thanking her over and over. He could stand here and repeat himself, or he could head up the stairs and confront Ria with the news. Swatting his hat on his leg once more, he turned on his heel and took the stairs two at a time.

Ria was sitting up in the feather bed, a tray of breakfast on the bedside table and Cricket gurgling and kicking his legs on the quilt next to her. She startled when Sett opened the door, then gave him a halfhearted smile. Sett dropped his hat on the dresser and crossed the room to sit on the other side of the bed. He reached over to tickle the baby's tiny foot.

"Good morning," Ria said softly. "You left early."

"Yes, I wanted you to sleep for a while. How are you doing?"

"I am all right. The dark woman brought me food. Look at this. Do you know what it is?" She held up a section of citrus.

"I think that's an orange. It's a fruit from California. They come in on the railroad."

Ria handed him the piece of fruit. "It's very juicy," she said.

Sett tasted it and nodded. How much he'd rather talk about strange fruit and put off what he had to say and what Ria didn't want to hear. He heaved a sigh.

"I talked to Sheriff Coleman. He had some information about a family from Denver who is looking for a missing child. The parents were killed in an accident last month. He's sending them a telegram."

"Then his parents are dead," Ria stated.

"Yes, but the grandmother is looking for the child. She's offering a reward."

"We don't want a reward!" Ria scooped Cricket up from the bedclothes as if Sett were about to grab him away. The baby let out a startled cry, but Ria hushed him quickly.

"I know we don't want a reward. I was just telling you because someone who offers that much money to get the baby back is certainly going to want him." Sett reached over to push a lock of Ria's hair back from her face. "Ria, please understand that I know how terrible this is for you. I wish there was something else we could do."

"We could have stayed home! We could go home now."

"The sheriff knows who we are and where we live."

"We could leave. We could go north, to Grandfather's country." Tears spilled down Ria's cheeks and she turned away from Sett, cuddling Cricket into her arms.

Sett clenched his fists in frustration. Ria's shoulders jerked slightly. She was silently sobbing at the same time as she quieted the baby, and he was afraid to even try to comfort her. He helplessly stared at her sleep-mussed hair, the thick braid that he used to playfully tug. Those early years together, just the two of them, enjoying the first calm pool in lives that had been separate turbulent floodwaters—it had been beyond anything he'd wished for. He'd worked on the cabin, building his barn and corrals, and Ria furnished their home, tilling a garden and taking delight in every turnip and carrot—an effortless partnership. When had that changed? When had Ria stopped laughing? A long time before Cricket, that was sure, but now he looked at a crying woman who would not look back. The partnership was waning, and when they had to return the child to his rightful family, Sett feared it would end completely.

He did not discount her mention of going north to the Blackfeet reservation and the only family she possibly had left. It had been her solution years before, when she tried to escape the cruel men who had enslaved her—the same men, it turned out, who had killed Sett's family. That she had turned back to help Sett, when she finally had the opportunity to run, he could not take for granted. But now her loyalties were elsewhere. What reason did she have to stay here? Sett felt like a traitor, a jailer. If she left him, he would deserve it, and he could picture himself going back to that wandering existence that had so haunted him before she came into his life. He did not want to return to those aimless days; he wanted to go home, to his own home with his own wife and family. He leaned across the bed, slipped his arm around her and the child, and pulled them close. He expected resistance, but Ria let herself lean against him, though the tears increased.

"There are so many people here," she whispered between sobs. "They stare at me. I don't know what to say."

Her words did nothing to ease Sett's regret. He'd had no business bringing her here. Ria had spent her whole life in the mountains, living in a trapper's small lodge with her mother and siblings, and then on the isolated homesteads. He could not expect her to suddenly fit into a life she had never known. He didn't know what to say, so he squeezed her closer instead.

"Last night, those men were going to fight with us because I am Blackfeet. They will take Tapikamiiwa away because I am Blackfeet." She struggled to turn and look at him accusingly. "That is why they will take him. Tell me, is that the truth?"

Sett released her and lay back on the pillow. Ria waited for his answer, her tear-filled eyes adding final remorse to every choice he'd made.

"That's part of the truth, yes. Most folks around here hold a grudge against Indians. But it isn't just you. With my history, they wouldn't give me the baby either. I spent ten years in prison, remember? I helped rob a stage and kill a man."

"You did not. You didn't know what was happening."

Sett was surprised by the outraged quickness of her response. He said, "Well, you are not all Blackfeet. You are the daughter of a Frenchman named LaBlanc."

Ria's steady gaze held his. In her arms, Cricket fussed at being held so tightly, and she relinquished her stranglehold on the child, placing him in the nest of bedding between her and Sett. The baby flailed his arms and puckered his pink lips at being released, but Ria ignored his demonstration and focused on Sett's face.

"I need to be more white?"

"You need to be yourself. But no one will know who you are if you stay locked in this room or won't talk. The Kellys are good folks. So is Sheriff Coleman. I think they would help us all they could, if they had the chance." Sett desperately hoped he was not lying to her, that he was not overly raising her hopes, but the tentative offer of her partnership was too irresistible to ignore. Even if they failed, he'd rather it was Ria and him, together.

Ria now looked down at the smiling infant and pursed her lips in thought. She said, "The people here call me Mrs. Foster." She turned a questioning gaze on Sett.

"I told them you are my wife."

"Did you pay Augie for me, then?"

Sett cringed inwardly. It was so easy to forget that Ria's upbringing had been very different from his. She had been sold as a wife when she was barely in her teens only to find that the "rich farmer" already had a wife and she'd been bought as a slave. She had not believed Sett, at first, when he tried to explain that according to American law, a man could only have one wife. Now Sett realized that he had made a mistake in not talking about it with her further—in not asking her to be his wife and doing things properly, instead of just drifting happily along with the arrangement.

"No, I did not pay Augie anything. I should have asked you, but . . ." He swallowed before continuing, "I guess I just figured that as long as we were together and happy, that was enough. I consider you my wife. Maybe you don't want to be."

Ria stared at him a long moment, her dark eyes measuring his sincerity. Finally, a small smile teased the corner of her mouth. "I want to be. I am. I have been very happy with you, Sett. I just want to go home now and be happy, you and I and Tapikamiiwa."

Sett reached over the baby, cupped his hand into Ria's thick hair, and pulled her into a soft kiss. "I know," he said. "I know that is what you want. But we must work together now, if there is any chance. And if not, if . . . if we lose Cricket, I still want you to come home with me."

Ria pulled back away from him. Her silent stare did nothing to assure Sett that his partner was back.

THIRTEEN

Mary Alice busied herself through the morning helping the cook with the baking. There was something about the ache in her fingers from kneading dough and the soft flour scent of the baking loaves that was so much more satisfying than adding up columns of figures. Now Mary Alice sighed as she settled herself at the desk and opened the ledger book. How could it always be the end of the month, with bills to be sent and rents to be tallied and abrupt notes to be penned to those who were falling behind?

The McFee empire was vast. Benjamin had seen to that. Mary Alice knew that her beloved Benjamin had not wished to leave her to deal with this, but when he left this life was not in his control. Their son William was a great help in many ways. He was an excellent negotiator and was the best at settling disturbances between the management and the employees, both at the mines and at the ranches. The miners accepted him, slapped him on the back and trusted him to deal fairly. The cowboys admired his storytelling and willingness to be the brunt of a joke. It was something that his father had excelled at too, but it was not Mary Alice's ken. What crusty ore-monger would trust a gray-haired old woman to understand his position, and what young bronc rider would have the courage to put a lizard in her bedroll? So Mary Alice had inherited the bookkeeping—the cheery business of sending out bills, confronting debtors, and sleuthing out irreconcilable balances.

Mary Alice tapped the bottom of her ink bottle before opening the lid and fitting it neatly into its base on the desk board. She stared down at the tiny markings in the ledger book then leaned forward to adjust the lamp.

When Amanda had married David Bruce, both Mary Alice and Benjamin had been overjoyed. It was a lovely match—a man whose intellect and breeding matched their daughter's in every way. David was a businessman, a young man with grand intentions and a good start. As soon as they were married, Amanda had taken over his books and worked as a partner beside her handsome husband. They were so much like the young Mary Alice and Benjamin McFee that Mary Alice relished the thought of them one day running the combined McFee and Bruce empires. But that dream was no more. There were no Amanda and David to take over now. It was Mary Alice, who could not read the ledger book without her spectacles and good light, and William, who cared way more about talking to people than profits. Mary Alice sighed again, adjusted her spectacles, and tackled the accounts receivable.

A rap on the door startled her out of her figuring. Mary Alice capped her ink and carefully laid her spectacles on the desk. Outside the door, a freckled-faced lad in a plaid cap and not enough coat shivered in the wind, a folded sheet of paper clutched in his reddened fingers.

"Telegram for Mrs. McFee," he stated when Mary Alice opened the door. He held the paper out for her.

"Come in out of the wind, young man." Mary Alice ushered the boy into the foyer while she retrieved her spectacles. Fumbling to unfold the crumpled page, she tipped the paper toward the window for light. She read the message then read it again, before folding it carefully and placing it in the pocket of her skirt.

"Will you take a reply?" she asked the messenger.

"Certainly, ma'am!"

Mary Alice went back to her desk for pen and paper, wrote out a few short lines, blotted the ink, and folded her note in quarters. Handing it to the boy, she dug in her pocket for some coins and pressed them into his palm. "Here, young man. Will you do me an extra favor? On your way back, run by the Smiling Scotsman Mine office and give a message to Mr. William McFee. Tell him he is needed immediately at home. Can you remember that?"

"Yes, ma'am! I'm good at 'membering. That's why Mr. Chase at the telegraph lets me deliver telegrams for him."

"Excellent! In that case, after you have delivered that message and the telegram, go to the railroad station and tell the stationmaster that Mrs. McFee wishes to book passage for two on the next train to Verdy. That is a place in Montana Territory. Find out when the next train leaves and return here with that information. There will be another coin for you." Mary Alice squinted at the grinning boy's ruddy face. "And I do believe I have a greatcoat that my son long outgrew that should fit you well."

"Montana Territory. Next train. Got it! Thank you, ma'am! Thank you very much! I'll be back in a flash!" The boy spun around and dashed out the door into the blustering wind.

Mary Alice had just finished packing the small valise when she heard the door slam and Willie's footsteps pounding up the stairs.

"Mother! There you are! Are you all right?" he panted from the hallway. Mary Alice was briefly alarmed at his wheezing and red face. Then she realized he must have run all the way from the mine. His shoes were splattered with mud and so were the bottoms of his trousers. He hadn't even bothered to put on a coat.

"William, I'm fine." She started to pull the telegram from her skirt pocket.

"A boy came running into the mine office, yelling that there was some kind of emergency and I was desperately needed at home," Willie gasped. "I thought something had happened . . ."

"Oh, my. Well, something has happened, but I didn't mean to alarm you. Here." Mary Alice handed him the message. "I've booked passage on the next train west. We leave tonight at nine."

Willie read the message through and looked up at his mother. "This certainly is the most promising lead we've received, but do you think it truly warrants traveling to this . . . Verdy, Montana? Perhaps we should get some more information from this . . . Sheriff Coleman?"

"I've telegraphed that we will be arriving on the next available train."

William stared at his mother. For the first time in weeks, there was color in her cheeks, and her eyes sparkled with their old light.

"I have business meetings tomorrow, things to take care of . . ."

"There is a boy down in the kitchen who will gladly take a message to cancel your appointments."

"But, that's a long ways for an unknown . . ."

"Willie," Mary Alice interrupted, "this child is the correct age and gender, of fair skin and hair, and we are dealing with a man of the law, who has seen the child! Not some scoundrel. He says right there that the child was found in the same mountains where Amanda . . . where the accident happened. And to our great good fortune, the couple who found him brought him to the sheriff. This is little Andrew Benjamin, Willie. I can feel it in my bones."

Willie looked unconvinced. "Mother, you have always

been a most practical woman. Since when do you go running off into the wilderness based on 'a feeling in your bones'?"

Mary Alice squared her shoulders and looked up at her son. "Since now. Go pack your things."

FOURTEEN

Eliza Jones had developed a habit of marching down the boardwalk with her large satchel in front of her like a shield. It helped to part the unruly pedestrians that crowded the main street, and it added to her formidable appearance—high-necked black dress and somber hat, black gloves and sturdy shoes; not an ounce of frivolity to her. It was a costume carefully chosen when Mr. Jones had decided to become a man of the law, and one which she would gladly abandon if she could convince him to purchase a train ticket out of this hellhole.

Ahead, she spotted her husband leaving the railroad station. Eliza quickened her pace and called, "Yoo-hoo! Deputy Jones!" in a voice that made every passerby on the street swivel their head. The deputy paused, waiting for his wife, though he appeared none too overjoyed to see her.

"Eliza. Where are you headed?" he asked when she caught up to him.

"Oh, back to the hotel, I suppose. I was just calling on Mrs. Coleman, arranging the details of the Ladies Reading Club for tomorrow."

Jones nodded. Eliza was very good at being part of the community events, managing to appear the civic-minded peace officer's wife without ever actually contributing so much as a tea cake. He considered how he might avoid returning with her to the chilly hotel room and wished he had left the station by the side door.

"We had an interesting conversation, Mrs. Coleman and I. About that Injun girl."

Sketch Jones grumbled, "Really?" He did not want to stand around chatting with his wife, but she had managed to reel him in with that revelation.

Eliza nodded and curled the ends of her lips up into a smirk. "Must we stand out here in this miserable wind? A cup of coffee would be most pleasant."

Jones started for the door of the nearest saloon, then thought better and turned abruptly into the neighboring restaurant, holding the door for his wife against the gale. The room was quite crowded, but Eliza marched to a single empty table under the front window. A tiny woman with flour-dusted hands came out of the kitchen and nodded when Deputy Jones ordered two cups of coffee. Sketch turned his attention back to Eliza. "So, what is the news?"

"Well, it seems that the fine Mrs. Lieutenant Kelly is rallying a cause to allow Foster and his squaw to keep the babe. She can argue like a lawyer, that one, for all her pretty manners. She says that the squaw lost her own child and is rearing this one as her own and that it would be harmful to separate them now—that the babe has suffered enough. She also insists that the woman is actually French! Can you believe that? And Mrs. Coleman said that the sheriff is inclined to agree."

Sketch clenched his jaw and growled low so the nearby diners would not overhear. "I don't doubt it. John Coleman's a damn Injun-lover. He sat right there in his office with that murderer and chatted like they was old buddies. Kept calling the squaw 'your wife' as if he thought they's honestly married. I don't trust Foster an inch. He's got Coleman hornswoggled." Sketch paused while the diminutive cook returned with the coffee. When she'd turned away, he cleared his throat. "Well, I got news too. A telegram came in this morning. The child's family was found, in Denver. The grandmother is on the train right now. A wealthy woman, sounds like."

Eliza set her cup back on the table. "How do you know this?"

It was Sketch Jones's turn to look smug. "I know how to do my job, Eliza, in spite of your doubts."

Eliza clenched her fist on the cup handle but decided to return to the main point of the conversation. "It is just unthinkable that a decent woman might be convinced to give her own grandchild over like that."

Sketch gave a snort of disgust. "Ah, the grandma will get the baby. She's rich. For enough money, Foster will hand over the child. He'll figure a way to profit by all this, just like before."

"Before?" Eliza Jones asked.

"Wherever Foster is, people disappear. And he turns up with their horse or their clothes. Or their money." He drummed his fingers on the table, coffee forgotten. "It would be a damn shame for a crook like Foster to get that reward."

Eliza pressed her thin lips into a disapproving line. "Yes. And not at all in the best interest of the child. I do believe, Mr. Jones, that perhaps a Citizens' Committee should intervene. For the child's own good." She stared down into her coffee cup, deep in thought. Then she said, "Yes, for the child's good. I'm sure that the grandmother will be most grateful if the child were safe, in more pious hands." Eliza stood and straightened her heavy skirts. "The sooner the better, I think."

* * *

Ria peeked out the window of the second-storey room. There was a view up the steep street, which ended at the rubble of a mine dump. A few other houses sat beyond the one the Kellys rented, but none were so large or neat. Each had a shed or barn and a privy in the back. This edge of town had a forlorn, windswept look, the stiff breeze whisking any loose debris away. Other than a cluster of leafless willows in the draw below the mine, there were no trees. Ria wondered if there had ever been any—were they all cut for firewood and to construct the sagging pole corrals? It called to mind her tiny cabin hidden in the grove of aspen under the sheltering bluff, and she felt very homesick.

She craned her neck to look down at what could be seen of the Kellys' backyard. A large barn was partially in view, the corrals newly repaired with bright peeled poles. The door to the barn was propped open, and after a moment Sett appeared, pushing a barrow of dirty straw and manure. He upended it on a pile at the side of the property. He'd removed his heavy coat while doing the work of cleaning out the horse stalls, and his breath steamed in the frigid air as he pushed the barrow back for another load. Coy trotted at his heels, worried to let him out of her sight. The dog glanced around, searching for her, Ria realized. Her homesickness was joined by guilt.

A chirpy hiccup brought Ria from the window. Cricket was awake and busily kicking his feet in attempt to roll over on the bed. She smiled at the baby as he grasped her finger. But when she turned to the panniers that Sett had brought up to the room, Cricket's enthusiastic wriggling succeeded and the infant rolled dangerously close to the edge of the tall bed. Ria hurried back to him, setting him in the middle with a pillow on either side.

"Stay there now, little one. I need to look for something." She spoke in Blackfeet, her own birth language. Ria turned again to the rawhide carriers. In there, along with her cook kit and food for the journey, were the extra clothes that Sett had packed. In her stubbornness about leaving, she had refused to pack anything but her usual attire. It had been Sett who pulled the clothing from its case under the bed, and he who had folded it into one of the panniers. Now she retrieved the black wool skirt and the red blouse and laid them on the bed. The shirt seemed extremely bright—a summer bloom of color in the gray light of the town. Cricket paused his explorations to stare at it, reaching toward it and opening his mouth wide.

"Yes, Tapikamiiwa. It is like a ripe berry. But not good for you to eat." Ria pulled the gathered skirt on and fastened the buttons around her waist. The red shirt was not nearly warm enough by itself, so she tucked her nightshirt into the skirt and put the red blouse on over the top. She started to tie on her belt, but dropped it to leap to the bedside, where Cricket had wriggled his way once more to the edge. How much more sense it made to raise a baby in a lodge, where everything was low! Ria scooped the child up into her arms. He started to protest, the thin beginning of a wail quickly silenced as her fingers gently rested on his tiny nose. Ria admired the fact that he was such a fast learner, but she wondered if his lonely time on the pony, where his cries went unrewarded, had helped him to learn this vital lesson. She softly stroked Cricket's cheek and smiled at him, cuddling him close to her. Then she gave up on the soft feather bed and placed the baby on the braid rug on the floor.

"Here, look at this!" She pulled a shiny tin cup from her cook kit and placed it just out of Cricket's reach. He slapped out toward it.

Ria found her comb and smoothed out her hair. There was no way she could coil her hair up on her head, as she had no pins to fix it there. She finally settled for knotting the long braid at the nape of her neck, where it flopped heavily every time she shook her head. She hoped the leather tie didn't show.

She repeated Sett's words in her mind, chanting them to give herself courage. *You are the daughter of a Frenchman named LaBlanc.* She tried to remember her father, but all she could recall was his red beard and booming voice, and that he had left the lodge one winter's morning to check his traps and had never returned. Still, the only link to him she had—her name and the fact that he was her father—was important here in the white people's city. Terribly important.

She had to go down the stairs, had to talk to Mrs. Kelly. Perhaps had to meet other women in the town. The women were the most frightening. The men could be angry and violent, and might express displeasure with fists or guns or knives. Ria was familiar with all three. But the women . . . She was not at all sure how the women would deal with her. She doubted that they would all be as polite as Lieutenant Kelly and Sheriff Coleman had been.

Ria picked up her belt again and snugged it over the bright blouse. There was no looking glass in the room, and she was not accustomed to using one. She just looked down at herself in the red shirt and full black skirt, and loosened the belt a notch so that it didn't gather the material so tightly. The weasel-skin medicine pouch jutted out over the gathers of the skirt instead of laying flat as it did over her long shirt and leggings, and the fringed knife sheath would not rest against her hip, but she couldn't quite imagine going without it. Finally she sat on the side of the bed and laced up her winter moccasins.

She lifted Cricket up from the floor, pleased that every day he was heavier in her arms. Still, she knew what she must ask of their hostess as soon as she went down the intimidating stairway.

Belinda Kelly rolled up her sleeves and set to work with her feather duster. Martha was in the kitchen making a hearty stew in anticipation of Kiernan and Sett's return to the house at noon, and given that the Kellys had only one servant, Belinda felt it only fair to pitch in with the daily chores. Martha was a wonderful maid, and willing to cook too, and most of the time there was only Belinda in the rented house in Verdy. The lieutenant was most often away on his cavalry business. So the sudden influx of guests to care for left poor Martha scurrying. Belinda cheerfully did her part, whisking dust specks into the air of the parlor.

It was indeed a daily chore. When she had first arrived in the Montana mining town, Belinda had been amazed at how much grime sifted into the house; just the comings and goings of the booted men had her sweeping the front entry several times a day. The constant fires burning in the kitchen cookstove and the parlor stove created not only ash to be carried out in a bucket, but smoke which tinted the draperies. Beyond it all seemed to be a pervasive sootiness that blanketed the entire town. She would flick the dust off of her precious books, the framed daguerreotypes of her parents, the graduated set of crystal bells (with one distinctly missing—it had not survived the trip west), only to find that by evening all were coated again with the fine grit of Verdy.

Belinda had just finished with the crystal bells, setting the tiniest one back into its place on the knickknack shelf, when a movement from the stairwell caught her eye.

"Oh, Mrs. Foster? Please, come on down." She thought that the woman in the stairwell had drawn back into the shadows, so she set her feather duster on the casual table and went to the landing.

It was Mrs. Foster, holding her baby and biting her lower lip. Belinda smiled. "I see you are feeling better. I am so glad. Please, join me for a cup of tea. Or coffee, perhaps?"

Ria took a step into the light of the parlor. "Thank you," she said so quietly that Belinda could barely hear her.

Mrs. Foster was no longer wearing her Blackfeet

clothes, but her attire was startling nonetheless. Only excellent training kept Belinda from raising her brows. Her husband's friend's wife was swaddled in enough layers to make her look plump, and her hair was oddly arranged in a sagging bun. The beaded toes of moccasins peeked from under the overbearing skirt. Belinda had an almost overwhelming desire to grab Mrs. Foster's arm and bring her back up to the rooms, to help her fix her hair and offer her loan of clothes, but instead she focused on Ria's face and smiled. "How is the babe this morning?"

Ria's grateful expression told her that she had chosen the right tack.

"He is good. But," here Ria paused, swallowed, "he is hungry. I can't . . . I don't . . ."

"Of course. Here, come to the kitchen." Belinda put her hand firmly on Ria's elbow and propelled her toward the door at the rear of the dining room. "You have done so much for the child. He is happy and well. Here, Martha can heat some milk and barley gruel . . ."

"Is there any horse in your remuda that's not good-looking?" Kiernan said appreciatively when Sett clucked Fox Ears over and entered his stall.

Sett grinned. "Well, there's the pony . . ." He motioned his elbow toward the spotted Indian pony in the next tie stall. The pony responded by laying her ears back and wrinkling her nose.

Kiernan laughed. "She'd be better looking if she wasn't so nasty tempered!"

Sett ran a hand down Fox Ears's neck. The little red horse turned his head as far as the tie rope allowed to snuff Sett's shoulder. There was no doubt the horse liked the man, and the feeling was mutual. Kiernan leaned against the post and watched Sett check the horse's legs and feet with silent knowing hands.

"How much for that one?" Kiernan couldn't help but ask.

"Don't want to sell this one. He's Ria's. And he can about keep up with the bay mare."

"Damn, if he keeps up with the mare at all, he's quite a horse," Kiernan said with a chuckle. "Just makes me more eager to see what you've got out there. The officers at camp will be fighting over your rejects."

"Tell 'em to have their purses out." Sett straightened up and gave the gelding a final pat.

With a final word to Coy, who curled up in the straw of the bay mare's stall, Sett followed Kiernan out the door of the sheltered barn and into a biting blast of wind. The perspiration on his face instantly froze and his eyebrows and beard became frosted with ice. He shrugged his coat up around his neck and was glad the house was only yards away. He never would have considered going out of the home cabin without his hat and muffler this time of year. For some reason the closeness of the houses in town gave him a false sense of safety. Kiernan had pulled his wool cap down over his ears, but still he hurried to the lean-to at the back of the house and gathered a quick armload of firewood. Sett followed suit and then headed for the door to the kitchen.

Stepping into the warm air melted the frost as quickly as it had formed, and Sett, unable to wipe away the moisture while his hands were full, saw only a blur of bright colors in the room. Through a misty haze, he followed Kiernan to the corner and dumped his armload of wood into the wood box, then fished in his coat pocket for a bandana to wipe his face. The smudgy spots of color sharpened to reveal three women—the dark, ample Martha in her white apron; fair-haired Belinda in her green house dress; and the brilliant crimson blouse that he'd picked out at Miller's Post years before, gracing Ria's slight form as she sat on the bench by the kitchen worktable. A grin spread across his face. Just as he'd pictured it, the color brought out the rosy blush of her cheeks and made her brown eyes sparkle. For a moment, all he could see was Ria's shy smile.

Then Belinda's cultured laugh broke into his reverie. "Good day to you too. What are you gentlemen staring at?"

Sett glanced sidewise at Kiernan. The Irishman stood with a similarly foolish grin on his face.

"Well, saints preserve us," Kiernan exaggerated his brogue for effect, " 'tis the specter of such lovely ladies in our midst! And with babes in arms!" Sett pulled his eyes from Ria to realize that Belinda was holding Cricket, and a spoon.

Martha straightened up from her cookstove and brandished her wooden spatula. "No goggle eyes there, Mistah Kiernan! None of that in my kitchen. Y'all wash up now for some supper. Beans and ham bone." But the corner of her mouth twitched up into an amused curl. It was good for Miss Belinda to have married a man who so openly admired her. Even if he lived in such a godforsaken land. Martha remembered well holding Belinda on her lap, spooning gruel into her baby mouth. Miss Belinda could have done much worse. Now, if only she would have a child to care for and seal the union.

"Sett, we have orders to wash up, and I for one will not disobey them." Kiernan winked at the ladies before trooping through the door into the storeroom, where a washstand was set up beneath a small mirror. He motioned Sett to go first and leaned against the door with his arms crossed.

"Now that is a pretty picture, my wife holding a babe in her arms. We're waiting for that."

Sett splashed lukewarm water on his face and then rubbed with the towel. "Yeah. We were too." The tone of his voice brought Kiernan upright.

"I'm sorry. I forgot." Kiernan self-consciously unfolded then refolded his arms.

Sett nodded. "How long have you and Mrs. Kelly been married?"

"Almost a year. I got orders to come out West a few weeks after the wedding. I suspect her father had something to do with that. Belinda's family wanted her to stay home and wait, but she . . . she wants a family and there isn't going to be a family unless she is near to me. So here we are. I have to spend most of my time at camp or on patrol, but I sure get to see more of her with her here than I would if she'd stayed back East." Kiernan took his place at the washstand and soaped his hands. "I'm lucky. Very lucky."

Sett watched Kiernan splash water around.

"Yeah, I think you are. How does she like it here? I mean, Verdy must be . . . different for her." The image of Ria hiding in her shawl as they rode through the streets yesterday haunted him. He was surprised that the well-born Mrs. Kelly had befriended her so easily.

Kiernan was carefully soaping his neck and behind his ears. The fact that he was well-born was pretty evident too. Sett realized that he'd never really had a conversation with the man about anything other than horses. He rubbed at the grimy spots behind his beard.

"Well, she's involved with the Ladies Reading Club and some other group that wants to beautify the city. She tried to be involved with the church, but . . . ," Kiernan peered at himself in the tiny mirror, "she's not impressed with the clergy." He took the comb that was hanging beside the mirror and carefully parted his hair, combing each side down in straight strokes. When his presentation suited him, he turned. "She doesn't complain. It's not like her. But I think she is counting the days until this duty is up and we can return East. I can't blame her, but I don't want to go back. I like the space out here."

Sett nodded. It was more information than he'd really wanted to know. Still, the conversation, married man to married man, warmed him even if he had nothing to contribute. He wasn't the only one with problems.

Then Kiernan added, "If we had a little one, it would be different. I think she'd be all right here if she had a child to care for."

"Uh huh." Sett swallowed. He stepped aside to usher Kiernan out of the storeroom. "Be right out." As the door swung closed, Sett stepped up to the mirror and took the comb from its hook.

Martha had just set out a pudding when there was a loud knock on the door. Belinda reached for the serving spoon, nodding Martha to answer.

"It's likely that preacher again, asking for a donation," Belinda said as she dished up the savory mass of bread and dried fruit.

But it was not.

Martha appeared at the door to the dining room, her demeanor formal. "Sheriff Coleman is here, askin' to speak with the lieutenant." Her dark-eyed gaze shifted to Sett. "And Mr. Foster."

Kiernan began to rise, but Belinda interrupted. "We are just finishing our meal. Invite the sheriff in for a bit of bread pudding, please, Martha. The men can discuss business afterwards." Martha shrugged and closed the door behind her as she returned to the parlor. In moments she was back.

"Sheriff Coleman thanks you, ma'am. But he says he needs to speak with the gentlemen in private." She did not add "now."

Kiernan rose from his chair and raised his eyebrows at his wife's disapproving look. Sett got up and followed him into the parlor, where John Coleman stood waiting with his backside to the stove. The men nodded an abbreviated greeting.

"Sorry to bother you in the middle of your meal. Lieutenant, there's been some trouble out toward the fort. A young buck ran away from the Indian school couple days ago, heading toward the reservation."

Kiernan shrugged. "Not much new about that."

"Yeah, well, he must have met up with some friends, 'cause they had a run-in with some of your men. Guess who won."

Kiernan bit his lip and waited.

"One of your troopers is dead. One wounded. Shot with a little boy's arrow that the buck must've made after leaving the school. But a lucky shot. The man that was killed was hit in the neck." John Coleman left the warmth of the fire and paced around the room.

Kiernan squinted at the sheriff. "Thank you for bringing the message, but this is a military matter, and I will handle it. No concern of yours."

Coleman stopped in front of the lieutenant. "No. It is my concern. A civilian wagon was traveling with your troops, seeking safe escort. Now I realize you have a lovely young wife here at home, and it's tempting to spend your time here, but mark my words, Lieutenant, I will not allow civilians endangered due to your lax leadership. Your men are supposed to keep the Blackfeet in control. How in hell did they ambush your supposedly trained troops?"

Kiernan's face flushed beyond his usual Irishness. "Sergeant Means is an experienced . . ."

"Means is the dead man."

The silence throbbed.

Coleman turned away from Lieutenant Kelly, quite sure that his message was received. He spun to face Sett.

"Foster." The sheriff's voice softened slightly. "I have news for you too. The lady from Denver, a Mrs. McFee, will be arriving in Verdy on the train tomorrow night. You might want to prepare your wife. They are very sure that the child is theirs."

Sett nodded dumbly. It all came too fast here in town. "All right," he muttered.

Kiernan escorted the sheriff to the door. "I'll leave immediately for the fort."

"Good idea."

"I'd like Mr. Foster to accompany me. He knows the Blackfeet. He could have helpful insight."

Sheriff Coleman considered this.

"As long as his wife and the baby stay in town, that's okay with me," he said. He headed off into the brisk wind toward the center of town.

Kiernan watched him go. Sett stood behind him in the doorway.

"I should stay here, Kiernan. They're coming to get the baby."

"We'll be back long before that. I could really use your help, Sett."

Sett Foster nodded to himself. It was all turning bad.

FIFTEEN

Ria's breath frosted the windowpane as she watched Sett and Kiernan lead their horses from the barn and tighten the girths. Belinda stood at the other window, one hand pushing back the curtain and a small frown creasing her forehead.

"Why must they always ride off into this awful weather?" she muttered as if to herself. Ria said nothing. Until Belinda had mentioned it, Ria hadn't considered the weather to be bad—cold, windy, cloudy, but not snowing. It was just a typical late autumn day, one in which she would have bundled up and gone about her chores if she were home. Sett too would have been outdoors working.

Kiernan swung up on his horse and turned back toward the house, sending his wife a brief salute. Belinda waved back, smiled, and blew him a kiss. Sett led his mare forward a few steps, checked his girth again and mounted, never looking back. Ria didn't expect it. She could not ever remember Sett looking back once he had decided to ride away.

The men headed off down the street, soon receding

from the limited view of the window. Ria hugged Cricket to ward off the tightness in her throat. She would have much preferred to be riding into the wind with Sett, but the sheriff had been specific; she and Cricket must wait here in town until the woman from Denver arrived on the train. Sett had explained it to her when he returned, grim-faced, from the parlor. He had taken her aside, allowing the Kellys the same privacy, and carefully told her that there was trouble with the soldiers and that he and Kiernan would be back probably before dark, but certainly before the Denver lady arrived the next day. That was when the tightness had descended on her, strangling off the already difficult words. She had only nodded, unable to protest or complain. Tears glittered in her eyes, and Sett stroked one finger down her cheek before lowering his voice even more, to a whisper.

"You'll be safe here with Mrs. Kelly. Stay in the house. I'll come back as soon as I can." He tried to smile, to cheer her up. "Promise." It was an old game they played, Sett asking Ria to promise something. He was much better than she at keeping promises.

"Well," Belinda said with a little *humph*. "We have a day without men. If this weather was more hospitable, we could go to the mercantile and see that new lot of fabrics. Instead . . ." She stepped into the middle of the warm kitchen and pursed her lips. "Martha, please put on all the kettles and then drag the bathing tub out here. It's so nice and warm in here, perhaps Mrs. Foster would enjoy a bath, and we can wash each other's hair. How does that sound, Mrs. Foster?" Ria moved away from the window and nodded at her hostess. Taking a bath indoors seemed an odd idea, but she could not find the voice to question it. Martha began filling all available pots and kettles with water and stoking up the stove, while Belinda bustled around collecting linens and cakes of scented soap, which she showed to Ria with pride.

"Lavender. My dear mother sent this out last month. How I missed my lavender soaps and toilet waters!"

Ria sat on the bench and bounced Cricket on her knee. The child gripped her finger and grinned, which Ria returned. Once the men were out of sight, Belinda seemed quite overjoyed to have the afternoon for themselves, and her chatter distracted Ria from her worries. When Martha dragged the galvanized oval basin from the pantry, Ria's eyes rounded. So that was how Mrs. Kelly meant to have a bath indoors! Ria was familiar with bathing in the creek, the water icy even in mid-summer. Occasionally she and Sett would ride down to the beaver ponds on a hot day. The water in the ponds would warm up some in the sun. In the winter, bathing consisted of scrubbing with a wet cloth, and washing one's hair was a rare treat. Now Belinda was dribbling oil from a tiny bottle into the tub as Martha poured in steaming kettles of water, adding some from the cold water pail as Belinda expertly tested the temperature of the bath with her little finger. A lovely floral scent invaded the room usually devoted to the hearty smells of cooking.

"Ah, the lavender is relaxing already. Mrs. Foster, your bath is ready!" Belinda held out her arms to take Cricket. "When the water cools a bit, we can give the little one a bath too!"

"Miss Belinda," scolded Martha with humor, "poor little boy will smell like flowers!" She and Belinda both laughed.

"Oh, it won't last. Here, Mrs. Foster, let me help you with your . . . things." Belinda realized that unlike her own dress, which buttoned up the back with the help of her maid, Ria's clothes were entirely under her own control.

Ria stood dumbfounded, staring at the steaming tub and the two women waiting expectantly. She had never thought about being shy—as a girl she had run around naked as all children did. If she had been at the riverside, bathing with the women of her mother's family, she would have peeled off the bulky skirt and shirts without a second thought. Certainly living alone with Sett, her state of dress had more to do with comfort and warmth than a desire to cover herself. But to disrobe so casually in such a situation? Her hesitation was taken as bashfulness.

"I'm sorry, Mrs. Foster. Perhaps this isn't comfortable for you! How about if Martha and I go collect some clean clothes for us all, and you just give a call if you need anything? I can bring little Cricket with me, and we can bathe him later in the wash pan?" Belinda waited until Ria nodded again, then she smiled widely and motioned Martha to place the soap and towel on a chair beside the tub. "Enjoy your bath, Mrs. Foster. Take your time—we have plenty of water—and just give Martha a call if you need more hot water, or help rinsing your hair." She bustled out of the kitchen, leaving the door slightly ajar.

Ria waited for a moment, staring at the tub. It was the first time she had been completely alone since she left home. The pinging of the stove and the rattling of the roof in the wind seemed like silence. For a moment she worried about Cricket, but then he could be in no better care than Mrs. Kelly's. Ria sat on the bench and unlaced her moccasins.

Even when she was naked, the kitchen was warm, and the water so hot that she eased into the tub slowly. With her knees bent, the water lapped her shoulders and a curtain of floral perfume rose around her. She sighed and leaned back against the raised lip of the basin. It was amazing! She had never thought of building a pond in the house and wondered if Sett knew about bathing tubs. The warm water was soothing, easing the tightness that burdened her, and she began to hum as she sloshed the water gently. Holding her breath, she sank below the water and wet her head. Taking the fragrant chunk of soap from the chair, she lathered her hair, surprised at how many bubbles the soft soap made. Then she submerged again and again to rinse.

It was good she was not a large woman. To slide herself back down the wall of the tub, she had to bend her knees up out of the water. Ria wondered how a large woman like the maid Martha would fit into the tub; even Belinda was much taller than her, and so that must explain the offer of help with rinsing. For a moment, the image of Sett's long body folded up into the bathing tub made her chuckle—it brought back the memory of her early meetings with Sett Foster, of his pale skin goosefleshed as he bathed in the beaver ponds and how she had giggled. So long ago.

A gentle rap on the doorsill was followed by Martha's thick voice. "Miz Foster, anythin' you be needing? Miz Belinda tol' me to ask."

It was much easier to speak to the dark-skinned maid. Her English was no more precise than Ria's own.

"Bring my baby. Cricket needs a bath too," Ria said. She added, "Please."

A moment later, Martha returned with the child expertly carried in her arms. Ria sank down into the water until only her head and knees showed. Martha laid the baby on the table.

"You wants I take his swaddlings off for you?"

"Yes. Martha?" The warm water was like a sip of whiskey, it loosened Ria's tongue. "You are here with the Kellys. You work for them?"

Martha carefully avoided looking at the shy little missus in the tub while she peeled the baby's clothing off. The inner tunic was rabbit, soft fur against his skin. Martha was impressed with the fine stitching. She straightened up with the naked infant in her hands.

"Yes, ma'am. I been with Miz Belinda since she was this little and before. My momma was her momma's girl. I was born to take care of Miz Belinda." She handed Cricket into Ria's outstretched hands. She watched protectively as Ria let the baby's tiny feet meet the water. She and Ria both smiled at the expression that crossed the child's face as he kicked. Ria slowly lowered him down until he was sitting on her stomach, his back against her legs and her hands carefully supporting his body. Ria grinned in delight as Cricket splashed, his kicking heels just under her breasts.

"You knows a lot about babies, for one so young," Martha commented.

"I helped my mother and First Wife with the babies. I am oldest."

"But you not have babies yourself?"

Ria's smile dimmed. "I do not carry them long enough." A silence sat between the women, while both watched Cricket.

"Forgive me askin', but this First Wife, that be her name? She your aunt?" Martha asked the question while turning to fold the baby's clothing in a bundle to take to the laundry.

"First Wife was first wife. My mother, Sweetgrass Woman, was second wife." Ria thought a moment and said, "To the Frenchman LaBlanc. My father was white." She remembered Sett's warning, that here in town, she needed to identify with her white heritage. She also remembered Sett explaining that white men could have only one wife.

Martha nodded as if that might indeed matter. "No whites up close in my family. We all just slaves. Until the 'mancipation. But Miz Belinda's family is good. They take care of me all my life."

Ria sat up a bit in the tub and took her eyes off of Tapikamiiwa for a moment to look at the large black woman. There was a permanent sadness in her eyes, as if she'd been born with it.

"You are a slave?" Ria asked.

"Was. When I was little. I remember the day they tol' us we weren't slaves anymore. I was scared."

"Sett says I was a slave. I thought I was a wife."

Martha looked even sadder. "They's a big difference between being a slave and being a wife."

Ria wished she could ask the woman more. They had much more in common than she and Mrs. Kelly, but Martha turned her back and went to the stove. "More hot water, Miz Foster?"

Before Ria could answer, the peace was broken by a hard rapping at the front door. Martha started for the parlor to answer it, but Belinda appeared in the doorway.

"I'll get it, Martha. Stay with Mrs. Foster." A look of concern wrinkled her brow as she shut the kitchen door firmly behind her.

Ria started to rise from the water, but Martha motioned her back. "Don't fret none. Probably just another message for the lieutenant, and he's already on his way." But she stationed herself at the door with her ear to the panel.

Belinda's view through the lace-curtained window was crammed with people. In the front she recognized Eliza Jones, the deputy's austerely dressed wife. Behind her was the deputy himself with his badge prominently displayed on the outside of his long coat. More people crowded onto the porch behind them, some familiar, though Belinda was new enough to Verdy that she didn't remember all of their names. A trickle of dread went down her spine as she put on a pleasant, surprised look and opened the door.

"Good afternoon." She did not invite any of them in. They would not all fit in the tiny parlor.

"Mrs. Kelly." Eliza Jones tipped her head, but did not smile. "We are here to speak with Mr. Foster."

"Oh, I'm so sorry. Mr. Foster and the lieutenant left hours ago to attend to some business at the fort. You will have to speak to him tomorrow."

The deputy looked alarmed. "They wasn't supposed to leave town!"

"It was with Sheriff Coleman's consent."

The deputy grumbled. Eliza Jones stepped up to the

doorjamb. "May we come in, Mrs. Kelly? We have important business that must be dealt with today, and this wind is bitter."

Belinda agreed about the wind; it was quickly chilling off the house. She grudgingly stepped back.

"My parlor is small . . ."

"Oh, we won't be long." Eliza bustled through the door with the deputy and several others following. They crowded into the small room and turned as one to face Belinda.

"Where is the Indian woman and the child? Did they go to the fort too?" Eliza asked.

"No, they are here. Mrs. Foster is resting and cannot be disturbed." The intrusion of this small mob into her house grated on Belinda's sense of control, and she found herself clipping her words, with no smile left on her hostess face.

Eliza Jones cleared her throat as if preparing to launch into a sermon. "My dear Mrs. Kelly, this is a matter of some urgency and I fear we will have to disturb 'Mrs. Foster' from her nap." The way she said *Mrs. Foster* left no doubt of her disdain. "The child's rightful family has been found and will be arriving shortly. We've come to retrieve the child, so that the grieving grandmother will not be overly troubled about the conditions the poor babe has suffered."

Belinda scanned the faces in the room. The deputy was glaring at her, his wife had a smug smile, and Mrs. Coleman, one of the only others she could name, was wringing her hands and looking like she was about to cry. "Is that so?" Belinda said. "And to which better house is the child going?"

"He will be safe with the deputy and me until tomorrow's reunion with his relations," Eliza said.

"Oh." Belinda's icy tone matched the drafts that still swirled around the room. "I see. A room above a bar is a more appropriate home for a young infant. I understand perfectly."

"Good. Now, fetch us the child." Deputy Jones looked

pleased with himself, but his wife did not misinterpret Mrs. Kelly as he did.

"No, I'm very sorry, but I can't possibly give Mr. Foster's child away while he is off on an errand. You will have to wait until he and the lieutenant return." Belinda was quite sure that this delegation would not have come to the house if Sett and Kiernan had been there. In fact, it angered her that they would assume that she was such a sissy as to give in to their demands herself. She stepped toward the door to usher them out.

"Mrs. Kelly, you forget that the child is not Foster's!" Eliza's voice was shrill and loud and most certainly reached into the adjoining kitchen. "Are you aware of that man's history? Do you know that he is a disreputable convict, a violent man who robs and kills? How can you defend such a man?"

Now Mrs. Coleman was sniffling audibly. "Mrs. Kelly, please, we are only trying to spare the poor grandmother the grief of seeing how her flesh and blood has been living," she whined.

The deputy added, "And that squaw he calls his wife, you know as well as us they ain't married. She's just some dirty ignorant Injun."

Belinda did not want to argue with these imbeciles, but she could not help saying, "The babe has been loved and cared for. He's a happy, healthy child."

Sketch Jones muttered, "Suckling at that damned animal's tit. It's disgusting, it is."

Belinda Kelly's entire life had centered on being a lady. She had never stooped to cursing or ventured into impoliteness, but now she wished she had the lieutenant's shotgun, so that she could hurry these people out of her house with the fear of buckshot in their backsides. The small mob in her parlor was seething, and if she had not been so angry, she might have been afraid. Instead she straightened up to her tallest and pulled open the front door.

"I must insist that you leave, all of you." The deputy scuffed his boots as if he might step toward her. "Now." Mrs. Coleman hurried out the door, the rest following more slowly.

"We'll be back," the deputy threatened as he passed by her.

"You won't be let in. You are not welcome in my house."

"We'll see 'bout that."

Belinda slammed and bolted the door behind them. The group milled around in the street in front of the house for a while, Eliza lecturing them all, and then they headed up the street toward the center of town.

Belinda sank against the door, finally shaking and scared. She waited until every one of them was out of sight before opening the door into the kitchen. Martha turned quickly to her.

"Miz Belinda, that was a brave thing you done." She opened her arms to hug the girl she'd raised. Belinda sobbed for a moment into the black woman's shoulder.

"Where is Mrs. Foster?"

"Upstairs in her room. When the shouting started, I dried her off and bundled her and the babe up the back stairs. She didn't say a word, not one, but she was scared that they was going to take the little one right now."

"I'd better go tell her they are gone, and that she is safe."

"Yeah, but you know, Belinda, that they's not gonna let her keep that baby." Martha hardly ever called Belinda by only her given name. It was Martha's way of saying this was important. A tear slid down Belinda's cheek again.

"Yes, I know," she whispered. "But I didn't want them to take Cricket like that. Not like that." Martha patted her arm. "Here, I'll bring some tea up for you. It settle you both." She turned back to the stove.

Belinda went back out to the parlor, glancing out the

window as if afraid that the townspeople would be back on her steps, then she climbed the narrow stairs. At the top landing, she knocked gently on the door to the guest room. There was no response.

"Mrs. Foster? It's Mrs. Kelly. Are you all right?" she called. "Mrs. Foster? Everything is okay now." Belinda turned the doorknob and opened the door slightly, peeking in. Then she pushed the door open all the way and stood in shock. Martha came up the stairs with the tray and stood just as quietly behind her.

The red blouse and skirt were tossed on the floor as if discarded in a hurry. Sett's belongings were heaped on the quilt-less bed. The pillowcases were missing. The one window, which faced the barn and the willow-shrouded creek, was open, the curtains flapping in the wind, and Ria and Cricket were gone.

SIXTEEN

The expanse of prairie hung like a dreary painting outside the Pullman car's window. Mary Alice stared out at it for hours. The train seemed to crawl across the canvas with barely noticeable progress, yet on the occasional broad curve she could look ahead and see the engine steaming and chuffing. Only the rapid clicking of the wheels led one to believe that the conveyance was actually moving. The mountains in the distance seemed no closer than they had when the porter brought the box dinner hours earlier. Across from her, William napped with his head leaned back on the horsehair bolster, his mouth slightly agape and soft snores issuing intermittently. Mary Alice was extremely grateful to have been able to procure a private compartment with a curtain. She could never have slept in the direct view of the other passengers.

She returned to gazing out at the barren landscape. She imagined Amanda, flush with excitement, making this same journey with her new husband. Amanda had always had a taste for adventure, and nothing would do but that she accompany David to the new mining project in the West.

Had she had any inkling that she would not return home again? Mary Alice hoped not. Amanda's letters had been filled with joyous discoveries; descriptions of the beautiful mountain scenery, the rowdy mining camp, the promising ore at the mine. There had been the special letter informing Mary Alice that she was to be a grandmother. There had been no hint of sadness or homesickness. Perhaps Mary Alice should have traveled to Montana Territory to see her new grandson rather than request that Amanda come home. If someone was going to die on that journey, wouldn't it have been better for it to be an old woman whose life was nearly over anyway, rather than the young couple with the child, all brimming with life?

Night was falling, though the setting sun could not be seen through the flat gray sky. The view out the window shaded darker, until Mary Alice could see only her reflection in the glass. The train seemed to be going faster now, the *clackety-clack* of the wheels bearing them briskly along toward the hidden mountains. Toward a motherless baby, a child lost. Mary Alice tried to imagine little Andrew Benjamin. He would have his mother's bright blue eyes and his father's high forehead. He would have pale translucent hair, just like Amanda's as a babe. He would be cheerful and strong, and with this image of her grandson so vivid in her mind, she wondered where he was just then. Was he warm and well fed? Was there an attentive woman to rock him to sleep?

William shifted in his seat, trying to ease a kink in his neck without truly awakening. Mary Alice wished she could sleep, but the rhythmic motion of the rails did not lull her. She stared at the window, keeping company with the old woman in the glass.

The army camp hardly looked like a fort. Other than the tall square of the blockhouse, it could have been someone's barns clustered together on the flat above the river. Horses milled around in a crude corral, and the grounds were empty in the brisk wind. Sett and Kiernan slowed their horses to a walk when they crested the rise and the fort first came into view. It was not good form to gallop into camp unless the Blackfeet were on one's tail, and with most of the Blackfeet on the reservation, that was unlikely. That, and Kiernan had a look of true reluctance at returning to his post.

Sett let the big mare settle in beside Kiernan's horse as they walked the last mile. He couldn't think of anything reassuring to say to his companion, so he was silent. In fact, he questioned again why he was here, other than that the lieutenant perhaps didn't want to ride alone. Men killed on his watch. His responsibility, when he was in town with his bride. Sett didn't envy the lieutenant at all.

"We'll put up the horses then go to my quarters. I'm sure whoever has placed himself in charge will be right prompt in finding me there," Kiernan muttered under his breath as they rode into the deserted yard.

"You mean you don't know who's next in rank? I thought the army had that all organized." Sett stopped in the lee of the stable lean-to.

"Yeah, officially they do. I promoted Means to Sergeant because he was the only one who'd give me the time of day. They've all been out here longer than me, and there's some who think I promoted him over them. And I did. It's a rough lot, this bunch."

Sett pondered this a moment and shrugged his coat up around his neck against the wind. "So, you want me out here so that you have a backup."

"Well, yes." Kiernan had the decency to look chagrined. "I just need to learn what happened and send a detail out after the culprit. That'll give the men something to do."

"So we can go back to town? Might not be that easy."

The lieutenant dismounted and started to lead his horse

into the shelter. "Come on, Sett. I need a favor. The men know you. It will keep things simple."

Sett did not move. His reins rested comfortably in his hands; it would only take a twitch of his fingers to be heading back to town. He said, "I'm just a rancher, a colt-breaker from the Cottonwoods."

Kiernan paused, looking straight ahead at the block-house. "Sure, that's what you are. Now. You're also a man with a white baby and a half-breed wife. And a past. I'm calling in a favor, Foster. This would all go a lot better if you were standing behind me."

Sett groaned. *Ria and Cricket, safe in Kiernan's home.* He said, "I'm no gunslinger, Kiernan."

"I know. If you were, you'd be carrying a .45 instead of a knife. There's not going to be any gunplay."

Sett waited, letting his thoughts twirl like the dust that was kicking up across the barren parade ground. Snow would be falling soon at the line cabin. It would be buried, hidden from all but the most knowing eyes. How he wished he and Ria were there now, hidden with it. Hidden with the child Ria so desperately wanted. Hidden from hate and duty and favors called in. Sett Foster sighed, ran his hand down the thick winter coat on the neck of his bay mare, and swung his leg over the cantle to follow Lieutenant Kelly into the stable.

The officers' quarters consisted of nothing more than a tiny two-room cabin. In the windowless back room, a bunk nestled against one wall and a table with a washbasin abutted the other. Pegs lined the back wall for clothing. In the front room, a battered desk and chair faced the door from the center of the room. One window faced the parade ground, and a well-worn bearskin served as a rug. An American flag hung limply from a stand in one corner; a cold stove occupied the other. It made for a sad comparison to the comfortable home that Belinda had made in Verdy, and no wonder to Sett that the woman had refused to live at the fort. He waited while Kiernan lit a lantern, though it was barely after noon.

"You want me to start a fire?" Sett asked with a nod toward the stove and full wood box. Neither he nor Kiernan had removed their coats or mufflers, and wouldn't want to until a fire had been roaring for at least an hour.

"No, don't bother. We'll be gone before it gets warm." Kiernan took a journal, quill, and ink pot from the desk drawer and seated himself in the chair. No sooner had he touched quill to ink than a sharp knock rattled the door.

"Yes." Kiernan said loudly without looking up.

"Corporal Gorney to see you, sir."

"Come in."

There was only the one chair in the room, and Sett glanced around uncomfortably for a place to stand. He stationed himself against the wall by the cold stove, aware that he filled the place where the territorial flag should be. To have something to do with his hands, he pulled his tobacco pouch from his coat and started to roll a cigarette.

The door pushed open, and along with a grizzled trooper who Sett assumed was Gorney, two other soldiers crowded into the tiny room. Gorney's arm was wrapped in a sling, a dirty bandage binding his shoulder. Kiernan capped his ink bottle and leaned back in his chair.

"I received word that there's been an incident. You are one of the injured, Corporal? Are you all right?" The concern caught the soldiers off guard and they looked sideways at one another before Gorney answered.

"Yep. It'll heal. Took an arrow in my arm. Just a flesh wound."

"Good. Make sure to change the bandage regularly, and if you need a doctor, don't hesitate to say." Now Lieutenant Kelly focused his gaze on the two troopers who glared at him from behind Gorney. "Privates Jenkins and Rattigan, correct? Were you also involved in the altercation?"

Jenkins and Rattigan appeared surprised to be called

by name. Sett sealed off his cigarette and slid it into his pocket, lighting up in front of the enlisted men not seeming protocol. The men's eyes flicked to him questioningly, but Sett had to admit, Kiernan was doing a better job of keeping them on their toes than Sett had expected. Both troopers' disgruntled expressions faded as Kiernan stared steadily at them, awaiting an answer.

Jenkins spoke first. "Well, of course we was there. All of us was there. Except you. Sir." There was a slight sneer at the end of his sentence, and the man leaned forward over Gorney's shoulder as if he would prefer to be in front. Gorney shrugged the man back, and Sett thought that these men had more respect for the corporal than they did for the lieutenant. Kiernan must have agreed, for he focused again on Gorney.

"What happened, Corporal? Start at the beginning," he said.

Corporal Gorney removed his gritty cap and ran a hand through shaggy gray hair. "Well, we was out on routine patrol, as you ordered. We was going south along the road, and only things we saw was freighters and the coach. One of the wagons had some trouble with a mule, and they were traveling along with us. So we came along in that canyon above the river, where the pine trees are down by the road, and all of a sudden Means, who was riding in front with one of the freighters, lets out this beller and I sees an arrow sticking in his neck! None of us knew where it came from, and we scattered into the cover. I mean, none of the Injuns use arrows anymore!"

Jenkins broke in, "Well, this one did! And damned good shot with it too!"

Kiernan tapped his fingers on the desk. "An ambush. What then?"

"We sat pretty still hoping that the Injuns would show themselves, but it was quiet as a church. Means had fallen from his horse, and so I decided to go get him. That's when I took this arrow in my arm."

Rattigan spoke for the first time, and Sett realized that the man was barely out of his teens. "That time we could see where the Injun might be hiding, and so we fired into that brush. But we missed him. Or he moved." The young man lapsed back into silence and Gorney took over.

"'Bout then, some rocks up the canyon came loose, and so we thought there was more than one. We all settled in for a battle, but none ever come. There was some rustling up the ridge, loose rocks and such, and then nothing. No attack. No reason. We sorta holed up there for a while waiting, trying to do for Means what we could do, but it was hopeless. Bled to death."

"Hmmm, so this ambusher fired two arrows and both hit?" Kiernan asked.

"Yup," Gorney said. "And when we pulled the one out of my shoulder, it was just a little boy's arrow, just a stick with a point on it. Probably Blackfeet, but hard to say. No markings."

"We don't even know for sure if it was Indians," Kiernan mused.

"Oh yes we do, Lieutenant!" Jenkins growled. "You might not be able to tell Injuns from anyone else, but us who's been fighting them all our lives sure can!"

Kiernan turned a steady gaze at the angry trooper. Sett could see the veins bulging in the lieutenant's neck as he controlled his demeanor. "All right, Jenkins. Why did these Indians attack a detail? Even if there were several, they were outnumbered. And the Blackfeet are confined to the reservation. It would be a rogue bunch, and seems like they would be doing a lot more damage than this."

Jenkins leaned over Gorney's shoulder again. He glared at the seated lieutenant before answering. "They had a reason, and they got what they wanted. They stole Sergeant Means's horse. They got his kit and his rifle too. Maybe they was shooting arrows 'cuz they didn't have guns. Now they do."

"You feel they ambushed the detail in order to gain horses and firearms?"

"Hell, yeah!"

Kiernan nodded at that. "How far did you track them?"

Now Gorney shuffled his boots. "We didn't follow 'em. We brought Sergeant Means back here and escorted the wagon into Verdy. We're a small detail, didn't want to divide up too much." Jenkins nodded. Rattigan clenched his jaw.

And didn't want to take responsibility for making a decision, Kiernan sighed to himself. He turned in his chair to address Sett. "You have any questions, Foster?"

The three soldiers stared at Sett, as if they'd forgotten he was stationed in the corner. Sett fished the cigarette out of his shirt pocket and scratched a lucifer on the cold iron of the stove. He hadn't expected to be addressed in this conversation, and took his time lighting his smoke before answering Kiernan's query with one of his own.

"Only one horse missing?"

Kiernan looked back at Gorney.

"Yeah, the sergeant's horse ran down the canyon when he fell. We found where it stopped, and where someone caught it and rode off."

"Sounds like there was only one ambusher to me," Sett said.

Gorney started to sputter a denial, but Jenkins pushed ahead of him. "Damn well was more of 'em! Was at least three. We heard 'em and took the shots." The man stopped and squinted at Sett. "Or maybe you think you know a little something about ambushes?"

Sett tipped his hat down and took a long draw on his cigarette. He knew a lot about ambushes, actually, but not for the reason Jenkins had finally recognized him. He said softly, "Just an opinion, Jenkins."

Kiernan Kelly cleared his throat. "Okay, dismissed,

men. We'll be riding out at first light, so pass the word. If anyone has more information, I'll be here."

Gorney started to ask a question, but the lieutenant turned away from him to address Sett, and the three men stomped out of the tiny office.

"Guess I'd better get that stove going after all," Kiernan said. "Looks like I'll have to go see for myself. I could sure use your scouting ability, Sett."

Sett opened the firebox lid and started selecting kindling. "Sorry, Kiernan. Can't do that."

Kiernan sighed loudly this time. "Yes, I know. At least you can tell Coleman that I'm on it, and tell Belinda that everything will be okay. This just doesn't sound like an Indian raid."

"It ain't. The Blackfeet are all up on the reservation, and we'd hear if there was a rogue bunch. It's probably one person, one clever person, who needed a horse."

"But attack a detail of six soldiers, and a couple of civilians? That would be foolish."

"Just waiting for the next riders on the road. Your men happened along in the wrong place at the wrong time."

"But whoever did this was way outnumbered!"

Sett held his cigarette down to spark off the tinder in the stove. "Yeah, worked perfectly, didn't it?"

SEVENTEEN

Ria wrapped the shawl tighter around her damp head. The icy wind made her head ache, but she did not want to stop to seek shelter yet. Fox Ears plowed steadily into the storm, the little spotted Indian pony trailing reluctantly, and Coy walking resolutely, directly behind the windbreak of the horses. The comforting warmth of Tapikamiiwa, bundled under her shirt, gave Ria reason to go on, heading northwest into the blooming storm that had been threatening all day. Twilight came early, with the clouds blocking the sun, and she knew she needed to stop for the night, but she also needed to put as many miles between her and the angry people of the town as possible. She didn't know how soon they would have started out after her.

She'd been surprised at how easily she slipped into the barn, collected her horses, and sneaked into the willow break behind the house. The townspeople must all be like Mrs. Kelly and avoid going out into the weather. The ones that had come to the door, the ones who wanted to take Tapikamiiwa away, had been too preoccupied with themselves to consider that she might be leaving as they entered.

Just as well. Perhaps no one would find her trail until morning and she would have a strong head start. If it snowed, the sheriff would have to guess which direction she had gone.

Sett was the only one who could track her, and this was an unsettling prospect. Hot tears joined the beads of sleet on her cheeks, the only expression of sorrow she allowed herself as she battled into the storm. Sett could track her, surely would track her, but likely would also lead the angry people to her to take her baby away. For all the part of her that longed to see Sett around every corner of the trail, she had to most carefully avoid him. And that was quite a challenge.

The terrain she traveled was unfamiliar, though Ria knew where she was headed. Her mother's people were at the reservation, far to the north. Surely there, someone would know her. Someone would help her. She focused on this thought as she guided her horse along a faint trail that followed a rocky reef. There were few trees in this rolling land. The main road ran along the more gentle slopes above the river, but Ria did not want to meet up with travelers who might identify her. She skirted instead along the base of the bluffs, trying to stay concealed from the road by riding just over the crest of the hill. The wind pelted her with ice pellets, but no snow would collect up on this bare ridge. It made for easier going, but with the rapidly diminishing light, Ria started looking for a sheltered place to spend the night.

Cottonwoods and willows grew in the watered ravines, and she turned Fox Ears to slide down a steep bank. The wind halted abruptly, the stinging snow of the ridge replaced by lazy flakes that settled on Ria's eyelashes and on her horse's red mane. After the hours in the wind, it seemed suddenly warm, but she knew better—this was the soft killing cold. One could go to sleep and never wake up.

The small creek at the bottom of the ravine was not frozen yet, this being the first real storm of the winter. Ria dismounted and led the horses to drink, her feet numb from the long hours in the saddle. She untied her coat and took Tapikamiiwa from his sling under her shirt. He blinked and wrinkled his face as if to cry, but did not make a sound. She pulled the rabbit fur hood over his ears and tied the strings under his chin.

"You are a brave little one," Ria murmured. She held the child up so he could kick his legs. She was glad that the maid, Martha, had not taken Tapikamiiwa's clothing to be washed. The long rabbit-fur-lined shirt and soft booties that laced up his chunky legs would help him stay warm. That is, if she could stay warm too.

The horses finished drinking and began to feed on the willow withes that lined the creek. Ria looked around for her dog, surprised that Coy was not beside her. She whistled softly, and the dog appeared from the brush just up the canyon, but quickly turned and went back into the thicket. Curious, Ria stood up and followed her, holding Tapikamiiwa close so he would not get scratched by the branches. Emerging from the brambles, she saw what had attracted Coy away from her: a rocky overhang carved out by the creek, its sandy beach blackened by the charcoal of old campfires, with a pile of firewood stacked under the lip to stay dry and, Coy's main point of interest, a midden of old bones tossed in the farthest corner. It must be a trapper's winter camp, a place to return to when working a trapline. Ria remembered LaBlanc leaving for weeks at a time in the middle of winter. He must have known shelters such as this one.

Ria returned to the horses and led them one at a time through the thick brush to the campsite. Spots did not want to push into the branches, and Ria broke off a switch to swat her on the rump. The exertion helped warm her hands and feet, and before unpacking the horses she lit a fire in the blackened circle of rocks. Hobbled and turned loose, the horses went back to foraging along the stream and Coy gnawed on one of the dry bones. Ria folded the blanket she had taken from the bed at the Kellys' to make a safe place for Tapikamiiwa to lay while she stoked the fire and heated some water.

Tapikamiiwa fussed on his blanket, and when Ria picked him up, his tiny hands were icy cold. She leaned back against the panniers and pulled the blanket up around the two of them, opening her shirt so the babe could nurse. She would have to find something else to feed him, but for now it was a comfort to them both. Exhausted, and sitting still for the first time since her flight out the window of the Kellys' house, Ria sighed and took stock of her situation. Her food supply was limited. She had only what had been left in the panniers, she'd had no time to pack more, but she could crumble some jerky into hot water to make a broth. She had the blanket and her warm clothes, but she would need to make some mitts for Tapikamiiwa's hands and her own. She wondered how many days' ride she was from her mother's people. She wondered if anyone would remember the small daughter of Sweetgrass Woman. She had been so young the few times she had visited her cousins. Ria leaned over to add more limbs to the fire.

Coy brought her bone over to lay on the edge of the blanket with them. Occasionally, the little dog would prick her ears, listening. Ria listened too, but even the roaring wind of the storm was far away. She imagined Sett stepping into the circle of firelight, strong and warm and coming to take her home to the cabin on White Buffalo Mountain. She yawned and blinked her eyes against drowsiness. The orange flames crackled and hissed as occasional snowflakes sneaked under the outcropping and the heat from the little blaze reflected on the rock wall, making a small haven of light and warmth in the lonely darkness.

Sett Foster let his horse choose the pace along the road into Verdy. At the first rise overlooking the town, he pulled up. It had been a long time since he'd ridden into a town at night, and the lights twinkling under the starless sky made the world seem suddenly upside down, as if at any moment he would realize he was riding on the lip of the horizon and could tumble off. The unfamiliar constellations of light were set in crooked rows and much larger than Sett had expected. Verdy had become a small city, and it sprawled across most of the eastern slope of the narrow valley. Somehow, it appeared even bigger at night. Sett shook his head and shrugged his collar up against the cold wind.

As the road dipped down to the streets of the town, he picked out the Kellys' house. Lights were in all the windows, to welcome him and Kiernan, he supposed. There was even a lantern in the barn, casting a thin strip of light on the frozen ground outside. Sett dismounted in the yard and pulled the barn door open with a gloved hand. He started to pull his muffler away from his face but stopped and dropped his hand toward his knife sheath. The barn was too quiet—no greeting nicker from Fox Ears, no wagging tail from Coy. A man stood by the lantern, his back to Sett, unrecognizable in a bulky coat and Scotch cap. At the creaking of the door, the man turned.

"Sheriff?" Sett removed his hand from his knife. "What's going on?"

"Come on in out of the wind, Foster. We have a problem." John Coleman stepped forward to hold the door against the wind as Sett led the big mare into the shelter. A glance at the empty stalls made Sett's pulse quicken.

"Where're my horses?" he demanded. "Where's Ria?"

The sheriff shook his head. "Don't know. Was hoping they were with you." There was no doubt in John Coleman's mind that Sett Foster was surprised; there was no mistaking the shock on the man's face. Foster stood clutching his reins as if he might wheel and head out the door right then, to begin a search. Coleman knew it was too late for that. The sheriff stepped over and laid a mittened hand on Sett's elbow. "Take it easy, son. We'll head out after her first thing in the morning, but tonight's too dark to get anywhere."

Sett relaxed his grip on the reins and shook his head in confusion, then in anger. "Who took her?"

"No one took her. She left by herself. With the baby." Coleman paced a few steps. "There was a bit of confrontation, not with my approval. Seems a group of concerned citizens felt that the child would be, um, safer in their care. They came to Kelly's this afternoon. Your wife apparently ran, with the child. I was hoping she had followed you."

Sett's eyes were dark with rage. "We agreed no one would bother her, as long as she stayed with the Kellys."

"I know. I apologize for that. But we've got to figure out where she went and bring her back. I figured there was no point in beginning a search before you got here. You would know where she'd likely go. There's a posse ready to go at daybreak."

Sett turned to unsaddle his mare. The sheriff studied him as he loosened the girth and pulled off the saddle. The mare was eager to get to her feed, and Sett worked quickly and silently, not letting his rage show in the movements toward his horse. He had a pretty good idea where Ria would head, but damned if he was going to lead the sheriff and a posse to her after they'd broken their word. He'd go after her alone. With a final hand on the mare's neck, he turned back to face the sheriff.

"I have a message for Mrs. Kelly, from the lieutenant," he said. "And I want to know everything. When she left. What she has with her."

Sheriff Coleman nodded and took the lantern down from the peg to lead the way across the frozen yard to the Kellys' kitchen door.

Belinda sat up from her needlework before the sheriff tapped lightly on the door. Martha got up from her bench to stoke the stove and stir the soup she'd kept warm for the men. John Coleman stepped in and dampened the lantern. Sett stomped mud from his boots before entering. Belinda craned her neck to peer behind him for Kiernan, and her frown deepened as Sett closed the door.

Without preamble he said, "Miz Kelly, Kiernan had to stay at the encampment. He's leading a detail out tomorrow to track whoever ambushed his men. He asked me to tell you it shouldn't take long and he'll be back as soon as he can." Sett's voice was quiet, controlled. If he was angry with her for allowing Ria to leave, he wasn't going to show it. Belinda rose from her seat and put her needlework aside.

"Thank you, Mr. Foster. Please, remove your coats, both of you. Martha has some hot soup for you." She busied herself setting out spoons to keep her worry from showing. John Coleman took off his coat and hat and hung them on the pegs by the door. Sett stood stock-still, the frost on his jacket melting in the warm kitchen air and dripping down onto the plank floor.

"Ma'am. About Ria. I want to know what happened. Now."

Belinda took a deep breath. She glanced from Martha to the sheriff before starting to speak. "This afternoon . . ."

"Foster, take off your coat and sit down," John Coleman broke in. "We'll discuss this in a civilized manner."

"Civilized, like giving your word? Civilized, like the good people of this town coming here to take my wife's baby?" Sett's voice was still controlled, but this time the control was deadly. He glared at John Coleman. "My wife is out there somewhere, and I want to know why. Now."

Coleman stood his ground. "Foster, stormin' out there in the dark isn't going to fix anything. We got to think about what we're doing, not just react."

"That's damn easy for you to say." Sett clenched his jaw and balled up his fists.

Belinda's eyes flew wide. She feared the men would

come to blows right there in her kitchen. Martha, holding two steaming bowls of soup, backed up into the pantry to be out of the way. Before she could think about it, Belinda stepped up to Sett's side and laid her hand on his sleeve.

"Sett," she implored in a soft voice. "Please. There's a lot to explain, and it has been a long day for all of us. Believe me, we have done all we can for Mrs. Foster. We searched for her until dark."

Sett looked down at the woman, so tall and fair compared to Ria. Her green eyes were brimming with tears, and he could not imagine her beating the brush in the cold wind, searching. He started to jerk his arm away.

"Yes, and gave her a good head start," John Coleman said dryly.

Sett glanced back at Kiernan's wife. There were still tears welling in her eyes, but there was also a glint of determination. He suddenly had no question as to whose side she was on. He relaxed his hands.

John Coleman did not miss that look either. The genteel and cultured Mrs. Kelly had already thought best to delay informing him of the Indian woman's flight for several hours, waiting until nearly dusk to send her black maid to the sheriff's office to summon him. She had explained with some hand-wringing that she had thought that poor frightened Mrs. Foster just wanted a little time alone and would return to the house shortly. She did not hesitate to lodge complaint again Deputy Jones for being party to the Citizens' Committee, nor did she neglect to mention that Sheriff Coleman's own wife was also one of the emissaries.

Sheriff Coleman now sat at the head of the table with his hands around a coffee cup, listening and biting his lip while Mrs. Kelly detailed the afternoon's events for Sett Foster. It was the same smooth story she had woven earlier, but this time Coleman had the feeling that there were certain details she was leaving out—leaving out because the absence of those details meant something to Sett Foster.

He also noted that Foster asked few questions, and there was no speculation beyond Mrs. Kelly's concern about the weather, as to which direction the Indian woman might have gone. The evening was growing late, and the sheriff had to be up by dawn to leave with the posse, but Foster seemed determined to out-wait him.

Sheriff Coleman stifled a yawn. The maid was pouring Foster yet another cup of coffee, but Coleman waved her away when she offered the pot to him. He'd come to a decision, an unpleasant one, and now he had to carry it out. He stood up and reached for his coat.

"Foster, we have an early appointment with the posse," Coleman said as he shrugged on his coat.

"Yeah. I'll be ready."

The sheriff tugged his Scotch cap down over his ears. "Well, I need to be certain of that. You understand?"

"I give you my word on it," Sett replied.

Coleman sighed and reached into his pocket. "Foster, I'm really sorry about this, but you're going to spend the night in the jail. Just so I can be sure where you are."

Sett didn't move from the table.

Belinda leaped up from her seat. "Sheriff Coleman, this is a terrible affront to a grieving man! Mr. Foster has not broken any laws. You can't just arrest him! Mr. Foster is my guest, and I will not allow it!"

The sheriff pulled a pair of handcuffs from his pocket. "I'm not arresting him, if he goes willingly, Mrs. Kelly. It's for his own safety. You know the mood of this town. Especially if, for some reason, he wasn't here in the morning."

Belinda sputtered something about what the lieutenant would have to say about this, but Sett silenced her with a raised hand.

"Okay, Coleman. You can lock me up if you want. Hell, you're armed and I'm not. You're not wrong; I wasn't planning to be here in the morning. But let me warn you, my goal is to find my wife. It's not to lead you and your posse to her."

"Fair enough, Foster. We'll deal with that tomorrow. Get your coat and your bedroll."

An old claustrophobia crept into Sett's chest as soon as the lock turned on the door. He was the only occupant in the jail, and he tossed his bedroll down on the bunk nearest the potbelly stove. Coleman had been congenial enough, only asking Sett to surrender his Winchester to be locked up in the safe in the main room. A young deputy was on duty, snoozing with his feet on the sheriff's desk when they had come in, and Coleman had specifically ordered the man to bring Sett anything he needed, within reason, and to make sure he was comfortable.

"Get some rest, Foster. We got a long day ahead," Coleman said as he dimmed the lantern to a low glow, but Sett could not make himself lay down on the bunk. He paced the confines of the cell, the familiar pattern of twelve steps, turn, twelve more, lulling him into a trance that brought him back to those other cells, those endless days of pacing and waiting. He had fully intended never to be in a jail cell again. He had worked so hard to that end, and here he was. His footfalls made a path in the sawdust on the floor.

He replayed Belinda's telling of the day's events. She was worried about the storm, about Ria being alone in the icy grip, but that was not what concerned Sett. Ria could take care of herself; she had her warm clothing, her horses, and her dog. Sett did a mental inventory of the food that had remained in the panniers—not much but enough, and with the cook pot she could heat water. Sett did not question Ria's resourcefulness, or her experience of living in the wild, but her own determination might well be her downfall.

The sheriff had hoped that Ria had run to find Sett, but of course she had not done that. Belinda had suggested that Ria had gone home, heading back to the cabin in the

Cottonwoods that was two days' ride to the southeast. Sett would be surprised if the small woman had chosen that predictable course. No, he was quite sure which direction she had gone: north, into unfamiliar territory, into the maw of the storm. She was on her way to her grandfather's people, a people now confined to the reservation. A people Ria had not seen since she was a young child.

Had she any idea of the conditions on the reservation? Did she understand that even if she found her distant family, there would be nothing they could do to help her? Sett pivoted at the end of his circle, pacing back to the center of the jail cell. He stopped, grasped the bars, and leaned his forehead against the cold steel. Damn, he should have stayed in the Cottonwoods. He should have given in to Ria and not insisted on his own honor-bound course. They would be sitting in front of the woodstove right now, Ria crooning to the baby and Sett planning his next horse hunting trip. Instead . . .

Instead, he had to figure out a way to give the sheriff the slip, to find Ria without leading the posse to her. Then to get away and head somewhere new, for he was sure that his quiet life here was over.

EIGHTEEN

Sett didn't think he had drifted to sleep, but he must have, since the voices in the other room startled him. In the windowless jail, there was no telling if it was near dawn. Sett listened carefully to the voice of the young deputy, who sounded as if he had just been awakened too. Finally the door was dragged open and the young man poked his head into the back room.

"Foster, can you read?"

"Yup. Pretty good."

The deputy came in and handed Sett a note. "That servant gal of the Kellys' is here, says this note gives her right to give you a package from Mrs. Kelly."

Sett looked at the fine writing paper and neat hand. It was addressed to Sheriff Coleman or the deputy in charge and requested that the package of food and supplies be delivered to Sett before he departed.

"That's what it says," Sett told him. "Is Martha still here?"

"Yup. You wanna talk to her?" The deputy motioned the big woman into the room. "This ain't normally something

I'd allow you, but Coleman was clear that you ain't under arrest. He just don't want you leaving without him."

"Thanks." Sett turned to Martha. "And thank you for coming. What time is it?"

"Jus' afore dawn, Mr. Foster. Sheriff should be here shortly. Miz Belinda thought these things might come in helpful to you. There's some rations and some medicines." Sett cocked an eyebrow at her. Was she trying to tell him that Ria was injured? But Martha just placed the package on the bench outside the bars of the cell. She then took a smaller package from the pocket of her coat. "This is for your breakfast. In case you're hungry 'fore the sheriff gets here." Now Martha held the bundle through the bars and Sett took it gratefully.

"Thank you, Martha. Please thank Mrs. Kelly for me if I don't see her when I get my mare."

"Yes, sir. She didn't 'spect you'd have time to talk." Martha put her hands into the pockets of the coat and turned to go. "God bless you, Mr. Foster."

When the deputy turned to let her out the door, Sett asked, "Turn up the lantern a bit, will you? I don't think I'll be sleeping again." The deputy did as requested and shut the door behind them as they left.

Sett untied the strings of the small package and found a waxed paper–wrapped bundle of fresh biscuits that were almost warm, slathered with butter. Slices of ham were folded in another paper, and in a third, carefully overwrapped to keep the grease of the food from damaging it, was another sheet of the fine writing paper. Sett put the food aside and tilted the paper toward the light.

Dear Mr. Foster,

I am most concerned about the welfare of Mrs. Foster and the child, but am also certain that the best possible course is for you to locate her rather than the search party. The citizenry here was most unkind and ill-disposed toward Mrs. Foster, and I'm sure it frightened her into leaving. I will do everything in my power to aid you and Mrs. Foster.

You know that she left several hours before the sheriff began his search. I told the sheriff that she had left openly by the back stairs, and that I assumed she was using the necessary and so did not immediately have cause for concern. That was a lie. Mrs. Foster left out the window of your room. She took with her extra blankets and sheeting from the house along with her Indian clothes and those for the infant. She has no food. Earlier in the day she asked for milk for the child, but she has none now.

I have clung to the theory that she is returning to your ranch. I will continue to do so. I will send Kiernan to your aid as soon as he returns home. Mr. Coleman informed me that the child's family will be arriving on the noon train. I will be there to meet them.

God speed to you, Mr. Foster.

Most humbly,
Mrs. Kiernan Kelly

Sett carefully refolded the paper and tucked it into his shirt. So Ria had fled in panic, bringing with her only what she could grab from the room. He suddenly lost his appetite for the ham and biscuits. Sitting on the edge of the bunk, he glared at the locked door into the sheriff's office, alternately wishing Coleman through the door so that they could begin their search, and counting each second of head start that Ria held, hoping it gave her enough of an edge that no one could find her.

No one but him.

A large crowd of men and horses gathered in front of the Kellys' house on the edge of town. Grim faces swaddled in hats and mufflers turned as one to watch Sheriff Coleman and Sett Foster walk down the street, the sheriff leading his horse. It looked like a lynching party, Sett thought, but he strode alongside Coleman with his kit over his shoulder, as if he were every bit as in charge as the older man. He could not think of any other way to approach it.

"Where were all these yahoos when we were looking for Digger Dick last year?" John Coleman grumbled under his breath. He stomped up to the assembled men and squinted at them in the early dawn light.

"You all here to volunteer for the posse?"

The group nodded, or mumbled, and a few said, "Hell, yeah."

Coleman turned his back on them and said to Sett, "Go in and saddle your horse. We'll head out as soon as you're ready."

Sett nodded and opened the door to the barn.

"I'll keep an eye on Foster." Deputy Jones dismounted from his horse and handed its reins to his neighbor.

Coleman said, "No need, Sketch. I need you out here to select men."

Sketch did not remount his horse. "I think they all should go. Then there'll be enough if we has to split up. 'Sides, they all just want to do their civic duty, opposed to some others here."

Coleman drew in a deep breath. Here it wasn't even sunrise yet and the day had already gone to hell. "Now, look here, Sketch . . ."

"Okay. Let's ride." Sett Foster led his tall bay mare from the barn, checked her girth one last time, and swung up as she danced in place.

The posse looked almost startled at his reappearance, and Sett brought the eager mare into circles as her back warmed under the saddle. Sketch hurried to his horse, but Coleman took his time mounting up. As if by unanimous decision, the ragtag posse swung around to head south. All but the sheriff. He waited, watching as Foster sifted out the big horse. The man could ride anything, by the looks of it. And that mare would outrun most anything. If hard riding would play into the coming game, John Coleman would bet on the horse rancher from the Cottonwoods.

Some of the posse had started down the street, Deputy Jones in the lead. Sett brought his horse under control alongside Sheriff Coleman.

"They goin' south?" he said ruefully as he turned the mare's nose into the brisk north wind.

A smile touched Coleman's eyes. "Be nice, wouldn't it?" he sighed. He urged his horse after Sett's. They had barely gone three strides when a squeaky yell sounded behind them.

"Deputy Jones! Men! That way!"

The posse stopped, looked over their collective shoulder, and then turned to gallop back past the house to catch up with Sett Foster.

From the window, Belinda Kelly observed the disorganized men and smiled sadly at the scene. "God go with you," she whispered against the cold glass. Then she turned and tied her apron strings tighter. "Martha, I'll clean up here. You go change the linens in the spare bedroom and sweep the parlor. Then ready my good green dress. I need to be at the train station at noon." Belinda lifted the kettle from the stove and headed into the pantry to wash dishes.

Dawn did not catch Lieutenant Kelly asleep. He was lying, quite awake, on the scratchy bunk in the dingy officers' quarters. He was fondly remembering listening to a distant reveille, from a much superior bunk, in the junior officers' barracks at the Academy. He could almost smell the welcoming scent of coffee drifting up from the officers' mess downstairs and the polite good-mornings from the other young men who shared his room. While none of that compared to greeting the day beside his beloved Belinda, it was still a most pleasant daydream.

There was no trumpeter here among his small detail, and so the most official sound to announce the day was the horses in the barn stomping in greeting of their morning feed. Kiernan figured that the men would have cowboy coffee on somewhere, but he could not smell it and probably would prefer not to. He sat up, pulling his boots on before allowing his feet to hit the splintery floor. Dragging his coat on over his union suit, he stretched as he headed for the stove. His head bumped the low ceiling, and all the rudeness of this post fell upon him like a shroud. He paused to look at himself in the small mirror that hung above the washstand.

"Good morning, sir," he muttered to the disheveled, bleary-eyed visage that looked back.

Stove stoked and water heating, Kiernan returned to shave and dress. He knew he had to make an early appearance and get the troops moving. The snow last night would have blotted out many of the tracks, but maybe they could still find some information about the ambushers. And he would have to assign a burial detail. Perhaps if they got back in time today, he could hold services for Sergeant Means.

The lieutenant made it to the yard early enough that most of the men were still finishing coffee and just starting to saddle. No one had been assigned to tack up the commanding officer's horse, and so Kiernan did it himself. When he led the horse from the barn, Corporal Gorney had the men somewhat assembled in the snow-dusted yard. With hardly a nod, Gorney wheeled the detail around and headed down the road.

The troopers traveled silently through the icy morning, the only sounds being the hoofbeats of the horses and the jangling of spurs and hardware. The snow had stopped, leaving a crisp frosting on the plains around the fort and a thicker covering over the mountains. The road wound across the flat before dropping down to follow the river. Most of this country was so open and windswept that one could see for miles, but after more than an hour of steady trotting, the road narrowed into a steep canyon, the slopes forested with fir and pine. The road hugged the bank under a rocky outcropping, the underbrush as tall as a man's head. Gorney raised his hand and slowed.

"Right around this turn, Lieutenant. Isn't that right, men?"

"Yeah. Means was in the lead," Jenkins said.

Kiernan moved to the front of the column. "Okay, let's take a look." He rode around the corner and paused. Yes, good place for a surprise. The thick trees and the curve of the trail would suddenly expose a traveler to anyone waiting in the rocks. In fact, the ambusher might have no clue as to who or how many people were on the road. Kiernan wondered about Sett Foster's theory that there was only one attacker, and that it had been a random choice. "Who was closest to Means?"

"Me, sir," Gorney said. "I was just a little behind him, but by the time I saw what happened, he had the arrow in his neck."

"Anyone else see it?"

The soldiers shook their heads. One, from the rear of the group, said, "I didn't see nothing except everyone diving for cover."

Gorney pointed out the brush and rocks on the lower side of the bank where the men had taken refuge. He dismounted to demonstrate how he had crawled out to where the dying sergeant lay. "And then I got shot too. From that direction." He pointed up toward the outcropping.

"But I heard someone moving over there." Jenkins pointed another direction. "Never saw the bastard though."

"There was someone down the canyon a ways too. Someone caught Means's horse down there and we didn't see anyone running that way."

Kiernan duly listened to each man's recounting of the attack, but somehow Sett's confident assessment kept repeating itself in his mind. The wind was kicking up snow, and the temperature was dropping again as the sun went behind a cloud. Kiernan was tired of standing around here with nothing to see.

"Let's see what we can find on down the canyon." He spurred his horse.

The site where Means's horse had been caught and mounted was blown bare of snow. A few scuffling tracks in the frozen mud were pointed out as the telling evidence. Kiernan dismounted, Gorney and Jenkins alongside. The three men knelt down to examine the days-old tracks.

"You're sure that these are the culprit's tracks? No one else walked here?" Kiernan had to ask.

"Course not, Lieutenant! Ain't the first time we've tracked an Injun, ya know." Jenkins's attitude was starting to wear thin. Kiernan again wished for Foster's expertise, but he muddled ahead on his own.

"This looks like the print of a leather heel." He pointed to one of the few clear parts of the tracks. "Which tribe wears boots?"

Gorney leaned closer to examine where the lieutenant pointed. "Hmm. Does look like a heel."

Jenkins got up and grunted. "They was shooting arrows."

Kiernan rose too. "Well, we can agree that someone caught the horse and rode away. Let's see if we can figure out which direction they went. Spread out and look for other tracks."

Hours to the north, Sheriff Coleman was also in a frustrating search for some sign of passage. Foster seemed willing to ride hard along the road, though he declined to say exactly where he was headed, and he did not argue when

Coleman suggested that the woman would have avoided the well-traveled road. Coleman was beginning to wonder if his trust in Foster had been that misplaced; if the man was deliberately leading them beyond where the half-breed woman would be. Certainly the grumbling from the men in the posse voiced that opinion, but none of them got disgruntled enough to quit and go back. The sheriff sighed again to himself. Searching for a pretty young woman was more appealing than last year's foray after a grizzled prospector who'd banged his partner in the head with a shovel.

Ahead, Foster moved his horse along in a big ground-covering trot. Most of the others pushed their horses into a slow lope, or tolerated the painful gait in an effort to save their mounts. If the hard riding bothered Foster or his horse, it didn't show. The mare had broken a light sweat on her neck, which frosted her dark hair, but otherwise she seemed as fresh as she had when they set out hours earlier. Coleman was glad to be on a decent horse, but if they didn't rest soon it would be cruel to the other animals.

Deputy Jones pushed his horse up alongside Coleman's. "How long you gonna let him lead us on this goose chase? That girl can't have gone this far by now, not off the road."

Coleman had to agree, but he just gave a curt nod and moved to catch up with Sett.

"There's a crossing up here a ways. We'll stop there and rest the horses," he said as he pulled alongside. Foster's beard was frosted from his breath. He nodded but kept his pace. Coleman said, "If your wife crossed the river, likely she'd do it there. Maybe someone saw her."

"Maybe."

NINETEEN

Mary Alice held her coat on her lap and waited for Will to return from the baggage car. She wished to waste no time disembarking, and so she'd sent her son to make sure their bags were ready and that the handlers were well tipped to see them safely and quickly off the train. The conductor had come by to tell her that they would be arriving in Verdy on schedule, just a little past noon. Mary Alice craned her neck to see forward, up the canyon, where the billowing steam locomotive puffed up the grade.

The railroad line wound up from the plains, curving its way from the broad valley floor into a wide canyon lined with groves of bare aspens. They passed occasional mining claims with small, bleak cabins and great piles of gravelly earth, so different from the neat farms and homesteads that lined the route across the plain. Now, as the train approached Verdy, the mines became more numerous and small communities huddled alongside the tracks. They were cold and windswept places, with an abundance of taverns and plenty of mud.

"Our bags will be first out the door, Mother," William

said cheerfully as he slid back the curtain to the berth. He sat down opposite her, his cheeks red from his forays across the open gangways between cars. "The conductor says we should arrive in a few minutes."

"I had expected a bigger place," Mary Alice said.

"I suspect Verdy itself won't disappoint you. Well, at least in size. The conductor says there are over ten thousand people living there now. There's an opera house and a dozen hotels. He recommended one, the Silver Palace, as the best." William shrugged his muffler away from his neck and removed his gloves. "I would like to take a day trip out to Irish Gulch, see the endeavor that had David and Amanda so excited. It is part of our holdings now or, more correctly, part of little Andrew's holdings, and I would like to inspect it if we are to administer it correctly."

Mary Alice scowled a bit. "I hope not to spend much time here, Willie. We can claim Andrew and head back. Perhaps on tomorrow's train. We have no idea of the child's health, and the sooner we get home, the better."

William pursed his lips and looked sadly at his mother. He reached across the berth to pat her hand. "Mother, this might take time. Please don't get your hopes up too much. We aren't even sure . . ."

"I'm sure. I can feel it in my bones!"

William patted her hand again but said nothing. It was that great force of will that had carried his mother through the trauma of her daughter's sudden death and had set her on this path. He knew she could not stand to think about waiting any longer to see her grandson.

The locomotive blew a long whistle as it crossed the wide, muddy road that had been parallel to the tracks. Ahead, the city of Verdy dug into the slopes of the canyon, tents and cabins on the edges giving way to a long street that was lined with larger, more prosperous-looking buildings. Near the top of the street, a gleaming ivory building stood out—the new territorial courthouse, still under construction.

The railroad station was a long, low building with a wooden dock that teemed with the citizens of Verdy. Mary Alice studied the crowd intently. There were miners and teamsters waiting with dray wagons for their supplies, passengers waiting to depart, and more people waiting to greet arrivals. Errand boys scurried through the crowd. One old Indian, wrapped in a red trade blanket, stood alone at the end of the dock. Some rather scurrilous-looking fellows lounged near the station, their hands in their pockets. Three overly dressed women with bright painted lips gathered by the nearest building, a saloon by the looks of it.

There was no one there carrying a baby.

William saw the searching look in his mother's eyes and stood to help her with her coat. He braced himself on the back of the seat as the train lugged to a stop alongside the platform.

"Welcome to Verdy, Montana Territory!" the conductor sang out as the doors were pulled open. Mary Alice waited for the motion to cease completely before rising from her seat. William guided her down the aisle and stepped down to the platform before her, while the conductor took her arm to hand her down safely.

"Have a nice stay, Mrs. McFee," he said. "Best of luck to you."

Mary Alice nodded her thanks and quickly battened her hat more firmly on her head with her scarf. The brisk wind was breathtakingly cold, though the sun was shining. She took a few steps and turned her back to the wind.

"I'll get our bags," William said. It was so cold that Mary Alice only nodded again.

She surveyed the crowd once more. Many of the men and some of the women were hurriedly making their way up the street toward the saloon; a few others were greeting friends or directing the unloading of goods. Then Mary Alice noticed a striking individual, a young woman leaving the doorway of the station and heading directly for her. Tall and dressed in impeccably tailored hunter green wool, with a wrap of brown and green plaid, the graceful woman at first appeared out of place in the general roughness of the crowd. As she came closer, she smiled pleasantly.

"Mrs. McFee? Welcome to Montana Territory. I am Mrs. Lieutenant Kelly. Sheriff Coleman asked me . . ." The young woman turned her eyes to some hullabaloo behind Mary Alice, and her smile froze.

Mary Alice heard a strident voice calling, "Mr. McFee, sir!" and she turned around to see a small group of people standing with the conductor, who was pointing out William. The group hurried toward William, but a grim-looking woman separated from them and started toward Mary Alice with a determined stride and a tight-lipped smile on her face. As she neared, the smile turned to a smirk and she met the young woman in green's gaze with open distaste.

"Why, how nice of you to bother coming out to meet the McFees, Mrs. Kelly. But there was no need. The Citizens' Committee has everything arranged. You may go now." Up close, Mary Alice could see that the woman's austere black dress was badly frayed at the collar and cuffs, and her wrap appeared quite inadequate for the cold. Yet she stepped in front of the younger woman and rearranged her expression into a sickly smile.

"You must be Mrs. McFee. My name is Mrs. Eliza Jones, I am Deputy Jones's wife. I am with the Verdy Citizens' Beneficial Committee, some of whom are speaking with . . . ," she cast a quick glance at Mary Alice and then at William, "your son, is it? We were expecting your husband. Here, come with me out of the cold. You must be exhausted after your trip and all the troubles that have befallen you . . ." She took Mary Alice's elbow and tried to lead her away. Mrs. Kelly had not moved and was glaring at the intruder with sparkling green eyes.

Mary Alice looked at her. "I'm sorry. You were saying? About the sheriff?"

Mrs. Jones tugged harder at Mary Alice's sleeve. "Come, we can talk inside, where it is warm. Where are you staying? We can arrange a room for you . . ."

Mary Alice was now fed up with the prattling woman. "Madam, please. You have interrupted us. I wish to hear what Mrs. . . . Kelly, was it? . . . has to say." She pulled her arm away from Mrs. Jones's clinging fingers.

Mrs. Kelly turned her attention back to the older woman, tipped her chin in acknowledgment, and said, "Thank you. I was saying Sheriff Coleman asked me to meet you, as he has been called away on urgent business."

"Oh yes! Urgent business!" Eliza Jones spat. "Tell her exactly why the sheriff had to leave. Go ahead. Tell her!"

Mary Alice stared at the sparring women, one so cultured and controlled and the other so vehement.

"What is going on here?" Mary Alice demanded.

"Mother." William hurried up beside her and took her arm. "Mother, we need to talk. There is bad news about . . . about the child."

The remainder of the Verdy Citizens' Beneficial Committee was composed of several men, with one plump hand-wringing lady among them. They positioned themselves behind Mrs. Jones, apparently in support of her cause.

Mary Alice glared at Mrs. Jones. "What it is it? Where are the authorities? Why in the world isn't there someone in charge around here!"

Eliza cleared her throat. "The child, who I'm sure is your daughter's—I can see the family resemblance . . ."

Belinda Kelly interrupted, though she was quite aware that it was not seemly. "My, Mrs. Jones, where did you see the child? I was not aware that the mother and babe were seen anywhere in Verdy except in my home."

Eliza Jones sputtered. "Why, the sheriff saw them. Clearly. And so, I suppose, did my husband the deputy . . ."

Belinda cast a last withering glare at Mrs. Jones and turned back to the woman from Denver. "Mrs. McFee, I beg you take your time considering this situation. It is a complex . . ."

Mary Alice held up her hand. Belinda fell silent. "I will ask questions. You all may answer. Simply, please." She shrugged her coat higher around her shoulders, and William dropped his hand from her arm as if he were as chastised as the others. "Where is the child now? Mrs. Jones?"

Eliza could not resist the shadow of a smirk. "We don't know where the child is. The Injun woman who found him run off with him yesterday. The sheriff and a posse are out tracking them."

Mary Alice gave a curt nod at this information. "Mrs. Kelly, I assume you have a different version?"

"Ma'am, the young woman, Mrs. Foster, cares for the babe as her own. She was frightened yesterday when this group of 'citizens' showed up and demanded that she turn the child over to them. She has gone into hiding. The Fosters, the couple who rescued the child from the wilderness, were staying at our house when it happened. I was witness."

"Witnessed her leaving and covered up for her to give her a head start!" Eliza snorted.

"Mr. Foster himself is leading the search party. I have no doubt they will return soon," Belinda added.

"Oh, please," Eliza said. "You have done everything in your power to meddle with the safe return of this infant to his rightful . . ."

"Uh hum," Mary Alice said. "And is there any suspicion as to where this woman has gone?" She aimed her question at the Citizens' Committee in general.

"The sheriff and posse headed north, at the suggestion of Foster. He must have reason to go that way," a fellow replied.

Now Mary Alice turned to William. "What is north of here, Will? A city?"

"No, Mother. Mostly wilderness, some mining camps.

Probably some small homesteads. I think the reservation is several days' ride away too." He looked to the Committee for confirmation.

Silence broken only by the squeaking of a windblown sign whipped around them with the cold. Belinda looked the older woman in the eyes. There was sadness and disappointment there, and worry and a certain fatigue. Belinda said, "This is a great disappointment for you, but I must tell you, I know that Mrs. Foster is not only a very devoted mother to this child, but also well versed in wilderness survival, as is her husband. I believe with all my heart that the baby is safe with her. She just became frightened, and it was both her and her husband's wish that they could keep this child to raise as their own. It has been a difficult time for all."

For a moment, Belinda Kelly thought that Mary Alice McFee might have sympathy in her eyes, but the deputy's wife fixed that.

"She keeps calling that half-breed 'Mrs.' and saying they're married! That's a lie, and she knows it. We are talking about a convicted murderer and his Injun squaw. There's no honor there, and no reason to trust them! All we can do is pray that the posse runs her down soon."

Mary Alice felt her son's hand grip her arm again, and she wondered if she were swaying. It was all so much, and this biting cold was beginning to seep even through her heavy garb. "Will, please let's proceed to the hotel and think on this." William immediately motioned to the porter waiting by their luggage and gave a dismissing nod to the assembled group.

"The lieutenant and I would be honored to have you as guests in our home," Belinda offered. "I have rooms prepared."

Eliza was scowling. There was no way that she could offer to be a similar host. She could not even recommend their hotel.

Mary Alice didn't have a chance to respond. William said, "Thank you, but we have made arrangements. If there is any word from the sheriff, we will be at the Silver Palace. We'd appreciate immediate notice if there is any news, regardless of the time of day." With that, he guided his mother after the porters, who led the way up the main street.

Belinda watched them leave, her spirits as weather-beaten as the windblown street.

TWENTY

Ria stood next to Fox Ears and Coy on the bluff, her dismay so complete that she forgot to worry about being skylined. Below her, the wagon road that she had been paralleling dipped down a long ridge and seemed to end at the bank of the wide and muddy Missouri River. A cluster of buildings sat by the abrupt end of the road on this side. Another building could be seen directly across. A large raft was tied up to the near shore.

Ria had been watching the ferry for several hours now. Again she watched as two loaded freight wagons lumbered to a halt in the yard below. A tall man came out of one of the cabins, and much gesturing and nodding took place. Then the teamsters urged their teams and wagons onto the raft, and slowly the conveyance took to the current. She had not figured out yet how it was made to move across the river, because that was not what mattered. She was quite sure, absolutely sure, that she would be expected to pay something for the ride across. And she had nothing with which to pay.

Finally, the ferry was bumping up against the far side of

the river and the freighters were on their way. The ferryman waited there as a group of horsemen approached. Again there was hand waving and discussion, but eventually the four riders got aboard the ferry and the craft began to make its creeping way back across the roiling river.

Ria remembered the river from her childhood. LaBlanc's lodge stood every summer along the Missouri, while in the winter they would travel inland to the better trapping grounds. She had even crossed the river a few times, usually in bull boats made by lacing hides to a bent willow frame, but once on mule-back. That crossing was vivid in her memory—her mother had held Ria's small brother in front of her in the saddle, and Ria had clung on behind. The overburdened animal struggled though the water and reached the far shore a mile below where they had started the crossing. The four of them had been soaked to the skin.

Ria's eyes never left the progress of the ferry, but her hands instinctively found Cricket's warm body under her shirt. It was bitterly cold. She could not attempt to swim her horses across the river and risk Cricket getting so wet. She watched the horses on the raft as it drew closer. One of them was tossing its head nervously. Ria wondered about the spotted pony, Cricket's pony. She wondered if she would get on the ferry, if she would jump overboard . . .

Coy started a low growl and the hair on her back rose. Ria took her eyes from the river to look behind her where her dog was staring. Both horses turned and pricked their ears, but Ria saw nothing except the groves of stunted firs among the rocks. Coy's growl intensified, and Ria hurried to get her toe in the stirrup and swing up on Fox Ears. She glanced back down at the settlement. The ferry was landing, but no one was pointing up at her. She wondered if someone had spotted her and slipped away to apprehend her. She had not seen anyone. Now a streak of fear made her heart race, and she tried to choose an escape route between the ferry settlement and whoever was sneaking up on her from the back trail. She urged her horse over the edge of the bluff to the east, where the hillside was steep and littered with boulders but the trees were not far away. The spotted pony dragged back on her rope, then leaped down after. Coy took the lead, still with her hackles raised, and made a beeline for the nearest trees. Fox Ears slid down the incline on his haunches, and Ria shoved one hand against the saddle horn to hold herself back in the saddle, and with the other cradled Cricket's vulnerable body, her palm cupped over his head. Pebbles and dirt cascading ahead of them made the marks of their passing very plain to see.

Ria reined up once they reached the trees. The land was still steep, but she did not want to risk tripping her mount on the roots and fallen limbs. She angled across the grove, trying to bear back toward the south before finding a drainage where she could drop down toward the river again. Finally they came upon a small elk park, and Ria dismounted. She tried to listen, but the blood was pounding in her ears so hard that she could hear only her own heartbeats. The horses stood blowing, their breath billowing in the icy air, and Coy panted but still stared up the way they had come. Ria took the empty cradleboard from the spotted pony's saddle and rested it against a stump while she unlaced it and spread the rabbit fur–lined flaps. She unbuttoned her shirt and untied the sling that held Cricket to her chest.

"Now, little one, you must ride where you are safer," she whispered. The baby shook his arms and kicked for a minute in the chill air, his cooing and chirping bringing a softening to the woman's face. She chose a soft cloth and changed the baby's swaddling, and wished she had time to let him suckle, but knew her own fear would not allow that. She bound the child into the solid framework of the cradleboard, trusting that the strong curved lathes would protect his skull and the outer ridgepoles would dampen any blows, and she slung the carry-strap over Fox Ears's saddle horn and remounted, ready to flee.

Where? Sunlight filtered through the forested side of the mountain, and with her breath calming, she could hear no pursuit, yet she was sure it had existed. Coy still glared and growled, and Ria was certain she would not be acting so if it were Sett coming upon them. Sett alone. There was no chance of that, and so she had to keep running, and now, while staying ahead of whoever was tracking her, she must figure out how to cross the river. She scanned the perimeter of the small park, trying to choose a direction.

"*A'sitápi na'á.*"

The voice startled Ria so badly that she let out a small yelp. Coy immediately began to growl fiercely and stood stiff-legged and staring up the slope.

"Little Mother, I mean you no harm. Do not run away with your little one, putting him in danger."

The voice seemed to echo from above; there was no clear direction to it. It was a soft, quiet voice. And it was speaking Blackfeet.

Ria's legs shook so hard that her horse grew nervous and danced in place. Ria peered up into the dense forest, squinting to catch sight of the owner of the voice. Time seemed to slow, and the air was buzzing with her dog's continuing growls and the crunching of the pine needles beneath Fox Ears's hooves. There was a flicker in the dappled shadows, and a figure appeared as if forming out of mist; a thin young man in an oversized coat, belted with a piece of twine around the waist. His straight black hair had been chopped abruptly just below his ears, and his large dark eyes sparkled with an oddly mischievous glint. Now, as Ria's eyes grew accustomed to the shadows, she saw that he was leading a horse. She realized she was holding her breath, and let it out in a little gasp.

"There, I am not here to hurt you. I saw you watching the ferry. You want to cross the river too." He stepped slowly closer, as if he were sneaking up on a fawn. At the edge of the clearing, he stopped and waited.

Ria nodded. "Yes."

"Where are you going, all alone?"

Closer now, Ria could see that he was perhaps her age or a bit older, but he was very thin and his clothes very worn. A knife sheath was threaded onto his twine belt and there was a rifle in the scabbard on the saddle. His language was natural, comfortable, and she guessed that he was Blackfeet, or half-breed like herself. She said, "I am going to my grandfather's people, on the reservation."

He laughed, the sound seeming very loud among the trees. "Me too. We can cross the river together."

"I cannot pay."

"Do not worry. I have a plan." Now he stepped right into the clearing, and Coy circled him suspiciously, but he gave her little regard. "Are you hungry? I have some jerky here."

The thought made Ria's mouth water. She dismounted and tied Fox Ears to a limb. She took Cricket's cradleboard from the saddle, intending to chew some of the meat for him. The young man was searching through his saddlebags. The horse was large and well appointed, wearing saddle, bridle, and saddlebags, and suddenly Ria recognized the tack. It was the same as Lieutenant Kelly's, with the brass medallions on the cheek-pieces and brow band. The young man held out a strip of dried meat, and Ria could not stop herself from taking it, but before biting into it she asked, "Where did that horse come from?"

The young man laughed again. "A bluecoat soldier gave him to me, for my journey." Chewing his jerky, he leaned down to look at Cricket's tiny face. "Does your baby have a name yet?"

"Yes, Tapikamiiwa," Ria said.

"A good name. The priests at the school named me Michael, after one of their angels. But that won't be my name when I get back to our people."

"What will it be then?" Ria scooped a bit of chewed meat onto her finger, to wipe on the baby's lips.

"I'll change it. I'll change it to something suiting a warrior." Michael's voice turned bitter. "The priests don't let us choose our own names. They don't let us live as Blackfeet. But that will change now." He offered Ria another strip of jerky and stared at her soberly. "You ran when you heard me coming. Is someone chasing you?"

Ria was crouched down by the cradleboard. She almost dared not look up at him. "Yes. White people want to take my baby."

Michael nodded as if that made perfect sense. Then the mischievous gleam was back, and he said, "They are chasing me too. Let's get across the big river before nightfall." He grabbed the saddle horn and swung up on the horse without using the stirrups. Ria hurried to hang Cricket's cradleboard back on Fox Ears's saddle and gather up the spotted pony's lead, and then she followed the young man on down the drainage toward the river.

The ferryman was gray-haired and grim. He glared at Michael and Ria, shifting his eyes from the cradleboard to the ugly spotted packhorse to the dog, who sneered back at him. They all stood silently in the yard, with Michael carefully keeping his horse behind Ria's and the packhorse.

"Tell him to take us across," Michael said to Ria in Blackfeet.

She glanced at him, startled. "You don't speak the American words?"

"Yes, but I have vowed not to. Just tell him."

The idea of negotiating with the ferryman was frightening, but Michael caught her eye and encouraged her with a lift of his chin. He pointed to the other side of the river and drew an encompassing circle around them with his finger.

"How much to cross?" Ria whispered.

Michael shook his head at her. "Not how much. Just tell him to do it!"

Ria summoned her voice. "We want to cross," she said. The ferryman gave a short "Ha!"

"Don't want no damn Injuns on my ferry. Ya can swim across like the rest."

Michael had moved his horse so close to Ria's that his leg brushed hers. He whispered, "Yes, when the priests brought us down here, we boys had to swim the horses across. The priests and the girls rode on the ferry. Show him your baby."

Ria turned Fox Ears slightly. "It is cold and my son would be wet," she said.

The ferryman waved a dismissing hand. "Nah, go away." He started to turn.

In desperation, Ria said, "Please, sir. I know . . . I know we do not look . . . right. My name is Marie-Amalie LaBlanc. We need to cross." Michael's knee bumped hers so hard she was sure there would be a bruise, but before she could respond to him, the ferryman turned back toward her. He squinted up at her, judging, she was sure, the lightness of her skin and the freckles across her nose. She shrugged her hood back.

"Okay," the ferryman said finally. "That will be four bits apiece for you and the saddle horses, and two bits for the packhorse and the dog. Pay now."

The first burst of joy at the ferryman's agreement was immediately replaced by the demand for money. Ria turned in the saddle to raise her eyebrows at her new companion, only to see the rifle coming up out of the scabbard and swinging up across the neck of her own horse. "Tell him we will pay on the other side."

Michael cocked the rifle. There was no need to translate to the pop-eyed ferryman. After a stunned moment, he scurried to the docked ferry and waited by the belaying rope.

"Go," Michael said with another bump against her knee, and she urged Fox Ears forward up the ramp. But the spotted pony would have none of it. She balked at the foot of the planks, tossed her head and rolled her wild eye and threatened to pull the rope out of Ria's hand. Coy jumped over the ramp completely, then stood barking on the raft. Michael rode his horse up behind the spotted pony, and while still holding the rifle in the ferryman's direction, he beat the pony on the rump with the free end of his reins. Still the pony would not budge.

"Leave her!" Michael ordered. The ferryman looked to be escaping in the melee, and Michael left the pony to train the rifle more accurately upon him.

"No!" Ria flung herself off of Fox Ears, running down the ramp with her shawl in her hand. At the pony's side, she tossed the shawl over its head. With it blinded now, she stroked the scrawny neck for the first time. The pony had always tried to bite her before. Then she led the spotted horse up the ramp and next to Fox Ears.

Her Blackfeet accomplice inclined his chin toward her, clearly impressed. He backed the well-trained cavalry horse up the ramp while keeping the ferryman in his sights. He motioned to the man to come aboard and crank up the gangway.

The raft swayed and bounced even at the dock, and the ferryman scuttled around, checking cables, adjusting lengths, and securing the gangway, before finally casting off the mooring line. With a stomach-sickening lurch, the ferry entered the river current and began its slow way across. Ria stood next to the horses' heads, the pony still under her blindfold and Fox Ears swiveling his namesakes nervously. Coy found a safe-looking spot in the corner and huddled up. Of them all, only Cricket was calm, his blue eyes wide, his cradleboard rocking with the raft.

They were maybe twenty feet from shore when the ferryman made a small feint, and then vaulted over the side.

Splashing in what was still shallow water, he dog-paddled back toward the shore. Ria was aghast—who would run the ferry?—but Michael just sat atop his horse and fired the rifle. The spotted pony flinched at each loud crack, and Ria tried to soothe her. The young Indian missed all three shots, but he laughed as the ferryman scrambled up the landing and ducked behind the nearest shed.

After the booming of the gunshots, there was near silence as the river splashed against the side of the raft. The cables tethering the ferry to the main cable creaked, and slowly, almost imperceptibly, the craft moved farther from the shore. Michael placed the carbine back into the scabbard and dismounted his horse. Ria stood close to Fox Ears, sheltering the precious cradleboard between her body and that of the trusty horse. She struggled to hold back tears. The river was immense, and the rolling water jostled the raft, which she now thought was quite adrift. She was afraid to look downriver, her memory being of rocks and rapids as the waterway narrowed. She wished for the tiny comforting cabin against the backbone of White Buffalo Mountain, for Sett coming in with an armload of stove wood, even for the warmth of Belinda Kelly's kitchen, but here she was, floating on rushing water of who knows what depth . . .

"That was good." Michael had come up on the other side of the horse. "But I need to practice with this rifle. The priests did not let us learn to shoot." He gave a short, bitter laugh. Ria raised her head from where she leaned it on her arm, over Fox Ears's back. She stared at the young man in disbelief.

"How can this be good? Without the ferryman, we are stuck out here!" she asked, trying to control the fear in her voice.

The young man shrugged. "We are going across, see?" He pointed at the now distant landing. "The water pushes it. His problem will be getting it back." Michael gave another disdainful chuckle. "Maybe he will have to swim again."

Ria looked back, and indeed the ferry was proceeding across the river under its own power, the current on the angled raft pushing it forward on its tether. She looked the other way and the bank was nearing. She could see the sandy slope where the ferry slid up onto the shore. Now it seemed that the ferry was picking up speed; perhaps the current was stronger here. At least there was no one waiting for the ferry on the far side.

She realized that the Blackfeet man was staring at her. He cocked his head, squinted a bit. "You said a name back there. You said you were LaBlanc."

Ria nodded. "My father. I have not used that name in many years." In truth, she had not been called Marie-Amalie since she was a tiny child. Her father had christened her so, but her mother and siblings used the shorter endearment. She was not sure why she'd called it up in that moment of desperation, other than it was a white man's name, and not Sett's.

"I knew LaBlanc," Michael stated. "He was the red-haired trapper. He was married to my aunt."

Startled, Ria stared over her horse's back at him. She searched his face for some familiar feature. His hair was thick and black as a raven's feathers. His eyes too were the coal black of the Blackfeet. But with his eyebrows tilted up in that roguish angle . . . There was a sudden flash of memory, a boy yowling in pain and shaking a fox-bitten finger.

"You are Pine Leaf!" she cried, and the young man grinned.

"I was called that, yes. You are Sweetgrass Woman's daughter. The one who wanted a pet fox."

Now Ria could not suppress a smile. What fate had brought this man to help her? First Wife's nephew, a boy several years older than her, one who had known her when she was a toddling child, as small as Cricket!

"Oh, yes. It has been so long . . . Do you know, is my

mother still alive? Are Talking Crow's people at the reservation? I . . ." Ria's words were cut short by a strong jolt. She clung to Fox Ears's saddle horn to avoid being tossed down upon the deck. The pony lost her balance and knocked into Ria so hard that it took her breath away. Michael Pine Leaf was gripping his horse's stirrup and trying to move its hoof off of his foot. The ferry had come to land, rather harshly, on the far bank.

Ordinarily, the ferryman would have been shortening the tethers as they approached, easing the craft up onto the sand in such a way that the ramp met the ground solidly, but now the raft swung back and forth with the current, first meeting the bank, then bobbing away. It strained at the cables like a living thing, and only by grasping the side rail was Michael able to make his way to the winch that let down the ramp. Its workings failed him, though. He had not ridden the ferry on his first crossing, but swum alongside with the horses. Now he had no hint of how to crank down the series of gears that would lower the ramp. The horses were struggling to stand, and the dog had climbed to the edge of the low wall, ready to leap toward the solid riverbank. Michael pulled a hatchet from his belt and hacked the rope until the ramp dropped with a great splash into the water. The ferry bucked and pulled, and a gap of several feet appeared and then disappeared between the end of the ramp and the solid shore.

"Let's go. Jump," Michael pulled his way back to the horses and forcibly lifted Ria into her saddle. He took the pony's lead and spurred his mount toward the gap. The cavalry horse jumped, his hooves scrabbling on the slick planking of the deck, but the blindfolded pony did not. She slid into the deep water, her front legs grappling at the bank and her hindquarters submerged as the ferry came rolling forward again. Ria cringed; she knew that the ugly spotted horse would be crushed, and instinctively she dropped her hand to where Tapikamiiwa hung safely on her saddle. But Michael had dallied the lead, and was pulling while the wave ahead of the submerged ramp picked up the back end of the little horse and she scrambled up onto the solid ground.

"Come on! Jump!" Michael called again. The ferry swung out, and on its next inward push, Ria urged Fox Ears forward. Eager to join his herd-mates on shore, the red horse soared over the closing gap, with Coy alongside. Ria clung to his mane and to the edge of Cricket's cradleboard. They landed with a thump on the sandy shore.

"Good!" Michael grinned. "And your son is a brave little one." For Cricket was wide awake, but no sound issued from his lips.

Ria slumped over Fox Ears's neck. She felt that all the strength had been drained out of her, that she might slide off the horse with her weak legs. She gasped for breath in the cold air.

"Look." Michael was pointing back across the river. The small figure of the ferryman was standing on the bank, watching. A group of riders was coming up the road to the ferry, very quickly. Ria sat up and wished she had Sett's monocular. She could not make out who was riding so fast.

"Are those the ones looking for you?" Michael Pine Leaf asked.

"I don't know." They watched as the ferryman gestured. Certainly, he was telling whoever it was that they had stolen his ferry. The men were far away, and dusk was falling, but she did not recognize Sett Foster or his distinctive big mare. "I don't think it is me they are looking for. "

"Then, it is me. I did not wait to see how many were following." Michael took the hatchet from his twine belt again. Dismounting, he examined the cables and wheels of the mooring. He chose the largest cable and began to hack at it with the blade. It took time, but it frayed with each blow, and finally, with a loud pop, the tugging ferry broke loose. It twirled once, as if reluctant to leave, and then careened into the main current. Now all the riders on the far side were gazing out across the water, as the raft picked up speed and finally bounced against a rock before disappearing around the bend.

"Let's go, Little Mother." Michael swung back up on his horse. He urged it up the road, and Ria glanced back once at the congregation of riders on the south bank before reining her horse after him.

TWENTY-ONE

Riding in the dark on the unfamiliar road, Sett slowed enough to let the sheriff travel alongside. The posse had dwindled to a handful of men, and those had given up grumbling, though the deputy occasionally let out a disgusted snort.

"How much farther to that ferry?" Sett asked John Coleman.

"Getting close now. That bluff over there overlooks it." The bluff Coleman indicated rose dark against the starlit sky. The well-traveled freight road glimmered in the clear night, a pale trail through the sage and brushy trees. Coleman said, "Up here, we'll cross a little ridge and see the river, then drop down to the ferry."

At the crest of the ridge, the party pulled up. The land sloped down sharply toward the river bottom, and the wide, shining water snaked its way across the broad landscape, opening up a view of rolling, open country bathed by the rising moon. But the beauty of the scene was broken by John Coleman's sigh.

"Uh oh. Something's going on."

The men crowded forward, looking down the long slope toward the ferry landing. A half dozen campfires burned, faint figures moving around in the firelight, and it appeared that every light in the ferryman's home was burning too. The smell of smoke drifted up to the ridge, and Sett could see faint flickering of other fires in the trees.

"Maybe there's a wagon train waiting to make the crossing." Sketch Jones suggested.

"Could be. Seems like quite a bunch of them for this time of year though," Coleman said.

There was a clicking noise in the darkness. Sett Foster was extending his monocular. He peered down at the camp by the river for a long time, before snapping the collapsible brass tube shut and stowing it away.

"That's a cavalry camp by the river," he said quietly. "Issue tents and regulation pickets."

The road dropped down to the river through a wooded canyon, and they came into the first encampments there. Sett slowed to a walk. Coleman and Jones joined him. The first camp they reached was a freighter, two heavy wagons and teams of oxen. The drovers jumped up from their rolls by the fire and squinted at the arriving men.

"Yer outa luck. The ferry's gone!" one of them hollered at the passing riders. Sett rode forward, not stopping to ask for any details from these at the end of the line. The next camp was also one waiting to cross the river.

"Might as well turn back, men. There's no crossing here."

"Camp at the end of the line, buckos!" one man yelled, until Coleman turned to flash his badge and mutter, "Official business."

Sett held his mare to a sedate pace, in spite of his screaming nerves. The echo of his horse's hoof-falls reverberated in the clear night as loudly as the blood pounding in his ears. He rode forward, dread residing at the back of his neck.

The buildings of the ferry landing came into sight, and the small cavalry contingent was bivouacked in the yard. The ragged posse entered the line, and Sett pulled up and dismounted. Several of the cavalrymen were on their feet. Sett recognized one.

"Gorney," he said. "Is the lieutenant here?"

Gorney came forward as the sheriff dismounted. "Yup, he's in talking to Lastrop." Gorney took one look at the worn-out men of the posse and turned to his detail. "Men, help with these horses, and get some coffee."

Sett remembered the young soldier from the fort when he came forward.

"Take your horse, sir?" Rattigan offered.

Sett shook his head. "Thanks, I'll look after her. What's going on here?"

The young man sighed. "An Injun stole the ferry. Took it across and then cut the cable. Ferry's gone. Injun's gone."

Sett felt that dread on his neck turn ice-cold. "When? What Indian?"

"Prob'ly the guy we were tracking. The one that shot Sergeant Means. Sounds like he was riding Means's horse. We weren't sure it was an Injun, because he was wearing shoes." Sett didn't follow all of the younger man's logic, but there was a lightening of the dread when the Indian was described. But the boy went on. "Thing is, we were tracking one guy. Sounds like there were two of them stole the ferry, with a couple of horses and a dog. They shot at old Lastrop. Lucky thing he wasn't killed."

Sett shoved the mare's reins into the young man's hand. "You hold the horse, right here, until I come back." He spun toward the ferryman's house and was on the porch in three long strides.

"Wait, Foster!"

Sett ignored the sheriff's call, raised his hand, and knocked once on the door before throwing it open.

Kiernan was sitting at a long table, cradling a steaming

cup in his hands. The ferryman, a tall, thin man with sparse gray hair, sat across from him, his wife at his side. Kiernan looked up at Sett's sudden entry, stunned.

"Sett! What are you . . ." He trailed off as John Coleman and Sketch Jones burst into the small room behind Sett.

"I could ask you the same thing," Sett growled. "But I already heard." He turned to the shaken ferryman. "Describe the Indians, the ones who took your ferry."

There was something in Sett's eyes that was about as frightening as the gun that had been fired at him that day. Lastrop shakily set his coffee cup on the table. "There was a young buck and a woman with a baby. And a packhorse and a dog. The buck held a rifle on me. They crossed the river, then cut the ferry loose. The woman did the talking."

Sett stood there, astonished. Kiernan slowly rose from his seat.

"Sett, what's going on? Why are you here?"

John Coleman stood at Sett's side. The shock in the man was palpable, and Coleman put his hand on Sett's elbow. "Foster, why don't you sit down and we'll get to the bottom of this." Sett did not move but stared at the wall behind Kiernan Kelly as if he could see the whole tableau being played out upon it. Kiernan Kelly turned to the sheriff.

"Coleman, what's going on? What are you doing out here?"

"Mrs. Foster left Verdy yesterday with the child," Coleman stated. Deputy Jones let his lip twitch at the reference to "Mrs." but Coleman ignored him. "She ran, and we've been looking for her."

"Looks like we found her, too," Sketch Jones added.

"Not soon enough. They've been on the other side of the river since before sunset, and it's a long way around to the next crossing," Kiernan said. He couldn't take his eyes from Sett Foster's face. The tired, restrained look had been replaced by a clenching jaw and darkening eyes, a look unlike any he had ever seen on his friend's features. He wished Sett would say something, would react in some way besides this dark silence. He asked, "Why in hell . . . ?" He glanced at the ferryman's wife. "Sorry, ma'am, but why would she be with our fellow?"

Coleman shook his head, then reached up to remove his hat and run his fingers through his salt-and-pepper hair. "Don't know, Lieutenant. You're after the one who shot your sergeant? We've been heading toward the reservation, because that's where Foster was sure the woman would go." The sheriff replaced his hat and sighed.

The old ferryman had been watching the exchange with interest. He said, "The woman said her name, some French name. Claimed she was white, but she was dressed like a squaw. Good with a horse too."

Sett finally broke his silence. "LaBlanc," he said.

"That's it," the ferryman agreed.

"So we know it was her," Kiernan said. "Coleman, how best do we get back on the trail?"

"We'll have to go back to the fork, head west and cross at Canyon Ferry."

"Hell, that's a day's ride!" Kiernan said.

"You could meet up with the railroad, flag 'em down, and take the train," Lastrop suggested.

"Nah, we'd have to leave the horses to do that, and we'll need them once we're there." Coleman accepted a cup of coffee from the ferryman's wife.

"We gotta send a wire up to the garrison at the reservation," Deputy Jones insisted. "Get them watching on their end." Coleman nodded at him. Jones was a pain, but that was a good idea.

"Swim the river."

Sett's whispered words were nearly ignored as the other men argued the best plan, but Kiernan heard him distinctly. He said in a low voice, directed only at Sett, "It would be suicide to swim that river in this weather. There's no way to dry out on the other side."

The ferryman's wife held a cup of coffee out to Sett, but he ignored her. Instead he focused on Kiernan Kelly, standing in front of him and the only one listening to what he was saying. "Got to, Kiernan. Got to stay on her trail. Before, I knew where she was heading. Now I don't."

"You have no idea who this Injun is she's joined up with? Tell me honestly, Sett. This fellow killed Means just to get his horse. You were right. There was only him and it was probably just opportunistic. Lastrop described him laughing the whole time. If you know anything about him, you better tell me, because I intend to find him and bring him in."

Sett became aware of the poor woman standing in front of him with a hot cup of coffee, of the eyes of the ferryman, the sheriff, and the deputy now all turned toward him, of Kiernan Kelly's earnest face. It was suddenly very hot in the crowded little house. Sett took a deep breath, struggling for air.

"Got to take care of my horse," he said, before he spun on his heel and stalked out the door.

Sett had rubbed down the mare and staked her up in the aspens when he heard John Coleman approach. He'd spread his bedroll in the shelter of a leaning tree nearby, in sight but away from the tents of the troops. "Foster, we've decided that first light, we'll split up. You and Jones will go with Lieutenant Kelly to Canyon Ferry and then continue the search. I'll take the rest of the posse back to Verdy. I'll wire the post at the reservation and deal with the McFees and then head for the agency, meet you there."

Sett nodded, then assumed he could not be seen clearly in the dark and said, "Sounds like a plan."

"Good," Coleman said. He started to turn away but hesitated. "Foster, this is a bad turn of events. I don't know what's the truth behind it, but just so you'll know, I'm praying for your wife's safety."

Sett nodded again. This time he hoped the sheriff would just know. He watched the man's dark form recede into the trees.

Sett didn't sleep but sat up in his bedroll, leaning against the tree. The moon had fully risen and cast a gentle light on the river and the land beyond. The fires in the encampment burned down, and the horses settled in at their pickets. Sett waited until the moon was full overhead then he crawled out of the bedroll and pulled it out straight. He placed his rolled up socks into his boots and laid them on the bedroll. Then he stripped off his long coat and his wool shirt and folded them beside the boots. He pulled on his fur-lined moccasins, and shivering in the deep cold of the October night, he rolled everything tightly into the canvas-lined bedroll. He caught up the mare and quickly saddled her, tying the bedroll in front of the pommel instead of behind and folding his rifle into a square of oilcloth before shoving it into the scabbard. He gave a glance back toward the encampment. No movement there. He led his horse upstream, through the trees.

"Where ya going, Foster?" The voice was ahead of him, drifting out of the dapples of moonlight under the trees.

"Taking a walk, Jones. What are you doing?"

The deputy stepped out from the shadows. "Watching you. You think we wouldn't post a guard on ya?"

"Nope, didn't expect Coleman to post a guard. I'm a free man, here of my own free will. Don't need a guard."

The deputy snorted. "Yeah. Well, Coleman's a trusting old fool. I'm not. So why're you sneaking away in the dark, tell me that?"

"Not gonna tell you anything, Jones."

"Hmmm. Be that way. Guess it's because you don't really know anything, anyhow. Seems like that 'wife' of yours had some surprises for you, too. Didn't know she had a young buck in the weeds, did ya?"

Sett dropped the mare's rein and let his hand fall near his sheath knife. "I don't know what's going on, but I'll find out."

"Oh, I'll bet you do. Bet you find out where she's been all those days you come into town with your damn mustangs." Jones stepped more into the open. He had his revolver in his hand. "Okay, now turn around and head back for camp. You might be slipping off to join up with your little slut and her friend, or you might be slinking off home to lick yer wounds, but not yet. Not while I'm around."

The blade of Sett's knife glinted in the moonlight. The sight of it brought a short grunt from the deputy. "Good move, Foster. Now when I shoot you, I can honestly say it was self-defense."

Sett dove into the shadows at the man's feet; the mare spooked back, and the cracking brush made a small chaos of noise. Jones squinted into the darkness, trying to find him, stepped back, and had his leg yanked out from under him. The revolver fired, the shot wild into the canopy overhead. Then Jones felt himself jerked against a tree trunk as Foster's arm folded beneath his chin, the cold blade of the knife at his throat.

"Damn you, now you've done it," Sett hissed into the man's ear. Through the trees, both of them could see the soldiers rolling out of their tents, arms drawn. The barn door flew open, the men of the posse silhouetted against a hastily lit lantern. The ferryman appeared at his door in a nightshirt, rifle in hand. There was a long silence, broken only by the bay mare's uneasy movements in the underbrush.

Coleman stepped forward. Sett could discern the lanky figure of Lieutenant Kelly behind him.

"Foster! You all right?" Coleman called into the trees.

Sett let his knife rest on the skin of Jones's throat.

"I'm all right," he called back. He waited a moment. "Did you set a guard on me, Coleman?"

There was a murmur of discussion in the camp.

"Should I have?" Coleman said back. One of the posse approached Coleman, gesturing into the trees. "Is Jones with you, Foster?"

Sett let out a short laugh. "Yeah."

"Send him back here. I promise he won't bother you again."

Sett leaned closer to the deputy's ear. "If I were a wise man, I'd make sure of that myself. Now, toss your piece over there in the brush and you walk back to camp, slowly." Jones lobbed the revolver away. Sett dropped his knife from the man's throat. Jones took several shaky steps, then broke into a run.

"He's getting' away, Coleman! He's running off!"

Sett wished it were light, so he could throw his knife. Instead, he called to his horse and pulled himself up into the saddle. The encampment was now in an uproar, Coleman swearing at the men and Kiernan's voice calling orders, all while Jones crashed through the brush like a frightened elk, yelling.

Sett urged the mare out onto the riverbank. The sandy shore was gentle on this side, the silver water lapping the gravel with an alluring calm. Sett did not pause but sent the big mare into the water, the first icy rush of it taking his breath away. Then the mare plunged into the deeper channel and the current grabbed them. She angled upstream, her body bobbing below the surface. Sett grasped the saddle horn and allowed himself to float alongside the swimming horse. His hands quickly started to numb, and he twisted the leather saddle strings around one wrist. He gave the mare her head.

He looked back once, seeing the fires in the camp all stoked into life, and the men pacing the shore, gesturing across the river. Then he turned to focus on the far shore, to keep his head above the water, to kick feebly when he could remember to, and to trust his life once again to the horse swimming strongly alongside him.

Over the rush of the river, he did not hear the shouts when another rider followed him in.

TWENTY-TWO

Ria dropped the reins on her saddle horn and let Fox Ears follow their guide across the plain. She tucked her hands into her coat for warmth and to support Tapikamiiwa in his sling under her shirt. It was much too cold to leave him in the cradleboard, though she worried about the dangers of riding through the unfamiliar terrain in the dark.

Michael Pine Leaf left the road as soon as they were out of sight of the river, and they had paused long enough for her to nurse the baby and eat some more of the soldier's travel rations before starting cross-country. Now he led them confidently across the rolling hills toward the north. The moon sent enough light that they could travel, and though Ria was tired to her bones, she did not ask to stop again. Lost in her own haze of weariness, she was startled when Fox Ears came to sudden halt.

"Look, Little Mother. Do you recognize it now?" The young man gestured to the distant horizon. "Those are the old hills, our people are just beyond them. We will be there by tonight."

It took Ria a moment to realize that by "tonight," he

meant another day's travel. She wondered if he planned to stop at all. She squinted at the far hills. "I do not recognize them. I do not think I have ever been there," she said.

"You must have been here. It is our people's land," Michael Pine Leaf stated.

"I grew up in the trapper's lodge on the river. Then I lived far south of here."

"Well, you will recognize it when we get there." He gathered his reins up to go.

"Michael, will we stop and rest soon? Tapikamiiwa is hungry."

The young man spun his horse around to face her. "Don't call me that! That is a white-eyes' name, and it is not my name."

Ria cringed back from his vehemence, the anger clear on his moonlit face. Then, just as quickly, he grinned at her. "Of course we will stop soon. I just wanted to use this bright light as long as we can. We will go down into that canyon, see? We will stop there." He turned back to the trail.

The horses picked their way down a long slope strewn with boulders, the shadows like black holes in the landscape. Ria struggled to stay awake, to be able to react if her horse stumbled or startled. Once in a while the pony would pull back on her tether, or a loosened rock would clatter away into the darkness, but otherwise they rode in silence, accompanied by glittering stars. At the bottom of the hill, the Blackfeet turned up into a side canyon dense with chokecherry brush. The branches slapped at Ria's face, and she shielded herself with her scarf. The young man finally pulled up next to a huge leaning boulder.

"We will stop here," he said.

Ria dismounted and started to unsaddle her horse. The man reached for the reins.

"I will take care of the horses. I will hobble them right

here. You can lay out your bed there under that rock. It will be out of the wind."

Ria smiled at him gratefully.

"Should I make a fire?" she asked.

"No. In case someone is looking, we are more hidden without it. There is more food in the saddlebags." Pine Leaf indicated where he had propped the cavalry saddle next to the boulder. Then he pulled the saddle off Fox Ears and leaned it against another.

Ria didn't really mind not building a fire. She was so tired that all that mattered was caring for Tapikamiiwa and sleeping. She laid her robe and blanket in the dry gravel under the rock. Chewing on a mouthful of jerky and sipping water from the army canteen, she loosened her coat and turned the baby so he could nurse. She worried that she didn't really have milk for him, but so far he seemed sated and healthy. By the time the young Blackfeet man had returned from hobbling the horses, Ria was rolled up in her robe, sound asleep.

Mary Alice had not slept well, and as soon as was seemly she pulled the cord that summoned the hotelman to her door. She ordered tea for herself and coffee for William, along with a light breakfast, and then settled herself on the settee in the parlor room to wait. She could hear William stirring in his bedroom. He had come in late, long after she had gone to bed. About the time the waiter arrived with the tray of breakfast, Will appeared. His shirt was untucked, his braces hung down around his hips, and his stocking feet padded across the cold floorboards as he made a beeline for the coffee urn. Still, he did not forget his manners, and he turned toward Mary Alice.

"Good morning, Mother. Did you sleep well?" he asked as he poured first her cup of tea, then his own coffee.

Mary Alice was shocked to see a dark bruise along her son's cheekbone. As he lifted the teapot, she noticed that his knuckles were scuffed. Mary Alice swallowed her immediate reaction and said, "No, it was not a good night." Mary Alice took the proffered cup. "I just could not help thinking of little Andrew, wondering where he is . . ."

William took a long sip of his coffee. "Yes, it is the talk of the town. Emotions are high on the subject. There was quite a brawl in the saloon next door. I'm afraid my presence started it."

"My goodness! Why?"

"The bartender knew who I was, and then the subject of my nephew's 'rescuers' came under debate. Everyone seemed to want to advise me on how to proceed . . ." William let his voice drain off as he tipped his coffee cup again.

"So what do the townspeople say?" Mary Alice set her cup back on the tray. She did not want Will to see her hands shake, and she wasn't sure she could keep the cup from clattering on the saucer at that moment. She waited for her son to swallow his coffee; he looked like he needed the strong brew this morning.

"Well, many are on the side of that Citizens' Committee. They argue the woman who has Andrew is an ignorant half-breed, one who's lived with several different men in the past. And the man, Settler Foster—you might remember reading about 'The Boy Outlaw,' the one who helped rob the stage line with the Kennady band nearly twenty years ago? They hung all of them except the boy. The judge granted him a lenient sentence. Well, that same boy is now the man who found Andrew."

"Oh, my. This is not good. Do they say . . ." Mary Alice's throat tightened with her thought. "Does anyone think he had a hand in the accident?"

"No, no one is suggesting that. This Foster has a homestead south of here. He sells horses to the cavalry. Good horses. He is popular with the officers around here for that reason."

Mary Alice sighed. At least her grandson was not in the hands of someone who'd murdered the baby's parents. "So this outlaw desires the money?"

"I don't think so. There are many opinions, but few seem to think he is in it for money. Some say he is too well-to-do already for a mountain rancher, but that sounds like speculation. Some think the woman just wants to keep the child, and the debate is whether it's moral for a white child to be raised by a heathen Indian." Will shrugged a bit and flashed a quick grin accompanied by only a slight wince. "Then I said I wasn't that worried about the heathen part, but blood was thicker than Irish whiskey and we'd like our flesh and blood back, and the whole room took to fisticuffs—the Irish against everyone else!"

Mary Alice stared at her son, momentarily speechless. She picked up the cooling tea, then set it back down without even taking a sip. "So that was the fight? Over that?"

Will grinned again. "Well, it was late and everyone was well into their cups. I think the brawl would have started if I'd said 'Roses are red.' "

"This is truly a lawless, godforsaken town!"

"Oh, I don't know about that. They live by morals of their own making, that is true. But I like it. I can see why Amanda and David settled out here. There are few rules, and even those can be bent, and that clears the way for many opportunities. On that subject, I met one of the supervisors at David's mine. Very bright fellow, name of Jordane. He offered to show us around. I for one would like to see what it is we are to manage from so far afield." William finished his coffee and put the cup back on the tray. He shrugged his suspenders up over his shoulders, the tails of his shirt still hanging out, now all bunched up. He looked like a youngster still learning to dress himself.

Mary Alice thought he was quite cheery considering his

late night and obvious blows. She pursed her lips. She considered saying something about wishing to be on the first train back to Denver the moment little Andrew was laid in her arms, but she withheld the words and sipped at her tepid tea while her son went to wash up and shave.

She could hear him whistling to himself as he lathered up.

TWENTY-THREE

The mare reached the far bank upriver from the ferry landing. Her hooves met the soft silt of the river bottom and she lurched up to the more shallow water. Sett grasped the saddle horn tighter and searched for the off stirrup with his toe as the mare struggled in the soft footing. He could feel the churn of her legs next to him, and he forced his cramping muscles to pull himself up against the saddle as high as he could. To slip under those thrashing legs would be fatal.

The riverbank rose steeply from the choppy water, and Sett looked for a landing spot, somewhere the slope of the bank was gentle enough that the mare would be able to climb up out of the river, but he was not able to guide her while clinging to the saddle horn. Finally his groping foot found the stirrup, and he pulled himself up into the saddle. The cold air slapped his wet skin—it had seemed warmer in the water—but once on the mare's back he could see the dug-out ramp of the ferry landing, and he headed her toward it.

He dismounted as soon as the horse was on solid footing. Water streamed down her sides, and she planted her legs wide and gave a hearty shake. Sett leaned against her familiar warmth as water pooled in his moccasins and around his feet. He feared if he let go of the saddle his shaking legs would fail him. He knew he must get moving, to warm both the horse and himself, but first he would wring as much moisture out of his shirt and trousers as he could and put on the hopefully dry boots that he had wrapped in the canvas bedroll.

He led the mare across the landing in the darkness and tripped over something hard and coiled. It was the ferry cable, sprung back to land from where Ria's companion had cut it. Sett carefully led the mare wide of the offending cable and wondered just who this mystery man was.

The ferry had anchored to a blockhouse, and Sett found a narrow bench on which to sit and pull off his wet footwear. He fumbled with clumsy fingers at the laces, finally loosening them enough to peel the soggy hides from his feet. He unbuttoned his trousers and peeled them off too, then wrung them hard in both directions before tugging them back on. The mare was shivering now; standing in the frigid night air was quickly chilling her, and Sett hurried to unwrap his dry boots.

The mare spun around, snorting, to face the river. She arched her neck and bugged her eyes at the dark flowing water. Sett, for the first time since plunging into the river, looked back. The fires in the camp on the other side were blazing high, the shadows of men could be seen flitting between them. The men seemed to be congregating on the ferry dock, and there was much movement, but Sett could hear nothing over the rushing of the river. He was surprised that the mare could hear anything either, but she most assuredly heard something. She stood snorting at the water, quivering with fear instead of cold.

Then Sett heard it too; the frantic splashing of an animal in the water. He leaped up, barefoot, and grabbed his rifle. At first he could see nothing in the dark water, only moonlight glittering off the deceptive ripples at the sloped ferry landing. But the mare was staring downriver, and when Sett squinted along the bank below the ferry landing, he saw it.

The river made a sharp bend just below the ferry crossing, the broad width of it narrowing down into boulder-strewn rapids and the bank becoming steep and undercut. There, struggling in the deep current under a bank of six or more feet, was a horse. Its white-rimmed eyes were bright with fear, and its distinct white blaze gleamed in the moonlight.

Sett leaped up on the mare and found his rope, but it was a useless soggy mass. Still he made a loop and urged his mount along the bank above the frantic horse. The mare was wary of the bank; in the dark the edge between solid footing and the drop-off into the water was nebulous and hard to see. When Sett was just above the tiring animal, he called out, hoping to hear an answering voice, but only the horse's sputtering breathing and the churning of the river returned his call. He tossed his wet lasso toward the animal's head. It fell into the water. The horse spooked back, losing its small traction on the river edge and swinging into the stronger current. The swimming horse turned downriver, moving fast now with the flow.

Sett urged the bay mare into a gallop, racing along the high bank in the darkness without any thought beyond catching that water-logged horse before it entered the rapids. Ahead the current had created a backwater, and he prayed the horse would slow there and he could guide it up out of the river. The bay mare ran as only she could, her shivering ended by the exertion. She slid on her haunches down into the marsh where the backwater had carved out its hollow. Sett threw his rope again. This time it settled around the neck of the wild-eyed horse. But the animal was so frantic, it would not follow the lead of the rope. It bellowed and rolled sideways in the water, unable to turn toward something it found more frightening than the current. Sett thought for a moment it had broken a leg or was tangled up. He dallied the rope around the saddle horn. His fingers were so numb from the cold that he could only hope that he hadn't dallied it around his finger. He backed his mare to tighten the rope.

As the horse in the river came around, Sett saw what so blighted it. Along the horse's side a dark form bobbed, a man's hand wound tight in the saddle strings just as Sett had wound his own hand when he swam beside his horse. Only this man did not swim and kick and hold his rifle high. As the horse came broadside in the current, the body slipped back under the water and under the horse. Again the animal turned with the current and was swept back out into the faster water.

The rope yanked the saddle horn so hard the big bay mare nearly lost her footing. She too was tired from the swim and cold and run in the dark. Sett urged her ahead a little, but there was not far he could go. The backwater had carved out above a rocky point; there was no following the river as it dove into the narrow rapids. Sett dropped his dally and heard the rope hiss into the river after the disappearing horse. In a few heartbeats, the exhausted animal disappeared into the roiling water.

Sett leaned over his mount's neck, his cheek resting on the coarse mane. His breath came fast and painful, his hands were chillingly numb, and he could not feel his feet in the stirrups anymore. Sett shut his eyes tight, but the last vision of the ill-fated horse remained bright in his mind; the blaze face, the S-shanked bit, the horrible dark body floating at its side.

He moaned.

"Oh, God. Kiernan. Why?"

TWENTY-FOUR

Dawn crept cold and gray into the river bottom. Corporal Gorney stood next to the sheriff on the dock, and the two men peered across the river.

"I think we might as well go. It ain't getting any warmer," Gorney commented. His breath fogged with each breath.

"Yup, I know. At least you can see where you're heading." The sheriff squinted hard at the far bank.

Gorney nodded. "They aren't there, Sheriff. They wouldn't have waited around. Foster was eager to keep on the trail."

"Yup, and your lieutenant was eager to keep up with Foster," Coleman said.

"So he said." Gorney paused. It wasn't his place to second-guess his officers, but he doubted he himself would have had the guts to go diving off into that icy blackness. He was too familiar with the cold out here, and too aware of how quickly one succumbed. He had not even spoken to the lieutenant last night when he had realized that, in the midst of the chaos that ensued when Foster went into the river, the handsome young man had tossed the saddle on his horse. He'd stood dumbstruck as Kelly stuck his toe in the stirrup and told Gorney that he was in charge; to bring the men across the river as soon as possible and follow the trail. Gorney had not said a thing to the rash young officer, not even to suggest that the man remove his heavy boots before entering the river.

Gorney seriously wondered if he would find Lieutenant Kelly on the other side.

"I'll gather the men," Gorney said at last.

The eight soldiers of the detail were mounted, all in bare feet or wearing moccasins if they owned them. Ammunition and firearms were wrapped in oilcloth. They shivered in the morning air.

Coleman and the posse were also mounted up, ready to ride back to town. Sketch Jones made his way toward Coleman, and Coleman just shook his head. The man had his kit bundled up in his oilskin, his feet wrapped in dirty rags.

"I'm going to ride with them, Sheriff." Jones didn't even try to make it a question. Coleman didn't want to argue about it. Jones was a troublemaker, but damned if he hadn't been right about Foster last night.

"Okay, Jones, but no freelancing. You follow orders from the lieutenant as if he were me. Understand?"

Jones smirked. "Sure, Sheriff." He turned to follow the soldiers up the bank of the river, where they would start their cold swim with the current.

The corporal was the first to reach the far landing, though Deputy Jones was right behind. Gorney tried to keep his horse to one side of the slope out of the river, but Jones pushed his horse up out of the water in the middle of the landing, and dripped and trampled on any telltale sign on the muddy bank. By the time the rest of the detail was out of the water, shivering and shaking their arms in an attempt to return circulation to their numbed limbs, Gorney realized that finding any sign of Foster's, or the lieutenant's, emergence from the river was going to be impossible.

He had to just assume, as Deputy Jones seemed to, that the men had ridden on quickly. Gorney directed his men to wring out, put on their dry footwear, and proceed leading the horses. Gorney started up the rise from the river at a fast walk, and Jones caught up to him.

"We'd move faster mounted, Corporal!" Jones said.

"We'll dry and warm up faster marching," the grizzled old campaigner retorted. Jones didn't say any more but occasionally grumbled as he climbed the bank with the troops.

A half mile above the river in a grove of aspen, they met the first camp of travelers waiting to cross on the ferry. The sight of the waterlogged soldiers brought the freighters up from their campfire.

"Where's the ferry?" one of them asked, but a glance across the river in the early light answered that question before Gorney could get the story out. Jones took it upon himself to ask if the freighters had seen or heard anyone ride by in the night.

Nothing, the freighters answered. But then, they had arrived after dark and slept hard.

Gorney turned back toward the river.

"Where the hell ya going?" Jones demanded. He pointed up the road as if Gorney were lost.

"You think those Injuns kept to the road, do ya?" the old soldier barked. Jones hesitated. "These bullwhackers came in late, long after them Injuns. But they was here when Foster came across." Only the young trooper, Rattigan, noted that the corporal said nothing about Lieutenant Kelly. "Foster's goin' to find those Injuns, so we are going to find Foster." Gorney turned back down the track, this time going slowly.

Finally he saw what he was looking for—the tracks sunk into the berm of the road, the trail leading off up a wide coulee. Gorney called a halt. Jones and Rattigan came forward to examine the trail.

"Must be them, several horses," Gorney said. Jones had to nod in agreement. "Mount up, men. Now we're goin' to ride."

The detail left the road, moving fast along the trail that was too many hours old. And none but Gorney and Rattigan noticed that there appeared to be only one horse following the first set of tracks.

TWENTY-FIVE

It must have been a dismal camp. Sett found where someone had spread a bedroll in the dry gravel under the tilting rock. The sand was scuffed with footprints, and he could tell where the saddles and pack saddles had been stowed against the rock to make a windbreak. A short distance away, signs showed where the horses had been hobbled to graze.

Sett poured some grain out on the ground for his mare and squatted under the tilted rock. He studied the sky from this vantage point, imagined Ria seeing the same view, hours earlier.

Judging from the horse sign, Ria and her mystery companion had spent only four or five hours here, just long enough to sleep a little and let the horses rest. He hoped that she had something to eat. His own stomach growled, so he gnawed on some jerky himself, barely tasting the spicy meat. The mare was still eating, and Sett knew that if he wanted to move as fast as he wanted to move, it was time well spent to let the mare have her grain. He paced back and forth in the small open space under the leaning boulder.

At the one side, a sour smell met his nose. He didn't pause at the first pass, but on the second go-by the smell stopped him. He kneeled down. Under some sagebrush was a stinking wad of moss, a soiled baby swaddling. It brought the entire situation into focus: Ria, carrying the young child. Some stranger now in charge of them. Them somewhere in this wide wilderness.

He turned to catch up his horse.

It was all a nightmare, this ride. If he thought about what lay ahead on this trail, he chilled.

When he thought about what lay behind . . .

At least now it was daylight. He would not have to ride through the dark with soggy ghosts at his heels.

The mare had finished off her grain. By all good reason, he should have let her rest and browse a bit, but he did not. He tightened the girth, led the mare a few yards up the draw, and mounted up. The trail was not hard to follow. Sett urged his tall, lean horse into a long trot again.

Early afternoon, the sun came out. The air warmed up enough that Ria pushed back her hood and uncovered her head. She let Fox Ears lag behind her guide. They were a sad little crew, the young woman on the red horse, the ugly spotted pack pony, and the tired dog who padded directly in Fox Ears's hoofprints. Ria did not mind being far behind. As long as she could just see Pine Leaf well enough to follow him, she could avoid listening to his constant monologue. When she rode near him, he spoke continuously about the soldier's rifle, his new prize possession, but for all the talk about the soldiers and all the men he had so cleverly fooled to gain the horse and the gun, he never once seemed to look behind to see if they were being followed.

Ria looked often. She would pause at the top of each ridge to gaze back along their trail, but there was no sign of any movement. She almost wished there were.

Tapikamiiwa had been fussy that morning. Now he was too quiet. Several times they had rested and she had put him to her breast, but he quickly lost interest in sucking. She had nothing for him, and her worry made Pine Leaf's prattling even more unbearable.

The landscape here was mostly bare, long, rolling swales. To get out of the wind, they rested behind rocks or banks, but Pine Leaf never wanted to take the time to build a fire and heat up some food. The thought of even plain stewed jerky made Ria's stomach growl, and she thought she could coax Tapikamiiwa to take some broth, but Pine Leaf kept up a steady pace along a trail that only he could see. Ria wondered if they were truly heading toward her grandfather's people, or if she was just wandering after a lost crazy man, for now she was sure that Pine Leaf's time in the white school had warped his senses.

Fox Ears began a climb up yet another barren hill, and Ria saw that Pine Leaf had stopped his horse just below the summit. He was looking back at her, waiting.

"Look, Little Mother," he whispered when she got close. He pointed down into the next ravine.

Below, nestled by a line of chokecherry trees near the creek, was a shanty cabin, a thin line of smoke issuing from the chimney. In the yard, a sturdy woman was splitting firewood. The sharp whack of the ax carried up through the clear air. Ria could see several children, small enough to be playing in the dirt rather than helping with the chores. One older child was picking up the split wood and stacking it in a low lean-to on the side of the cabin.

"Look!" Pine Leaf said again. "There is a cow tied in the trees. Milk for your baby!"

Ria saw the cow, a skinny old brown cow. She was surprised that Pine Leaf should think of Tapikamiiwa. She had not confided her worries. Her heart swelled with gratitude; had she thought so low of her own cousin?

Then she noticed Pine Leaf fingering his new rifle, and

the memory of him firing at the old ferryman came glaring back. That had only been yesterday. How did he plan to get the milk from this poor woman?

Ria said, "If I go down and talk to the woman, show her my baby, maybe she will give me a little milk."

Pine Leaf laughed. "She will chase you away with the ax! I will go get it for you. And maybe some meat too."

That made Ria uncomfortable. She shifted Tapikamiiwa in his sling. He kicked against her hand feebly. "We should stay together. If her husband is around, maybe he won't shoot at me."

Pine Leaf considered this. "If she has a husband around, why is she doing this hard work?"

"I cut firewood all the time. Sometimes Se— my husband is busy doing other things."

"Humph," Pine Leaf snorted. "If you have a husband, he must be off doing other things now, or he would be here to protect you."

Ria bristled at his tone. "He would be here if he knew where I was."

"Oh. So you ran away from this good husband? Why did you do that? Does your good husband beat you? Does he lock you outside in the cold? This husband of yours sounds so good, maybe I will shoot him if I see him!" Pine Leaf shook the rifle stock in the scabbard.

Ria stared in shock at her mad companion. His black eyes flashed, and he brandished the rifle and looked around as if he expected Sett to come riding into view. Ria glanced around too, a small terror growing in her that maybe Sett was close by, that Pine Leaf had spotted him when she herself had not. She thought that if Sett appeared, she would throw herself on Pine Leaf, knock him off balance, stick him with her knife . . . but then Tapikamiiwa squirmed against her chest and she knew that she would not throw herself off of her horse. And she knew that Sett was far, far behind them. He would have been halted at the ferry, along with the cavalrymen.

She said in a quiet voice, "No. He will not come here."

Pine Leaf stabbed the rifle back into its scabbard. "That is right. I don't believe there is a good husband. I think you are alone. You need someone to take care of you. Just look, without me you would have never made it across the river." Ria nodded, and watched a pleased expression cross the dark young face. He went on, "When we get to the reservation, I will speak to your family about you. I can marry you, take care of you. After I go on my quest and get my new name."

Ria was aghast. She realized her mouth was hanging open, and she shut it quickly. "You . . . you are my cousin!"

Pine Leaf shrugged. "I am your mother's co-wife's nephew. We are not related." He turned away from her to stare down at the homestead again. Now the woman had chocked the ax in the block and was gathering up the last of the split wood. "Let's go, while she is still outside." He launched his horse off the crest of the ridge, in such a rush that stones clattered down the slope and the woman raised her hand over her eyes to peer up at them. With a wave of her hand, she ushered her children into the cabin.

Ria paused on the ridge. Pine Leaf was already halfway down the slope. Maybe if she turned and galloped away right now, she could get away from him. In many ways there was nothing she wanted more. Then Tapikamiiwa kicked against her again, and she could not turn and run. She needed the milk from the skinny cow, and perhaps, if she was there, Pine Leaf would not hurt the farmwife.

Pine Leaf stopped before crossing the small creek. He waited impatiently as Ria took a slow and careful route down the hill.

"Hurry up!" he called to her in Blackfeet.

The homestead woman stood with her back to the door of the cabin, her hand still raised to shield her eyes. As Ria drew closer, she looked right at the woman. Ria admired her. She was brave.

"Why are you going so slow?" Pine Leaf said angrily.

"I am not going to trip my horse and hurt my child just because you have no patience." Ria pulled up beside him, and Coy posted herself in front of Fox Ears and growled. "This white woman is brave. I think if I ask for milk, she will share some with us."

"No, you are too cautious. I will do the asking, and I will ask for more than a little milk!"

"How will you do that, Pine Leaf? You have vowed not to use the white man's words."

The young man swung his mount around to face her. His face flushed red, and he grabbed the rifle stock. "Do not call me that! That is a child's name! You will learn respect before I take you as wife. You, unworthy woman who does not deserve a real man's attention!"

Ria stared back at him, her eyes glittering. She thought that he might hit her with the gun, and she remained as still and impassive as a snake watching its prey, but inside her heart was pounding. Ria glanced behind her cousin, at the woman still standing guard in front of her home. The woman was watching their argument closely. Ria said quietly to Pine Leaf, "We came here to get milk."

He winced, and released his grip on the rifle. He turned back to the homesteader. "Yes, we will get milk. You talk, but remember, I know the American words. I will know what you are saying."

Ria unbuttoned her coat, and shifted Tapikamiiwa in the sling, so he could be seen. Then she urged Fox Ears toward the creek, calling out to the woman as she rode. "Heyo, there. We have come a long way. My baby is hungry. I would . . ." Ria paused. She had been going to say "beg," but the sound of the big soldier horse right behind her made her think again. "Ask, ask for some milk from your cow."

The farmwife tipped her head, squinting at the odd entourage coming into her yard. She said, "Stop zare. I vill bring milk from the cold house."

Ria pulled up in the middle of the creek, but Pine Leaf pushed past her and up onto the bank.

"Tell her we want other food too. Meat, and bread. And bullets. Find out if they have any bullets for the rifle."

"Cousin, we need only milk," Ria whispered in Blackfeet.

"No, we need everything. Tell her!"

Ria looked the woman in the eyes. There was curiosity there, but not fear. Ria did not think that this woman would give them any ammunition. There was something about the straight line of her back and the tilt of her chin, that reminded Ria of . . . herself. Yes, she herself had once stood protecting her home like this.

That memory, so distant now. Ria thought how much had changed, since that day when she had picked up a rifle as tall as herself, leaned it against a window ledge, and sighted on the front buttons of a stranger who had come into her yard. She had not known then where that encounter would lead, but she had been fully prepared to protect her home and the people in it.

Then that memory sharpened, becoming so oddly acute that she was in it, and she remembered the stranger's long sweeping glance at the window where she was hiding, and how she knew that he knew she was there.

She could not help it. She swept her gaze away from the brave woman, to the window of the tiny shanty, and it was there: the silent barrel of a shotgun resting in the corner of the sill. She came back to herself with an icy chill.

"Cousin, we must go," she said under her breath.

Pine Leaf looked at her incredulously. "What is wrong with you? Are you afraid of this lonely woman who does not even have a man to help with chores? We came for food and milk, now find out where it is!" He spun his horse first back toward Ria, then back to the defiant woman. "Tell her now, to go and get the bullets. I know they have them!"

"Cousin, remember if they have ammunition, they also have guns." Ria began backing Fox Ears away. She whistled low, calling her dog with her. Instinctively she pulled the heavy wool of the coat back over Tapikamiiwa. The brave woman was now looking from Ria to Pine Leaf. She never glanced toward the window, and Ria took that to mean that she indeed figured she had a backup.

Pine Leaf was livid. He screamed at Ria, "Get back here! Tell them to get the bullets! You cowardly woman, no wonder no man would keep you!" He pulled the rifle from the scabbard. "Go then, run away. I will take what I want." He raised the rifle over his head and spurred his horse across the yard.

The blast of the shotgun reverberated in Ria's ears. Fox Ears spun around and lunged out of the creek, dragging the packhorse after him. Coy dove into the chokecherries. There was a short commotion in the yard—Ria heard the scrambling of the cavalry horse and then the door of the shanty being yanked open and a shouting, childish voice—but mostly she heard her own grating breath as she clung to the saddle horn and felt a stinging burn on her ear. Ria reached up to the burn, and her hand came away bloody.

She wanted to run and run and never look back, but she did not even know where to run to anymore. She turned to head Fox Ears up the draw, hoping to find shelter in the thick growth of chokecherries. Tapikamiiwa kicked his heels into her ribs. She could feel his straining body against hers. He was frightened and close to crying. As was she.

Fox Ears swerved suddenly. A man was standing on the trail right in front of her, a big ruddy-faced man with a rifle, a pair of sage hens hanging off of his belt. Ria yanked Fox Ears to a stop. The spotted pony blundered into him from behind, and Coy let out a yelp. The farmer swung the rifle at her, aiming at her heart. Aiming at Tapikamiiwa.

"Vait! Stop!"

The voice pierced like another pellet from the shotgun.

The farmwife had run across the yard and was standing now by the edge of the creek. She had her hands cupped around her mouth, so her voice would carry. In a strange language, the woman called up to her husband. The man held his shot, but peered up at Ria with cynical eyes. He spoke curtly and gave a short tilt of his head toward the ground.

Ria's heart pounded. She could hear the woman running up the draw through the dry grass. The man in front of her motioned again. He wanted Ria to dismount. She slipped off her horse, and her knees gave out. She huddled on the ground, Fox Ears standing guard over her, Coy bracing herself and growling. Ria started to pull her coat loose, and heard the man thumb the hammer. She froze.

"Nein!" The farmwife huffed up to them. She spoke a rapid string of words in the strange language.

The man's reply was gruff but worried. The farmer did not lower his rifle. He gazed at his wife with concern.

The woman struggled to regain her breath after the run up the draw, and she nodded. Then she pointed back down into the yard.

Ria could not understand what they were saying. She was surprised that white people didn't speak the American words, but she thought the woman was defending her. Or at least keeping her from being shot. Her gaze followed the woman's pointing finger to the cabin yard.

Pine Leaf lay sprawled in the dirt. A young boy stood nearby, still cradling the shotgun. The boy shifted his weight from foot to foot, as if a part of him wanted to run from the bloody body and another part wanted to stay and lay claim.

Ria bowed her head. Tears leaked from her eyes, but she

was not sure if the tears were from sorrow or relief. The couple stared down at her silently, waiting.

Finally, Ria opened her coat and lifted Tapikamiiwa from the sling. He kicked and strained against her hands, so long in the confines, and so near her frightened heart. She heard the farmer let off the hammer of the rifle, and shift it aside.

She heard footsteps in the dry grass, but she did not look up. She could see the edge of the woman's dusty skirt and her heavy brogans.

"Zat man, he vas your husband?" the farmer's wife said down at her.

Ria shook her head, whispered, "No."

"Your brother?"

"No."

"You travel vit him?"

"I had to." Ria rocked Tapikamiiwa and felt more than heard his muted howls. It was a silent sob, and Ria bent her head over her child and joined him. The fear and tension of the past few hours released now, she gave in to painful weeping.

Then the woman knelt beside her and, with an awkward gentleness, daubed with her apron at the blood from Ria's nicked ear.

TWENTY-SIX

John Coleman had a plan as he entered the town of Verdy. He'd go first to the telegraph office and send a message to the garrison at the reservation. Then he would send a more detailed letter with the first stage heading north, or if he had to, he'd hire a fast rider. Once the important message was on its way, Coleman would go to the McFees, whom he assumed would be easy to track down at one of the better hotels. Coleman was not looking forward to that meeting. Next, he would stop by Lieutenant Kelly's house and advise Mrs. Kelly that her husband had continued north in the company of Sett Foster, in pursuit of their now-mutual quarry. And finally, he would go home, to have a hot meal and a few hours' sleep before heading out in the morning to the reservation. But this well-laid plan was not to be.

The dwindled number of the posse declined further as they reached the outskirts of the city. Men peeled off toward their homes or to a favorite saloon. A few called good-bye to the sheriff. One or two offered to accompany him the next day, but Coleman thought that by dawn even those would think better of it. So, as a cold wind snapped up the street and the gray afternoon descended on the mining town, John Coleman and his plan rode alone. Ahead, the Kellys' fine house stood out among the less pretentious dwellings. The front door opened, and Belinda Kelly hurried onto the porch. She waved at the sheriff, beckoning him to stop. Coleman groaned to himself. He couldn't tarry and still catch Sam at the telegraph office. Still he slowed his horse and called out to the woman.

"Mrs. Kelly, your husband went on ahead with Foster. I got to take care of some business, then I'll come fill you in."

Mrs. Kelly left the porch and made her way out to the street, a shawl clutched against the whipping wind. "Sheriff, you need to know that the McFees are here, at the Silver Palace. They are quite anxious and wish to hear from you immediately. Also . . ."

Coleman interrupted her, let his horse inch up the street rather than pulling it to a complete stop. "I'm sorry, ma'am, but I got to get to the telegraph office and get a message sent. Now."

"It's as bad as that?"

Coleman reined in his horse. Yes, it was as bad as that, but he really didn't want to go into it with this woman. He wanted to continue with his plan. "Well, the sooner I get the message sent, the sooner they'll get it."

"Who? To whom are you sending a message? The McFees are already here. Where is the child? Where is Mrs. Foster?" Belinda Kelly stared up at him with her green eyes, a wisp of hair blowing loose from her bun. "Is Mrs. Foster all right? Is the child safe?"

Coleman sighed. He let his horse start to walk out again. "Don't know. Never caught up to them. Your husband and the soldiers are still on the trail, with Foster." That was only a portion of the truth, but Coleman hoped she would wait for the rest. He knew the woman would think it rude, but he turned his back on her and continued down the street.

Around the corner, the main street was rather quiet in the late afternoon chill. Coleman had a hope that he could make it the three blocks to the train station and telegraph office, but he had gone less than half a block when he was hailed again.

"There he is! Yoo-hoo! Sheriff Coleman!" Eliza Jones called from the boardwalk. She was with a small group of the Citizens' Committee in front of the hotel. "Sheriff, this here is William McFee, from Denver. He's the lost baby's uncle."

Coleman sighed and looked down at the indicated young man, who was sporting a brand-new greatcoat. Coleman gave a curt nod of greeting. "McFee. I'm on my way to the telegraph office, for some urgent business. Then I will be back to fill you in on the developments."

McFee started to say something, but Eliza Jones broke in.

"Developments? Why, you must have found them. You've been gone nearly two days! You didn't let that rascal Foster give you the slip?"

McFee held up his hand to stop the tirade. He turned to the sheriff. "Go on and send your message. I'll go with you, and you can fill me in."

Coleman nodded again and started his horse down the street, while McFee returned to the boardwalk.

"I'll show you where the telegraph office is," Eliza offered.

McFee said, "Thank you, but I found it this morning by myself and can certainly find it now." The young man's face was grim. He was imagining how his mother, who was at that moment having her tea in the lobby, would take any news other than the fact that her grandson was arriving in the arms of a successful posse. William thought it best if he got the news from the sheriff and broke it to his mother himself. He headed down the boardwalk toward the train station at a brisk walk.

Eliza Jones was not happy to be so dismissed. Here she had only wanted to help, and yet the young man seemed ungrateful of her offer. Eliza rubbed her cold hands together and watched William McFee disappear down the street. Then, glancing the other way, she saw the fine wool shawl and deep green coat of Belinda Kelly, making her regal way toward the entrance of the Silver Palace. The woman was walking with great purpose, and Mrs. Jones forgot about William McFee's slight and hurried to get to the tearoom of the hotel, sure that the meddlesome Mrs. Lieutenant was bent on ingratiating herself into the plan that Eliza had so carefully made.

John Coleman made it to the telegraph office just as Sam was locking the door for the night.

"Open back up, Sam. Official business."

The young McFee arrived moments later and politely waited without saying anything while the sheriff stared at the telegraph form and the grumbling stationmaster relit the lamps and unlocked his equipment.

"Where's this goin', Sheriff?" Sam asked.

"The garrison at the reservation. Address it to the commanding officer." Coleman continued to stare at the blank paper. There was too much to say in such limited space as the telegraph provided, but he'd been composing the message as he rode. He put the lead to the paper and quickly wrote. Coleman held the paper up to the lamplight and pursed his lips. He handed it to Sam. "This make any sense?"

The stationmaster squinted at the message. He read it out loud, "'Half-breed woman and baby stop detain stop traveling with man stop dangerous stop no harm to woman baby exclamation details to follow stop.' Yah, if you want every squaw with a child held in jail till you get there."

"Better to have too many than not the one we want. Send it. How soon can I get a message out by stage or rider?"

The telegraph operator started to tap at his keys. "Stage leaves first thing in the morning. You want it to go sooner, better hire some young tough."

"I'd like it to get there before me, and I'm going tomorrow."

William McFee broke his silence in the back of the room. "Book me on that stage, to wherever this is."

Coleman turned to examine the young man. "You're welcome to ride along with me, McFee. You are being very rational about this, more than I expected."

William started to nod, but then the door to the station burst open and the wind blew in Mary Alice McFee, followed in a pack by Mrs. Lieutenant Kelly, Mrs. Jones, and several of the Citizens' Committee. Sam startled from his tapping only for a moment.

"Mother! It's freezing outside. You shouldn't be out without your coat!" William said. Then he realized with chagrin that it sounded exactly like something his mother would say.

Sheriff Coleman realized that the lady had, indeed, rushed out of the hotel without so much as grabbing her wrap, and he started to shrug off his coat, but was beaten to it by William. William draped his new plaid greatcoat over his mother's shoulders but avoided meeting her eyes. Mary Alice was giving one of her famous stern stares, but this time it was directed at the sheriff.

"Where is my grandson, Mr. Coleman?" she delivered in a cultured and quiet voice lined with rime.

From behind her, the arched eyebrows of Mrs. Kelly asked a similar question, and the faces of the Committee had an accusing look.

Coleman sighed. He must be getting old, he thought. Instead of finding all this exciting, all he wanted to do was get a good night's sleep. It looked like the feather bed in his little house was still a long ways away tonight.

"I don't know," he said honestly. "The woman crossed

the Missouri River yesterday just before dusk. They cut the ferry loose after them."

"See! That Foster is not to be trusted!" Eliza Jones fumed.

"Wasn't Foster, ma'am. We don't know who the girl hooked up with, sounded like an Indian. Anyway, they got across and succeeded in slowing everyone else down. Mrs. Kelly, we met up with your husband and his detail at the ferry. They were tracking the man that crossed with Mrs. Foster. Late last night, Foster and the lieutenant forded the river and continued on the trail. This morning, Deputy Jones and the rest of the troops followed."

Belinda Kelly closed her eyes. So the sheriff didn't know where Ria Foster was, nor did he know where Kiernan was. She swallowed against a lump in her throat.

"You are here sending a telegram, Sheriff. Do you know where they are going?" Mary Alice McFee asked.

"We suspect they are heading for the Blackfeet reservation. The woman has family there. Foster was quite sure that was where she was headed," Coleman answered.

"And, you, of course, believe him!" Eliza Jones spat out.

"Yes, ma'am, I do!" Now the sheriff raised his voice. This was getting out of hand. "It would only take one look at Sett Foster's face when he found out about the ferry to know . . ." Coleman shook himself into control. When he spoke again, it was with a cold and quiet detachment. ". . . to know. I've sent a telegram alerting the post at the reservation. I, and it sounds like Mr. McFee here, will be heading out first light tomorrow. Now, I am going to go have a hot meal and get some rest, and I recommend the same to you all."

There was a moment of silence in the cramped stationmaster's quarters.

Mary Alice asked, "Is there a stage to this reservation?"

"Yes, ma'am. Leaves tomorrow at seven," Sam said quickly.

"Book me on it." She opened her purse.

Eliza Jones stepped forward. "Mrs. McFee, this is a wild and unlawful country. I don't recommend that you travel alone, and it sounds like your son is going with the sheriff."

"Yes," one of the men in the Committee inserted. "It is not a safe place for a woman traveling alone. Just look at what has already taken place."

Mary Alice glanced first at her son, and then at the sheriff. "I think William should go with the sheriff. They will arrive much sooner than the stage."

"I'll go with you," Belinda Kelly said.

"Oh no! I would be glad to go!" Eliza Jones sputtered, but she did not reach for her purse, as there was nothing of value in it.

"Sam, I will pay now for my passage." Belinda pulled her purse from its string on her wrist. It opened with a determined snap.

Coleman was exhausted. He wanted nothing more than to be done with all these people and to be propping his aching feet up against his stove, but he couldn't help but take pleasure in the look of defeat on the deputy's wife's face when Belinda Kelly paid in gold coin for her ticket on the morning stage.

TWENTY-SEVEN

The farmer's cabin was one large room divided by a blanket hung on a cord, and it seemed to overflow with children. The rafters had been floored in and several of the older children slept up there. A baby and two others slept on a cot next to the main bed, and the farmwife, who had introduced herself as Mrs. Gunderson, had shown Ria where she could spread her bedroll in front of the stove. It was cramped and warm and full of the sounds of the sleeping family, the man's snores bellowing from behind the blanket divider. Still, Ria had slept through the night in exhaustion.

She woke before daylight to help Mrs. Gunderson prepare breakfast while Mr. Gunderson and the oldest boys went out to feed the livestock. They had eaten the meal in silence, and now Tapikamiiwa and the youngest baby were being entertained by a little girl of maybe five years of age while Ria and the missus began to clean up and the older children scattered away to their chores. The babies lay on the cot in the corner of the room and the little girl moved pinecones and twigs and told a long story in a language that

Ria did not understand. The woman's English was limited, but her husband made no effort to speak in English at all. He sat at the end of the long trestle table and finished his coffee, eying Ria skeptically. Suddenly he asked a terse question.

"He vants to know where you are going," Mrs. Gunderson said.

Ria stacked the wooden plates on the shelf behind the stove where she had seen the woman put them the night before. "I am going to my grandfather's people, on the reservation. Maybe my mother is there."

The woman translated for her husband, who grunted and asked another question.

"You take him, the dead man, vith you?" Mrs. Gunderson seemed a bit embarrassed at her husband's directness. Ria stared down at the dishrag in her hands. She wiped at a platter distractedly. Last night, laying in her warm bedroll in front of the stove, she had tried not to picture Michael Pine Leaf, First Wife's nephew, who was out in the woodshed wrapped in a canvas tarp. She did not want to think about packing the body onto the horse, or having to unpack it if she stopped for the night. Michael Pine Leaf had suggested that they were near the reservation, but Ria had no idea how far it really was, or how long it might take to find Talking Crow's people. It would be best to leave him here, bury him here, but she did not know how to ask that of these people.

Her silence must have stretched too long, for Mr. Gunderson suddenly broke into a long tirade in the strange language. His wife nodded a couple of times and then scowled at him. The man stopped talking but glared back at her.

"He says, he does not think you take the man. He says, you too small to lift him. But if he and Karl bury him, it vill take all morning. He has vork to do this morning. He has important vork to do, and he does not have time . . ." Mrs. Gunderson's voice trailed off, but Ria could figure out what else Mr. Gunderson had said. He did not have time to take on the responsibility for another woman and baby. He wanted her to go away and quickly.

"Tell him, if he will bury Michael Pine Leaf here, I will give him the horse, the one Michael rode," Ria said.

The farmer's expression softened when his wife translated. Then he squinted and grumbled something.

"He says, and the saddle and bridle that the horse wears?"

Ria nodded. "Yes and the saddle." She knew that the horse was not hers to give; it belonged to some bluecoat soldier like Lieutenant Kelly. But Ria had no way of returning it, and she had enough to handle with her own horses, her dog, and Tapikamiiwa. She dried off the last platter and turned to check on the baby. "I will pack my things. Maybe I can be to the reservation by nightfall."

Mr. Gunderson wanted to know what she'd said, and then he nodded and spoke again in a less angry tone.

"He says, the reservation is just over the pass. He vill send Thomas to show you the way. He and Karl can dig the grave."

Mr. Gunderson rose from his bench and got his hat and muffler from the peg by the door, then went out into the yard.

Mrs. Gunderson faced Ria, and her eyes were concerned. "Vat if you do not find your family? Do you have . . . someone you go back to?"

Ria took a deep breath. She watched Tapikamiiwa reach for the pinecone doll that the little girl was holding. She realized that she had no count of the children here—there seemed to be one of every age, from the oldest boy who'd shot Michael Pine Leaf, down to a baby just older than Tapikamiiwa, and Mrs. Gunderson's waist was thick again. In many ways, Tapikamiiwa fit into this fair family better than he did with her. His light fuzzy hair and pink skin made him look like a sibling to the rest of the children. She reached down to scoop her child up.

"I have someone. But I cannot go back." She hugged Tapikamiiwa close and went over to roll up her bedroll. It took only a few minutes to pack her things, and Mrs. Gunderson helped her carry them out to the barn.

The man and son had chosen a spot out of sight of the cabin, on a low ridge crowned with a single pine tree, and were digging with a pick and shovel. Ria bit her lip and tried not to look at them. She greeted her dog and was pleased to see that the horses were finishing a feed of oats. A boy of about seven years helped saddle Fox Ears, but Ria packed the spotted pony herself. The pony tried to bite everyone else. She hung the cradleboard on the pony and placed Tapikamiiwa in her sling before turning to Mrs. Gunderson.

"Thank you," Ria said.

The woman murmured a soft phrase in the strange language. "Be careful," she then said in English.

Ria mounted up, and the young boy took off at a fast jog up the track. He motioned to her. Ria followed, not looking back at the small farmstead until she reached the brow of the ridge. There she paused and turned back toward the remains of the only one of her family she had seen in more than ten years, now lying in an unmarked grave under a lone pine tree.

Mary Alice McFee settled herself into the forward-facing seat of the stage. A rather dapper gentleman, a banker he'd said, had suggested that the ladies be allowed the better seats. Mrs. Kelly sat next to her, and across in the rear-facing seats, sat the banker, a tired-looking mine foreman, and a grizzled fellow who'd barely nodded a greeting. Mary Alice pulled her shawl closer about her shoulders. She noted that Mrs. Kelly was wearing a heavy woolen greatcoat, perhaps one of her husband's, along with a shawl, muffler, and gloves. From outside the stage, she could hear the baggage being tossed into the boot and several passengers climbing up to the top of the coach.

"Have you traveled overland by stage before, Mrs. Kelly?" Mary Alice asked quietly.

"Yes, in the short time that Kiernan and I have been out West, we've been stationed at three different posts. Most of my travel has been by stage, other than the time I had to ride in the freight wagon." Belinda smiled slightly. She placed a gloved hand on the older woman's elbow. "It's a rather rough ride, I'm afraid. And cold. But I packed an extra blanket so please let me know if you get chilled. We can share it."

Mary Alice sighed. She was not looking forward to traveling in this conveyance. She said in a whisper, "My daughter and her husband died when their coach overturned." With a sickening jolt, the stagecoach rolled forward and Mary Alice feared she would slide off the seat. She grabbed the leather strap that hung from the ceiling of the coach and held on.

"The driver is making time here while the road is good," the banker said cheerfully, his feet braced a polite distance from the women's and his hand grasping his leather handhold. "He'll slow down some when the road gets bad. I've traveled this route many times."

"Oh my," Mary Alice said under her breath. The stagecoach was lurching madly, its apparent purpose being to toss the passengers from their seats. Mary Alice wondered briefly how those people on the top of the stage stayed aboard, but then she decided that she should concentrate on keeping her seat until the stage reached the bad section of the road and slowed down.

Mrs. Kelly, on the other hand, was making conversation with the other passengers, when she could.

"Are you also going to the Belknap reservation, sir?" she asked the banker between bounces.

"No, my destination is Great Falls. We have a branch office there."

"That is farther than the reservation, is that right? I've heard my husband speak of it." Belinda managed to sound both polite and interested in spite of the rattling coach.

"Yes, it's to the west, so I will be parting this lovely company before you reach your destination. You're traveling to the reservation? Whatever for, may I ask?"

Belinda Kelly cast a sideways gaze at her traveling companion, who appeared to be quite overawed with this trip even though it had barely begun. She did not want to answer for Mrs. McFee, but the lady did not appear ready to answer for herself.

The mountain man broke the silence. "They's goin' after that Injun, the one that stole the baby. That right? Verdy's talking about nuthin' else!"

Mary Alice managed a weak nod. "My son and Sheriff Coleman left this morning before dawn, and we will meet them there."

"My husband is also on the way with a cavalry detail," Belinda added.

"Coleman's a good man," the banker said.

"Yeah," the grizzled fellow growled. "Good luck. With Foster in on it, they ain't much chance of finding 'em." He shifted in the seat until his shoulder was wedged against the wall of the stage. Then he deliberately closed his eyes and pulled his hat down over his face.

The rest of the passengers lapsed into an uncomfortable silence, pierced only by the incessant screeching of the wheels and brakes of the stagecoach. Mary Alice grasped onto the handhold and leaned against Mrs. Kelly, who braced back against her. She had prayed many times in comforting surroundings—the elegant church that McFee money had helped build in Denver, the quiet of her own home—but now she prayed more fervently than ever before in her life, here in an icy cold, jouncing, rumbling stagecoach as it made its way north.

TWENTY-EIGHT

The sky was clear, but the cold snapped in the air. The dry grasses were sparkling with frost, and the big mare's whiskers were glazed with ice crystals. Sett could even feel its weight on his eyelashes. He had wrapped his scarf around his face and over his ears and jammed his battered hat down over it, so the only skin showing was around his eyes. He was riding again, following the hard, frozen tracks on the trail, but every few miles he dismounted and led his horse. It was the only way to keep his feet from freezing.

He would have preferred snow to this deep cold. It would have been warmer. He imagined every possible situation that Ria and the child could be in; huddled under brush? Trying to ride through the night? Walking to stay alive? And the mystery man, was he helping her, or was she in even more danger than from just the elements? The old trail followed a fairly direct route, deviating from the direct north-east line only to wind down into a valley and then up the other side. With each ridgetop, Sett paused and scanned ahead with his monocular. He had to wipe the lens often as it fogged up in the cold air, but the plains were still and empty of life. Even the antelope were holed up somewhere. It was not a day for traveling.

The pale sun was high when Sett pulled the mare up on another low hill. He did not need the monocular to see the farmstead below him along a creek. Smoke puffed from the chimney, and the thin snow in the yard was trampled with tracks. A large pole corral held two horses and a cow, all three huddled against a windbreak that attached to a sturdy barn. The trail veered down the hill toward the farm, and Sett sent his horse down it.

Halfway down the slope, he saw tracks forking off, going a short way toward a knoll. The tracks were very fresh, probably made that morning, and it appeared that something had been dragged along in the snow behind the walkers. Sett rode a little ways in that direction, and then stopped short. On the crest of the knoll, freshly turned earth was guarded by a single tree. A grave. A very new grave.

Sett's breath stuck in his lungs. He rode closer. There was no headboard, only the narrow mound of frozen dirt clods that lay dark against the crust of snow and dried grass. It was too large a grave to be a baby's, unless . . .

Sett whirled the mare around and headed for the farmhouse at a gallop. The mare broke through the ice on the creek, splashing and cracking her way onto the bank. Sett knew better than to gallop into a yard without warning, so he hollered out as he pulled the mare up.

"Hello! Hello!"

The barn door flew open and a man stepped into sight. He was muffled about the face, as Sett was, so that his features were hidden. But the shotgun that he held in his hands was easily recognizable. The man had pulled the mitt back from his right hand, and his fingers were poised on the trigger. Angrily, the farmer yelled back at Sett, though Sett could not make out a single word.

"Wait, wait," Sett said. "I don't mean you no harm. I'm looking for someone, a woman. With a little baby." Sett raised his hands away from his rifle scabbard. The farmer gestured with the shotgun. He wanted Sett to go away, that much was evident. Why he was so angry, Sett could only guess. He could not understand a single word the man said.

"The grave, up there," Sett pointed up at the long pine. "Who is it? A woman?"

Now the man took his fingers from the trigger and pulled his mitten back over the hand, though he did not lower the gun. He spoke rapidly in the strange language, nodded once toward the animals in the corral, and then again toward the grave. But Sett could make no sense of it.

"The grave," Sett asked again, pointing. Then he crooked his arm as if holding a baby, rocked it a bit. "Mama?" The farmer paused his ranting and looked curiously at the big man on the horse.

"*Nein*," the farmer said. He pointed at a large horse in the corral and began to explain something in a more controlled voice. Then the man motioned behind him and a boy came forward to join him in the doorway of the barn. The farmer patted the boy's shoulder proudly, pointed at the grave, and again at the horse. Then the man nudged the boy with his elbow.

"Pa says, tell you it's an Injun in the grave. He tried to rob us. That's where the horse come from."

Sett relaxed his hands. He felt like he'd been holding his breath ever since seeing the grave, and now he sighed in relief. Just to be sure, he asked, "It's not a woman?"

The boy shook his head. "Injun. Crazy man."

Sett squeezed his eyes shut for a moment. Thank God.

Now the farmer lowered the shotgun, but he did not invite Sett to dismount or come inside to warm up. He spoke to his son again.

"Pa says, what do you want?"

"I'm looking for someone, a young woman with a little baby. Have you seen them?"

The boy looked discomfited as he translated to his father. The older man squinted at Sett again. He pointed down the track that led to the reservation.

Sett followed his direction. "She was here, then?" The farmer just continued to point.

"She showed up with the Injun . . . ," the boy started to say, but the father elbowed him none too gently.

Sett persisted. "Was she all right? Was she hurt?" The boy looked like he would like to answer, but the father just grunted and continued to point.

"Pa says, she went that way this morning. The horse is ours now."

Sett reined his horse in a tight circle. He didn't understand this man's language, or his inhospitable attitude, but hopefully he wasn't sending Sett off on a wild goose chase.

"Tell yer pa thanks for me." Sett turned his back on the hostile farmer and urged the mare into a lope.

TWENTY-NINE

The first dwelling that Ria found was abandoned. The door hung open in the wind, the yard strewn with litter and old clothes. Packrats had built an impressive lair in the wood box. Ria dismounted only long enough to decide that she would ride on, at least until sunset. She'd rather camp in the weather than stay in the haunted-looking cabin.

The track was deeper past the abandoned cabin, but still seldom used. It wound along a bottomland until, over another low ridge, she spotted another small building, a simple square log cabin. This one had some sheep in a corral, and more exciting, a lodge was set up next to the building. In the early twilight, the skins of the lodge glowed like a lamp, the guiding light signaling a traditional home. Ria had not seen a real Blackfeet lodge since her childhood; the sight brought tears to her eyes.

"Look, Tapikamiiwa!" She loosened her coat and held the baby up so he could have his first view of a true lodge. "Look, it is our people!" Then she dismounted and strapped him into his Blackfeet cradleboard, so that they would meet these relatives in proper form.

She did not have to call out as she neared the lodge, for a skinny brown dog ran out barking. Coy started to growl, and then several more dogs appeared from inside the open door of the cabin. The flap of the lodge was pulled open, and an old man stepped out. He was wearing an odd mix of white man's clothing—a vest and shirt, trousers, and a campaign hat—with tall winter moccasins and a bone breastplate. He was not wearing a coat, though the wind was bitter. It appeared he had put the breastplate on rather hurriedly, for it hung a bit lopsided. He waited in the yard and called his dogs back.

Ria rode up to him.

"*Oki*, Grandfather," she said formally in Blackfeet.

"*Oki*, Daughter," the man replied. "Where are you riding this time of day, all alone with your son?"

Ria smiled. She was glad now that she had taken the time to add a boy's decorations to the cradleboard. "I have come a long way, seeking to visit my mother. I have not seen her since I was very young. Her name is Sweetgrass Woman, the daughter of Talking Crow."

"Oho, then. Maybe I know her." The old man shuffled forward and waved toward the lodge. "Get down, Daughter, and rest. My wife has a stew, a little thin, but warm. I will put your horses in the shelter, here." He took Fox Ears's reins after Ria lifted Tapikamiiwa's cradleboard from the saddle. He led the animals into the cabin.

"Watch out for the spotted pony," Ria started to say, but the pony had already begun her teeth-bared swing toward the old man's arm. He was ready for her and met the soft upper lip with the point of his elbow, without looking around.

He chuckled. "This chestnut is a fine horse. We don't see this kind of horse here much anymore. The pony, she belongs here!"

Ria waited while the pack of skinny dogs circled around Coy, sniffing and bracing. Finally they grew bored with the new dog, and Coy disappeared under Fox Ears's legs, to curl in the thin straw that covered the dirt floor of the cabin. The old man tied the horses to rings nailed into the walls and hung the saddles over a limb that was suspended from the rafters with braided lines. There was a scrawny old mule in the cabin, and all the dogs returned to their nests in a small pile of hay. Ria wondered at the size of the hay pile. It was nowhere near enough to feed even the sheep for the winter, but there did not seem to be any more stored in sight.

Her host chatted cheerfully as he tossed a few handfuls of the hay to each horse. "The gover-mint built this fine house for us, but my wife doesn't like it. It is square, and the door is in the wrong place. She is very traditional, you see. So we live way out here, far from the agency. We don't get our share of the food they hand out. So we eat better than most!" He laughed.

Ria could not help smiling a little too. She retrieved the jar of milk that the farmwife had given her. She took the loaf of bread that the woman had slipped into her pack too. Then she followed the old man into his lodge.

It made her choke up, a great welling of her heart filling her chest. She held Tapikamiiwa so he could see. The smoky interior of the lodge was cluttered, household items hanging down from ropes that crisscrossed between the long poles, sleeping pallets with battered old robes against the wall. A fire burned in a ring of stones, and a couple pots of something simmered alongside it. The woman who stirred the stew wore a threadbare, quilled shawl, her gray hair hanging to her shoulders. She looked up as Ria entered, saw the baby, and smiled. She had very few teeth.

"Wife," the cheerful old man said, "this young daughter is looking for her mother, Sweetgrass Woman. I will take her there after we have something to eat."

The woman continued to smile. She motioned for Ria to come in and sit. Ria went around the fire clockwise, without thinking about it. She sat in the guest's place. The man walked around too and sat on a well-used cushion.

The woman did not speak much, but she offered to warm the jar of milk in the pot of water that was sitting on the fire stones. She ladled some steaming brew into a tin cup and set it near Ria to cool. She handed another full bowl to the man. Then she asked to hold the baby. Ria took him from the cradleboard and handed him into the knowing arms of the grandmother. Tapikamiiwa kicked and waved and smiled up at the mimicking toothless grin and delighted eyes. Ria was so overwhelmed that she could not speak. It was like stepping into her past, the smells and sounds and sights of her early childhood. She almost expected First Wife and her batch of siblings to come tumbling through the door, but instead she sat with the lonely old couple and listened to the man's rambling tales.

Their names were Snow and Whitefoot Hare Woman, and they lived here at the edge of the reservation, as far out as they could. They had no more living children, maybe some grandchildren, but they did not see them anymore. The priests had taken them away. Sometimes Snow would work for the trapper. Sometimes he hunted for himself. As long as the agents didn't find out, what harm was it? And a rabbit was good game nowadays. They lived so far out, by themselves, that they had managed to live a long time. They did not catch the fever disease or the coughing disease. Finally he said, "There is a woman with that name, Sweetgrass Woman, who lives by Alder Spring. I think I heard that when I was in at the agency."

"Is Alder Spring far from here?" Ria asked. She picked up the cup of stew, now finally cooled enough to sip. It was indeed very thin, in fact not much more than broth with bits of some root vegetable floating in it. There was not any fat.

Ria offered the loaf of bread and took a chunk for herself after Snow and Whitefoot Hare Woman had broken some off. It at least soaked up the broth.

"Not far. I can take you there tonight. It is clear and a good night for traveling." Snow took some more bread and dunked it into his bowl.

Whitefoot Hare Woman was offering her withered old finger for Tapikamiiwa to grasp, and she squinted at him as he gripped.

"Strong boy, this one," she said. She leaned closer, still smiling and cooing at the child. "His father is not one of the People."

Ria paused with her cup halfway to her lips. "No, his father is not." At least she did not have to lie. She set her cup back down and reached for the baby. "Here, I will feed him now."

Whitefoot Hare Woman did not hand him over. She picked up the jar of milk and tore off another chunk of bread. "Rest, Daughter. It has been a long time since I had a baby to feed, and this one looks like he eats well. Look at his pale round cheeks! What bright eyes. Like cornflowers." She expertly shifted Tapikamiiwa in her arms and offered him milk dripping off the bread, which he eagerly took.

Ria sat for a moment before picking up her broth again. She could not take her eyes from her child, in the arms of the dark old grandmother. There was a strange feeling, an unpleasant feeling, that now usurped the euphoric glow that had held her since she stepped into this lodge. She desperately wanted to grab Tapikamiiwa away from the kindly woman, to swaddle him again in her sling where no one could see him.

Snow began another rambling story, something about how many soldiers were stationed at the agency and how the agents themselves were not all bad people, but they were too gullible and easy to rob. Unfortunately, the white men got to them first and robbed them before the People had a chance to. Ria listened with only half an ear, sipping the watery stew and watching as Whitefoot Hare Woman lifted Tapikamiiwa upright and jiggled him. The woman's hands were sure and gentle, and Tapikamiiwa seemed very taken with her wrinkled face. Ria finished her broth and waited until Snow paused in his story.

"I am eager to see my mother. Is it truly so close that we could go tonight?" Snow stared at her. Ria felt her cheeks flush. It was extremely rude to interrupt an elder, especially one who had been so kind. She dropped her gaze down to her hands, folded in her lap. "I must apologize, I am rude. It is just . . . I have not seen any of my family in many years, since I was a young girl. And I have traveled a long way." Now this, she thought, was a lie. She had seen Michael Pine Leaf. But he was, as he had explained, only her father's first wife's nephew, not really related. He didn't count.

Snow inclined his head in acknowledgment. It was odd for a young woman to be traveling this time of year, all alone. And even odder, he noted, for her child to be so white.

"Yes, Daughter, we can be there in a short ride. This Sweetgrass Woman also lives outside the agency, but not far. I will go saddle the horses." Snow pulled himself to his feet and found a wool coat hanging on one of the pegs, then slipped out the flap of the lodge. Whitefoot Hare Woman had finished changing Tapikamiiwa's wrappings, and she pulled the cradleboard toward her to strap the child in. Ria wished she would just give Tapikamiiwa back, but she didn't know how to ask for him. She picked up the jar with the milk.

"Thank you, Grandmother, for helping us," Ria said.

"I enjoyed it, Daughter. He is a fine young boy." Whitefoot Hare Woman offered up her toothless grin, first to Tapikamiiwa in his cradleboard and then to Ria. But she raised her bony finger and wagged it. "But I warn you,

Daughter-who-is-running, you cannot keep him under your coat forever. If the white-eyes at the agency see him . . ."

"Thank you, Grandmother," Ria repeated, hoisting the cradleboard to her shoulder. She turned to slip out through the lodge flap. By the fire, the old woman slowly shook her head and sighed.

THIRTY

The night was icy and clear with a biting wind, but Ria hardly noticed it. She left Tapikamiiwa in his cradleboard, but draped a blanket over him to shield him from the cold. Fox Ears followed the old man's mule willingly, and Ria was left with her own rising excitement. She would soon see her mother for the first time in so many years that she could barely count them. There was the year that she had left the trapper's rendezvous, her mother going west with a new man and Ria going south with the American husband. Then the next year Ria had lived at the American's homestead, miserable and wishing for a way to leave. And the year after that, Sett Foster had ridden into the yard, and Ria's life had taken an abrupt turn for the better.

Ria tallied the years on her fingers. So many years. She wondered about her baby brother and half-sister. First Wife's daughter Yva was two years younger than Ria. Was she still living in the family lodge, or did she have a family of her own by now? And the baby, Jean Pierre, he would be a big boy. She realized that she had not thought of her siblings as grown-up; they had remained little children to her.

And her mother, was she still the most beautiful woman at any gathering? Was her hair still sleek and ebony?

Ria's heart pounded in her chest. She wished that the old man would hurry his mule along, but then she chided herself. It was fully dark now, and to rush down the trail would be foolish. Snow had said that it was not a long ride to her mother's, and so she must be patient. But then she wondered, when she arrived at her mother's door, would she be recognized? Had she changed very much in the years? Ria knew that she had. She had grown up too and was no longer an innocent girl. Now she was a woman, a wife, and a mother. She carried her own scars, some obvious and others deep inside.

Ria raised her hand and stroked one fingertip across her tilted left eyebrow. She knew its odd angle sometimes drew stares. She knew that had Sett been there, he would have gently pulled her hand away if he saw her tracing the old injury. She wished for a moment that she were arriving with her husband at her side, then she pushed the thought away, at the same time dropping her hand away from her face. He could not be here, or she would not be here. There was only one way, and she had made her choice.

The sound of the wheezing mule broke through the steady wind. Snow had stopped on the trail ahead.

"We are here," he said, pointing with the brim of his hat. Ria rode up beside him to where she could see.

It was a barren, windswept place. A small log cabin with no windows sat alone in the middle of a brown meadow. A few scraggly trees marked the spring. Ria could not see any livestock, or any place to keep them. Across the clearing, the bare poles of a lodge pointed starkly up at the sky, the white of the dry wood reflecting the starlight. The place appeared abandoned, except for the thin strips of light that seeped out of the missing chinking between the logs of the cabin and around the single door.

Snow must have felt the disappointment in the young

woman. He said, "Sweetgrass Woman has no one to help her, I think, and keeping a true lodge is hard work."

"So, my brother and sister are not here?" Ria said.

"I do not know of a brother. The sister, she may be at the agency now." He started his mule toward the desolate dwelling. "Come, I will stay with you to the door and turn your horses out so they can find some shelter. There is a coulee above the spring where the wind is not so strong." Ria followed him into the yard. At the door, Snow dismounted and held Fox Ears's reins while Ria took the cradleboard from the saddle. Coy stayed protectively close, her hair raised at the quiet cabin. Perhaps she expected dogs to come out barking or perhaps she too was discomfited by the eerie stillness.

"I will leave your panniers and your saddle here by the door, so that you may get them easily," Snow said. Ria began to protest, but he interrupted, "No, I will not go in. But I will announce you." He stepped up to the door and scratched his fingers across the dry wood.

"Sister. Sweetgrass Woman. It is your neighbor, Snow. I have someone here to see you," he called in a carrying tone. The old man held his ear close to the door, to hear a reply. Ria heard nothing, but Snow went ahead and pushed the door open. Faint light fell into the night, splashing across Ria's legs and the cradleboard which she held in front of her. She was frozen in place, her heart skipping madly. Snow took her elbow and gave her a gentle shove through the door. "Go now, Granddaughter." He closed the door behind her.

There was a lantern hanging from the rafters. It threw a dim light around the room and into Ria's wide eyes. For a moment she felt blinded, then she heard a soft cough and the rustling of someone moving in the corner.

"Who is it?" a whispered voice said.

Now Ria saw her, a thin woman raising herself on one arm from a sleeping pallet on the floor. The long hair was streaked with gray; the woman's skin was sallow and stretched tautly across her high cheekbones. She coughed again and peered across the room with rheumy eyes.

Ria choked, her throat tightening. "Mother. It is me, your daughter, Ria."

The woman squinted, pushed herself up further from the bed. "Daughter? Come closer."

Ria crossed the room, still holding Tapikamiiwa in his cradleboard. She saw now that there were other sleeping pallets against the wall, and an oil-drum stove, and a nearly empty wood box, but the woman was alone.

At the woman's side, Ria propped the cradleboard against a bench and kneeled down. The woman was so thin. She leaned near to look into Ria's face. Then Sweetgrass Woman let out a little sob.

"My girl! My eldest daughter! I did not know if you still lived!" Sweetgrass Woman started to topple back down onto her bed, and Ria grasped her bony shoulder to ease her. Her mother hugged her close, weeping until she started to cough again, a painful wracking sound.

"Mother, you are ill. Let me make you some medicine." Ria was already groping for her medicine bag, hanging ready at her waist, but it was buried under the layers of blanket and coat and shirt. Sweetgrass Woman did not release her.

"You may make it, but it is the sight of you that will cure me." Sweetgrass Woman finally lay back on her bolster, but her eyes did not leave her oldest child's face.

"I will make it anyway. It will help you breathe." Ria rose and explored the cabin. There was a barrel of water in the corner and enough sticks to strike the stove into life. She chose carefully of the herbs in her pouch and then went to drag the panniers inside the door. When she opened it, Coy was waiting, curled up in the meager shelter of the panniers. Ria motioned the dog into the room.

Sweetgrass Woman smiled weakly. "I would know that

you would travel with companions!" she said as the dog found a corner by the now-blazing stove.

"My horse is outside, and Tapikamiiwa's," Ria said, while rummaging in the pannier.

"Tapikamiiwa, that must be your son. Let me see him."

Ria left her pack and unlaced the cradleboard. Tapikamiiwa kicked his legs at the freedom, and Sweetgrass Woman stretched her hands out to hold him.

"What a fine strong boy! You are still married to the American farmer, then?" She ran her bony hand over the child's glossy white hair.

Ria looked aside. "No, that was not a good man. I was not his wife, only a possession." She drew a deep breath before continuing. "But he is gone now. I have . . . had a very good man as husband. But Tapikamiiwa and I are alone now. That is why we came to find you."

Sweetgrass Woman looked back up at Ria, peering at her intently in the dim light of the cabin. It sent a familiar tingle down Ria's back—how well she remembered thinking that she could hide no secrets from her mother. But it was different now; she was an adult, a wife, mother. Ria got up to test the tea and asked, "Do you live here alone? Where is my little brother?" She left out asking about Ross, Sweetgrass Woman's second husband, the one who had sold Ria to the American farmer.

Sweetgrass Woman was smiling at Tapikamiiwa, but her expression changed when she replied. "Jean Pierre was taken away to the boarding school. They said he would come home in the summer, but he did not come last year. The agent says that he gets reports from the school and that Jean Pierre is good. I do not know what that means."

Ria paused. Was the boarding school the same one that Michael Pine Leaf had run away from? She asked, "Do you ever see First Wife, or my sister Yva?"

Sweetgrass Woman waited a long time before answering. "First Wife died in the cold winter, but Yva is here.

She lives here with me, sometimes. She has not been home today. She is at the agency." Sweetgrass Woman took a deep breath, and it made her cough. She turned away from the baby and covered her face with the blanket. Ria knelt by her and held the cup of hot tea until her mother had recovered enough to take it. Ria took Tapikamiiwa onto her lap and rocked him. Her mother sipped at the soothing liquid. She smiled a little, in thanks. Then she said very quietly, "Yva is . . . lost. Lost to the white man's whiskey."

Ria was stunned. She remembered how men acted when they drank whiskey. The idea of a woman acting that way was profane. A long silence stretched between them, only Tapikamiiwa's cooing filling the void. Finally Sweetgrass Woman shifted on her pallet and took another sip of her tea. "I came back here after one winter with that man. Neither of us found good husbands at that rendezvous."

Ria nodded and lay her baby down next to his grandmother. "I will make some food for us and heat some milk for Tapikamiiwa." She went back to her packs.

Sweetgrass Woman again studied her daughter, and Ria busily poured water into two kettles and pulverized some jerky for broth. She knew the question was coming and wished she could avoid it.

"Are you ill, daughter? Why are you not nursing your son?"

Ria stopped rolling the dried meat between her palms for a moment. Then she resumed and said casually, "I do not have enough milk, but Tapikamiiwa is doing well."

"Your husband must be an American. Is he pale-haired too?"

An image of Sett Foster, his hair and beard the color of dark honey, flashed into Ria's mind. In that vision, Sett was muffled against a cold wind, the long strands of his hair escaping from under his hat, his dark hazel eyes searching for her in a bleak landscape. She said only, "Yes, he is an American. He raises horses to sell to the army. We have a ranch in the mountains far to the south." Then she was dismayed that she had said too much. Her mother's gaze warmed her back. When Ria turned back to them with the bowl of milk, her mother was still staring at her.

"That is a long ways to travel. How did you know I was here?"

Ria sat down on another pallet. She was suddenly very weary, and she realized that it was late at night now and she had traveled far in the one day. But she could not ignore her mother's questions. "I was hoping to find Grandfather, or any of my family. But on the journey, I met First Wife's nephew. Do you remember Pine Leaf when he was a boy? He knew you were here." She offered Tapikamiiwa some milk in a horn spoon.

"Where is Pine Leaf? Is he with you?"

"No." Ria swallowed against the lump in her throat. "No, he is dead. He . . . he was not in his right mind and he attacked a man."

Sweetgrass Woman murmured sympathetically, but the news did not deter her from her questioning. "So, you left this good man, your husband, and traveled a long way in the winter, with a small child that you cannot feed. Why? Is your good husband the father of this child? Is he looking for his son?"

Now Ria knew that her mother could still read her mind. She knew too that Sett was certainly looking for, not his son, but her. And she knew, as well as she knew Sett, that he would not stop until he found her, or died. Ria dropped the spoon back into the bowl though Tapikamiiwa was still hungry. She hung her head to hide the tears. It had been foolish to come here, foolish to have thought that she could run away from such a problem. She began to cry.

Ria's mother reached over and took the baby from Ria's lap. She picked up the bowl and spoon and began feeding him. She did not look at Ria for a long time. Finally she said, "My daughter, I feared I would never see you again, so I am very glad to have you here. But you must tell me. Is this your husband's son?"

Ria could only shake her head.

Sweetgrass Woman offered a final spoonful to Tapikamiiwa, then lifted the baby to her shoulder. She rocked him and patted him, smoothing his shining white hair with her hand. She said quietly, "Marie Amalie, is this your own son?"

Ria had not been called that name since she was a small child, and even then it was her father, the red-bearded Frenchman, who most used the formal name. Ria choked back her sobs.

"Yes! He is mine! He is mine now. He is Blackfeet. Look at his cradleboard! I am now his mother."

But Sweetgrass Woman was sadly shaking her head. Tapikamiiwa was falling asleep. He blinked his bright blue eyes as his grandmother laid him next to Ria on the pallet, then he smacked his pink lips and drifted off. Sweetgrass Woman moved over to sit beside her weeping daughter.

"Here, now, daughter. You are tired. Here, now," she crooned. She wrapped her skinny arms around Ria, stroking her hair just as she had stroked the baby's. "You have suffered much, alone, I think. Here, now. Lie down and sleep. We will deal with it in the morning."

THIRTY-ONE

Corporal Gorney's breath froze on his beard as he huffed up the trail. He'd ordered the men to dismount and lead their tiring horses up the long slope, and from the low muttering, he guessed that some of them cursed him. But, with this bitter cold, Gorney knew that walking was the only way to prevent frostbitten toes. The sky was dark with clouds, and now Gorney's thoughts were on finding some sheltered place to bivouac before the snowstorm began. At the top of the rise, he paused.

"Well, I'll be damned!" he mumbled through his scarf.

Young trooper Rattigan stopped beside him. The two men stared silently down into the valley as the rest of the detail caught up, with Sheriff's Deputy Jones still mounted on his horse. As each man peered down into the shadowed valley, he joined the first two's silence. There, twinkling like stars, was lamplight in a pair of windows, the bright squares shining on the thin covering of snow in a bare yard.

Gorney slapped his hands together, his handmade mittens making a muffled pop. "Let's hope they have a barn or shed we can camp in tonight. Men, mount up!"

Gratefully the troopers swung into the saddle and started down the trail in pairs. Sketch Jones rode alongside Gorney.

"We better approach with some caution. Foster could be there," Sketch Jones said.

"Could be he is," Gorney replied gruffly. "I'm more worried about that murdering horse thief. I don't see Foster firing on us."

"I wouldn't doubt it. Who knows what Foster is up to? He could be in cahoots with that Injun. This whole thing could be a ruse to steal away with that white child. I don't trust a thing about him." Jones's horse stumbled on a steep drop in the trail, and the man savagely yanked up on the reins. Gorney clenched his teeth but said nothing.

One of the men behind them said, "What about the lieutenant? He'd be there with Foster."

Jones gave a depreciative snort. "Good old Lieutenant Kelly? That sap. He'll let Foster get away with anything! He's just a damn green Easterner, all excited to befriend a real desperado . . ."

Gorney pulled his horse up short, so that the man behind him nearly bumped into the horse's tail. "Don't you speak ill of the dead, Deputy! I won't have you callin' a ghost down upon my men and my duty!"

"Dead? He's probably down there toasting to Foster's brave escape!" Jones sneered. "Or maybe flirting with the squaw, or . . ."

Gorney spurred his horse toward Jones, but he didn't get there first. Trooper Rattigan, his pink-cheeked face shining pale in the gathering darkness, had his sidearm pointed into Sketch Jones's face.

"Take that back," the young man hissed in a trembling whisper. "Take it back and apologize. Lieutenant Kelly was a fair and respectable officer. And I agree with Gorney. I won't have you callin' his ghost."

Jones stared for a long while into the large-caliber revolver. The barrel glinted in the dim light. Finally Jones raised his hands. "All right. I apologize to . . . whoever. But what are you talking about, his ghost?"

Rattigan slowly holstered his gun. "Don't take an expert in reading sign to see that the lieutenant never came out of the river," he said quietly. The young man turned his horse and rejoined the line. Jones looked over at the corporal.

Gorney just nodded. "Nope, don't take an expert." He moved his horse back down the trail toward the cabin's lights.

The cabin yard was well trampled, the darkness of frozen mud standing out from the shining snow. Gorney halted his command across the creek. They could see the small barn and the lean-to with a corral. Wood smoke drifted out of the cabin's stovepipe. The occupants were most likely having their evening meal; the smell of bread drifted out with the smoke. The faint sound of a chair leg scraped on the floor. A child's voice, high and piercing, was shushed to silence. Gorney waited at the edge of the creek, and then he shouted out, "Hullo, in the cabin!"

It was as if the cabin suddenly held its breath. The slight noise inside stopped. Then a man's voice yelled through the door in a strange language.

Gorney glanced around at his men. "Anyone understand that?" One fellow in the back said, "I think he said to go away."

"What language is that?" Gorney asked.

"German, sir. I think. My grandma was German."

"So tell him we are the United States Army. Tell him we're looking for . . ."

"I can't talk it!" the soldier said. "I just know a few words when I hears 'em!"

"Humph," Gorney said. He shouted at the house, "We're the United States Army, Cavalry. Tracking an Injun horse thief."

The man in the cabin reissued his original demand.

Gorney tried, "This is Corporal Gorney with the United States Cavalry. We are going to camp in your barn tonight and move on at first light!"

"*Nein!*" the cabin occupant yelled, along with a new string of words.

"He says someone is dead, sir. Something about a savage," the soldier said.

"So now what?" Jones sneered at the corporal. Gorney tried to ignore him. He turned to his men. "Rattigan, go check the barn. Portney, find a place to tether the horses." He turned back toward the cabin and said to Jones, "We're going to camp the night in the barn. At least we'll be warm and out of the snow. This German fellow won't speak our language, but he seems to understand it well enough, or someone in there does. He'll just have to let the U.S. government take its turn tonight."

Trooper Rattigan came trotting back from the barn. He stopped next to Gorney, his breath frosting in the night air. "Corporal, the barn . . . Sergeant Means's horse is in there!"

Snow had begun falling as Sett and the mare skirted a rocky outcropping that ran for miles along a canyon. The heavy clouds blotted out all chance of starlight, and the world became black-and-white, with the trail rapidly disappearing in front of them. Sett let the mare choose the way. She seemed to find the road easier than he did, and so they were both startled when a tumbledown log wall appeared just before them.

What had perhaps been a barn was now just rotting logs, one end completely dissolved into the earth and the other tumbled over, at the tallest about four feet high. The wind had piled a drift against the outside of this wall, and a small bush had grown up at one end, making a low, dry place beneath the overhang of the fallen logs. Sett dismounted and leaned to peer under. He struck a match, its flickering orange flame casting enough light to see into the pitch. The hole was unoccupied, other than a large packrat nest under the bush.

Sett stared into the shelter for a long time. Somehow, he had wished that his match light would show him what his tired mind most wanted: Ria curled up there in the closest thing to shelter he'd seen since riding away from that lonely homestead in the afternoon. Sett sighed.

He wanted to continue on, to follow the trail until he found the spot where Ria waited. He knew, he prayed, that she was somewhere near, that she was waiting for him. That she would welcome him when he finally found her.

But the night was deep and cold, and the bay mare was standing head-hung, and as much as Sett wanted to ride farther, he started to unsaddle. He piled his gear inside the overhang and poured a generous feed of grain onto his saddle blanket for the mare. He found his tinder and started a small fire using the convenient supply of dry sticks in the packrat nest. Then he crawled into the collapsed timbers and huddled on his bedroll.

The snow danced down outside the shelter, and the bay mare finished her feed and paced around the small enclosure of the fallen barn until she found a spot out of the wind. She put her rump toward the storm and cocked a hind leg, resting gratefully. The snow began to pile up along her back.

Sett fed his fire and realized that it was warming the small overhang enough that he pulled off his gloves and found a can of beans in his pack. He drank a cup of hot water, watching the snow pile on the logs, and finally slid into his bedroll and into an exhausted sleep.

John Coleman and William McFee had switched to fresh horses at a roadhouse at mid-afternoon. They left word for

Mary Alice, who was following by stage, then continued at a blistering pace to the garrison at the reservation, arriving there well after dark. John Coleman was pleased with young McFee. The fellow had uncomplainingly ridden along, occasionally asking about the name of some unique butte or outcropping. In fact, William seemed to be enjoying himself in spite of the bitter cold and hard riding. He handled his horse in fine manner and even expressed delight when a sudden downpour flattened out the brim of his new hat.

"There, now perhaps I'll pass as a frontiersman," Will had laughed. "As long as I don't say anything, I suppose!" Coleman could not help but chuckle himself.

"McFee, I've no doubt you'll make a frontiersman, with a little practice," Coleman had said. And he meant it.

Now, bunked in a shared room at the garrison's simple officers' quarters, Coleman lay awake on his bunk and listened to Will's steady breathing.

The sheriff was exhausted, but his mind still zipped along. The stage, bearing the ladies, would arrive late the next morning. He knew they were laid over at the same roadhouse where he'd left the horses, and he hoped that Mrs. McFee did not find the accommodations too rustic. Especially since the roadhouse was palatial compared to what they would find at the reservation.

The garrison buildings were grouped around a beaten-earth parade ground, with palisade walls between the buildings and a square guardhouse at each corner. In the evening, livestock was driven into the stockade and a large gate swung shut, locking out the poor Indian wretches who begged alongside the road and slept in tattered teepees around the periphery of the outpost. Along with the officers' cabin and the agent's office, a long barracks housed the enlisted men and there was a mess hall that doubled as a church on Sunday and a social hall on Saturday night. Smaller cabins lined one side of the enclosure, the homes of the men with families. Dogs, chickens, and pigs huddled under the eaves. A kitchen was situated next to a slaughter-house. It was a crude village.

Still, it was much better inside the garrison than out, where the Indians lived in squalor. Dependant on their rations of beef and flour, they lined the road to the garrison. Some had begged for tobacco as Coleman and McFee rode in. Others glared at the men murderously from under the folds of a blanket. Others were lying in the ditch, passed out from drink. One had curled up with a sow in a brush shelter. Coleman noticed that McFee went silent at that point; all joking ended.

Now Coleman pulled his bedroll up against the chill in the room and worried. He worried about where they would house the two ladies when they arrived. He suspected that Mrs. Kelly would accept whatever room could be had at an officer's home, but Mrs. McFee? Coleman remembered that the McFees had taken a room at the finest hotel in Verdy. There was little fine china here. Then he worried about the child they had come to save. In which of those hovels was that child hidden? The commanding officer had received Coleman's telegram, but other than asking in the immediate vicinity, he'd had no news to report about any suspicious new women with babies. And finally the sheriff worried that he'd been misled, that the woman was not even headed here. Sett Foster had led him astray. Foster had met up with her and headed into the Western mountains. He'd be laughing at the gullible sheriff from some hideout. He'd be in Canada.

Coleman's only consolation was Lieutenant Kelly, who was there with Foster, making sure he did right.

THIRTY-TWO

A small noise woke Sett, but when he strained to hear it again, the silence suffocated him. An odd gray light seeped through one wall, and Sett remembered that he was in the cave-like tumble of logs. The snow had drifted up over the opening. His fire was barely warm. Sett scrambled up out of his blankets and knocked snow away from the top of the wall with his bare hands. A blast of cold air and the brilliant blue of clear sky welcomed him.

Outside, the fine bay mare snorted and Sett recognized what had awakened him. It was well after sunup. How could he have slept so long? He wrapped his scarf around his face and jammed his hat down on his head, then stood up.

The mare snorted again at his sudden appearance. The sun glare on the snow forced him to close his eyes. When he squinted them back open, his hopes sank in his chest.

A shimmery white expanse of fresh snow stretched around him. The sun was just showing from behind the trees, and as the day imperceptibly warmed, the snow piled on the pine branches slid off with a plop. The mare had trampled the knee-deep snow in her corner. She looked rested and ready. The blue sky heralded at least a few hours of dry weather. He was maybe only hours behind Ria. He should be riding.

But where to? Sett could not move. He stood there in the powdery dry snow, little mounds of it still sticking to his hat brim and the shoulders of his coat, and gazed around at the trackless expanse. The faint trail that he had been following, the tracks of one shod horse and a barefoot pack pony, were now obliterated by the snowflakes.

It was not hard to head north, and so that is what he did, following by logic and ease the most likely path of the trail. Occasionally he would come across a blaze on a tree or a spot where someone had chopped some branches, but the mountains seemed deserted of life. Sett figured he must be on the reservation land now, as he wound down out of the deep snow and onto a rolling plain. Here the snow was less, but the wind blew unheeded. There was no sign of the trail, and Sett knew that he'd lost it and lost Ria.

He gave the bay her head and let her drift to the east, as if the strong wind were blowing her off course. He even let her choose the gait, and for a long while the mare moved at a brisk walk along a gradual ridge. It didn't matter where the mare took him now. It was all the same. He'd lost Ria's trail. He'd failed.

Somewhere he would cross a road, or run into a settlement of some sort, and then he'd head to the garrison at the reservation. His best chance of finding Ria now was to be there when they apprehended her, for surely she could not hide forever. Sett's hope of finding her first, of somehow easing her through the coming ordeal, was buried under two feet of snow up on the mountain, and so he turned the navigation over to his horse and gave himself time to brood.

He wondered how close he was to the garrison at the agency. Was it east or west of him, or still to the north? He wondered where Coleman was, and how far behind were the cavalry? He tried not to think about where Kiernan Kelly was or how Belinda Kelly would get the news.

Sett could well remember receiving news like that himself. It had left him gasping and choking. But Mrs. Kelly was too much of a lady to run out the door and retch. She would faint, Sett feared. He hoped that Martha would be there to catch her.

The mare paused before heading down a well-worn game trail, which dropped off a steep bank into the creek. The fast-moving water was free of ice, and the mare paused for a drink. Sett sipped from his canteen too, though he was not really thirsty in the cold weather. It was just something he did from habit.

The mare crossed the stream and bounded up the trail on the far side. Breaking out onto a meadow, she took off at a trot, shaking her head and looking at the horizon with pricked ears. Sett let her move along, covering a lot of ground without knowing where they were headed. At least the vigorous pace kept them both warm.

On the other side of the little valley, the mare swerved down a narrow gully. The footing was tricky, and Sett pulled her to a walk again. The mare held the bit and tossed her head.

"Ho, there, mare. What's your hurry?" Sett said aloud to her. He knew well the mare's habit of whinnying at other horses, and wondered if there was a wild herd nearby. The mare moved eagerly down the coulee bottom, along a thin line of willows and hawthorn. Ahead the coulee widened out again, and now the mare fluttered her nostrils. Sett stopped her, dismounting to stand by the horse's head. There was something ahead that excited her, and Sett wanted to know what it was before he rode into the middle of it.

Keeping one hand short on the reins, he led the mare to the edge of the thicket. The coulee widened out into a sheltered meadow, the dry fall grasses poking up through the thin snow. There in the yellow grass, were two horses, one a red chestnut and the other a small, ugly spotted pony. Sett could not restrain his mare completely—she nickered just loud enough for the two horses to hear, and they lifted their heads and stared up at the mare and the man in the brush. Then Fox Ears whinnied, pranced in a small circle with his ears and tail up, and finally he was off at a gallop toward his stablemate and friend, the tall bay mare.

There was commotion, loud voices, and Coy growling steadily nearby. Ria struggled to rouse herself, but the hard hold of her nightmare dragged her back. It was not until the distant reedy wail of a baby filtered into her dreams that she came awake and sat bolt upright in bed.

Blinking her swollen eyelids, she frantically searched for Tapikamiiwa in the shadows of the cabin.

There he was, silent and wide-eyed, in the arms of Ria's mother. Sweetgrass Woman shook her head, stroked the child's white hair, and motioned for Ria to be silent.

From outside the cabin door the piercing cry continued, accompanied by the harsh voices that had invaded Ria's dreams.

"Now, yer lucky we hauled you out of there, Yva. Ya owe us now, right?" a man's voice growled near the door.

"Both of us, remember? And we know you know that," another man said.

"So, next time you're in, you owe us. But leave that squalling baby with yer mother. We won't be rescuing you again."

Ria could not hear any replies, but the pitiful wailing of the baby continued and the sound of it drew her out of her bed.

"No, daughter. Leave it!" Sweetgrass Woman said. "Do not let those men know you are here!"

Ria shook her head like her dog after a rain shower. "Who is that? What baby is crying?" she asked.

"It is your sister, come home from the agency. Leave it. She and her daughter will be in soon," Sweetgrass Woman begged, but Ria went to the cabin door.

"How can she not comfort the child?" Ria asked. There being no windows on the cabin, she cracked the door and peered out. It had snowed in the night, and in the slight slice of the yard that she could see, two men sat on horses, and hidden behind them was a woman in a scarlet and black skirt, the edges in tatters and hanging down into the mud. The continuing cries of a very young infant pierced the scene.

"I pay, I pay!" a woman's voice shrilled, but then the speaker staggered on the muddy ground and the man on the horse reached down to grab her sleeve to steady her.

"Yeah, I've no worry about getting what you promised, Yva. But I like my women to be awake when I'm fucking 'em. Get on in the house and leave that damn squallin' brat home next time you come into town." The rider hoisted the wearer of the red dress back onto her feet and then turned his horse. He glared at the partially opened door of the cabin.

"You heard all that, squaw? Next time you send the girl in to make your money for you, keep the damn kid here. It's dangerous for all of us."

Now Ria could see the woman, a small thin girl in a garish white man's dress. The screaming baby was slung over her hip, and the woman paid no mind to the child. She was reaching up as if to cling to the rider's pant leg, forcing her lips into a smile. Ria pulled the door open and stepped across the sill, but she stopped when the taller man stared at her.

"What's this?" he growled.

Ria froze, then felt Sweetgrass Woman's hand clasp the back of her shawl. With surprising strength, her mother pulled her back into the cabin.

"You stay with your child, Marie Amalie. I will do this."

There was an undeniable order in the frail woman's voice. Tapikamiiwa was lying on the cot at the rear of the cabin, and Ria gave one look into her mother's eyes and then turned away from the door to return to the boy.

Sweetgrass Woman pushed open the door and stepped into the yard.

"Daughter, Yva, bring the baby to me," she said. She clutched the door frame for support.

The men in the yard laughed. "Yeah, Yva. Give the baby to yer mother, and then maybe you can pay that debt right now!"

Sweetgrass Woman said, "Bring me the child, but you are not bringing those men into my house."

The girl in the red dress turned viciously toward the older woman. "You! Don't you tell me what to do!" Then she swayed again, nearly dropping the baby.

"Just give her the kid, sweetheart," one of the men said.

"Yeah, hand it over and then we can get on with it!"

The tall rider dismounted from his horse. Yva tripped toward him, threw her arm up as if to embrace him, but instead he snatched the squalling baby from her.

"Give . . . her . . . back!" the drunken girl demanded, but she tripped on the long skirt and went to her knees in the snow. The man moved two long strides to the door and handed the noisy baby to Sweetgrass Woman.

"Take it inside and bolt the door. And don't let her bring that baby into the garrison no more. She about got arrested just for having that baby." The man pushed Sweetgrass Woman back through the door and pulled it closed behind her. He went back to Yva, kneeling in the muddy snow.

"This is a rude place, darlin', but I think we'll collect what you owe right now." The other man dismounted from his horse.

Sweetgrass Woman stood with her back against the door. She rocked the crying infant almost frantically. Ria sat at the back of the cabin, cradling the alert Tapikamiiwa in her arms and staring at her mother. There were tears in the older woman's eyes, but she made no sound and stayed resolutely by the door as if she were afraid that Ria would try to escape or the men would try to come in.

"Is that my sister's husband?" Ria finally asked.

"She has no husband," Sweetgrass Woman replied.

"Is he the father of her baby?"

"No, I do not think so. I do not know." Now Sweetgrass Woman bent her head over the whimpering child. "Poor little one, no one wants you," she whispered.

Ria stood and placed Tapikamiiwa on her cot. She crossed the dirt floor to her mother and held out her hands. "Let me have her." Sweetgrass Woman jerked her head up. She stared at her oldest daughter.

"I still have some milk," Ria said. She took the featherweight bundle from her mother's arms and peered down into the tiny pinched face of her niece. Then she went back to the pallet at the back of the cabin and left her mother guarding the door.

THIRTY-THREE

"I think we are there," Belinda Kelly said after she dropped the dusty black curtain back over the window of the stagecoach. She looked over at Mrs. McFee.

"Oh, thank the Lord," Mary Alice whispered.

Belinda was worried about the older woman. She knew that neither of them had slept much the night before in the shared scratchy bed at the way station, and the constant joggling of the coach allowed for no rest during the trip. And now, as the coach approached a forlorn group of buildings that sat unprotected on the windswept plain, she carefully pulled the shade closed. Better if Mrs. McFee did not see the desolation of their destination, at least for a few more minutes.

The passengers they had started out with in Verdy had all changed course, with the banker catching another stage at the roadhouse, and the rough-looking frontiersman disappearing to God knows where. For the morning's journey to the agency, Belinda Kelly and Mary Alice McFee had been alone in the swaying coach. Belinda desperately wished she could plead poor Mrs. Foster's case here, without any participation from others, but seeing Mrs. McFee's pale face and dark-circled eyes, she did not have the heart. So conversation remained limited, and Belinda peeked out of the curtain often, praying that the stage driver's assurance of arriving by noon was accurate.

It was. The sun was high and shining thinly through piercing cold air. As the stage slowed to a stop at the edge of the parade ground, Belinda saw that they had a welcoming party. Sheriff Coleman and William McFee waited in the lee of a log building and stepped out quickly as the stage rolled to a stop. There was no sign of Kiernan. He must still be on the trail.

"Look, your son and the sheriff are waiting for us." Belinda pushed the curtain back a little, and Mary Alice leaned forward to catch a glimpse of her William.

"Dear boy. Willie has always been such a good child, always caring." She sagged back into the seat. Belinda raised her gloved hand to the window, to wave a greeting to the men. William McFee did not look like a "dear boy" to her. He fit in quite well next to the sheriff; a man dressed for the country, with an easy and confident carriage. The door of the coach opened and Sheriff Coleman stuck his head inside.

"Good morning, ladies. I hope you are both well?"

"Yes, thank you, Sheriff." Belinda took his offered hand and let him step her down from the coach. William took her elbow to guide her to what served as a sidewalk as the sheriff helped Mrs. McFee disembark. William quickly took his mother's arm.

"Mother, are you all right? It must have been a tiring journey."

Mary Alice sighed. "Yes." She shrugged as if to shake off the pains of the travel and then turned to look around the desolate agency headquarters. The stockade that protected the buildings offered little shelter from the wind, and dust devils swirled across the parade ground. A few soldiers were heading for the stables, and at first Mary Alice didn't realize that what appeared to be heaps of blankets or garbage against the walls were actually humans, Indians, huddled in a long line that led to an open doorway.

Sheriff Coleman's eyes followed her gaze. "They are waiting for rations. Supposed to hand 'em out last week, but the supply wagons were delayed."

"Oh, my. Where do they live?" Mary Alice forgot her weariness for a moment; the idea of the people in rags waiting for days against the buildings for their share of food made tears well in her already tired eyes.

"Most live here, near the agency. Some live out in the hills." The sheriff guided Mrs. Kelly toward a door. "This way. The agent, Mr. Roberts, is waiting for us."

It was a blessing to go into the agent's office and be out of the wind. Belinda and Mary Alice sat gratefully on a sturdy bench cushioned with a buffalo hide. It was quite comfortable to not be constantly pitching around in the stage. The room was small and decorated with hunting trophies. An enormous elk rack hung on the wall behind the agent's desk. There were several hats hanging on the antlers. The agent himself leaped up and greeted the newcomers warmly, even ordering his servant to bring in hot tea. When it arrived, though, it was in tin mugs that were so hot that Belinda could not hold hers in her hands. She finally set the mug down on the bench beside her, and Mrs. McFee did the same.

"Has there been any news of my grandson?" Mary Alice said once the general pleasantries were done.

"Nothing definite." The reservation agent spoke with a hint of a foreign accent. He had seated himself behind his desk, beneath his elk. "We thought yesterday, perhaps, we had found something. A young breed girl who fit the sheriff's description. But when my men checked it out, it turned out her baby was a girl. So they let her go." He folded his hands on the desk, pleased that he had at least some information to make it appear that he was doing something. "The word is out among the soldiers as well as my men. We'll look at every baby that comes through!"

Mary Alice nodded.

Belinda Kelly took the opportunity to ask, "Has there been any word from my husband, Lieutenant Kelly, or his troops?"

The agent shook his head. "Not yet. Sheriff Coleman was expecting them to arrive today, if they weren't delayed. It snowed pretty good in the mountains yesterday. That could slow them down."

Belinda hid her disappointment, but it was not like this was the first time the lieutenant had been on business that did not follow a set schedule.

Sheriff Coleman said, "I don't really expect them, unless Foster arrives too. They'll stay on his trail, and it's possible that he isn't coming here at all."

"You mean, we were deceived?" Mary Alice sat up straighter on the bench. William put his hand on her shoulder.

"No, I think he means to track down his wife. He thought there was a good chance that she was coming here, but we don't know where she is. If she went somewhere else, then Foster will follow her."

"And the lieutenant will follow him," Belinda added.

Mary Alice McFee sighed. Her fatigue resurfaced, and she wished only to have a quiet place to nap for a while. William patted her shoulder, and Mrs. Kelly took up the mug of tea and handed it to her.

"Here, Mrs. McFee. It is cool enough now and will refresh you," Belinda said as she offered the lukewarm cup.

"Mother, there is a positive side to all this." William McFee stepped around to face her. "Because Foster and the soldiers have not arrived, it likely means we are ahead of them. They are traveling cross-country, and in the weather, while we sped here by the main road. Even if the woman does not turn up here at the reservation, we are that much closer to wherever she does surface. I've spoken with the soldiers stationed here. They are ready to ride at a moment's notice when Mrs. Foster is located. We will find little Andrew, Mother. I promise that."

Mary Alice gave a tight-lipped smile up at her son.

"Will is right, Mrs. McFee. We got some of the best tracking your grandson, and none of 'em men who give up easily." Sheriff Coleman sincerely hoped he was speaking the truth.

Will reached to help his mother up from her seat. "Now, I think we have found the most suitable lodging available for you. Perhaps you would care to rest after your stage journey?"

The lodging was indeed the most suitable that Will could find on the fort compound. A large woman, her hands and arms red and rough from doing laundry for the soldiers, showed them into the former storeroom behind the stove in the mess hall. A lantern hung from the rafters, and two small, well-bedded cots lined the wall. Will had cleaned it out himself that morning and found an extra wool blanket to put down on the floor as a rug. It was only a short walk across the parade ground to the latrine. Belinda Kelly recognized it instantly for what it was: a thoughtful labor of love. Most often visitors were housed in the officers' homes and ended up sharing a bed with strangers. Will even introduced the washerwoman, and directed them to call for her if they needed anything. Belinda was sure that Will was paying the woman well for the extra service.

Mary Alice did not see quite so quickly how much effort had been made on her behalf. However, she did see a quiet, stable bed and a chance to rest, which she took gratefully.

* * *

A gust of wind followed the reeling girl through the door. Ria instinctively curled over the tiny child at her breast and drew the blanket up to shield her.

"Who are you?" Yva demanded, her eyes darting from Sweetgrass Woman and Tapikamiiwa to her unrecognized sister at the back of the dim cabin.

"Yva, close the door!" Sweetgrass Woman said, turning now to protect Tapikamiiwa from the draft. The girl did not move. The back of the red dress was wet from the snow, her hair straggled down into her face, and her cheeks were flushed with something more than just cold. She seemed oblivious to the bitter wind that blew on her back.

Yva stared dumbfounded, gazing first at Sweetgrass Woman and then at Ria. Finally she focused on the child in Sweetgrass Woman's arms. "And who is that? Where is my baby?" Her voice raised in anger, and she took a few steps into the room.

"Yva, sit down," Sweetgrass Woman said, though the girl paid her no heed. Sweetgrass Woman shut the door.

"Where is my baby?" the girl demanded. "What have you done with my baby?" She spun around, gazing wildly around the cabin. The quick turn made her lose her balance and she caught the wall to keep from falling.

"It is all right, sister. I have your daughter here," Ria said quietly. She pulled the blanket away to reveal the nursing infant.

"Yva, you do not recognize your older sister, my daughter Ria. Remember her from the lodge on Old Man River, a long time ago?" Sweetgrass Woman gently bounced Tapikamiiwa in her arms. The boy's blue eyes were wide with the excitement at the new people and the shouting.

Yva squinted at Ria suspiciously. "Where did that white baby come from?"

"Mine, my son. His name is Tapikamiiwa. What is your daughter's name?" Ria spoke very calmly, hoping to quiet both her drunken sister and the babe at her breast. But Yva was not ready to be calmed.

"Give me my baby!" She weaved across the dirt floor toward Ria.

"It is all right, I have milk and she is hungry . . ."

"No! Give her to me now!" Yva grabbed Ria's sleeve, jerked it hard. The force pulled Ria from the cot and the baby let out a thin howl at being so rudely interrupted. Ria caught herself from falling and kept the crying infant tucked safely in her arm. Her sister did not release her hold on Ria's sleeve. She shrieked more loudly than the child and tried to yank Ria off balance again, one hand grasping toward the baby.

"Give her to me, give her to me now!"

Coy darted out from under the cot, growling at the girl who was grappling with Ria. Yva aimed a kick at the dog, missed, and nearly fell.

Ria was aghast. She could not believe that the girl cared so greatly for her daughter when the poor child was so hungry and unkempt. She could not help but clutch the baby closer, protecting her from the wild woman who was her mother.

"Yva! Daughter! Stop this!" Sweetgrass Woman's protests fell on deaf ears. Yva now reached up and grabbed Ria's braid, pulling her hair so hard that Ria's head snapped around.

"Ow!" Ria swung around and hit her sister in the ribs with her elbow. It knocked the wind out of Yva, ending her shrieks with an *oof.* Yva collapsed in a heap on the floor.

Ria stared down at her and rocked the baby. Her sister was thin and not very strong, and she was very drunk. It had perhaps been unfair to hit her when Ria knew that she herself was hardened from hard work, but the silence was worth it. Yva now only sat and wept.

"I want my baby!" the younger girl sobbed. "I just want my baby."

Ria leaned down and lay the infant in her sister's lap. "Here, Sister. I am sorry that I hurt you."

The baby girl had stopped crying, but Yva did not pick her up and cuddle her. She continued to weep, sitting there on the floor, and she let the baby lay kicking on the sodden wet fabric of her skirt.

Sweetgrass Woman came over and held Tapikamiiwa out to Ria. "Here, I will help her to bed." She guided Yva to a cot, carrying the tiny baby for her. Yva was unconscious as soon as she laid down. Sweetgrass Woman left her baby next to her and covered them with a blanket before turning back to Ria.

"She will sleep for a long time now. In a little while, we will take the baby again, when Yva doesn't know."

"She does this often?"

Sweetgrass Woman shook her head sadly. "It is like an illness, the white man's whiskey disease." Sweetgrass Woman paused to cough gently. "First Wife and I shared this cabin, but First Wife died in the cold winter, and so now Yva spends her time at the fort, where there are many men to buy whiskey for her. Sometimes she comes home like this. Sometimes she does not come home. Sometimes she leaves her daughter here and forgets about her."

Ria gave Tapikamiiwa a squeeze, and he responded with a squirm and a smile. She could only shake her head in wonder at the passed-out girl on the cot.

"I could not do that to my child," she said.

"No, you would not, Daughter. I can see that."

Ria took a deep breath and glanced around the cabin again. "Are those men gone? I need to go to the latrine."

Sweetgrass Woman paused for a moment at her language. "Yes, they are gone now. There is a line of willows behind the cabin."

Ria nodded, found her sling for Tapikamiiwa and her coat. Calling her dog, she went outside into the trampled snow of the yard and headed through the useless sunshine toward the thickets.

Sett finally found a spot where he could see the cabin door and still have the horses hidden in a coulee. He was not as close as he would have liked, but well out of rifle range. He was not sure if that was good or bad. No one could fire upon him, but he could not fire at the cabin either.

He waited, squatting in the low-growing clump of sagebrush with the snow freezing his feet and the wind whistling by his ears. He had seen the riders approach the cabin, and saw the woman in the red dress. He watched the motions, the staggering, the swagger of the riders, and the girl being half-dragged up the bank toward a thicket. Finally the two men had ridden away to the northeast. The girl in the red dress had gone into the cabin some while ago. Smoke puffed out of the stovepipe, but otherwise the cabin sat silent and frustrating, with no sign of Ria. Sett shifted his weight to the other knee. He prayed he wasn't sitting up here in the brush for nothing.

The door of the cabin opened, and the little merle dog trotted out, raised her pointy nose, and sniffed the breeze. The sight of her gladdened Sett's heart. He nearly stood up and whistled, but better judgment stayed him. The next figure out the door was swaddled against the cold in a heavy coat and shawl wrapped up over her head, her dark skirt brushing the instep of her moccasins, her arms folded protectively over her chest. He knew her immediately, knew the way she walked, the length of her steps, the sweeping cast of her eyes as she scanned the horizon before proceeding across the barren yard. The relief of finding her sank into his stomach. He sighed but did not move.

Ria pulled the door closed carefully behind her, walked across the yard toward the willows, and disappeared into them. Not long after, she appeared again, shielding her eyes with her hand and looking up the coulee toward where he had found the horses. She did not go in search of them, but walked directly to the cabin and let herself back in.

Sett eased from his sparse hiding place, his knees cramped from kneeling in the snow for so long. He made his way back to the horses tied in the brush.

"She's there," he told the bay mare.

"She's down there, with Coy," he said to Fox Ears.

"Tapikamiiwa is with her," he whispered to the spotted pony, who laid back her ears and threatened to bite.

THIRTY-FOUR

The day passed slowly. Sett had returned to his precarious hiding spot in the sagebrush, though this time he brought the canvas from his bedroll to shield his feet from the cold. He waited a long time, until the door opened again and another woman came out and made the short trip to the willows. This woman was a stranger and walked cautiously through the melting snow as if she was afraid to fall. Sett saw the door open slightly, as someone inside the cabin watched the old woman's progress. Later in the day, the door swung to let the dog out again, but none of the women came out. Sett glanced at the sun, now hazy behind some high thin clouds. He was beginning to feel confident that the only occupants of the cabin were the three women, that no men were concealed in there. He watched as Coy sniffed the wind again, then headed straight toward his hiding spot.

The dog took her time coming across the yard, but once she was in the sagebrush, she stopped and paused to scent the air. With increasing speed, she trotted through the sagebrush. Sett saw her appear and disappear in the clearings, and he knew that she moved with purpose. It was not the first time that Coy had tracked him down. In fact she almost always met him on his way home, long before the cabin was in sight. And the dog was particularly fond of the bay mare, making her bed in the straw of the mare's stall whenever possible. Sett stayed right where he was, until the dog trotted up to him.

"Coy, it's good to see you," Sett uttered as he rubbed the dog's ears. "You've been taking care of Ria, haven't you? I wish you could know how glad I am to find you."

Coy grinned up at the man as if she did indeed know how glad he was, then she went to greet the horses by lifting her nose up to theirs. The bay mare let out a low nicker at the sight of her.

Now all Sett had to do was figure out how he was going to approach Ria. She couldn't run again—he had her horse—but there was no guarantee that he would receive a warm welcome. He waited in his scrubby blind as the sun made its early descent toward the mountains. The old woman came out and Ria was with her, but after the old woman was back inside, Ria stood in the yard and whistled for her dog. Coy, sitting next to Sett in the brush, looked from the woman to him, but did not respond to the summons. Sett could see the worry in Ria's gestures as she turned in several directions and held her hand to shade her eyes. She finally turned and went reluctantly into the cabin.

Sett stood up. His knees ached and his calf muscles twitched. Coy did a little prance around him in the mud.

"Well, guess we go in?" Sett asked the dog.

She agreed.

The sun was setting, shadows stretching long from his feet and the feet of the horses, extending into the sagebrush along the eastern slope of the little hollow where the cabin sat. Sett walked through the damp sage, leading his mare with Fox Ears and the spotted pony tethered behind. Coy walked with him, aware that this was a special stalk. As the entourage entered the clearing of the cabin's yard, Sett paused. The horses came to a halt behind him.

Sett did not know how to call out to the cabin. *Hello the cabin!* did not seem to fit. Neither did, *Ria, come out!* or *I'm here*. He wondered for a moment if there was always a trick to announcing oneself to a cabin, in particular where one might not be welcome. He wondered just how unwelcome he might be.

Coy did not worry about her welcome. She had heard Ria calling her. She marched up to the cabin door and said, *ROOF!*

The door swung open quickly, as if Ria had been waiting for that *roof*. The woman immediately bent down to the dog, and then her head tipped up, looking out across the barren little yard to the man and three horses, standing there at the edge of the shadows. Coy's tail was wagging as Ria's hand paused along her neck. Sett thought that he could hear heartbeats, and he wondered if they were his own, or if the accumulated thumps of the horses, the dog, and his wife were in sync.

Ria stared at him as one would at a ghost. Then she took a step backward into the cabin, her hand on the door preparing to shut it against him.

Sett sighed; this might be so.

He sighed again and could not stop his hand from reaching out toward her.

Ria left the doorway, walking at first slowly then with more speed through the melting snow. Coy cavorted alongside, and as Ria approached the edge of the sage, she was running, running to him. She threw her arms around his neck, and he clasped her around the waist, lifting her up out of the muddy snow and burying his face against the rough wool of the blanket around her shoulders. Her weight was nothing, her scent was everything. Slowly, slowly, he swung her around, so glad to have her near again. So without words.

THIRTY-FIVE

"Mrs. McFee? I'm sorry to wake you." The polite voice of Mrs. Kelly pierced Mary Alice's deep slumber. She started to roll over, the lumpiness of the mattress bringing her awake faster than Belinda's gentle urging.

"Sheriff Coleman was just here to report that my husband's cavalry detail is approaching the fort! He requested us to come to the agent's office as soon as you were ready. Mrs. McFee, are you all right?" Now Belinda's voice took on a note of concern. Mary Alice blinked her tired eyes and waved her hand above the scratchy woolen blanket.

"Yes, my dear, I hear you," Mary Alice mumbled. She never liked being seen when she first awoke, but now was no time for vanity. "Please, help me up. This bed is of dubious worth." Mrs. Kelly offered her hand and helped the older woman to sit up on the side of the cot. "Don't tell Willie I said that. I know he worked hard to procure this private room for us."

Belinda could not suppress a smile. "Yes, it is much preferable to most of the accommodations here." She had spent some time walking around the garrison, if only to give Mrs. McFee some privacy for her nap. But the sheriff's news, that a small mounted detail had been spotted on the road to the south, had brought Belinda quickly back to the small room. "I brought some hot water and a basin if you would like to wash up." She indicated the wash bowl on the only table in the room. She did not want to rush Mrs. McFee, but her eagerness could not be contained. Mary Alice looked up into the young woman's face.

"And is your husband with this detail of men?" she asked.

Belinda shrugged. "Possibly, though Sheriff Coleman said that the lieutenant had gone ahead with Mr. Foster. We do not have any way of knowing if the detail has found them. Or the one they were seeking."

"Ah, but we are both eager to find this out, yes?" Mary Alice heaved herself up from the cot and went to wash up and to tidy her hair.

The eight soldiers and their corporal rode into the garrison by twos, with Deputy Sketch Jones riding alongside the corporal at the head of the line. They came in at a walk, each tired, bedraggled man silently keeping his thoughts to himself. Corporal Gorney led the men in his command toward the agent's office, as that seemed to be where there was a gathering of people awaiting their arrival. The small porch was crowded. Gorney recognized the sheriff from Verdy and the commanding officer of the fort, along with a couple of other soldiers. There was also the Indian agent—a hefty fellow in a bearskin coat—and a young man with a newish hat. Then Gorney squinted in surprise. There were two women—one young, tall one, the other older—waiting with the men. Gorney marched his horse right up to the railing.

"Corporal Gorney, sir, reporting in from detail." Gorney saluted the officer of the fort. The captain returned his salute.

"Send your men to the stables to put away their mounts,

Corporal. Davis here will take your horse. We'd appreciate a briefing at once, if possible."

Gorney dismounted and handed his horse to the waiting trooper. Unfortunately, Deputy Jones did the same. Gorney was getting sorely tired of the deputy, sorely tired indeed. He wished that Lieutenant Kelly were here; then he would be the one to have to break the news to the sheriff. Gorney glanced at the two women in the group. Who were they? Most likely, they were here about the baby, and Gorney didn't have any good news there either. That baby was still hidden in some Injun's coat somewhere, out in the snow. He stomped his boots on the porch to loosen the mud before entering the cramped agent's office.

The office was not really big enough for this many people. The sheriff directed the ladies to the bearskin-covered bench, and the agent seated himself underneath the overbearing mounted head of an elk, which took up way too much room. The rest of the men crowded along the walls. Gorney found a spot near the potbellied stove, and his wool trousers began to steam.

The agent addressed him. "Corporal, first, let me introduce the ladies. Mrs. McFee is here from Denver. That is her son, William, over there. She is the missing child's grandmother. And this is Mrs. Lieutenant Kelly, who accompanied Mrs. McFee. Of course you know the lieutenant."

Gorney's eyes flicked wide. He touched the brim of his hat and muttered, "Nice to meet you, ma'ams," but his mind raced in a mad circle. *Mrs. Lieutenant Kelly! Oh, shit.* She was staring up at him with large green eyes, a bit of her pale blond hair showing from under her hat and scarf. Well, Gorney mused, he could certainly understand why the lieutenant had wanted to spend most of his time in town with his bride. What was Gorney going to say if she asked him where Kelly was?

"Looks like your men had a hard ride, Corporal. What did you find out?" Sheriff Coleman said.

Gorney took a deep breath and pulled his attention away from the Mrs. Lieutenant. "We tracked the pair of Injuns to a homestead about twenty-five miles south of here. There, we found Sergeant Means's horse, in the possession of the homesteader. The farmer didn't speak English, and he wouldn't give up the horse. He claimed it was given to him in payment of some sort. He also said that the man we were seeking, the one that ambushed and killed Means, was dead. He showed us a fresh grave."

Sketch Jones broke in. "The corporal here decided that we didn't need to take the horse, even though it's evidence. And we got no proof that there's a body in that grave . . ."

Coleman nodded tersely at his deputy. "Sketch, let the corporal finish, and then you can fill me in on our part." He turned back to the corporal.

"Well, the deputy is right, in a way. It was a little tricky dealing with that farmer. He was not a friendly sort, and everything was translated through a young boy."

"Any sign of the woman and the baby?"

Gorney shook his head. "Appears she was there with the Injun, but rode on the next morning. Problem was, it snowed heavy up in the mountains that night. By the next morning the trail had been covered."

"Any sign of Sett Foster?"

"Nope, not after the snow. The homesteader's kid said a man came by the cabin too, but he kept moving. Probably was Foster."

Coleman looked grim. The agent drummed his fingers on the desktop. The sound reverberated through the packed room.

Mary Alice and William spoke at once.

"So there is no news of little Andrew?"

"So we have no idea where the Indian woman is?"

And Belinda Kelly asked, "Did the homesteader mention the lieutenant being with Foster?"

All eyes shifted back to Corporal Gorney, who stood

steaming by the stove with his campaign hat in hand. He wrung the hat hard, and a few drops of water splattered onto the floorboards.

"Umm, no," he said simply. "No, I'm sorry but we lost the trail yesterday in the snow."

Gorney avoided Mrs. McFee's gaze and was grateful that the Mrs. Lieutenant turned away to ask something of the sheriff.

"You may go, Corporal. Get dried off and get something hot to eat from the mess. We will find you if we have any further questions." The officer in charge waved his hand dismissively. Gorney wasted no time heading out the door.

"Sheriff, I'd like a word with you," Sketch Jones said. Coleman nodded.

"You may use this office, Sheriff. I am on my way out," the agent offered.

"I'll escort the ladies back to their quarters," the captain offered. "And please join me for dinner at the officers' mess." He made a small smile, "Which, of course is the north end of the regular mess hall, but nearest the stove!"

"The corporal there gave a pretty thin description of what went on," Jones started as soon as the ladies were out the door. Coleman took the chair from behind the agent's desk and pulled it up to the stove. He guessed he should have offered it to Sketch, who was just as wet and bedraggled as the soldiers, but the man seemed more intent on pacing back and forth over the bearskin rug. Coleman propped his boots on the rail around the stove and waited.

"That foreign farmer what had Means's horse had the bridle and saddle too, along with the saddle blanket, all with U.S. Army brands, and would that lazy corporal do his duty and seize 'em? No! He was afeared of that loudmouth fellow. Couldn't even speak English! Nope, old Gorney there, he . . ."

"Sketch, we aren't out here to help the army recover

horses. We're looking for Sett Foster," Coleman interrupted. "What do you have on him?"

Sketch clenched his jaw. "Yeah, well, he was just as soft on that one. It did snow, a lot. We was slogging through it over knee deep up there in the high country. But as we came down, there was a place where a trail took off. Snowed over, for sure, but a trail. Corporal Gorney rode right on by. I pointed it out, and there's one soldier, pretty quick kid name of Rattigan," Sketch figured he didn't need to mention that the kid had been quick to draw his sidearm too, "who also noticed it. The kid agreed with me, it looked like something big had headed off there, maybe a horse. But nope, the corporal said it was an elk trail! Besides, we were heading in here, to the warm, dry barracks. To hell with tracking Foster."

"Think you could find this trail again, Sketch?"

"If it don't snow or blow, that Rattigan kid could find it."

"Might not be worth all the backtracking. I'm thinking that the woman, Mrs. Foster, has probably holed up somewhere, maybe with her family. I'm thinking we should be looking from here."

Sketch stopped his pacing and now stood near the blazing stove. He scowled down at his boss, sitting with his feet up as usual. "There's something else that the corporal decided not to mention."

Coleman waited. Finally he said, "What, for God's sake? Sketch, you get on my nerves sometimes with all your suppositions."

"Ain't a supposition. Ask that trooper Rattigan. When Lieutenant Kelly jumped his horse into the river that night, heading after Foster, he never come out on the other side."

Coleman sat up straight, put his boots on the floor. "How do you figure?"

Sketch smirked. "No tracks on the far bank other than

Foster's and the earlier tracks of the Injuns. No tracks anywhere except Foster's. And that damn farmer, the boy there said one man came looking for the Injun woman. Not two."

Sheriff Coleman leaned forward and placed both hands over his face. He sighed. "And Gorney knows this?"

"Oh yup, he knows. He just wasn't going to be the one to tell the pretty widow."

Coleman rubbed his palms up over his eyes, trying to ease the headache that increased with every bit of new information. Finally he looked up at the gloating deputy. "Well, we aren't going to tell her either. At least not until we have something more certain."

Sketch started to protest, but Coleman raised his hand. "No, I will not bear that kind of news to that poor woman until we know for sure. The lieutenant might be on his way here right now, and that's how we are going to play it." The sheriff scowled at Jones. "And, Deputy, I am not kidding on this. Not a word from you."

Jones snorted. "Fine, Sheriff, if that's how you want it. But every one of those troopers knows the same thing. How long you think that's gonna stay a secret in the barracks?" He turned and headed out the door, letting an icy draft swirl in around Coleman, who sat with his forehead in his hands.

THIRTY-SIX

Ria's thoughts finally settled into some order. From the first rush of fear at the sight of Sett beckoning, to the wonderful warm relief as he held her close, she felt whirled and twirled until dizzy. Now Sett sank down to his knees and placed her gently on her feet. The moments ticked by; tears iced up on her cheeks, and she thanked whatever grand fate had guided Sett to her. She had run from him, but it did not matter. He had found her. No matter how bad things might be, or might become, it was better to be with him.

Ria opened her eyes. The horses were staring at them, Coy was wagging her tail. They were her family, and from now on she would not forget that.

Sett leaned back to hold one of her shoulders with each hand and peer into her face. He reached up to wipe the tears away with his thumb. He pulled the shawl closer around her neck and stroked her cheek gently.

Ria did not know what to say. For all the thoughts, all the feelings that she wished she could share with him, nothing was ready to be said.

"Are you all right?" Sett asked.

Ria sniffed and nodded.

"Is Cricket all right?"

Ria first stiffened. He wanted to know where the baby was, so that he could take him from her. But Sett's eyes were dark with concern. Ria said, "Tapikamiiwa is well. He is there in the cabin, with my mother."

Now Sett gave a slight smile. "Ah, so that is why that woman is watching me so closely." He tipped the brim of his hat toward the cabin. Ria turned and saw Sweetgrass Woman standing in the doorway, one hand on the sill, peering intently at the pair of them, a small smile on her face.

Four adults and two infants in the one-room cabin made for quick intimacy, even though Yva's presence was simply as a snoring figure under a blanket. Sett found a seat on an upturned log in front of the stove, letting his wet clothing dry while Ria went back out into the gathering darkness to care for the horses. Sweetgrass Woman spoke no English, and so Sett made no attempt at conversation after Ria introduced them, but the woman hobbled around the stove and soon produced a steaming cup of broth for him, the product of Ria's supply of dried meat. Sett smiled and nodded to her gratefully.

"*Kóópis*," he said in Blackfeet. "Soup."

If his small command of Ria's first language surprised her, she did not show it. Instead, she went to the cot where the babies had been confined in a makeshift crib by placing firewood logs under the edges of the blanket. The old woman lifted Tapikamiiwa from his bed and carried him over to Sett. She held the child up as if displaying him to her son-in-law and spoke at some length. Sett understood only a few words—"blue," "wants," and "no"—but he watched her intently as she spoke, not sure if he should shake his head or nod. Then Sweetgrass Woman slung the child onto her hip and reached out with one hand to snatch the empty soup cup from Sett. She then deposited the baby into his lap, where he had to hold the child or drop him.

Sett swallowed hard and held the baby as if he were poisonous. Sweetgrass Woman glared at him and gave a sharp "Humph!"

Sett wished Ria would come back in from the horses, but until she did, he would have to deal with a mother-in-law he had never even imagined. He glanced first at the resolute, gray-haired woman, then down at the chuckling child in his lap. This surprised him.

Tapikamiiwa was apple-cheeked and grinning. After the long journey, the child seemed happier and healthier than ever. His pale blond hair had grown, and the pink of his skin glowed in the lantern light. Sweetgrass Woman had launched into another long tirade, motioning at the baby and then toward the doorway where Ria was soon to return. Sett decided that holding the child could not be any more difficult than holding a squirming pup, and he bravely hoisted Cricket by taking hold under his arms. He listened to Sweetgrass Woman's directions and admired the child. Now he could pick out other words—"father," "mother," and again, *saaaa*, "no."

Sweetgrass Woman returned to the makeshift crib and picked up the other baby. Sett could only assume this child belonged to the sleeping girl on the cot, who must be very ill for she had not moved since he had entered the cabin. The tiny child immediately began to cry when her grandmother picked her up. Sweetgrass Woman rocked her, bouncing as best she could on the balls of her feet. She made her way over to Sett and turned to show him the baby's wrinkled, sorrowful face. She continued talking, as if he understood it all. That was how Ria found them when she returned, Sett holding the gurgling Tapikamiiwa and Sweetgrass Woman looking on with a self-satisfied smirk.

Sketch Jones was not sure why the troopers had been in such a rush to get to this miserable fort. The barracks were drafty. The men had stuck wads of grass in the walls where the logs had shrunk. The mess hall was almost as cold, and the food was a steaming mass of meat and beans. Mostly beans. Even the coffee was bad.

Jones found a spot to sit at one of the long tables, far away from the officers' mess at the end of the room nearest the stove. Coleman was down there, with the two ladies and a bunch of fawning officers. It about made Sketch Jones lose his appetite, as if the food itself wasn't enough. But Jones had been out on the patrol as long as the troopers, so he ate the meal and swigged down the watery coffee in silence. Two other men in civilian clothing—rather dirty, ragged clothing, but at least not uniforms—sat across from him, eating with grim looks on their faces. Finally the shorter one mopped his plate with a biscuit and then pushed it back.

"Now, was that the venison we brung in yesterday, ya think?" he asked his companion.

"Couldn't say, the way Cookie boils it." The second man pushed his empty plate away too. "Thought I was hungry, but I'll pass on seconds. Next time, we gotta just figure a way to snare off a haunch for ourselves, maybe find one of the Injun gals to roast it up for us."

"Yeah, what you think they'd do if they saw some fresh meat?"

"Don't know, Shorty. Might be grateful. Real grateful," the second man sneered.

"The ones you'd want to be grateful wouldn't know how to cook it. You think that skinny girl knows how to cook? You need to find a fatter squaw." Both men guffawed at that.

Jones pushed his plate away too and picked his teeth. He watched the two hunters as they stretched and joked.

"Hey, there anywhere to get a drink round here?" Jones asked.

The hunters stopped their private conversation and

stared at Jones across the table as if seeing him for the first time.

"Well, there just is, and that's a real good suggestion. I could use a drink. How about you, George?"

"You bet. Come on, mister. It ain't fancy, but it's better than this den."

Jones rose from his seat and followed the pair out into the dark shantytown outside the fort.

The saloon was down a shack-lined alley on a narrow path barely wide enough for a wagon. The end wall was cobbled together from logs and boards, but the rest of the construction appeared to be canvas. The door was heavy, made from long planks. Small white letters that could only be read from up close spelled B-A-R. Above the lettering was an odd bright blue drawing of what Jones assumed was a pig or maybe a fat cow.

The talkative man pointed at the drawing. "That's a bear. It's the Blue Bear Bar." He laughed as if it were a huge joke. Inside was so dim that Sketch had to stop for a moment to let his eyesight adjust. The room was long and narrow, and planks setting on barrels made a trestle across the short back wall. Behind the planks was an old man who had one arm. One man sat at a bench at the bar and a few leaned back in chairs near the stove. The men nodded at the two hunters as they took a place at the main bar. A bottle of whiskey was placed in front of them.

Jones took the bottle, poured a stiff drink for each of them. "Thank you, fellas. This is more like it." He took his glass and the bottle, and settled in at a chair in the corner, carefully setting the bottle on the floor by his chair. The two hunters exchanged a glance.

"Likes his solitude, I guess," George said and shrugged. He picked up his drink and turned in his seat. "I don't see Yva yet. Ya think she's still out at the hogan?"

"When was that, yesterday? She's probably still sleeping it off."

"Yeah, well, we might have to go get her. I'm not real fond of that Irish gal. Too sharp-tongued."

"Too fat, ya mean. Ha!"

Jones downed his first shot of whiskey and then sipped at his second. The conversation of the two hunters turned to favorite whores and the general quality of the fort's creature comforts, and Jones let his eyes wander around the room. The other men in the bar were drinking, not talking. Most met his gaze as his eyes passed over them, but a few dipped their hats. Jones suspected that word traveled pretty fast out here and that they knew he was a deputy sheriff. It made him feel superior, that he struck fear into some just by being there. Maybe one of them knew where that Injun gal was. Maybe they were some cohort of Foster's? Wouldn't that be a coup, to find the squaw? It wasn't just for the reward, either, it was the right thing to do. Best for the baby by far, and likely to increase Sketch Jones's standing. Jones sipped his whiskey and considered what all he could do with some money and some credibility.

A couple of men finished their drinks and left quietly by the heavy door. Jones noted that they were the ones who hadn't met his gaze. *Humph.* Jones let his chest swell a little.

If he found that baby, then he could run for sheriff. Bet he'd win too. And he knew damn well that he'd do a better job than old Coleman. Be more righteous. More on top of things.

"Wonder where that other gal come from?" The cheerful hunter's volume was increasing as his whiskey decreased. His voice broke into Sketch Jones's reverie. "Never seen her before, and with her looks I would've remembered!"

"The old woman rushed her back into the shack damn fast, didn't she? We wasn't supposed to see her," the other man said, emptying his glass and casting a quick glance toward the deputy and the bottle.

"Why, you think?" Shorty drained off his whiskey too.

"Don't know, just what the old woman said there, about a baby or something."

"Well, that brat of Yva's was making a holy racket."

"Well, it was damn strange."

Jones pricked up his ears. Of course now that he wanted to hear what the men said, they both turned away and mumbled. Jones reached down for the bottle and stood up.

"Another one, gentlemen?" he asked as he approached the bar.

THIRTY-SEVEN

The morning dawned flat and cold, and Sett broke through a hard crust on the trampled snow in the yard. The pile of broken branches outside the cabin was so small that he headed up the hill toward a cluster of pines to scavenge up more wood. There were little pickings close by, and Sett could easily see that the old woman, Ria's mother, was too frail to carry wood very far.

Besides, hiking up to the crest of the rise satisfied him; he could take a look around the country, likely see the horses in the coulee, assess the dismal-looking weather, and take a few deep breaths outside of the worn air in the cabin.

It was too close in there, the human scents competing with wood smoke and an occasional waft of stew.

He had bedded down last night on the floor in front of the door, Ria next to him nearer the stove. She had brought Cricket to bed with them, and Sett lay awake most of the night, afraid that he would somehow crush the baby. He got up once to stoke the fire, but could find no logs larger than kindling in the box. And in spite of how vigorous Sweetgrass Woman had been the night before, in the morning she could barely get out of bed, and her coughing defied even Ria's hot teas. Yva—Ria had called her "my sister" but then explained that the girl was the daughter of LaBlanc's other wife—mostly sat in a sullen silence on her bed, barely moving until the unhappy baby began to cry. If Ria started to lift the child, the skinny girl would jump up and snatch the child away, setting off renewed wails and angry voices.

Gratefully, Sett reached the stand of trees. As he had thought, the women had not come this far, and there were several armloads of good-sized sticks. Before collecting the firewood though, he turned to peer off into the steel gray sky to the west. It did not look promising.

To the north, the horses grazed in the shelter of the coulee bottom. Sett fished in his pocket for his eyeglass and looked at the horses that much closer. Each was head-down, chewing where the snow had blown off the dry grass. Sett collapsed the little spyglass and turned back to gather a load of wood. A movement down the slope caught his eye—Ria and Coy, walking up the hill toward him.

"I will help gather wood," Ria said when she reached him.

Sett nodded. He watched as she spread a well-worn hide out on the ground and began piling wood on it. He started gathering a pile of sticks too, and quickly realized that with the hide, she would have a much bigger, not to mention easier to carry, bundle than he would have.

Suddenly Ria sat back on her heels and looked away across the rolling land. It was quite a different view, with the horizon far away and melting into the stormy sky.

"My mother tells me she talked to you last night." Ria turned to face him, staring into his face as if waiting to gauge his honesty. He did not say anything. "She said you agreed to a plan."

Now surprise darted across Sett's eyes. "A plan? I didn't

even wink because I couldn't understand what she was saying!"

Ria stared at him for another few moments, then she turned away. "You would not agree, if you had understood."

Sett wanted to reach over, touch her shoulder, get her to turn back toward him. He sat there on his knee, his arms full of sticks. "It was about the babies, wasn't it? Something about both of them?"

Ria nodded assent, carefully keeping her face turned north as she leaned forward to pick up another branch. "Yes."

"What is it?" Sett started to drop his firewood, to take the wood out of her hand, to make her look at him.

"It is nothing you need to worry with." Ria stood and stepped out of his reach. She hoisted her hide-bag of wood and started down the hill. Sett grabbed up some of his sticks and followed her.

He caught up with her halfway to the cabin, but she walked in silence all the way, her moccasins scrunching in the snow and the ridiculously large bag slung over her shoulder, while he walked along with an armload of twigs.

They had no more than dumped the firewood into the box by the stove than Sweetgrass Woman raised herself up onto one elbow and asked a short question in Blackfeet. Ria's back stiffened.

"*Saaa*," she replied.

Her mother sighed. She turned toward Yva, who was sitting listlessly on her bed, the baby on the blanket beside her. Suddenly Sett thought, *Where is Cricket?* He glanced around the cabin, then realized that Ria was carrying him under her shirt, had been, along with that load of firewood.

Sweetgrass Woman started into a long monologue, punctuated by coughs and sips of tea. After a moment, Yva looked up at Sett with open malice.

"She want me to tell you her talk." It was the first time Yva had addressed him, up to this point ignoring him as if he would soon disappear.

"*Saaa!*" Ria said so loudly that Sett jumped. She hardly ever spoke above a whisper. "No, you are wrong that he agreed. He will not do it."

Sweetgrass Woman frowned. She continued to dictate to the younger girl. Yva smirked a little at Ria's distress. How upset she was! How afraid of this man of hers! Yva wanted to know what secret Sweetgrass Woman had that Ria so didn't want her husband to know.

"She say, ask him! He tell Sweetgrass Woman no if he will not help."

The uproar, and the intensity of the voices, set the tiny baby off again, and Yva ignored the howls. This time Ria did too, though she rocked Cricket under her shirt as she began to argue again.

"That does it!" Sett thundered. He immediately felt a wash of guilt as the women fell into silence and stared at him as one. Yva even picked up her daughter and shoved her under her shirt. He turned to Ria, and this time with his voice much lower as he said, "Tell me what is going on. Now."

No one spoke. Ria glared at him.

"Tell me, Ria." Sett heard Sweetgrass Woman say something behind him.

"My mother . . . Sweetgrass Woman wants us, you and me, to go to the fort, with Yva's baby, to show the soldiers."

There was a gasp from Yva, and she launched into indignant Blackfeet. Sett was confused. "Why?"

"To show them the baby is a girl. Then they would let us go, and we can go home."

Sett squinted at her. "And where would Cricket be?"

"Here, with my mother and Yva," Ria said.

Yva jumped up from the bed. "No! You not taking my baby away to the fort!"

Sweetgrass Woman grasped Yva's hand and tried to pull her back to the bed, explaining something in an insistent voice. Sett looked at Ria questioningly.

"Sweetgrass Woman says, once we prove that the baby is not the one they seek, they let us go and we trade back."

Yva continued to protest, but both Ria and Sweetgrass Woman watched him. Sett pulled the hatchet out of the chopping block and then struck it back in.

"Hell, Ria," he sighed. "Too many people know that Cricket was with us in Verdy. They saw him."

Ria did not waver. "But they will not be here. We will not go back to Verdy."

Sett was slowly shaking his head. "Is this what your mother said I agreed to?"

"Yes."

He could not believe it, that she had presented that whole plan last night while he sat and grinned at the baby like an idiot. He guessed because he had smiled, she assumed he agreed.

"I'm sorry, Ria," he said. "I don't think it would work. We have to take Tapikamiiwa back." He turned to Sweetgrass Woman, shook his head sadly, and firmly said one of the few words he knew in Blackfeet: "*Saaa*."

Tears brimmed in Ria's eyes, but she only nodded and turned back to the stove. Yva sat back down with a snort. She was still muttering about using her baby as a decoy, but she also was cheered by the thought that they would soon be going to the fort, and so she would have a ride. Sweetgrass Woman said nothing. She was not going to defy her son-in-law, but her eyes remained glittering and determined.

THIRTY-EIGHT

The two hunters were a surly pair when Jones met them outside the barracks in the morning. Although they had readily agreed to take him to the cabin—they were going there anyway to retrieve their favorite whore—now they glared at the deputy as he sat on his horse waiting for them.

"Good morning, fellas," Jones said.

The one called George grunted. "Yeah, is for you I s'pose. How come you didn't mention that reward last night, for the half-breed squaw, the one with the baby? The men in the barracks are talking about nothin' else!"

Jones blinked at them in the flat gray light. "Well, is that so?" He let his long coat fall back to reveal his badge, pinned on his vest. "This could be a wild goose chase. We could ride all the way out there and it's not the right squaw. Not like you saw her up close. Or knew who she was." Jones smirked a little as they mounted up.

"If it is her, we should get a share of the reward," Shorty stated.

"If it is her, we'll see about it. I'm sure there are others here who can guide the whole posse there, especially if everyone is talking about it!" Jones snapped back. The hunters grumbled some more, but they turned their horses toward the southern hills and Jones followed them through the frigid morning air.

"Now, where do you think the deputy is heading off to?" Sheriff Coleman said softly to Will McFee from the door of the army stables.

"He didn't report to you, huh?" Will replied. He had removed his stiff new gloves so that he could bridle his horse, and he hurried to put them back on. Trooper Rattigan came over, leading his horse.

"Ah, not hard to guess that, Sheriff," Rattigan said. "Good Deputy Jones was drinking with those gents last night, and the two of them returned to their bunks about three sheets to the wind and very talkative. They're heading the same place we are."

"That's what I was afraid of," Coleman said. "Let's go." He led his horse out of the steamy, warm barn into the blast of cold air outside, Will and the trooper right behind.

Sett Foster hiked up the coulee carrying a sack of grain for his horses. The silent cold settled like a fog around him, making every footfall and crinkling bit of grass sound like a symphony. Everything seemed frozen to stillness, with only the cheerful wanderings of the dog to break up the spectral quiet. Once past the narrow ravine above the cabin, the coulee opened out into the tiny meadow, and Sett found the horses sheltered in a dense grove of hawthorns. The bay mare nickered as he approached.

"Hey, horses," Sett crooned as he joined them in the thicket. He poured out a measure of grain for each horse, some extra for his bay mare, and then squatted down out of the wind to roll a cigarette while they ate. The horses looked good, considering how far they had come so fast. Sett had been worried about the bay mare. He did not remember ever using her so hard, and she was gaunted up, but she ate her grain with gusto and seemed happy to be with her stablemates. Fox Ears had held up quite well, though Sett could see that he was in need of a new pair of front shoes, and the spotted pony looked much the same as always; in fact she laid her ears back at him and rolled the white of her eye menacingly as he poured out her grain. Sett noticed that while Coy moved comfortably between the bay mare and Fox Ears, picking out bits of grain, she avoided the nasty pony completely.

"I guess that bad attitude is for a reason, Spots. You don't have to share your oats," Sett chuckled, then he went back to brooding. It was a raw day to be riding cross-country, and while he knew that it was in his best interest to get saddled up and head into the fort with Ria and the child, he hated to expose them to the weather. At the same time, he reminded himself, they had already ridden through worse, and if Yva could be trusted, the fort was only a couple of hours away. Still, Sett thought that he would wait one more day, let Ria rest here with her mother, though he wondered how restful it truly was, with all the bickering. In fact, sitting here in the cold stillness of the morning with only his horses and dog for company was quite relaxing. Sett finished his cigarette and gathered up the empty feed sack.

"Come on, Coy, we'd better go." The dog sneaked one more tidbit of grain from the mare's pile and then started back down the coulee with Sett. But as they entered the narrow spot, the dog suddenly stopped and pricked her ears. Sett froze behind her, then he heard it too: an angry yell, and then the distant reedy wailing of a baby. Coy took off at a run down the coulee, and Sett dropped the feed sack and ran after her.

Once clear of the ravine, he paused long enough to gasp for breath and to see just what he had not wanted to see: Three horses were outside the cabin and the door was swinging open in the wind. Coy never paused; she went charging across the yard, spooking the horses. Sett began his headlong run down the slope, his mind reeling with every step.

They'd been found, damn it, and while two of the horses were new to him, he thought he knew that rawboned gelding. Damn Sketch Jones—the last lawman Sett had hoped to run into again.

Sett cursed his heavy boots and long coat, which now seemed to throttle him, wrapping around his legs as he ran. The man suddenly bursting into the yard caused the three horses to spook back yet again, and now Sett could hear Coy's barking mixing in with the baby's cries and the loud angry voices, but he could not make out what the voices said for the pounding of the blood in his ears and his own ragged breathing.

He pulled his knife as he approached the door and heard a woman shout in Blackfeet, and then an agonized holler. Knife out of the sheath, he let out a bellow as he skidded into the open doorway.

Coy had one of the strangers by the leg, her growling intense as the man tried to kick her loose. The other stranger had grabbed Yva and was shaking her like a rag doll. From the pallet, Sweetgrass Woman tried to screen the wailing baby girl from the onslaught, but what most caught Sett's wild eye was Ria, a long stick of firewood in her hands, standing over a bludgeoned Sketch Jones, who rolled on the floor with his hands over a bloody ear. The man shaking the girl looked up in surprise as Sett charged through the door. He dropped Yva and turned to Sett, a knife in his hand. Yva crawled under the pallet, leaving her baby above with Sweetgrass Woman crouching over her.

"Who the hell are you?" The man was not a novice at brandishing his knife. Sett stopped in a crouch.

"I'd ask the same question," Sett growled.

Ria gripped her stick harder. She glanced across the tiny cabin at Sett. "They came in!" Ria motioned down to the deputy, who was slowly sitting up on the floor, one hand still over his ear. "This man, he came to Kellys' to take Tapikamiiwa!"

"Yes, that's Deputy Jones, all right," Sett muttered. Jones was fingering his ear where Ria's club had mashed his earlobe. She must have caught him a good one, as the deputy was moving none too quick. Sett glanced over at the man that Coy had cornered against the wood box. He was not moving too sprightly either, and Sett figured that Coy had gotten hold of more than just his pant leg, but he didn't want to discount him yet. From underneath the cot, Yva began a string of excited Blackfeet.

"Shut up, girl," the man hissed at her. To Sett, he said, "I don't know your stake in this, but you better be damn sure it's worth it."

"It's worth it," Sett replied. The man stepped toward him, knife blade flashing. The room was too tiny for much action. Sett feinted toward the open door and his opponent stepped into the middle of the cabin. Just as Sett prepared to step in again, he saw a flashing movement. Ria had swung her stick of firewood, aiming for the back of the attacker's knee, but Deputy Jones had thrown himself forward onto the floor, one arm extended, and grabbed the fringe of Ria's leggings. As her club came down on the tall hunter, so did she. A cry escaped her lips as she twisted sideways to protect Tapikamiiwa, still under her shirt, as Sett had feared.

The blow distracted the man and Sett stepped in with a left-handed fist to his jaw. On the floor, Ria rolled and recovered her stick, just as Deputy Jones took another hold on her clothing. She brought the limb smashing down on his fingers as they gripped the edge of her poncho.

The man in the corner jumped forward, and Coy latched onto his leg again with a loud growl. He staggered back into the pallet where Sweetgrass Woman was cowering, knocking over the poles that held her extra clothing at the head of the cot. She tried to shove him away with her thin hands, her voice joining Yva's in a shriek.

"Hold it there!" a voice from the doorway commanded. Ria brought her stick down once again, this time aiming for Deputy Jones's other ear. He let out a roar. Coy clamped down harder as her adversary beat her with his fists. Sett grappled with the man beneath him on the floor, trying to get his knife into a place where he could use it. The voice from the door was lost in the din.

Bang! The shot reverberated in the small cabin, and the fighters froze. Only the poor infant girl continued to scream.

"Stop, right now," Sheriff Coleman ordered, his revolver pointing up at the sod roof. Sett pushed himself back from the hunter sprawled on the floor. Ria pulled away from the loosened grasp of Sketch Jones. Even Coy dropped her death grip on Shorty's leg.

"Everybody up on your feet. Drop your weapons. You too, Jones. Yes, and you, Foster. And Mrs. Foster, please."

Ria let her stick fall to the floor, Sett placed his knife at his feet, then rubbed his bruised knuckles. The sheriff wagged his Peacemaker slightly. "Okay, Jones and your cronies, over here. Foster and your . . . ," the corner of Coleman's mouth twitched as he realized that the battalion on Foster's side was all women and dogs, "company over there by the cot."

Coleman stepped farther into the packed cabin, making just enough room for Will to peer over his shoulder at the startled group.

"Now, who wants to tell me just what is going on here?"

THIRTY-NINE

Corporal Gorney tried to duck his head and hurry across the parade ground when he caught sight of the Mrs. Lieutenant heading toward him, but he was not quick enough.

"Good Morning, Corporal," Belinda Kelly called out, increasing her pace so suddenly that the young officer who was escorting her had to do double-time to catch up. "Corporal, sir, I would like to speak with you for a moment, if I may?"

Gorney muttered under his breath, but there was no way to avoid the lady's questions, especially with one of the officers in tow.

"Yes, ma'am. Lovely morning, isn't it, ma'am?" Gorney gave the officer a short salute and stood straighter.

"Well," Belinda chuckled. The morning was not particularly pleasant at all. The sky was a flat gray and the wind whipped her scarf about furiously. "I suppose it could be snowing."

"Oh, it will, ma'am!" Gorney saw the officer squint at him suspiciously.

"Ma'am, perhaps you would like to talk to the corporal in the mess, out of the wind?" the officer said.

"Oh, I have just one quick question. Corporal, you are in my husband's command, correct?"

Gorney nodded, then added, "Yes, ma'am."

"But he did not arrive here with you." Mrs. Lieutenant Kelly raised her eyebrows and tilted her head.

"No, ma'am, he went ahead of us at the ferry, the night Sett Foster crossed the river. We followed the next morning, with the deputy."

"So Lieutenant Kelly is with Sett Foster?"

Gorney chewed the inside of his lip. Why was she asking? Had she heard the rumors? The lady was gazing directly at him, so he stared down at his worn boots.

"Answer the Mrs. Lieutenant's question, Corporal. That's an order!" the young officer said, with an affronted expression. He shrugged his coat about his shoulders.

"Yes, ma'am, he could be with Foster or . . ." Gorney trailed off.

"Yes?" Belinda asked.

"Right behind him."

Mrs. Lieutenant Kelly smiled, but it did not reach her eyes. "Thank you, Corporal." She resumed her course across the windswept yard with the attending officer at her elbow. Gorney watched her, wondering how come highbred ladies' skirts never blew revealingly around their legs, and deciding that it must be due to an abundance of undergarments, the likes of which he could only imagine.

Sett climbed up the coulee for the second time that morning, to catch up his horses. The young trooper, Rattigan, went with him, trudging along through the mud in silence until Sett looped his rope around the mare's neck and started back down toward the cabin, Fox Ears and Spots following. Then the trooper cleared his throat.

"So the lieutenant is not with you," he stated.

Sett stopped and stared out over the bleak windswept hills to the south. "No," he said.

"There's some figured he'd be here with you," Rattigan said. "But not me."

Sett shook his head, removed his hat, and slapped it against his knee before crushing it back onto his head. "Then you know what happened."

Rattigan stared out at the hills too. "Yeah. I was hopin' it wasn't true, but I knew it was. I could read the sign." The two men stood for a moment, the only sound the soft rustling of the horses. "He shoulda took off his boots," Rattigan finally said.

Sett pursed his lips and started back down the coulee without a word.

The cluster of men waiting in the cabin yard somehow made the place look even more desolate. Sett saw Sketch Jones vector toward the sheriff when he and Rattigan came into sight, but the two hunters were preoccupied with flirting with Yva, who was laughing for the first time since Sett had met her. Then he saw the tall hunter hand the girl a flask, and with a grimace Sett turned his back on them. Not that the sheriff and the deputy were any more pleasant a sight. Jones's voice carried loudly through the thin air.

"Don't be a fool, Coleman! We got to get that baby away from her right now."

"I don't think Mrs. Foster is going to try to run again, Jones. Not with all of us right here," Coleman said.

"You don't, huh? Well you obviously didn't get clunked with a stick, or bit. That squaw fights like a she-bear, and if Foster and her decide to cause trouble . . ."

"I'm not causing trouble," Sett said as he led the horses into the yard. "Ria will go with us. Just don't scare her again, Jones. You're the whole reason she ran off in the first place."

Jones balled up his fist, and Sett dropped the reins to the

horses he was leading. Coleman quickly stepped between the two men.

"Enough there! You two are gonna have to settle your differences some other time and place. Now, Mrs. Foster can carry the baby, but we do want to see the child before we head out. McFee here has the right, for sure." Coleman waved Will toward the cabin. "Foster, let's get this over with."

"Okay, but Jones stays out here," Sett said. He knocked on the door before pushing it open.

Ria was fastening the toggles on the panniers, and she stood up when the men entered the tiny room. She glanced over at Sweetgrass Woman, who was propped up on her bolster on the pallet. Ria looked scared, and Sett realized that Sketch Jones's shouting must have been audible even through the log walls.

"They aren't going to take Tapikamiiwa now," he said softly. "But this man here is Cricket's *aaáhs*, his uncle. He would like to see his nephew."

For a moment Ria's eyes widened in a fleeting panic. Her arms crossed over her chest protectively, and she glanced again to where Sweetgrass Woman was wheezing on her bed.

"*Aaáhs!*" the old woman said. "Show him, Marie Amalie." Ria turned her back on the men and unfastened her coat. When she turned back around she held Tapikamiiwa in her arms, the boy's wide blue eyes taking in the strangers with a serene gaze. Will McFee stepped closer and leaned down to peer at the child.

Please, Ria prayed to herself, *let him be the wrong one. Let this quiet man be seeking a darker child, a smaller child, an older child. Please*. The man leaned close to examine the baby, but he did not reach out to touch him.

"It is a miracle. Andrew, your hair is the same pale blond as your mother's, God rest her soul." Will straightened up and gave Ria a gentle smile. "He is in excellent shape, Mrs.

Foster. I can only thank you for caring for him so well, under such harsh circumstances."

Ria hugged Tapikamiiwa closer and tears leaked down upon his shining hair.

Sett stood back with the sheriff near the door, watching her and feeling helpless. There was nothing he could do, nothing anyone could do. Ria turned to pick up the cradleboard and Sett knew what she was thinking. Tapikamiiwa would ride to the agency in his Blackfeet cradle, maybe for the last time.

"Good, let's get going before it starts to snow," Coleman said briskly.

"Wait," Will said. "What about her? The old woman. She does not look well."

Sheriff Coleman paused in the doorway and pinched the bridge of his nose between his gloved fingers. He sighed. "Can she ride?" he asked Sett Foster.

Ria had gone over to her mother, holding a cup of water to the woman's lips. She caught Sett's eye and shook her head.

"I don't think so. She's weak from hunger," Sett said.

"Perhaps we could send a wagon out from the fort?" Will continued. "If there is something I can do to help, I'd like to. In thanks for Mrs. Foster caring for little Andrew."

Coleman wondered if he would ever be done with this odious task. Suddenly Will McFee didn't seem like such an easy fellow to get along with after all. "With the storm coming in, we'd be lucky to get a wagon here in a week."

"We can't just leave her here alone. There's not much in the way of stores here."

Ria set the cup down on the floor beneath her mother's bed. She beckoned for Sett to come nearer. She did not want to speak in front of all these strangers, even if they were being kind. "There are travois poles behind the cabin," Ria whispered when Sett knelt down by her.

* * *

Sett and Ria tied the panniers on the spotted pony and fixed the travois poles to the pack saddle. With all the bedding piled deep on the hide platform, Sett went back into the dilapidated cabin.

"*Na'á*. Mother." He easily lifted the frail woman and carried her out to the travois. Will McFee helped him tuck the blankets over her.

"Thank you for your kindness," Sett said quietly to the younger man. He could not help but like the fellow, even though the man was the cause of such grief.

McFee only nodded. "You've yet to meet my mother. If she ever thought that I'd left a sick woman out here, she'd have my hide!"

Sett looked over at where Ria was hanging Tapikamiiwa's cradleboard on Fox Ears's saddle. It had been many years, a lifetime in a way, since Sett had seen his own mother, but he could picture her as clearly as if she was standing next to him. He said to McFee, "Our mothers are probably quite a bit alike."

Will McFee's gaze followed Sett's. There was the half-breed woman, the one who had garnered so much scorn from the people in town. She was carefully arranging a wool blanket over the saddle, where it would cover little Andrew—what had she called him? Tapeeka-something? She had carried that child through weather and wilderness, and yet he looked as hearty as any babe in the civilized city. Will's attention returned to the big man standing next to him. Foster was also watching his wife, but his eyes were dark with sadness. If Will had known him better, he would have put his hand on the man's arm. Instead he said, "She's young. You'll have many fine children."

Sett Foster gave his mother-in-law's coverings a final tug. The woman appeared to be dozing, and that was good, since the ride into the fort was going to be both rough and cold. Finally he turned to stare William McFee directly in the eyes.

"I don't think so," he said.

There were loud voices from the hunters and a shrieking protest from Yva, who carried her baby slung under her arm. The infant had begun to cry again. Deputy Jones quickly joined the argument, mostly to insist that Yva do something to shut up the screaming child.

"Don't want to listen to this all the way back!" he shouted.

"Me neither. I'm tellin' ya, Yva, shut that brat up, or stay here!" The tall hunter pushed the girl away from where she was attempting to mount his horse. Yva stumbled and nearly fell, her voice rising again in a string of Blackfeet too fast for Sett to understand. John Coleman went over to negotiate some kind of truce and get his entourage on the trail, but the yelling continued.

Ria sidled Fox Ears over to the fine mare and hissed to Sett, "They give her more whiskey." Ria watched her half-sister trip again in the snow, this time nearly dropping the child that she so resolutely refused to give up. Ria bit her lip and looked at Sett next to her. Then she urged her horse across the trampled mush of the yard toward the screaming girl.

"Sister, I will carry your baby for you," Ria said, her voice both controlled and firm. The shouting stopped, and all involved stared at Ria as she held out her hands for the baby.

"No, it is mine! I will carry—"

"Think, sister. The baby is cold. I will give her back to you when we reach the fort. She will be quiet in my coat, and the men will not be so unhappy."

Yva stared at Ria for a moment, then she reluctantly handed her the crying infant. Ria turned her back on her sister and rode over to Sett, tucking the baby into her shirt as she did. The silence was immediate, and blessed.

"Thank you," John Coleman sighed. "Now, let's go before it snows."

FORTY

They did not get back to the fort before the snow. The heavy first flakes drifted down as they crossed the low ridge, but by then Yva and the hunters were far ahead, so far that Ria could no longer hear her sister's tipsy laugh or see the flask that the men were handing back and forth and for which her sister begged. Ria rode slowly, her blanket draped over Tapikamiiwa's cradleboard, the tiny niece snuggled at her breast. She led the spotted pony, with Sweetgrass Woman silent on the bouncing travois.

Ria tried to choose the smoothest path in the fading daylight, slowing Fox Ears and the pony in order to pick their way around a rut or rock in the flat light. She did not always see the obstacles beneath the gathering snow, and it hurt her to hear her mother's sudden gasp when the travois dropped into a hole or bounced over a frozen track. Sett and Will, flanking her as she rode, winced along with her, and once Sett had her stop while he retied the lashing that held the woman onto the hides. No one rebuked her slow progress; even the sheriff and the trooper rode ahead and pointed out the best way to travel when they could. But while she did not hear him say anything, Ria could feel the evil eyes of the deputy boring into her back.

Ahead, Sheriff Coleman pulled up his horse and waited while she caught up. It was nearly dark now, and far ahead Ria saw lights dimly flickering, a cluster of lamp-lit windows.

"That's the agency," Coleman said.

"Good to have 'er in sight before dark," Rattigan said. "We'll be there in an hour."

"Or maybe before morning!" Deputy Jones snorted.

"Shut up, Jo—" Sett started to growl but Will McFee interrupted him.

"We're traveling with a frail woman and two small babies here, Deputy. At my request. We'll go at the pace that Mrs. Foster feels she can handle." Jones grumbled something else that Ria could not hear. She glanced at Sett, the only visible part of his mufflered face being his eyes; and she hardly recognized the murderous look. Sett, who was usually so under control and calculating, would attack the deputy, Ria thought, if she and the pack pony were not between them.

The sheriff seemed to notice the same thing. "Why don't you go on ahead, Jones? Tell them we are coming in. Rattigan, you can go with him."

Rattigan shook his head under his scarf and campaign hat. "Yes, sir, but I'd rather stay with you. There's a dry wash to cross down a ways, and I'm the most familiar with the trail. Might be tricky with the travois. The deputy can go on, though."

Jones snorted again in disgust. "Right, I'm going to leave you all alone, so that Foster here can slip away. You think I was born yesterday?" He took up his position behind the travois. Ria saw Will catch Sett's eye and tip his head.

"Let's keep moving." Coleman urged his horse into the darkness.

The ravine was steep-sided, and the trail dipping into it too narrow to drag the travois without danger of it tipping. At least the spotted Indian pony was experienced and picked her way carefully along while Sett and Will each took a pole and lifted the travois over the worst parts. Sweetgrass Woman clung to the edges of the blankets and spoke to the men in Blackfeet. The only word Sett recognized was "good."

The road now widened out and became smoother as they neared the fort. Rattigan lit a small lantern, and it swung from his stirrup as he led the way. The distant flickering lights of the fort and compound slowly grew clearer, and Ria felt her chest constricting. She feared another city, another assembly of humans. More than that, it was the end, the place where Tapikamiiwa would be taken from her and she would return to the pitiful barren existence. Her teeth were chattering. Sett leaned over and pulled her blanket closer around her shoulders. Ria did not think he believed that she was cold.

But the flickering window lights were deceiving in the dark and snow. Almost before she realized it, they were passing by huts and shanties. It was not a big city like Verdy, but more of a small encampment with tents and pieced-together buildings. A few doors opened as their party passed through the shantytown that had grown up around the main fort buildings. Dark faces huddled in blankets, stared out at the odd travelers. A young man went running off ahead of them, darting into the dark. One noisy building had many lights, even a pair of lanterns hung outside, illuminating the doorway. A woman's husky voice was singing, off key and sluggish. Through the window, Ria could see the men, drinking, shouting, pounding the tables.

There was a commotion behind them.

"*Hai!*" a belligerent voice yelled. "*Hai!* You said you would give her back! Give her back now!" Ria pulled Fox Ears up, and Sett stopped short beside her. Ria turned in her saddle, but she knew what she would see. It was Yva, now wearing a new dress, a bright yellow one, with no coat or blanket. Her half-sister ran up the road to them, her hair flying. She pushed her way between Will's horse and Ria's and stared up with glittering eyes.

"*Hai*," she said again. "Give me my baby!" Here, close, Ria could see the front of the yellow dress, stained and wet. Yva looked as if she had just crawled out of a snowbank.

"Where do you live, sister? We can bring you both home," Ria said. She could feel the tiny niece at her breast, a warm curl against her skin. She did not want to hand the child over out here in the wind.

"I live there." Yva waved her hand. "Give her to me." Yva jerked hard at the blanket that covered the saddle and Tapikamiiwa. "You do not get to steal babies, you know. They say you steal babies!"

Sett jumped off his horse and grabbed Yva's arm. "Don't say that!"

From the travois, Sweetgrass Woman said, "*Saaa*, daughter. No." Will stepped his mount closer, keeping a close eye on Yva, lest the girl pull the covering from little Andrew's cradle.

Yva yanked her arm away from Sett. "Make her give me my baby!" Her shrieking brought the men out of the bar. The small crowd spilled into the street, jostling for a good view. Sheriff Coleman turned his horse around.

"That's enough now. Go back inside, nothing to see," he ordered.

"So that's the Injun that stole the white kid?" one of the men hollered. "So that there is Sett Foster? How'd ya catch 'im?" There was a general rumbling from the group of drinkers. Coleman turned to Ria.

"Mrs. Foster, maybe you'd better give your sister her baby," he suggested quietly.

Yva continued crying, but her mouth twisted into a smug leer. She snatched the little girl as soon as Ria had her clear of her coat. The shock of the freezing air jolted a screech out of the child, and Ria pulled off her shawl, to toss over her sister's shoulder.

"Please go inside, Yva. Please, take her in where it's warm," Ria whispered.

"Don't tell me what to do! I am her mother, her real mother! I do not have to steal babies." Yva turned her back and headed for the crowd of men.

Sett stood at Ria's stirrup, his hand gripping the thick wool of the blanket that wrapped her legs and sheltered Tapikamiiwa in his cradleboard. He looked up at Ria, who had glistening frozen tears on her cheeks.

Sett let Coleman herd the party along toward the fort. Yva's words rang sharply in his ears, and he tried to watch Ria without letting her see him looking, but she rode with her eyes straight ahead, as if she rode toward a gallows. The scraping of the travois poles and the muffled hoof-falls of the horses seemed to thunder in Sett's ears. As they entered the gates of the garrison, Rattigan paused.

"Where are we going, Sheriff?"

Deputy Jones gave one of his grunts. "Sheriff, you don't have a choice on this. We're here. Either they hand over the kid now, or they're going to the jail tonight."

"Wait a moment here," Sett said angrily. "I've been cooperating with you all along, Coleman . . ."

"'Cept when you went diving into the river," Jones sneered.

"I was only doin' a job no one else was gonna do," Sett hissed at Jones.

"And when you was holed up in the old woman's cabin. You weren't in any hurry to bring 'em in, were ya?" Jones let his hand slide down toward his sidearm.

Will McFee broke in. "Sheriff, I'm sure my mother would want . . ."

Deputy Jones swung with a fury toward the young man.

"Your momma would want that baby to still be here in the morning!"

"I should have slit your throat when I had the chance." Sett was down off of the big mare, his long coat open in the cold night air, his knife in his hand. He heard Will jump down beside him and thought fleetingly of unwelcome allies. Coleman reined his horse around, his gray eyebrows frosted under his Stetson, his hand resting on the stock of his rifle.

"Damn it, men! We don't have time for this!" he started, but Coleman did not get a chance to finish. Sketch Jones had pulled his gun and pointed it casually at Ria.

"Now, Foster, don't get hasty," Jones said. "You wouldn't want your 'wife' to get scared again and try to run."

Will said angrily, "This is absolutely unacceptable! How dare you point that gun—"

"Shut up, you greenhorn," Jones snapped. "If we did this your way, you'd never get that baby back. Now, 'Mrs. Foster,' hand over that papoose basket."

Ria sat, unmoving, on her horse, only her eyes flicking from one man to the others.

"Jones, you are way out of line!" Sheriff Coleman growled. He pulled his Winchester from the scabbard, but he did not want to start any shooting. The last thing he wanted was shooting.

Jones spurred his horse closer to Ria's, the black barrel of the revolver waving close to her head. "Now, I said. Hand it over!" Ria slowly pushed the blanket away from her leg. She never took her eyes off the deputy's face as her hand fumbled with the carry strap that looped around the saddle horn.

"Hurry up," Jones said as he leaned over to grab the braided leather strap. Ria's other hand swiftly came up from under the blanket. There was a faint glint of steel, and Sketch Jones let out a scream. His revolver fired up into the night, and with a throaty roar Ria's dog leaped up and latched onto the deputy's leg at the calf. Jones's horse jumped sideways, bumping into Fox Ears and spooking the spotted pony, who now pulled at her tether in panic.

Sett dove in, grabbing Jones's arm and pulling him from the horse. Sett's fist hit the man's jaw before he was on the ground.

"Stop this! Stop!" Coleman was shouting, but Will McFee had leaped on the fallen deputy with Sett and was delivering his own share of blows to the man's torso. Trooper Rattigan had grabbed the spotted pony's lead and was trying to hold her from running away with the travois. Ria spun Fox Ears around, pulling the blanket back down over Tapikamiiwa and sliding her knife back into its sheath. She called to her dog in Blackfeet.

Running feet and sudden light surrounded them as the soldiers burst out of the barracks. Strong hands pulled Sett and Will from the deputy, who lay moaning and bloodied in the mud.

"She knifed me!" the deputy was saying, one hand clutching at his ribs. A slight trickle of blood seeped through his gloves, but it was the bruises on his face that showed more in the lantern light. "She knifed me, the bitch!"

Coleman was down from the saddle. "Not well enough, Jones. What the hell were you thinking?" Coleman shook his head. "Take him inside. I'm assuming you have a doctor here?" Several of the soldiers hauled Jones to his feet and dragged him toward the barracks. Coleman turned to Sett and Will. He motioned the soldiers who were still holding them to back off. "And what the hell were you thinking, Foster? Now you don't leave me much choice."

Sett muttered something under his breath and picked up his hat from where it had been knocked to the ground. He looked over at Ria, the only one still on her horse. Her eyes were wide and frightened.

Will McFee finished wrapping his hand in a bandana.

"Sheriff, I don't want that man anywhere near my nephew, or the Fosters, again."

"That won't be a problem, McFee."

"And I don't think my mother would want them in a jail cell tonight," Will said.

"Now, that we don't have much choice on," Coleman replied. "Trooper, lead the way."

Sett's voice was quiet, but lethal. "This ain't a good decision, Coleman." But Ria interrupted him, her voice determined and controlled.

"Anyplace, Sett. Out of the wind." She turned large brown eyes on Sett, staring at him with such intensity that he turned and caught up the mare's reins.

FORTY-ONE

The jail was a low log building on the north side of the mess hall, the only windows tiny and high. Drifting snow had piled against the wall. The trooper carried the lantern in, with Sett and Coleman behind him. There were only two small square rooms with a sturdy door between them, an elaborate iron hasp making the door the least likely portal for escape. The floor was cobbled with stone, and an empty woodstove sat in the front room. In the back cell, bunk beds and a crude bench were pushed as close to the wall near the stove as possible.

Sett's breath frosted in front of him as he peered into the jail cell. "Ria's mother is ill. We can't bring her and the baby in here."

"I'll get a bucket of coals from the mess," Rattigan said. "We'll get a fire going."

"It'll take all night to get this place warm!" Sett stomped across the stone floor, picked up the water bucket that sat behind the cold stove. He turned it upside down, and the frozen water hung in it, suspended. "Lock me in here if you want, but my wife is not staying—"

"Foster, this is where you are." Coleman was exhausted, and finally losing his temper. "This is not Verdy. There aren't any hotels or well-heeled friends to put you up in style. Now, get a fire goin' and get your family unpacked. I want to be able to sleep some tonight and for once know exactly where you all are!" He gave Rattigan a curt nod, and the trooper hurried out the door. Just the two of them now, Coleman's expression softened. "Foster, I know this is a hard deal. I'll try to get a doctor to look at the woman, and we'll get you some hot food from the mess hall. But I am posting a guard on your wife, and you should consider this: The sooner she relinquishes the child to his family, the sooner you can all get out of here and go home. I think we are all looking forward to that."

Sett shrugged and stuffed his hands into his coat pockets. If there was one thing he could agree with the sheriff about, it was that he wished he were home.

Ria appeared at the door, helping Sweetgrass Woman as she shuffled into the dismal digs. Then she went back out and returned with one of the panniers. It struck Sett that while he had been in here arguing, Ria had been unpacking the horses. He stepped over to take the heavy pack from her.

There were dark circles under Ria's eyes. She helped her mother get settled on the lower bunk, piling the robes and blankets back up over her as her breath frosted in the cold air of the dingy room. The trooper returned with a pail of hot coals from the cook's stove, and two other soldiers followed him with armloads of firewood. There was very little discussion as the troopers got the stove going and helped bring in the rest of the packs. Sett went out to tend the horses, with Coleman following. Sett tied the horses into the stalls at the end of the cavalry barracks, and he realized that while Will McFee's horse was already there, there was no sign of Will.

Two troopers were posted as guards in the front room of the jail, and then Coleman beckoned to Sett.

"Come with me, Foster. We'll go get some hot food for you all," Coleman said. He led the way through the dark toward the mess hall door. Sett pulled his hat down lower as the cold wind whipped around the end of the building, his thoughts gloomy and many miles away. He was not looking forward to this night, when he would have to persuade Ria to say good-bye to Cricket. He marched through the mud behind the sheriff in silence.

It was not long after supper, and lanterns still burned in the largest room on the post, casting little slats of light across the snow. The door to the mess hall was wide, and Coleman reached to push the handle just as it swung open from the inside. Bright light flooded out. Coleman stepped back as he nearly collided with someone coming out in a hurry.

"Oh, my goodness, Sheriff!" Mary Alice McFee said, startled. She patted her chest as if to calm her heart. "Well, it's good it's you! I was just coming to have a word with you!" Mary Alice turned her stern gaze on Sett, who stood there numb. "And you must be Mr. Foster."

Will McFee was standing behind his mother. Sett nodded and touched the brim of his wet hat. A rather formidable woman, Mrs. McFee. Coleman had told Sett she was here at the post, but it was still a surprise to see such a refined woman in such a run-down place. Then Sett took in a sharp breath, because the McFees were not alone. Smiling brightly from behind them, her golden hair and green eyes impossible to ignore, was Belinda Kelly.

She smiled even more and craned her neck to look beyond Sett, into the darkness of the yard. "Sett, I am so glad you're here!" Belinda said.

Sett didn't think his heart could sink any lower in his chest. He knew who she was looking for behind him. He stood there dumb, both women staring at him, Mrs. McFee with a stark questioning gaze, and Belinda with her smile starting to twitch.

"Mrs. Kelly, what are you doing here?" Sett finally stuttered. His friend's wife's expression sobered.

"Why, I accompanied Mrs. McFee, on the stage. To meet . . ." Her sentence drifted off. "He is with you, right? Kiernan is with you?"

Sett finally broke out of his stupor. He had to step around Mrs. McFee, who followed his movement like an owl. He started to take Belinda's arm, hesitated, then did.

"Um, I need to talk to you."

Her eyes flew open and he felt her stiffen. "He was not with his men. The sheriff said he went with you, at the river."

"Ma'am, please. We need to speak, alone," Sett said softly. He could feel the sheriff and Mrs. McFee staring at his back. Will seemed to be gazing away in embarrassment.

Mrs. McFee finally broke in. "Mrs. Lieutenant Kelly? Would you like us to stay?" she asked.

Belinda finally pulled her eyes away from Sett's. She swallowed, but said, "No, please go ahead."

"Are you sure, ma'am?" Sheriff Coleman asked. Belinda nodded. Coleman turned to Mrs. McFee. "What may I do for you?"

"Will has informed me . . ." Mary Alice's voice was stern. She pulled her shawl up around her ears and marched out the door. "I want to see them. Right now."

Sett flinched and started to turn around, but Will McFee was by his side. "It will be all right," Will said before heading out the door.

The big door closed behind them, shutting off the blast of winter air. The hanging lanterns of the hall cast a flickering gold on the room. Sett thought it was an awfully bright place, compared to where he'd been the last few days. Still he would trade in a heartbeat to not be here in the glow and relative warmth if it meant he did not now have to do this. He would ride forever in the cold and dark if he could change this.

Belinda was staring up at him, and the longer he made her wait, the more tears welled in her eyes. She repeated, "He went with you, at the river?"

"Yes," Sett whispered. A pain like a wave crossed his face. "I didn't ask him to. I didn't want him to." He forgot that he was still holding her arm, and he clenched his fist. She pulled away from him.

"Mr. Foster, where is he? Tell me!" Now she gripped his sleeve, her hand thin and white against the stained canvas of his coat. She sobbed, "Is he dead?"

Sett looked up at the lanterns hanging in the rafters. Then he closed his eyes against the bright light.

"Yes," he sighed. "Damn it, ma'am, I wish I didn't have to tell you this. Kiernan followed me into the river, but he didn't make it across." He opened his eyes and looked back down at her. She was crying, tears streaming down her face. He wondered if he should do something, give her a handkerchief or something. He couldn't think of a thing on him clean enough to hand to her. "Can I get . . . Is there something . . ."

"How do you know? Kiernan is a strong swimmer. How can you say he's dead!" Belinda's angry voice startled him. Now she was shaking his sleeve as if she would like to rip his arm off. Sett tried to hold her arms.

"Please, Mrs. Kelly, I . . ."

"How can he just be dead? Just because you say so?"

"It's not just me. But I . . . was there. I saw him."

Belinda dropped his sleeve and leaned her head on his chest. Sett could feel her sobbing against his coat and again wished he knew what to do next. He finally rested his big hands on her shoulders. Her crying slowed and she asked, "You are the only one who knows?"

"No, that scout with Kiernan's detail, Rattigan. He thought so, and he asked me."

"Kiernan's men know? And no one would tell me?" Now Belinda produced her own dainty hanky from her pocket.

She held it up to her eyes and her breath heaved. "Oh, the moment he died I was no longer their responsibility! I hate this damn military. And don't be shocked at my language! I've spent my whole life with it, I can call it what I want!"

Was she hysterical? Sett wondered. Now he was a bit sorry that he had sent the McFees away. Likely Mrs. McFee had more experience in this sort of thing than he.

Almost as if she had heard him, the door flew open and Mary Alice and Will hurried in, shaking snow from their clothes. Mary Alice came directly to Belinda and embraced her. "Oh, my dear. We just heard. Come sit down. Poor girl." She guided Belinda toward one of the benches.

"Will, please bring my small valise." Will hurried to the tiny closet behind the kitchen where his mother and Mrs. Kelly had been rooming. "Mr. Foster, I suppose there is still hot water in the kitchen? We need some tea." Sett gratefully headed toward the back of the mess hall. When he returned with a kettle and cups, Mary Alice found a small brown bottle in her bag and poured a generous slug into one of the mugs, before handing it to Belinda. The young woman would barely move to take the cup.

"Here, Mrs. Kelly, drink this up now. It will help you sleep." Mary Alice pressed the cup into her hands.

"I don't want to sleep. I'll only have nightmares!" Belinda whispered, her voice husky from the tears.

"No, it will be all right. I will stay with you. You won't be alone," Mary Alice insisted.

Belinda took a small sip of the laced tea. She started to cry again. "What am I going to do? I have no place to go. How could he leave me like this?"

Mary Alice patted the widow's hand and pressed a damp cloth to her temples. "Now, dear, you know the lieutenant loved you." She looked up at Sett and raised her eyebrows.

How much she reminded Sett of his own mother! Though physically there was little resemblance—Rose

Foster had never owned one dress as fine as Mrs. McFee's traveling clothes—it was as if his mother looked through the woman's eyes. And he knew what she wanted. Sett kneeled down next to the bench so he could be eye level with Belinda.

"Kiernan wanted nothing more than to be with you, Belinda," Sett said. Then he ran out of words.

Mary Alice nodded. "Now, drink your tea, my dear. And don't worry about what will come. We will take care of it."

Belinda swallowed the rest of the tea, and finally her crying subsided and her eyelids started to droop. Mary Alice and Will helped her stand and head for the small room. Then Mary Alice turned back and peered at Sett as if she had forgotten he was standing there.

"Oh, you should go back. I imagine they are waiting for you," she said.

Sett stepped out the door into the frosty night. There under the lamp above the doorway was a familiar Stetson hat.

Coleman said, "Come with me, Foster," and the sheriff turned away to lead him toward a well-lit building across the grounds.

At first Ria had been unsettled by the staring glass eyes. Even Coy had growled up at the taxidermy head of a mountain goat, but as Will McFee and John Coleman had carried Ria's meager belongings into the unusual room, and helped to settle Sweetgrass Woman onto a comfortable cot with clean blankets, Ria began to think of the odd assortment of stuffed creatures and skins nailed to the wall, in threatening poses, as guardians, wild ones here to watch over her.

Ria kept waiting for the moment when they would demand that she hand over Tapikamiiwa. But finally Coleman ushered Will toward the door.

"There is food on the stove, and a soldier posted outside. If you need anything, just tell him. Otherwise, orders are that you are not to be disturbed tonight. Please, feel free to rest and eat, and wash up if you want," Coleman explained. Ria nodded, though she did not believe all of what he said. The sheriff turned to leave.

"Sir," Ria said, but when Coleman turned back to her she became tongue-tied as always. She blushed. "This place . . ." She gestured at the cluttered room with one hand. "What is this place?"

Coleman gave a short laugh. "This is the Indian agent's office, though it looks more like a hunting lodge to me. Anyway, it's the warmest room at this fort, and Mrs. McFee, um, 'commandeered' it for you."

"Mrs. McFee?" Ria asked.

"My mother," Will said.

Ria gave her nod again and the men left, closing the door carefully behind them. Sweetgrass Woman let out a pleased cackle. She was smoothing her hand across the fine wool of the blanket on the bed. "That stew smells good, Daughter."

Ria went to her pack to get bowls and knives.

It was very warm in the room, too warm to be wearing the layers of coats and blankets that she had been swaddled in for days. She took Tapikamiiwa from under her shirt and put him down on a huge skin rug on the floor. He wiggled and kicked and gurgled, happy to be free of the confining wraps. Ria helped her mother to a bowl of the rich meat and gravy and then had one herself. It made her belly hot and full like she could not remember. She removed the last layer of wool shirt above her light blouse and sat down on the hide rug beside Tapikamiiwa. He was trying to crawl, fascinated by the head of the bear that was still attached to the rug. He reached for the ears and the shiny ivory teeth.

"Look, he is a brave one. He is not afraid of the bear!"

Sweetgrass Woman said. She held out her bowl for more stew.

"No, he is not afraid," Ria agreed. She tickled the boy and pulled him back from the bear's head when he tried to chew on the ear.

Then there was Sett, standing in the doorway, wiping frost from his face with the back of his hand and staring speechlessly at her. The door was pulled closed again from the outside. Ria, warm and full and surprised, looked up at him.

"What the hell?" Sett said.

Sweetgrass Woman laughed again at the look on his face, a bit of the fat from the gravy running down her chin. Coy got up from her blanket behind the stove to greet him. Ria stayed, cross-legged, on the fur, one hand on the baby.

"What the hell?" Sett repeated. He pulled off his hat and coat and hung them on a rack of antlers by the door, gazing around in astonishment at the desk pushed out of the way into a corner, at the simmering kettles on the stove, at the basin of wash water and the clean sackcloth toweling waiting on a bench. He sat down heavily on the floor next to Ria.

"Is that coffee?" he finally asked.

"Yes, the cups are there." She pointed. "There is good stew in that kettle, and bread."

"What happened? When I started back to the jail, Coleman brought me here. I thought . . ."

Ria understood his confusion. It seemed like a wonderful dream, all this, but she knew it was not. Just like a dream, it would be over in the morning. She pulled Tapikamiiwa back from the bear's head again, picking up the huge paw to wave and distract him. The bear's long claws clicked on the wood floor. Tapikamiiwa started to wriggle toward it.

Ria said, "I thought they were coming for Tapikamiiwa." She looked down at the baby again, her cheeks red. "But it was a woman, *Aaáhs's* mother. She came in the room.

She looked and then she said," Ria deepened her voice to imitate the older woman, " 'This will not do!' And then she left. Very angry, I think. Then *Aaáhs* and the sheriff came and brought us here. This is the . . ." Ria tried to remember what the sheriff had told her, "agent room."

Sett leaned back against the bench behind him. He was suddenly so tired, so exhausted at being yanked through one knothole after another. He did not want to fight it anymore tonight. He watched Ria play with the baby, her face rosy with the warmth.

"Did she see Cricket? Mrs. McFee?" he asked.

"Yes," Ria said. "She looked, just like *Aaáhs*."

Sett sent a silent thank-you to Mrs. McFee for this respite, and he wished this were the end.

He rose to dish himself up a bowl of the meaty stew. Sweetgrass Woman held her bowl out again and laughed.

FORTY-TWO

Yva was roused from her stupor by a loud voice and banging at the door. "Hey, Yva! It's my turn!" The flimsy door shook.

Yva sat up on the chaise and nearly dropped the baby, whom she had forgotten at her breast. For a moment she stared at the infant, wondering why it was there, then she remembered; she had come back to town. The banging continued on the door.

"Hey, what you doin' in there? I gots a gentleman waiting."

Yva hefted the baby into her arm and pulled her shirt closed, but did not bother to button it. She needed to get out; Kate had a customer and Yva had better get to work. No money, no whiskey, and her head was beginning to ache. She grabbed her blanket and stumbled to unlatch the door.

"I'm coming," she shouted as she fumbled with the latch one-handed. She pulled the door open to face the pouting woman who shared the crib.

"About time!" the woman grumbled. She looked down at Yva's baby, who was starting to whimper. "Why'd ya bring her back here? You know the fellas don't want no baby aroun'." She pushed Yva aside. Snow swirled in the door. A man, so bundled up that Yva couldn't see his face, was right behind her. Yva felt a hand on her back, propelling her out the door.

"Ugh. It stinks in here," the man said as the woman shoved the door closed.

Yva bent into the gusting wind and pulled her blanket up around her head. She started for the saloon, only a hundred steps away, then stopped. She couldn't bring this baby in there. They'd kick her out. Especially when it started crying, and she knew it would. It was only quiet now from being fed. She needed someplace to leave the baby. She turned back to the row of cribs, the haphazard cluster of rooms and coops that stretched along the willow break. She picked one at the far end, near the creek.

The first door she came to had a lamp on, and she could hear grunting. She followed the short wall of the building to the next door. She could not hear anything. She tapped on the door. No answer. Yva had to lift the door to make it swing.

The room was empty and dark, but Yva felt around until she found a blanket on the bed. Yva wrapped her baby tightly in the blanket and placed her on the cot, then went out and lifted the door securely closed behind her. The child's weak crying quickly disappeared in the whistling wind.

Out in the storm again, Yva started back toward the saloon. The snow was blowing sideways, and the shadows loomed menacingly around her. She squinted through the storm to see the lights at the saloon—was that them, to her left? Or was that another shack? She tripped on something under the snow and fell. The cold snow on her face made her gasp, and she pushed herself up so quickly that she was dizzy. She hurried again toward the distant flickering light, or where she thought the light had been. She stuck her hand out, so sure it would meet the solid wood of the building. But instead, her fingers met the icy air, just as her feet went from under her and she slid down the steep bank of the ravine and into the slushy drifts of snow.

Her mother and Sett were snoring, each sleeping so deeply that they were breathing in rhythm. Ria sat against the bench, a pile of furs for a backrest. She had opened the door of the stove and sat staring into the flames, Tapikamiiwa asleep in her arms. He was getting heavy, she realized. He had grown while he had been with her, in spite of the difficulties. She looked down at his translucent eyebrows, the pinkness of his skin. He was beautiful. He was brave. He belonged to someone else.

She could see the family resemblance in *Aaáhs*. Tapikamiiwa's mother's brother had pink skin, and the beard that was growing in was light, much lighter than Sett's. Even in the few minutes that she had seen *Ni`itsa*, the grandmother, she knew where Tapikamiiwa's bravery and stoicism came from. And she had seen for herself that Will McFee was kind, and he would have learned that from his mother. Sett had told her before he went to sleep about how kind they were to Mrs. Kelly.

Sett rolled over and his snoring changed pitch. For a moment Ria thought he might be awake, but then his breathing steadied again. Ria wondered what she would have done, if it had been Sett who had drowned while following her reckless flight? She remembered Belinda's house, how kind the woman had been, all because Sett was a friend of the lieutenant's. Ria wondered if the McFees in their happiness would recognize all the sadness this had brought?

She stroked her fingertips up Tapikamiiwa's arm and

tried to picture what he would look like when he was walking, learning to ride, growing into a young man? Every image was hazy, as if the figure were disappearing into fog. She contented herself with memorizing him now, the freckles on his cheek, his smoky scent. She shifted her position, and the baby stirred but did not wake.

"No one needs help sleeping tonight, my son, except me," Ria said in her native language. "But listen now, and I will teach you a lullaby."

It was full daylight when Sheriff Coleman knocked on the door. Sett crammed his hat on his head and stepped outside to talk to him.

"There's a stage coming through this afternoon. The McFees are booked on it," Coleman said. "Mrs. McFee would like to come here, to your missus. I told her your wife might not speak much English, but she wants do it that way. Unless you object, I guess."

"You guess?" Sett said.

"I think highly of Mrs. McFee and of Will McFee, don't get me wrong. But that woman is strong-minded." Coleman cleared his throat. "Maybe you understand that."

"Maybe I do." Sett looked out across the parade ground. It was covered in a blanket of snow, and there was a cross of tracks where everyone had walked, but the sky was clear and the wind only slightly bitter. He turned back to the sheriff. "Once the McFees have the baby, are we free to go?"

Coleman nodded. "Yes, far as I am concerned the matter is settled. I expect the McFees to be along shortly."

Sett gritted his teeth. Here it was. He nodded tersely to the sheriff and went back in the agent's office.

Ria looked up when he came in. She was carefully pouring warm water into the washbasin. Cricket was naked, kicking joyfully on one of the towels laid out on the floor.

Sweetgrass Woman was out of bed, preparing to hand Ria warm washcloths to bathe him.

"Ria," Sett said, then stopped. What could he say? He tried again, "That was the sheriff."

Ria glanced at him then returned to her job. "They are coming?"

Sett said, "Yes."

"Good," Ria said. She was too involved with Tapikamiiwa to see the surprise on his face. Sett thought that perhaps she did not understand.

"Mrs. McFee is coming here. The sheriff says she wants to talk to you," he said carefully.

Ria said something to her mother in Blackfeet. Sett could not hear it. Then she said, "Good. I will talk with her."

Sett stared in disbelief. Then he said, "We can leave after, after they take him. Whenever you are ready."

Ria stood up, facing him. She glared at Sett, her eyes glittering with tears. "They cannot take him. I will not let them take him from me."

"Ria," Sett sighed. "Ria, we don't have a choice here . . ."

"They cannot take. I can give." She turned her back on him and sat back down beside the baby. She exchanged the cooling cloth in her hand for the warm one Sweetgrass Woman was wringing out. She pursed her lips and blinked.

It seemed to take forever for the McFees to show up. Sett began to pace in the small space near the door, and other than glancing his way while talking to Tapikamiiwa, Ria ignored him. She had washed the baby and dressed him in the finely stitched rabbit-fur shirt, with the soft fur against his skin. Then she washed herself and shook out her clothes and rebraided her hair. Finally she helped her mother, using a soft hairbrush to smooth the old woman's long hair. She straightened up the blankets on the cot and packed the bowls and cups away in the panniers. Finally she poured the last of the hot water into the basin and said, "Sett. Here, wash." Which Sett obeyed without thinking twice.

The tap on the door was sorely anticipated, and yet it made Sett jump. He went to the door and noticed that Ria and her mother both sat down, Ria holding the bright-eyed Tapikamiiwa against her shoulder. "Ria, they're here." Sett felt ridiculous having to say that. "Come over here."

Ria sat up straighter, but otherwise did not move. "This is my lodge for now. They come to see me." Sett did not know what to make of her, this one who moved with such a deliberate manner. Sett opened the door.

Will and Mary Alice were both dressed for traveling, Mary Alice with a fine woven wool shawl around her shoulders. Will extended his hand and Sett shook, before motioning them in. When Sett turned to face Ria, he finally understood. She had the seats placed in a circle with herself in the owner's place, the prominent bench with the buffalo robe on her right and Sweetgrass Woman to her left. He led Mrs. McFee sun-wise around the edge of the room and indicated her seat. The woman accepted the place graciously. Then Sett realized that Ria had not placed a seat for him or Will. He looked down at her with an apprehensive squint.

Ria hoisted Tapikamiiwa up, holding him against her shoulder. She said in very simple Blackfeet, "Sett, I want to leave now, soon. You get the horses?"

Sett didn't trust his Blackfeet that much. He asked in English, "Are you sure?"

Ria again sat up, as if settling her backbone into a taller person. "*Aaaaa.*"

Sett stared at her, as if he suddenly didn't recognize her. He turned to Mrs. McFee. "I'm going to go get our horses packed. I want to thank you, both, for your kindness to the Mrs. Lieutenant Kelly. And, well, for your kindness to us." He thought there were other things he'd like to tell them, but now he was the tongue-tied one. "I guess Ria wants to talk to you herself."

Mary Alice smiled, first at Sett and then at Ria and finally at Sweetgrass Woman, who smiled back. "That will be fine. I'm sure we have women's business to be discussed. Willie, why don't you go help Mr. Foster with his horses?" Will looked a bit startled, but he followed Sett out the door and stood on the porch beside him, scratching his head.

"Got any idea what that's all about?" Will asked.

"You got me," Sett mused. "But, sounds like we got a job assigned to us. Let's get the string packed."

The women sat in silence, Ria stroking Tapikamiiwa's back and rocking him. Finally she turned to Mary Alice McFee.

"You are *Ni`itsa*, the grandmother?"

Mary Alice tipped her head in acknowledgment. "Yes. I am Mary Alice McFee, Andrew's grandmother."

"I am. . . . I am Marie-Amalie LaBlanc Foster. I am Tapikamiiwa's mother. This woman," Ria used her chin to point to Sweetgrass Woman, "is my mother."

Mary Alice inclined her head in greeting and said, "Ah. My pleasure."

Silence strung between them like the strands of a spider's web. Tapikamiiwa made smacking noises with his lips. Mary Alice leaned a bit, hoping to see the baby's face, but Ria held him over her far shoulder.

Suddenly Ria asked, "Your daughter, she was married to a Blackfeet man?"

Mary Alice startled. "Oh, my dear, no! Her husband was named David Bruce. He was a Scot."

Ria looked perplexed. She looked at Sweetgrass Woman, and the old woman reached behind her to bring out Tapikamiiwa's cradleboard. She held it out for them all to examine. Ria said, "This is Tapikamiiwa's. When Sett found him, Tapikamiiwa was in a Blackfeet cradleboard, on a Blackfeet pony. That means he is Blackfeet."

Mary Alice examined the cradleboard as closely as the other two women, as if it might indeed hold some clue to this mystery. She noted the fine beading and the miniature bow and arrow dangling from the brow board. But she said, "His mother Amanda and father David were killed when the stage rolled into a river. I do not know how he came to be in the carrier." She leaned forward to study the cradleboard more closely, wishing she had her spectacles. "The beading is beautiful."

Ria said, "I put on the decorations for a boy. The cradle was unfinished." Sweetgrass Woman broke in, her voice reedy in a long string of Blackfeet. Ria waited, then said, "My mother says, we might never know how he got there."

"No. Perhaps that will always be his secret," Mary Alice said. She tried not to lean more, to try and glimpse the child's face as Ria shifted to set the cradleboard aside, but she suspected that her intentions were well read. "His name, Tappy Kami Wa?" Mary Alice asked.

"Tapikamiiwa. Cricket." Now Ria put her hands under the boy's arms and lifted him away from her shoulder, laying him down on the bearskin rug. The baby gave a delighted shriek and scrubbed his way toward the bear's ominous teeth.

"Andrew. Andrew Benjamin Bruce," Mary Alice said.

"Andrew," Ria said softly. "What does that mean, Andrew?"

Mary Alice watched in amazement as the baby—most certainly Amanda's son, for he looked so much like her—succeeded in grasping the bear's long tooth in his fist. She watched, transfixed. The child looked so healthy, so happy, after the mean journey he had traveled. She realized that Ria and Sweetgrass Woman were staring at her, awaiting her answer. "Oh, it is an old name in Benjamin's, my husband's, family. It means 'manly warrior.' "

Ria translated the name to Sweetgrass Woman and she

nodded approvingly. The three women sat in silence and watched Tapikamiiwa poke at the bear's sewn-shut eyes. When he tried to chew on the frayed ear, Ria picked him up and placed him in front of her on the tail end of the rug again. He immediately began working his way toward the bear's head.

"He will be crawling fast soon," Ria said.

"Yes, and before long he will be walking, and then, before we know it, he will be a grown man." Mary Alice sighed. "And he may well be adventuresome like his mothers. He may well come west again."

"You will tell him that he is also Blackfeet?" Ria did not take her eyes from the scooting babe. He was moving steadily away from her, focused on the fascinating animal head. Tapikamiiwa—Andrew—reached his goal and opened his mouth wide. This time Mary Alice rose and leaned down, her long fingers expertly taking the baby under the arms. She brought him back and placed him on the rug in front of Ria.

"Yes, Andrew Tappy Kamee Wa Bruce. You will have to teach me how to say his name correctly."

Ria swallowed against the lump in her throat. She lifted Tapikamiiwa, hugging him close for a long moment, letting her whole body rock while she spoke softly to him in Blackfeet. Then she stood in one smooth motion and handed the baby to her mother. Sweetgrass Woman stood slowly, rubbed her brown cheek against the boy's pink one, and then stepped over the bearskin and put Andrew Tapikamiiwa Bruce into his grandmother's arms.

Mary Alice enfolded the baby in her shawl, closing her eyes as she hoisted him to her shoulder. Amanda's son. Here in her arms at last! Her fingers stroked his fine white blond hair; she inhaled his sweet scent. Bittersweet tears dropped down on her grandson's head.

When she opened her eyes, the old Indian woman was still standing in front of her, tears streaming down her cheeks. The young woman, Mrs. Foster, had turned her back and was packing her belongings into the rawhide boxes that went on the packhorses. Mary Alice met Sweetgrass Woman's gaze, bright blue eyes meeting dark brown ones. Sweetgrass Woman nodded. Then Mary Alice turned and quietly left the room with Andrew under her shawl.

FORTY-THREE

Sett hoisted the packsaddle up on the spotted pony. Will stood near her head, and he deftly stepped away as the pony bared her teeth and darted her head to bite.

"Mrs. Lieutenant Kelly is going to join us as far as Denver," Will was saying. "She and my mother seem to have become friends. I believe my mother has invited her to stay with us for a while, until she decides what to do next."

"That's generous of Mrs. McFee," Sett said as he checked the lashings that would hold the travois poles in place.

Will continued, "I was pleased that it worked out. The Mrs. Lieutenant seems like the best of women."

"That she is. The lieutenant was a fine man, too." Sett noticed that Will's face colored a little. Well, if young McFee was taken with Belinda, that would not be the worst of situations. Sett finished with the packsaddle. "Well, we best be on our way. We can get to Sweetgrass Woman's cabin by nightfall."

Will said, "Foster, there's the matter of the reward."

"Don't want a reward, McFee. I didn't do anything deserving of a reward."

"Well, consider it your wife's then. She kept little Andrew safe to the best of her ability. Use it for her."

Sett snugged up the girth. "There isn't anything that Ria wants that a thousand dollars could buy. But do this for her. Raise that baby up the best you can. I think that's all she would wish for."

"That I can promise, Foster. Andrew will never lack for anything."

"'Cept a mother and a father." Sett untied the pony's lead and headed into the aisleway where the other horses were waiting.

"He'll have an uncle, an '*aaáhs*,' isn't it? I'll be the best *aaáhs* to him I can be." Will stared down at his boots for a moment. "And, well, Foster, maybe you'd rather never see me again. Can't say this has been the most favorable way to gain an acquaintance, but I'm intending to take a more active part in David and Amanda's mining prospects. That'll mean coming to Verdy on a regular basis. I'm hoping we might meet again, do business, under more favorable circumstances."

"I don't know anything about mining."

"It sounds like you have good horses to sell, though. That's always of interest."

Sett pulled his coat up. "That will be fine, McFee. I'll be seeing you then." He reached out to shake the younger man's hand, then wrapped his scarf around his face and led his horses out the barn door.

Will McFee stuck his hands in his pockets and watched the big man leave.

FORTY-FOUR

Ria was waiting by the door of the agent's office. She had pushed the desk back into place and carefully stacked the cook pots beside the door. She started carrying the panniers out the moment she saw Sett and the horses coming across the parade ground. She had seen the stage arrive in front of the mess hall, and seen the sheriff tie his horses at the rail. She wanted to be out of the fort before anyone else came to talk to her.

Sett took the panniers from her and hung them on the spotted pony. He helped Sweetgrass Woman out to the travois and settled her as comfortably as he could in the piles of blankets. Ria tried to help, but she could not resist watching the door to the mess hall, across the square. She did not cry. She thought she would not ever cry again, so dry and dusty was her heart. Sweetgrass Woman still sniffled and finally pulled her blanket completely over her head, though the day was warm by winter's standards. Sett spoke only when necessary, and Ria was all the more grateful for him, for what he did not ask of her right now.

Mounted up, the small party rode across the parade ground, crossing the tracks of the stage. Ria stared straight ahead, willing that they be invisible to the eyes which she knew were watching. They were nearing the first shacks of the reservation when her wishes fell through.

"Sett! Mrs. Foster!"

Sett pulled his mare up. Belinda Kelly was picking her way through the wet snow, holding her skirts up but splashing her fine leather boots with each step. She was wearing only her light shawl. She called again, "Sett, please wait!"

Sett dismounted. "Mrs. Kelly, go back inside. You're not dressed for the cold."

"No. I didn't want you to leave, without . . ." Belinda reached her hands out to take his gloved one. "Without telling you, thank you."

"Mrs. Kelly . . ."

"Please," she said. "Consider me your friend. As Kiernan considered you his friend." She dropped Sett's hand and stepped over to the side of Ria's horse. Ria did not want to look down, but she could not help it. Belinda Kelly's face was puffy, her eyes red from crying. Belinda reached up and laid her white hand over Ria's mitten. She glanced back at the empty cradleboard that hung on the spotted pony's saddle. "Mrs. Foster, Ria. I am so sorry."

Ria could not say anything at first. There were no words. She nodded, then looked down at her horse's ears. Finally she whispered, "I am sorry too. About your husband. He was good to me. You were good to me."

"Please know I am your friend, Mrs. Foster. Perhaps Sett didn't tell you, but I am going with them, the McFees. I will watch over the babe. I will tell you—I will find you—if there is ever a problem." Mrs. Lieutenant Kelly patted Ria's mitten.

"Mrs. Kelly?" Will McFee had followed her onto the parade ground. "Please come back in. Your shoes are wet and . . ." Belinda gave Ria's hand one last pat. She smiled sadly at Sett and let Will lead her back to the porch of the mess hall.

Sett mounted up and urged the fine bay mare onto the wagon road.

Ria had not seen the Indian shacks clearly on the dark night they had rode in. She recognized the saloon, with its double lanterns and the odd drawing of a blue pig on the door, but the ramshackle dwellings that lined the road saddened her even more. It was not what she had imagined, this reservation, so different from the warm homes of her people that she had pictured on her flight here. Staring eyes in thin faces, shy dirty children, men decimated by drink and disease . . .

Ria did not want to look.

Sett pushed the big mare into a faster walk. There were filthy white men too, standing in front of the bar, muttering desultory remarks as they passed.

"Did it again, didn't he? Foster riding free, probably with that reward in his pocket," one of them grumbled loud enough for Ria to hear. She focused her sight toward the low hills with the dotting of trees which lay to the south. Sett too kept his chin up and his gaze homeward, and Ria let Fox Ears follow him without interference.

They were nearing the end of the gauntlet, the edge of the tent city, when a man stepped into their path. He walked slowly, as if his feet pained him, and he carried something. The man stopped, blocking their way.

"Sett Foster," he said.

"Rattigan?" Sett asked.

Rattigan staggered toward them. Ria could see that his pants were soaked, wet above the knees, and she thought this a dangerous situation. The army scout walked as if he could not feel his feet, but he deliberately marched toward them. When he got to Sett's horse, he paused.

"I know you don't need any more bad news," he said. "But that girl, your wife's sister, she's dead." Sett was looking down at the trooper as if he didn't comprehend. The trooper said, "I found her when I was rounding up the troops this morning. She fell into the creek last night. Froze to death."

Ria pushed Fox Ears a bit closer, to hear what he was saying. Then she realized what the man carried in his arms.

"She abandoned the baby in one of the cribs. I searched and searched for her." Rattigan then walked past the fine bay mare and stopped at Ria's stirrup. He held up his burden, a well-wrapped gray blanket. Ria dropped Fox Ears's reins and accepted it with both hands. On the pommel of her saddle, she folded back the layers. The cold air alarmed the tiny girl, and she began a thin wail. From back on the travois, Sweetgrass Woman pulled the blanket away from her head.

Ria unbuttoned her coat, pulled her shirttail out to make a pouch, and put the tiny niece to her breast. The wailing stopped as suddenly as it had started. Ria pulled her coat closed.

Rattigan nodded once at her. Then he started his clump-footed walk back toward the fort.

The top of the pass held long views in all directions. The wind capered over the ridgeline, and Sett pulled up to let the horses rest. Ria's horse stopped alongside him.

The horses' breath frosted in the clear air, and the view in all directions was crystal. Ria pushed back the folds of her blanket in order to see the small movement in the distance: the black speck of the stagecoach crawling steadily away on the thin line of the wagon road. Sett and Ria waited, watching until the dark vessel crossed the divide, disappearing from their sight on its journey east.

Ria pulled her hood back up, folded her arms around the precious daughter under her coat, and turned away. Sett reined the bay mare, and Coy headed down the slope to guide the way home.